Fairy Court in Exile: An Epic Fantasy Novel of Civil War

Servants of the Moon and Sun: Book Three

By Joel C. Flanagan-Grannemann

www.ServantsoftheMoonandSun.com

Version 1.0 Published September 2023 in Seattle, WA

Edited by Jay-Jay Flanagan-Grannemann
TheHyphenatedEditor@ServantsoftheMoonandSun.com

Cover Design by 100covers
contact@100covers.com

DDC: 816.3 Flanagan-Grannemann

Suggested LC subject headings:

>   Interpersonal relations — Fiction
>   Women soldiers — Fiction
>   Soldiers — Fiction
>   Interpersonal relations and culture — Fiction
>   Civil war — Fiction
>   Mothers and daughters — Fiction

Library of Congress Control Number: 2023916510

Please sign up for announcements and updates at
www.ServantsoftheMoonandSun.com

ISBN: 978-1-7355384-7-1 Trade Paperback
ISBN: 978-1-7355384-6-4 E-Book
ISBN: 978-1-7355384-8-8 Hardcover

<u>Dedication</u>

This book is dedicated to my parents, Anita and Bruce.

<u>Author's Note</u>

For your protection, all Fairy names have been translated into your language.

Fairy Court in Exile:
An Epic Fantasy Novel of Civil War

Servants of the Moon and Sun:
Book Three

Table of Contents

Prologue
The Night of Black Wings

Glaive could take no more.

Before him, two soldiers of Air, their blue uniforms almost purple with blood, held the arms of a struggling Shrinekeeper. Her leather wings battered them, but they held her tight, forcing her to her knees.

"They will be buried," a sergeant declared, his hands still dripping with the blood of the two Shrinekeepers he had just killed. The blood from their slit throats joined that of the dead they had been trying to take back to the Shrine of the Goddess.

"Curse you!" the kneeling Shrinekeeper swore, her voice rising over the fighting. "They should be burned!"

"There's nothing you can do about it, old woman," the sergeant taunted. He spun the bloody dagger in his hands, then pointed it at her. "Join your pitiful Keepers."

"*Fire*," Glaive Sent.

His squad did not ask at whom.

The taunting sergeant fell, several black-tipped bolts protruding from his torso and chest. The same bolts he had been using to kill other Fairies in green and silver uniforms. The soldier holding the Keeper on the left fell to the flail of the sole Feather-wing in Glaive's squad. The other, Glaive killed himself. His sword sliced through the man's arm and into his torso. With disgust, Glaive pushed the body off his blade.

Around them, other soldiers of Air turned, and were shot down by the other members of Glaive's squad. For a moment, a bubble of peace formed amidst the chaos.

"Are you all right?" he asked the Shrinekeeper as she turned to look at him.

"I am," she assured him.

"Keeper!" Glaive gasped, as he realized who knelt before him. "You should not be here."

"I am needed here, to see that the dead are properly Returned," she said with all the serenity of her position, as she rose to her feet, ignoring the pools of blood and dead bodies all around her.

Glaive started to say something, but his soldier's intuition made him duck, pulling the Keeper back down with him. A bolt passed just over his head. There were multiple snaps as his soldiers returned fire.

"We have to get her back to the Shrine!" the Feather-wing with the bloody flail yelled.

"But the dead," the Keeper protested.

"Wedge!" Glaive ordered, ignoring the Keeper's words, and pulling her in front of him. His squad formed up around him, firing at their former brothers of Air. Moving swiftly, they headed for the Shrine of the Goddess.

☾ ෴ ☼

Glaive blocked the door.

"I need you to stay with them. Guard them, protect them, and go with them. Protect them even from themselves."

"I will not be held back. Not," she gestured behind him as the mob was gathering closer at the foot of the Shrine's steps, "when you need me."

"I need you with the Keeper."

"Don't hold me back," she spat. "Hook holds me back. Bastard thinks women can't fight or fly. I can do both. There will be a fight. You need me."

"There will be no fight," Glaive said calmly.

His tone jarred her back from her anger. What was happening began to dawn on her.

"I need someone I can trust."

She laughed. "Trust. Trust the one who was banished for bruising the ego of her precious little girl. Trust the one who had to disguise herself just to fly."

"It's not much of a disguise," Glaive commented with a smile. "I need someone who will get the Keeper and her people out safely."

"I wish I never told you about my family."

"I needed to know the strengths and weaknesses of my soldiers."

"It is not a weakness!" she replied hotly. "This is because of her?"

Glaive nodded. "I promised her I would do all I could to keep you safe."

"She still leads us around by our hearts."

Glaive only smiled again. A noise made him turn. His other four soldiers were forming a line. He turned back, his face hard. "Do I need to make this an order, soldier?"

"No." She touched his hand on the door frame. "Goddess guide you."

"Goddess protect you," Glaive said, and slammed the door.

"Stand aside, Lieutenant!"

"No. I will not."

"Obey my orders! There are rebels inside."

"You seek to defile the dead. You will not enter the Shrine."

"My purpose is immaterial. I have given you an order."

"It is my duty to deny dishonorable orders. This is a place of sanctuary. You seek to defile it."

"You will regret this."

"I will not," the Lieutenant declared confidently, as the other soldier descended the stairs of the Shrine of the Goddess. He watched as more soldiers of Air joined the more senior soldier. Their once bright blue uniforms were now splattered in blood, turning them purple in parts. The gestures of the denied Lieutenant became broader and angrier as he spoke to his soldiers below. The crowd grew.

"We will not be able to hold them for long, Lieutenant," the soldier in blue at his side said. "What do we do, Glaive?"

Glaive turned slightly so that he could see all the members of his squad. There had been five besides himself. Five soldiers of Air. Proud to wear the uniform. Proud to be the elite of the Fairy army.

Proud that they could strike fast and be gone before any reprisals. Glaive was proud that those who remained stood with him now. The only Fairies standing against the mob that Air had become. The only ones holding the doors against those who would defile the Shrine and the dead and wounded inside.

"Weapons?" he asked.

"Just our swords," the sergeant replied. "We threw away the crossbows and bolts Hook gave us."

Glaive sighed again. With no bows and only light armor, they would be no match for the mob gathering below. He could already see the crossbows being gathered and loaded.

"*Lieutenant Glaive,*" the Keeper Sent from inside the Shrine.

"*Keeper. Are your people still in the palace?*"

"*It has gotten worse. I have recalled all I could. We are gathering in the main Shrine.*"

"*How are the wounded?*"

"*There are no wounded.*" The Keeper's stark words sliced into him. "*The corruption has killed them all.*"

Glaive took a long breath. He looked over his four remaining soldiers. They had been together for a while and the six, now five, knew and trusted one another with their lives. They all looked at him with concern. Stretching his Power out, Glaive included all of them in the Send.

"*How long do you need?*"

If the Keeper was shocked by the quickness of his decision, it did not bleed into her response. "*As long as you can give us. The doors are Locked with a Ward anchored into the Shrine. I cannot open them again.*"

"*I. . ., we, understand,*" Glaive replied. The other soldiers nodded.

"*They will give you no mercy,*" the Keeper warned, more for herself than for him.

"*I know. Go with the Goddess, Keeper.*"

"*And She with you, brave Lieutenant.*" In a flash, she Shared a bit of lore with him. "*Her last gift to Her servants.*"

"Thank you," Glaive replied, understanding the information and Sharing it with the others. He felt a surge of humor and dark amusement from his soldiers as he gathered the Shared Weave into himself. The others did the same.

"Servants of the Moon and Sun," the Keeper pronounced, *"the Mother of Waves guides you."* Then she was gone, with a mental brush to each of them at their wings.

Glaive turned to face the mob. They had not yet set foot on the steps, but they filled the courtyard in front of them now. Crossbows were raised, loaded with black-tipped bolts. Swords and spears were being brandished wildly. Glaive heard the volume of the crowd's taunts rise. Behind him, his soldiers stepped into their usual diamond pattern, leaving a hole for their missing Sister.

Below, a few bodies were lying in contortions of death. Their wings were as black as the sky above.

"Be ready," he advised the sergeant directly behind him, who grunted in response.

"Here he comes again," the Fairy on his left warned. The unit's tension surged.

"Hold," Glaive ordered, gripping his sword. "He's just coming to yell again."

A short laugh moved through them as they watched the Fairy from before, now carrying a bigger sword, climb toward them. He stopped below the top step, out of reach of the five soldiers.

"No further, Morning-Star," Glaive decreed, raising his sword.

"Stand down, Lieutenant," the other Fairy ordered. "We will enter the Shrine."

"Why do you want to do that?" Glaive asked, almost conversationally. "There are only dead in there. No more soldiers to fight. The Shrinekeepers aren't to be a part of any fighting. It's always been that way. Why do you need to enter?"

"I have been ordered," Morning-Star replied, chewing his lip. "Stand aside."

"Who ordered it? Captain Hooklance? I haven't seen him since he left to get the prisoners."

"These orders come from the Three Sisters."

"I do not recognize their authority," Glaive retorted. "They are the Queen's sisters, not the Queen. They hold no power over Air."

"They have all the authority they need." Morning-Star was getting frustrated. "You are violating your Oath. I order you to stand aside."

"I might, if you tell me what you need the dead for."

Morning-Star narrowed his eyes. "I do not need to tell you."

"Then you must be ashamed," Glaive accused, pointing at him. "You are violating your honor and the honor of this Shrine." His voice rose, and his Power carried it to those below. "You want to deny these dead a Return." Below, the taunts began to diminish. "You used foul blades to kill your Brothers and Sisters, and now you want to bury them." He directed all his horror and disgust into his next words. His Power carried them to all those gathered below. "No. I am a Servant of the Moon and Sun. You will not enter!"

Morning-Star could hear and feel the mob behind him begin to turn. Beads of sweat popped out on his forehead. The five soldiers before him stood as solid as the stones of the Shrine. He wavered.

At that moment, a Send stabbed through all their minds. *"Attention all Fairies. Those loyal to Queen Zellandine should escape any way they can. The Three Sisters of the Queen seek to depose her. They are Blood Cult members, and pervert our ways. Flee, and resist."*

Glaive spoke into the sudden silence. "Now it makes sense. Not only are you traitors, but you break your covenant with the Goddess, too. Curse you. Curse you and your followers!"

Morning-Star turned, rage in his eyes. "Fire!" he screamed, as he threw himself to the ground.

Arrows arced and bolts flew. A downpour of sparks showered the five soldiers, as the blacksilk heads hit their iridescent Shield. Shocked, Morning-Star climbed to his feet again.

Glaive smiled. "Talon was his sister," he explained, with a nod to the sergeant behind his right shoulder. "She Shared how to work together to make a Shield. Very useful." Glaive gestured, and Morning-Star's sword slid away from him, clattering down the stairs.

"You can't hold forever," Morning-Star snarled. He turned and gestured to the crowd behind him. Another volley hit the Shield. Sparks, and the lightning of feedback, spread out from each hit. The soldiers grimaced, and the sergeant, who was leading the Circle powering the Shield, dropped to his knees.

Morning-Star smiled and raised his hand again. "Give up," he demanded.

"Lieutenant." The Keeper's Send brushed his mind. *"They are Returned. We are evacuating. She is with us."*

"Goddess keep you," Glaive replied. *"We are Servants of the Moon and Sun."*

"The Mother of Waves grant you a swift Return."

"We have served. We will serve again." The Send broke.

Glaive smiled as Morning-Star dropped his arm and a third volley arced across the sky. "We have served!" he called.

"We will serve again!" his soldiers answered. With a burst of silver light, they let their Shield drop. The impact of the missiles drove them back, slamming them against the doors of the Shrine. Glaive was thrown onto his back, a horrible pin doll, staring at the sky.

Blinking, Morning-Star listened as the rest of the arrows clattered on the stone. Then he laughed. Gesturing for the mob to follow him, he strode to the bodies. Looking down, he saw that Glaive was still alive. Bending down, he grabbed the blood-covered front of his uniform.

"Cursed, honorable fool," he taunted. "You think this will save you or those inside? You died for nothing. You will be buried so deep, no one will ever find you." Behind him, the mob gained the top of the stairs.

With surprising strength, Glaive grabbed Morning-Star's arm. He whispered, "I regret Returning you with me, but I am glad I will get to kill you again." His left hand opened. The Weave triggered. Five Silverfire suns exploded before the Shrine. Morning-Star barely had time to widen his eyes before he disappeared in the wave of flames. Building far beyond the Power of the five brave soldiers sacrificed, the Silverfire wave broke over the mob. They had time to scream as they, too, were consumed. A dark wail shivered over the courtyard as blackblades dissolved in the Silverfire, then it blew away on the night wind.

Chapter One
The Convoy

"They're late," Elanor said.

"They'll be here," Min replied serenely.

"They should have been here. . . ." Elanor paused to glance at the sun and its relation to the largest tree in the timberline across the small field. "A while ago."

"You know how long it takes to move Fairies and supplies through a Ring," Min reminded her, pulling her cloak tighter around her bulging belly. Despite the sun, it was quite chilly. Her body was still off, making the adjustments necessary to grow two new lives. Sometimes she was cold, and other times hot, and nothing in her training could regulate her temperature. Flora and Luna said this was normal, but they said that about everything. She pulled her thick braid of white hair over her shoulder and worried at the tie at the end.

"And they have to come through at night and get all the wagons loaded beforehand. Captain Narra is meticulous. He'll not risk any of his soldiers in an unstable Ring. There was probably just a delay. And it's a long way."

"Half a day's ride or fly, I know," Elanor said with a frustrated exhale. "And the wagons go slower, but they still should have been here by now." Her red hair was loose and blew around her like a cloud. Min had noticed that Elanor wore it down more often now, only braiding it if she had to fly or fight. Probably another way to distance herself from everything that had happened. Elanor's iridescent wings vibrated with nervous energy, especially the red one.

"Please calm down," Min pleaded in a low voice. She put her hand on Elanor's arm, and felt her start, then relax. "We must control that which we can control, and let everything else go."

"You need to take that advice," Elanor said with initial annoyance. Then she smiled and put her hand over Min's.

Min sighed. She knew it was good advice. Flora kept telling her that, too.

The draft beasts were slow. She remembered the trip across the plains to Summerwind's plantation. How the chora stank.

"They should have been here by now," Elanor repeated.

Min agreed, and they linked and reached out with their Power. Something hovered right at the edge of their reach. Maybe Narra, his flight, and the convoy.

Coming up behind them, Regent Titania declared, "They're late."

Min turned, letting go of Elanor's arm, feeling irrationally guilty and slightly embarrassed that she hadn't felt Titania make a door in the Wards.

"Regent," Elanor said, bowing slightly. "You should stay behind the Wards. This is a remote area, but your security is vital."

"They're risking their lives for me," Titania replied, stepping further out onto the field. "The least I can do is meet them."

Two Leather-wing soldiers stepped out of the Ward and flanked Titania. Their wings were stiff and ready. One of them glanced at Elanor and gave her a slight nod.

"And I am well protected. Isn't that right, EagleClaw?" Titania asked, touching the arm of the soldier on her right.

"Yes, Regent," EagleClaw agreed. "But the Ladies are also right. You should stay behind the Wards."

"Lady Min and Lady Elanor are too cautious. I trust in their Wards. They should, too," Titania said in mild rebuke.

Elanor flinched, and Min felt a spike of pain go through her head.

"With all due respect, Regent," Min said, "please don't call us Ladies. We no longer hold that position. When T. . . she left, we were released from her service."

"You are still ladies," Titania responded, scanning the distant trees and not looking at them. "Both of you. As your mothers would surely remind me if I did not address you with that honorific."

'Especially mine,' Elanor thought.

"I meant no disrespect, Regent," Min said swiftly. "It's just. . . ."

"What would you like to be called?" Titania asked, with a bit of humor coloring her aura. "Dame? Like Merry-Weather has taken a fancy to?"

"No," Elanor said quickly.

'Paramount,' Min thought, grasping her personal Wards tight to avoid even a wisp of that thought getting out.

"Well, when you decide . . .," Titania said lightly.

"Something is coming," EagleClaw interrupted.

Elanor and Min opened their Sight and looked toward the tree line. Two chora riders were emerging, followed by a wagon pulled by a grey beast with a single horn.

"Where are the others?" Titania asked.

"I can sense three more," Elanor said. "Still moving through the trees. Single file."

"And the soldiers?"

Elanor shook her head. Min frowned, and pressed her Sight to its limit.

"I can sense more at the end of the column," Min finally said.

Titania's hands clenched, and she moved to take a step forward.

"Something is wrong," the other soldier said, blocking her. He scanned the sky. "Narra should have flyers up." He touched the blue piece of fabric tied to his belt. "He always has flyers up."

"Maybe they're Shadowed," Elanor suggested.

"Something is wrong," EagleClaw repeated. "Regent. Please return to the Wards."

"What is it?" Titania asked, moving back, but only beside Min and Elanor.

Across the field, the riders were moving quickly. The wagon was almost keeping pace with them. The beast pulling it labored, but continued racing forward, urged on by the driver.

"Are they running from something? An attack?" Titania suggested.

EagleClaw could only shrug.

"Alert them," Titania ordered.

Elanor felt the edge of a wide Send. Her hands itched, and she wished she had brought her bow. She rested her hand on the hilt of her sword and readied a Shield.

At the lead soldier's raised hand, the riders stopped a few paces from Titania and the others.

"Lieutenant," Titania called out, seeing the rank badge on the uniform of the man on her right. "Where is Captain Narra?"

"He's in the rear. He thought someone might be following us from Derra-Fae. Wanted to make sure we'd lost them," the man answered easily, his hand resting on the pommel of his saddle.

The other man didn't look as relaxed. He fidgeted, his wings flexing.

"Send to him," Titania ordered. "Tell him to bring the rest of the convoy with all speed."

The wagon was getting closer, and Elanor could see the beast's hard breathing and its bloody hooves. The driver raised his hand.

Min, her Sight still open, Saw something, and she reacted as Raven had drilled into her.

"Shadow!" she yelled, and struck out with her Power.

A shimmer in the grass between the two riders became a Feather-wing in a dark uniform. He was flung back by the bone-breaking impact of Min's telekinetic push, his arms raised in the act of throwing. Something whined through the air, and Min felt a brush on her neck. She hammered the Feather again, driving him into the soft ground and sending up a spurt of blood and feathers.

At Min's shout, Elanor stuck out her hand. A line of Silverfire stabbed from her fingers, slicing into the rider on the right. Cut into two unequal pieces, his body fell from the chora.

"Down!" EagleClaw yelled, pulling Titania to the ground as the other rider raised and fired a light crossbow. The bolt dinged off Titania's hastily raised Shield.

The other soldier's hand snapped out, and two rods connected by a silksteel chain flew from it. The flail struck the rider, the chain wrapping around his neck. With a grunt, he fell from the saddle as his chora bolted. Running, the soldier leapt on the fallen assassin and began stabbing him with a shortsword.

Min screamed again. Whitefire stabbed from her hand, striking a spot behind Titania. With a wail, the figure of another Fairy — this one Leather-winged — appeared, immolated by the blinding white flame.

"Reinforce my Shield," Titania Sent to Elanor. EagleClaw scrambled off her, conjuring his own Shield as he moved to cover the other soldier.

Elanor threw all her Power into the shimmering barrier as more crossbow bolts hit it, sending sparks raining down.

"Blackblades!" Elanor yelled, fear in her voice. "From the wagon!"

Across the field, three Leather-wings were rising from the bed of the wagon, flapping their wings to gain altitude as the driver and another Leather fired at Titania and Elanor's Shield.

Before EagleClaw could get to him, the other soldier fell, peppered by bolts from the now hovering Leather-wings.

Images of Harpoon's body full of bolts filled Min's mind and she muttered, "Curse you motherless bastards." Her right hand stabbed at the wagon, and a line of Whitefire as thick as her arm streaked across the field toward it. As it struck the wood, the cart burst into flaming shards, and Min made an upward motion with her left hand. The flaming wood and the two burning attackers rose in a pillar of fire, catching the middle of the three Leather-wing crossbowmen. He screamed, flapping his now-flaming wings in a vain attempt to escape the conflagration.

Min brought her right hand down on her left, and the whole burning mass of wagon bits and Fairies smashed savagely back to the ground.

Silverfire from Titania's hands reduced one, then the other, hovering attacker to gleaming ash.

"More wagons!" Min yelled. She felt something warm running down her neck, and touched it. She was surprised to see blood.

Two more wagons were coming out of the woods, the beasts screaming as the drivers whipped them for more speed. Cloth coverings were thrown off as more Leather-wings in red armor stood up and leapt into the air.

Elanor's throat tightened as she saw that they were armed with crossbows. She reached deep into herself and released more Power into the Shield.

The Leather-wings in red didn't get high into the air before a series of Silverfire explosions blew them back to the ground. Elanor almost cheered as she saw four Feather-wing flyers streak up from their dive, turn, and head back toward their burning enemies. More Silverfire explosions peppered the ground.

"Send the other squad!" Titania yelled to EagleClaw.

Elanor yelled over the crackling of the flames and the screams of burning Fairies. "Regent! We must leave."

"More are coming!" Min shouted, running toward Elanor and Titania. She felt lightheaded, and stumbled on a lump in the grass. Elanor's Power reached out and kept her on her feet. She tried to yell for Titania to get through the Wards, but her mouth was suddenly filled with blood, and her voice was gone. She stumbled again.

Elanor's Power pulled the smaller Fairy into her arms. Blood stained Min's neck and chest, streaming from a cut along the side of her throat.

"You're hurt!" Elanor yelled in panic, pressing her hand to the wound. She tried to Heal it, but she had little Power left after maintaining the Shield against the blackblades. All she could do was slow the bleeding and keep Min upright.

Weaving as though she were drunk, Min tried to press her hand to the cut, but the Realm roared at her, and she slumped in Elanor's arms.

"Regent!" EagleClaw yelled. "Get to the Ring. Our flyers can hold them."

Titania held her ground, watching as another wagon appeared, driving around two others that were burning in the clearing. Bolts flew, seeking the swooping flyers. She saw one, then another, fall.

Rage like she had never felt before filled her, and Titania reached out, sending Silverfire stabbing across the field. It struck its target, but at that range, all it did was destroy a wheel and tip the wagon over, sending red-armored Fairies scrambling.

Titania cast again, streaking a line of fire across the grass. The wagon burst into flames, but more enemies were flying over the trees, heading their way.

Elanor yelled from the doorway she had made in the Wards. "Regent!" Min hung limp in her arms. "We have to go. Min's hurt, and we can't hold the Shield. The flyers will have to hold them."

"She's right," EagleClaw agreed. He pointed to two more squads of mixed Leather- and Feather-wing flyers moving to intercept the attackers. "We'll hold them, cover your escape, and then take the other Ring as planned."

"You are not sacrificing yourself for me," Titania decreed. "Do you hear me, soldier?"

"I don't intend to, Ma'am," EagleClaw said with a grin. "Just kill more of the False Sisters' troops." He touched the hilt of his sword.

"That's an order," Titania said. "Come to the mountain as soon as you and your soldiers are clear."

EagleClaw gave a nod and turned, running toward the battle.

"Come on," Titania said, scooping Min's limp form into her arms. They entered the faintly glowing dome of the Wards.

Elanor hurried to the center, and the large Ephemeral Ring there.

"I hate to lose this one," she grumbled, as she activated it and reached out for the Ring at the Exile Queen's mountain.

"EagleClaw will save it if he can," Titania comforted her, as she joined Elanor in the Ring. She began Healing Min as the Song of the Ring covered them and carried them away.

☾ ⌇ ☼

They were in the library of the Exile Queen's mountain, now one of the refuges of the Regent and the Fairies of the true Queen. EagleClaw sat in a chair by the Ring. He clenched his fists as Flora Healed the burns on his arms.

"Quit fidgeting," she complained.

"How many were in the convoy?" Steeltrap asked. She had been coordinating the defenses below and had rushed to the library when Flora had Sent news of the attack.

"Eighteen soldiers, including the Captain," EagleClaw answered. "And six wagons. So at least twelve more Fairies." He stopped, looking down as his burns faded. "Narra said he was going to bring some refugees, too. So there might have been more."

"How many did we lose?" Titania asked.

There was a sudden silence as everyone waited for EagleClaw to respond.

"Five flyers. All the rest escaped to the other strongholds. I had to destroy the secondary Ring, but the large one is safe."

"Goddess's mercy," Flora muttered. "That took weeks to make."

Elanor was kneeling over the prone Min. Beside her, Luna, despite her still-healing hands, was working to Heal Min. The bleeding had stopped, and the wound finally closed. Elanor sat back, relieved, as Luna, whose touch was lighter, worked on Healing the cut on Min's vocal cords.

"Who were they?" Steeltrap demanded, "and how did they find out about the convoy?"

Titania shot her a look to tell her that she was overstepping. Steel nodded, and stepped back, her hands hooked in her sword belt.

"We don't know," EagleClaw replied, after a glance at Titania. "Could have been near Derra-Fae, or on the road. There wasn't much left of the wagons," he said with a proud smile. "As to who. . . . Troops of the False Sisters. Tra's, by the armor."

"And the assassins?" Titania asked, visibly restraining her urge to pace.

"There was nothing left of the second," EagleClaw said, with an admiring glace at Min. "And there was nothing on the body of the first that identified him at all. Though it was pretty mangled." He looked at Min again, not quite believing that such a small Fairy wielded such Power. "His boots were still standing upright in the grass."

"And that tells us much," Titania said.

"Shadow Agents," Steel declared, and Titania nodded.

Flora looked up, confused.

"Shadow Agents are stripped of all rank tattoos, family marks, birthmarks, and identifying scars," Titania explained. "They do not exist."

Min opened her pale eyes and stared up into Elanor and Luna's faces. She touched her neck, then, with a scared look, darted her hands to her belly.

"They're fine," Luna soothed. "Too small to have really noticed, but they're unharmed."

Min tried to speak, but nothing came out.

"Don't talk," Elanor urged, gripping Min's hands. "Luna's Healing the damage. That blade almost took your head off."

Min's eyes got a little wider, and she squeezed Elanor's hand in response.

"You almost died," Elanor whispered, holding in a sudden rush of pain. "I can't lose you, too. . . ."

Min smiled weakly.

"Yes, Shadow Agents," Titania agreed. The anger in her voice was clear. She clenched her fists, then fixed her gaze on Elanor.

"Elanor, how are you doing on this mountain's defenses?" When Elanor didn't answer, her gaze still fixed on Min, Titania's voice rose. "Lady Elanor!"

"Yes, Regent?" Elanor said, turning her slightly guilty eyes swiftly back to Titania.

"The Wards?"

"We have a rough framework," Elanor reported, glancing down at Min, but Luna had just put her in a Healing trance, and her eyes were closed. Elanor looked back to Titania, floundering a little. "A rough framework, but it will take many Fairies to lay out the lines and power them."

"You and Min volunteered. You both know this mountain and its . . . peculiarities better than anyone else. If you can't. . . ."

"We can," Elanor interrupted with more confidence. "It will just take many hands, especially to set the stones."

"Good." Titania nodded. "Have a full plan, including how many you'll need, by the full moon. If I have to send for more Paramounts from other strongholds, I will. Paramount Conwenne is focused on Ring security right now, so her attention is split. I am relying on the two of you to keep our Sisters and Brothers safe."

It was only two days till the full moon, and Elanor knew she and Min still had much work to do. "We will not let you down, Regent," she promised with all the confidence she could muster.

"Good. I must attend to something, but when I come back, you can show me this rough framework."

"Yes, Regent," Elanor acknowledged with a swallow.

"Now." Titania's gaze swept over all of them. "Lieutenant Steeltrap."

"Yes, Regent," Steel responded, standing straighter.

"I'm making you Captain. You're stepping into Narra's place. Go immediately to Silverflow and coordinate the resistance there. The False Sisters are building up to strike. I can feel it."

"He was a great leader," Steel said, making the Sign of the Three, three fingers sweeping from her forehead to her heart. "I will do my best to live up to his example."

"May he Return swiftly," Flora beseeched, and the rest of the Fairies echoed her words.

"I need you to do more than live up," Titania said. "I need you to be ready to fight whatever the False Sisters throw at us."

"I will be, Regent," Steel swore.

"Now, I must go," Titania declared. "All of you have your orders."

"I'll accompany you, Regent," EagleClaw offered, standing.

"No. I need you to join Captain Shatterstaff and Halfwing at the cold stronghold. They've taken in many young Fairies, and they need more teachers."

EagleClaw looked a little disappointed, but he gave an affirmative nod.

"Plus," Titania said with a little smile, "where I'm going is possibly the safest place in the Realm."

☾ ∿ ☼

"How many did we kill?" Tra asked.

"The whole convoy," a Leather-wing Captain in red and blue armor replied. "At least thirty."

"But we lost the entire strike force," Tra said, her anger lashing out. "Captain Bardiche, that is a failure."

"My Queen," he said with a bow. "We captured or destroyed vital supplies. And killed one of their top Captains. Our losses were minimal, considering the amount of damage we did."

"We relied too much on the Shadow Agents," Dina said, looking up from her cup of wine. "We should have sent more soldiers."

"There was stiff resistance," Bardiche responded tightly. "More than we expected. At least five squads of flyers."

"You assured me your men were up to the task," Tra said coldly. "I cannot waste soldiers. And their bodies were burned, rendering them useless to us."

"Yes, my Queens," Bardiche acknowledged meekly, looking down at his feet.

After a prolonged moment of glaring at the captain with her blind eyes, Tra asked, "What else did you find?"

"It took a while for the three Paramounts to break down the Ward they had erected, and then we found nothing. Just the echo of where an Ephemeral Ring had been used." Bardiche's eyes filled with contempt. "Paramount Erikk thought he found a Ring Frequency. We sent one of my soldiers through an Ephemeral Ring. The whole thing detonated, and killed not just the traveler, but two more as well."

Dina laughed humorlessly.

"Were the Paramounts able to find anything of use?" she asked with contempt.

"No," Bardiche replied. "Only that they were here, and are now gone."

"Those three are spineless toadies," Tra cursed.

"They did break down the Wards around Miranda's private quarters," Dina reminded her, taking another drink.

"They also triggered a backlash that destroyed vital information and items that traitor had in her possession." Tra cursed again. She turned her sightless eyes on Bardiche. "Find Paramounts Erikk, Jarrad, and Aknavi. Cut off one's arm, another's leg, and the third's head. I don't care who."

Bardiche smiled cruelly. "Maybe I'll let them decide who'll lose what. It might be fun."

"I said I don't care, Captain," Tra declared languidly, waving him away. "Now go."

☾ ♒ ☼

"If it was Shadow Agents," the Mistress of Shadows said, her doubt coming through strongly over the Geode Web, *"then it was without my knowledge or consent."*

"I find that hard to believe," Titania responded, keeping a tight leash on her emotions. *"You have always assured us of the trustworthiness of your Agents. The last Queen hung many decisions on that assurance. Now, how can I trust anything you or they say?"*

"The False Queens have corrupted many," the Mistress admitted coldly. *"It is not surprising that some of my own Agents have fallen to their maneuverings and promises. You can be assured I will root out any traitors. In my own way."*

'Zell was right to mistrust her,' Titania thought, deep behind her Wards. 'She plays both sides, and also the middle.'

"See that you do," Titania replied, her thoughts as cold as the Mistress had been. *"If we are to fight those corrupt Fairies, I cannot be looking over my shoulder for assassins."*

"I can assure you, Regent, you will not need to look over your shoulder. I will deal with these rogue Agents." With that, the Mistress of Shadows cut the connection, and her Geode disappeared from the Web.

With a sigh, Titania returned her own Geode to its Warded chest. The weight of today's events was suddenly very heavy upon her, and she shut the lid harder than she should have. The metallic clang hurt her ears.

Going to the window, she looked out over the multicolored sand and rock formations carved by the constant wind. This was the only place she felt safe now. A tower in a remote part of the Fairy Realm, far from any towns or cities. Her hands gripped the windowsill.

"We needed every one of them so badly," Titania moaned, covering her sudden sob. The faces of those soldiers — Captain Narra, the unknown Fairies who just wanted to get to safety — they would be in her dreams tonight.

"Another debt the False Sisters will have to settle," she swore, pushing the grief and anger away. She needed to be calm, still. If she gave in to despair, she would never leave this desert tower.

"Then who would find me?" She almost laughed. "Only three people know this Ring's frequency. And two of them are dead."

Her eyes were drawn to the silver box that had appeared in her Ring a few days before. Titania couldn't bear to open it, to hear yet another last message from her teacher and friend. Miranda's contingencies had been many-layered, and her preparations vast. She knew one of the things that was in that box, but until they reclaimed Fae-Treval, it would be no more than a trinket.

'There are other things in there,' the memory voice of Zellandine reminded her. 'You are my Justice. Wield it.'

"But I can't, Sister. You're gone," Titania told her distorted image in the glass.

21

"Mama! Mama!" one of her twins yelled, running into the room.

"I'm right here, dear, no need to yell," Titania said, turning toward her son.

He was smiling, and holding a brightly colored ball. He threw it from one hand to the other.

"Mama!" he yelled again, showing off what he could do.

Titania wished in the deepest part of her consciousness that she could put a suggestion in his little mind that he didn't need to yell when she was standing right before him. But how could she? As Queen's Justice, she had banished Fairies for doing much less.

'There are times when they must be silent, or risk all our lives,' Oberon's voice reminded her.

He was right. There would be times when a baby's cry would mean danger, and possibly death, to them and others, but it still irritated her conscience.

"And I'm glad it does," she muttered, sitting down in her chair, and holding out her arms to her son. He grinned and leapt into her embrace. "Show Mama," she urged.

Laughing, he tossed the ball again, catching it and laughing some more.

Titania buried her face in his soft feathered wings and beseeched the Goddess that this cruel civil war would not last, and that her children would know only peace, not war.

Chapter Two
Under the Mountain

A hard knock on the door startled Min out of her concentration.

"Just a moment," she called. The bright Weave she was working on shrank under her hands. With a gesture, she sent it across the room to an open silver box. Another gesture shut the lid.

A harder knock came on the door.

"I said, just a moment," she called out, beginning to get annoyed. "I don't want to lose my hair in a burst of feedback." Settling back into her chair and easing the constriction of her dress around her middle, she thought with a sigh, 'You can't deny it any longer: you need bigger clothes.'

"Come in," she called, as she waved the door open.

A young Fairy girl burst into the room. Her feathered wings and red hair were in wind-blown disarray. Signing wildly with her too-long arms, she Sent, *"Show me where she died! I must See!"*

Startled by both the intensity of her Send and her wild emotions, Min held up her hands. "Too loud," she told her. "Too much." The two growing minds within her complained and kicked.

The girl shook her head. *"I need to See where she died. Who killed her? Show me!"* she demanded, motioning again, pointing first to herself, then at Min. *"I've been kept away. I need to know why she didn't come home. Didn't come back to me!"*

Her raw grief threatened Min's own fragile equilibrium. Her unborn twins pushed against her mind from within as the girl pushed at her from the outside, driving her into anger and despair.

"No," she declared, holding up her hands, palms out, left hand behind the right. "Control yourself, or I will Shield you and call the guards." Her aura lit up, and her Wards pushed back against the girl's raw Power. 'Who's been training her?' she wondered.

The girl's fists clenched, and her wings shivered, but her emotions slowly began to recede.

"Take a deep breath," Min advised her.

"I need . . .," she Sent, pointing to herself again.

"Take a deep breath," Min said again, more forcefully this time.

The girl complied, breathing deeply.

"Now let it out."

She did.

"Deep breath in," Min said, demonstrating. "And out."

The girl did as instructed. Her wings stilled, and the raging fire of her emotions began to bank.

"And once more, breathe in," Min said, smiling to herself, as she could hear Miranda telling her the same thing in days long past. "And breathe out." Min lowered her hands. "Good. Now, what is your name?"

"Obsidian," the girl Sent, as she traced the letters in the air with her hand, leaving a faint glow.

"Obsidian?" Min asked, puzzled at first, but then the image of the plantation at Riverbend entered her mind. "Oh," she said in realization. "You've grown. I'm sorry, I didn't recognize you."

Obsidian folded her arms and shuffled her feet. She was caught in the awkward time of life. Her arms and legs were too long, and her wings too short, but Min could see the potential in her. The resonance of everything she might be. Her Power burned brightly, but it was red, as red as her hair.

"Honor," Min said simply. "She helped save you." Obsidian nodded. "And she never came back as she promised."

Obsidian shook her head.

"Please sit," Min requested, motioning to the other chair in her narrow room.

Obsidian shook her head. *"I just need to know,"* she Sent.

"Please," Min said with more command. "Sit." She softened. "My back hurts, and looking up at you makes it worse." She gestured, and the books on the chair floated to the floor.

Obsidian finally sat, folding her legs first one way, then another. Her wings knocked against the chair back.

"It will get better," Min assured her with sympathy. "I had to grow into myself, too."

A swift denial came from the girl, who saw only beauty and grace.

"No, truly. I knocked over vases all the time." Min projected a memory of turning too quickly and sweeping everything off a table to crash and clatter on the floor.

Obsidian smiled despite herself.

"I would rather you speak," Min noted. "Your Sends are too strong, and they're making my babies restless."

Obsidian shook her head.

"Is your voice still damaged from the fire?" Min asked with puzzled concern. "It should have healed by now. Let me See." She held up her hand, reaching out toward the girl.

Obsidian sat up straight and raised her hands in the blocking motion Min had made earlier. Min's light probe skittered off her Ward.

"I just wanted to See," Min said, annoyed, but also intrigued by the strength of this girl. "There might be something I can do. I'm not the best Healer, but I can diagnose."

Obsidian shook her head again, and her Ward grew stronger.

"All right," Min relented, lowering her hand. "But you must lower your voice, so to speak."

Obsidian lowered her hands, and her Ward dropped away. *"How?"* she asked, making Min wince. She tried again. *"How?"*

"That's better," Min complimented. "Don't project. Think of your Send as a light. You've been shooting a beam at me. Make the light more diffuse. Like when the clouds cover the sun."

"Please, Lady Min," Obsidian asked. *"I need to know how she died. I'm sorry I barged in. Merry-Weather has me running so many errands, this is the first time I've been able to slip away. I would like to see her Return."*

"That's much better," Min replied, stopping herself before she said "child." She had hated it when adults used to call her that. "I understand. But I did not witness her death. I was injured, and have no memory of their Pyre. All I have was Shared with me by others."

"The others will not speak to me." Images of an angry Steel and a sorrowful Shield appeared in Min's mind. *"Lady Elanor scares*

me, and Captain Shatterstaff has been away. Please. Whatever you can give me, I would be grateful."

Despite the grief radiating from her in waves, Min smiled. "Elanor scares you? I will have to tell her. Why? She. . . ." Min stopped. She had gotten used to the storm that was Elanor on the best of days, but what would she be like to this very sensitive child?

"The memories are very strong and very difficult for me," Min began. The appearance of Merry-Weather at the open door interrupted her.

"That's where you went to," she said sharply. "I'm sorry, Lady Min." She turned her steel eyes to Obsidian. "This young one needs to learn manners. Come now." She motioned at the girl. "Leave the good Lady alone."

Obsidian stood out of reflex, knocking the chair back against the wall. Min's Power kept it from banging to the floor.

"It's all right, Dame Merry-Weather," Min said quietly. "We were just talking about one of our fallen Sisters."

Merry-Weather made the Sign of the Three. "You shouldn't be bothering the Lady, little miss. And you." She pointed at Min. "You have important work to do. It's late, and you should be sleeping." She grabbed Obsidian's arm.

Min and Obsidian shared a look. The quiet but focused thought she received from Obsidian made Min smile.

"I said it was all right," Min said, opening her wings just a bit. Merry-Weather stopped in the act of pulling the girl out of the room. "I was about to tell her, the memories are too strong for me now. It is very late," she said, nodding in agreement with Merry-Weather, who huffed. "But I can Share with her some of my good memories of her brave soldier. Tomorrow, if all her tasks are done to your satisfaction," another, more gracious, huff came from Merry-Weather at that, "I will be able to Share more. We will build up to the Pyre."

Merry-Weather let go of Obsidian's arm. "If you say so, Lady Min," she agreed with a frown. "I will be beneath the dome. When you're done," she looked pointedly at Obsidian, "find me there."

"Thank you, Dame," Min said, as polite as she could be. "Please close the door."

Merry-Weather did, with a loud harrumph.

"I will pay for that," Obsidian Sent, sitting back down.

"And you should. It is not polite to barge into a Lady's room," Min said, with an exaggerated imitation of Merry-Weather.

Obsidian laughed out loud. An odd sound, but still pleasant.

"She hasn't gotten used to the fact that I'm no longer one of her Ladies to command," Min told her. "But she deserves our respect and obedience all the same."

"Yes, My Lady," Obsidian Sent with a bow.

"Never call me that," Min said harshly. Strong images of fire and blood poured out of her, making Obsidian stand up straighter, a sudden fear in her eyes. The beginning of a Shield formed.

Min realized what she had done. "Just call me Min," she said gently, Projecting calm and quiet. Obsidian settled, and her Shield fell away. "We are all hurt. Its teeth bite me unexpectedly sometimes."

Obsidian nodded with understanding beyond her years.

"Now, come," Min said, offering her hands. "I will Show you the time Honor fell into the river trying to pick fruit." Obsidian smiled, taking Min's hands. Her aura flared as they Joined in a Circle.

☾ 〜 ☼

After Obsidian left, Min leaned forward in her chair, her head in her hands. She rubbed at her temples, and then her eyes.

Behind her, a panel in the wall slid aside, and Elanor stood watching her. Her hair was loose, and she wore only a short robe, carelessly tied. She watched Min with intense eyes.

"So, she's afraid of me?" she finally said.

"As she should be," Min replied, not looking up. "Your Silverfire cut that assassin in half."

"And you tossed the other one right out of his boots. And he was behind a Shadow." She crossed to stand behind Min. "Another headache?"

27

Min nodded and leaned back, her eyes still closed. She let Elanor massage her shoulders and neck.

"When Shield returns, she can Look and See if something was missed." Elanor's concern grew, as her hands worked Min's shoulders, pulling out the tension. Min's head lolled in enjoyment as Elanor's fingers rubbed up the back of her neck.

"I don't know what good it would do. I've Looked, and I See nothing," Min muttered.

"You shouldn't be having these headaches," Elanor told her. "More fuzzy vision?"

"No. Just the pain." Min leaned back into Elanor's hands. "Do you know where she is?"

"Somewhere south of Silverfire and Riverbend, but not as far as Paramount Holly's little town. The False Sisters keep attacking, and our people keep beating them back. With heavy losses on each side. Steel is with her."

"Poor Shield. She just wanted to find a quiet spot to contemplate her place in the Realm. Now she's one of the few who know how to fight the blackblades."

Elanor was silent.

"Has she found a way to save more?" Min asked.

"No," Elanor replied. "Removing their arms and legs is the only thing that works. No one has lived through a body wound."

Min leaned forward in sudden pain. Elanor rushed around and took her hands. She pressed into her mind, triggering pain blockers. Min took a deep breath as the agony abated.

"She was very intense," Min said when she could speak. "Strong. The twins accepted her quickly, though. Which is odd, but it was still exhausting. Thank you."

Elanor smiled. "That's what I'm here for." She paused. "So, she wanted to see how they died?"

Min nodded.

"And you didn't Show her yet?"

"No. I Showed her a better time. She was satisfied for now. But she won't stay that way." Min glanced at Elanor, a strange look on her face. "Maybe we should go. It might be good for us. See the place again. Mourn for real this time."

Elanor leaned back on her heels. "The cliffs." Pain filled her face. "I don't know." She reached back to touch her red wing. "There's too much pain. I don't know if I can take it."

Min smiled. "It was just a thought. I'd like to go back. See it again. Mourn, and celebrate their lives."

Elanor shook her head.

"But I have to finish these Weaves first," Min said, sitting up. "If the False Sisters keep pushing hard, it won't be long till they get here. We need to be ready."

"You are in no condition to keep working," Elanor declared, pulling herself out of the darkness. "You need to sleep. Or," she said slyly, running her hand up Min's arm, "we could go back to bed. Pleasure is a good cure for pain. At least it makes you forget for a time."

Min pulled back and folded both of her arms over her growing belly. "That was a mistake."

"We've been making many mistakes these last three moons then," Elanor told her, still smiling.

"I will not be your replacement for her," Min told her hotly.

"And I'm not him," Elanor shot back. "I thought the breasts would have been a hint."

"Just go," Min said, standing. "They're asleep. I should be, too." She went through the sliding door and closed it behind herself. A moment later, it opened, and a dress came flying out, hitting Elanor in the stomach. The door shut again with a snap. Still smiling, Elanor crumpled the dress into a ball and left.

Outside, in the hall leading to the library, Elanor caught a young Fairy running by.

"Please take this to the laundry," she requested, pushing the dress into his arms.

"Yes, Lady Elanor," the young man agreed, blushing at her barely closed robe.

She let him stare for a moment, then waved him off. She turned in the direction of the stairs down. Her room was the last one on the corridor. They had converted the small rooms leading to the Exile Queen's library into bedrooms for those now living in the mountain. Since she was pregnant, Min had the only one with an adjoining door. All the others had to sleep in narrow rooms with single entries. Elanor didn't care, as most nights she slept in Min's bed. But it was good that she kept a room for times like this, despite Flora's dark looks and Merry-Weather's constant needling that someone else could take it if she wasn't going to use it.

Elanor felt the Ring in use behind her and turned. Flora came striding down the hall.

"Where's Min?" she called.

"Asleep," Elanor called back.

Flora looked torn between happiness and frustration. "Good. I thought I was going to have to dose her tea. It's not good for the children for her to be working so hard."

Elanor walked closer to her. "I tried that. She sniffed it out and threw it in my face. Then I had to take my dress off." She shrugged, daring Flora to say something. "I got tired, but she was invigorated. Then that girl, Obsidian, came to visit her. Now, she's finally asleep."

"Well, I guess you must do what you must." Flora rested her fists on her hips. "Shatter needs a strong Power user who knows Rings at the Regent's stronghold. Min is asleep, and your mother is unavailable." She returned Elanor's challenging stare. "So, you will have to do."

Elanor glared at Flora. "What does she need?"

"I don't know. I was just sent to fetch someone. But it's important." She looked Elanor up and down. "I doubt it's bed play, so I would put some clothes on. And it's cold there."

"Stop criticizing me, Mum," Elanor said, moving to tighten the belt of her robe, but stopping before she did so.

"Then start making better decisions. Standing in the hallway like that! Our Sisters and Brothers are fighting and dying, and you stand there like some Human trollop." Elanor drew breath to speak, but Flora continued. "I don't agree with you spending time with Min. But she needs something to keep her stable, and you seem to do that, at least sometimes, but for Goddess's sake, have some decorum." She nodded to several Fairies, all watching the conversation avidly.

Elanor wanted to open her robe and flash them. She settled for snapping back at Flora. "Maybe she keeps me stable. Did you ever think of that? I've been hurt, too."

"We have all been hurt," Flora told her. She glared at the gawkers. "I'm sure there is something all of you should be doing. I'm sure it's important, and this delay is a hardship to your Sister Fairies." Looking guilty, they began to disperse. She turned back to Elanor. "We have all been hurt," she said again, softer this time, stepping closer. "I just worry about you."

"I'm worried, too," Elanor shot back, turning on her heel. She called back over her shoulder, "Tell her I'll be there as soon as I can find something decent to put on. Might take a while: all my trollop clothes are on top." She yanked her door open, stormed into her room, and slammed the door on Flora.

Flora sighed and turned, almost running into the young man holding Elanor's dress.

"I'm sorry, Mum," he said. "I need to take this to the laundry below."

"I'll take it," Flora volunteered, yanking it out of his hands. "You go and get dinner."

He bowed, and hurried off.

Flora looked down at the dress, and the spreading stain in the middle. "This will take more than soap to clean." She made the Sign of the Three. "Goddess help us." Then she went to the door closest to the library and opened it, entering her own room.

Chapter Three
The Stronghold

Elanor appeared in the Ring at the Regent's stronghold. She tried to move her feet, but a Ward held them to the floor. She smiled at the familiar touch of her mother's Weaving. Five Leather-wing soldiers were arrayed around the room. They watched, with drawn bows, as she traced the day's symbol in the Ward. In the corner, an Iridescent woman looked up. She nodded, and with a gesture, dropped the Ward. Elanor stepped out of the Ring, and spread her arms so the woman could run a glowing blue crystal over her. She felt the Finding Weave penetrate her clothes, seeking any hidden crystals or Wards.

"Nice sword," one of the soldiers commented, as the woman stepped back and returned to her place in the corner.

"From the armory," Elanor told him. She touched the hilt, which was shaped like dragon wings, with the pommel representing the creature's snarling mouth.

"Captain Shatter will meet you in the steel room," he told her, opening the door.

"Thank you," Elanor replied, pulling her cloak more tightly around herself. Flora had been right: it was cold here. The corridor was empty, and her bootsteps echoed on the stone. Loose pebbles rolled underfoot. Through the windows along the right-hand wall, she could hear people sparring. She looked, and saw young Leather-wings being put through their paces by Halfwing. She felt sympathy as he cracked one over the head with his wooden sword for not keeping his guard up. The boy stumbled, but got back up, holding his wooden sword higher.

Beyond the courtyard and over the wall, Elanor could see snowcapped hills. She still didn't know exactly where Titania's stronghold was. Secrecy was the best security, Shatter said. The mountains were beautiful. She just wished it weren't so cold.

With a glance at the sun, she hurried on. Behind her, Halfwing called, "Who do we fight for?"

"The Queen!" the children replied.

"Who do we defend?"

"Our Brothers and Sisters!"

"Who?" Halfwing called.

"Our Brothers and Sisters!" came the reply, louder this time.

"Who do we fight for?" Halfwing called out again, motioning for them to start sparring again.

"The Queen!" came the reply, mixed with the clash of wooden swords.

Elanor smiled, remembering when she had been that young. Then she frowned. All those memories included Talia at her side. She pushed them aside, and quickened her steps.

Around a corner, she came upon another door. Guarding it were two soldiers, a Leather-wing and a Feather-wing. The Leather-wing pointed her spear at Elanor.

Elanor held up her hands and traced the day's symbol in the air. Then she spread her arms again. The Feather-wing made a flinging motion at her with both hands. Elanor felt a dispelling Weave wash over her.

"Good thing I don't use my Power to keep my hair up," Elanor joked, as the Leather-wing opened the door.

The soldier ran a hand over her bald head. "I wouldn't know about that, Elanor." The Feather-wing did not look amused, and returned his gaze to the corridor.

"Is Shatter here yet?" Elanor asked the guards as she passed through the doorway.

"The Captain passed through a long count ago," the Leather-wing replied. "You'd better hurry." Then she shut the door with a bang.

"Motherless," Elanor swore, now running down the corridor that descended in a gradual spiral. The floor was slippery, and she had to grab onto the wall with her Power to keep her feet beneath her. Seeing a chance to make up time, she latched into the walls with Power from both her hands and let her feet slide. She picked up speed as the incline got steeper. She saw the flicker of light around the next bend and projected more Power to slow herself. Skidding on the stone, she came to a stop before another door.

"Having fun?" a Leather-wing asked her. He stood alone beside a large steel door. Elanor removed her cloak slowly. All around her, the subtle ripple of Shadow Wards proved her instincts right. A pair of unseen hands took the cloak, and she felt more running over her body.

"EagleClaw!" Elanor exclaimed. "I'm glad to see you. How was the cell we got you thrown into?"

"As you would expect," he bantered back. "Dank and musty. Like my first barracks. Took me back." He looked up at the ceiling. "You know, it might have been my first barracks."

"Quiet, fool," a voice snapped from Elanor's shoulder. She felt a pinch as hard fingers probed under her arm.

"And that reminds me of my first tumble with a boy," she said, addressing the person behind her. There was quiet laughter all around the room. A harsh Send cut it off.

A sharp-faced sergeant materialized in front of her and handed her back her cloak. "Shatter is waiting." He spoke with no emotion.

Elanor bobbed her head in respect to him and the rest of the unseen guards. EagleClaw opened the door and motioned her in. 'Nice sword,' he mouthed.

Beyond the door was a small circular room. As the door closed, Elanor felt the Wards snap back into place behind her. Four figures turned to face her.

The Regent — Lady Titania — crossed the small room and embraced Elanor. "I'm glad you could come. I have need of your skills."

"It is my honor, Regent," Elanor replied with only a slight smile. "I serve."

"And you honor us all with your service," Titania replied earnestly, pulling away. She gestured to the others. "I think you know the Captain."

"I've met her once or twice." Elanor grinned as Shatter enfolded her in a powerful hug, wings and all. "It's good to see you again," she said into the soldier's powerful shoulder. Unexpected tears filled her eyes. Shatter's normal sternness held a bit of lightness today. Pushing aside her tears, she Sent, *"I sense something new in you."*

"You'll find out soon," Shatter replied. *"Now wipe your tears on my shoulder. We have serious business."*

"Yes, Mother." Elanor did as she was asked and stepped back, her face and demeanor both properly business-like.

"This is Chameleon," Shatter said, gesturing to the tall, thin Leather-wing to her right. Chameleon bowed to Elanor. "He has brought information about a Ring we might be able to use. He's an Agent of the Mistress of Shadows."

Elanor hid the concern that information gave her and nodded back at the Fairy.

"Since the False Sisters have Locked all the Rings at Fae-Treval," Titania was saying, "this is welcome news. Despite the danger, we must explore this Ring." She gestured to the last Fairy in the room. "This brave soldier has volunteered to go through first."

The Leather-wing soldier stepped up and bowed to Titania and Elanor. "I serve, Regent."

Elanor looked the volunteer over, and her stomach cramped. He was young, had only a few scars, and smiled too much. "Thank you," was all she could say.

"Dark Glider was part of a squad of Air that came to us after the Night of Black Wings," Shatter told her. "They brought important information on the False Sisters and their allies."

"I was ashamed by what my Brothers and Sisters did that night," Dark Glider explained.

'Even his voice is young,' Elanor thought.

"And I needed to do whatever I could to fight them," he continued, with a bow to Titania.

Elanor caught a smirk from Chameleon, quickly covered. She glanced at Shatter, but the Captain was checking the soldier's gear.

"Do you have your Pyre?" Shatter asked.

Dark Glider pulled a silver disk from under his shirt and showed it to Shatter. Elanor felt a Weave containing Silverfire within the disk.

"It will trigger with your death?" Shatter asked, after touching the disk.

"It will," Dark Glider confirmed. "I will not have my body used by those foul ones."

"You can also throw all you are into it and make a larger explosion," Elanor told him.

"Yes," he acknowledged, his smile dropping. "I've been taught that, too. But I haven't been able to practice," he said, his smile returning.

"Time is short," Chameleon said. "I cannot guarantee the Ring will be secure past nightfall."

Elanor winced at the arrogance in his voice. She looked toward Shatter again, but she was still caught up in preparing the soldier for his mission. Elanor turned to Titania.

"Then we must hurry," Titania said. "Elanor, let us look at this Ephemeral Ring."

Elanor joined her in the middle of the room and knelt. "What do you need me to do?" she asked, putting her hands on the cloth.

"We need a Ward to hold anyone coming through this Ring. It isn't in the best shape, so I hoped your experience with Ephemeral Rings would be of help."

"Of course," Elanor said, and reached out into the Ring. "It has very little Power. One person at a time may travel, and then its Power will have to build up again. For a fifty count, maybe."

"That was my thought, too," Titania agreed.

"I don't think it will hold any Wards," Elanor said, thinking. "It might be better to create something here and keep the Ephemeral Ring inside it."

"Whatever you feel is best," Titania agreed, standing. "How long?"

"Not long," Elanor said. She reached into a pocket and pulled out a piece of white chalk. She held it up to the sky she could not see. "Goddess, grant us Power to defend our Sisters and Brothers," she entreated.

"Goddess grant," the others echoed.

Elanor poured her Power into the chalk, then began to draw a circle around the Ring. Her Power flowed into the line on the floor. Then she made another circle, about a hand-span further out. More Power went into that second circle. Then finally, a third circle. Acting quickly, but with precision, Elanor wrote in Old Fairy within each of the circles. With a final flourish, she sat back on her heels and held out her arms.

"Regent, Captain?" she asked. "Would you assist me in Powering this Ward?"

Shatter took her right hand and Titania the left, and they granted their Power to Elanor. She Wove the bright silver light of the Regent and the purple ('Purple,' she thought. 'This is new!)' light from Shatter with her own, and added it to the Ward. With a snap and the scent of rain, the Ward flared into place. Dark Glider let forth an impressed gasp.

"I have concerns," Elanor Sent to both Shatter and Titania, as their Power withdrew. *"I do not trust him."*

"Neither do we," both Sent back. *"Be ready,"* Shatter told her.

Shatter helped Elanor to her feet.

"You understand your mission?" Titania asked Dark Glider.

"Yes, My Lady." Dark Glider recited his instructions with the confidence of youth. "Go through the Ring. Shadow, and see if it's safe. Return in a fifty count." He gripped the dagger on his belt as he finished.

"Good." Titania turned to Chameleon. "The Frequency?" she requested, holding out her hand.

"Let me," Shatter said, smoothly stepping between Chameleon and the Regent and placing her hand on his shoulder.

"Of course," he said, Sharing the Ring's Frequency with her. Afterward, Shatter frowned for a moment, but quickly moved to Dark Glider and gripped his arm.

"Return to us," she ordered.

37

"I will, Captain," he vowed. Then, with a bow to Titania and Elanor, he stepped over the chalk lines and onto the Ephemeral Ring. With another smile, he disappeared.

Casually, Elanor put her hand on Shatter's arm.

"The Heir's quarters," Shatter Sent, counting.

Elanor suddenly went cold, and moved to stand with a clear view of the Ring. She noticed Chameleon had moved closer to the door. Titania had shifted so that she was on the other side of the Ring, furthest away from him. Elanor flexed her hands and prepared Silverfire.

"Forty-six," Shatter said out loud. The whole room tensed. Elanor raised her hands, and the Wards about the Ephemeral Ring lit up, casting a bright light around the room. Chameleon shaded his eyes.

"Forty-eight," Shatter said, stepping back from the Ring and closer to Chameleon as Titania's aura flared to life.

"Forty-nine. Fifty," Shatter said with finality.

Elanor held her breath. Nothing happened. She looked across the room at Titania, who narrowed her eyes. Shatter turned to face Chameleon. He shrugged.

Then the Ring flared to life, and a soldier in gaudy blue and red armor appeared. He held Dark Glider's head aloft, his blood dripping to the floor.

"We've found ways around your little Weaves," he said with contempt, throwing his trophy at the Wards. A shower of sparks lit up the room upon impact, but the Ward did not fail.

He glanced around the room. "I am the Captain of the Queens' Guard, Bardiche. You must be Titania."

"Hooklance couldn't come?" Shatter asked with venom.

"He's busy," Bardiche responded, not looking at Shatter. "I have come with a message."

"Speak it," Titania said, her voice contained.

"Surrender, and come back with me, and the rest of your people will be granted mercy." He paused, wiping at the blood on his bare arm. "Refuse," he smiled, his eyes beginning to glow red, "and all will burn."

"Your False Sisters have shown no mercy," Titania retorted. "They use those foul weapons and deny our dead a proper Return. How can we trust your words?"

He shrugged. "I'm just a soldier. I follow my orders. This is the message." He pulled a stone from the pouch at his side. "It took us a while, but we've mastered your little trick." He rolled the stone in his palm. "And ours are much stronger."

"We have nothing to say to a murderer like you," Titania said. "Go. Take that answer to your False Queens. We have seen how they keep their promises." She waved him away. "Go!"

Bardiche continued rolling the stone in his palm.

"You cannot break my Ward," Elanor told him. "It would just blow up in your face."

"Slut," he snarled. "I'll be glad when you come under my blade. It will not be quick."

"I know men like you," Elanor shot back. "It's always quick."

He spat on the Ward. "This has been your only warning," he swore. He glanced at the door. "I'll see you soon." He disappeared, and the stone hit the floor.

Elanor threw all her Power into the Ward. A flare of Redfire filled the space inside it. Acting quickly, Elanor compressed the Ward, pushing both it and the Redfire within into the Ephemeral Ring. She heard splitting stone and ripping cloth. Elanor screamed in rage, and Pushed everything she was and would ever be into the Ward. Silver light flared, overpowering the red, and then — with a bang — all the light disappeared.

"Damn," Chameleon breathed, throwing something with his right hand. A dark disk arced through the air toward Titania. He turned, throwing again, and was hit by Shatter, the impact driving him to the ground.

She struggled to keep his arms contained, grabbing his wrists and twisting. He grunted as Shatter's blows broke both his arms. He tried to say something, but Shatter drove her forehead into the side of his head. His skull cracked, and he fell unconscious.

Titania calmly gestured at both flying disks. Her Power diverted them into the walls, where she covered them in Shields, fearing another Redfire explosion.

"Shatter, move!" Elanor yelled. Shatter rolled away from Chameleon's unconscious form as Elanor conjured a dome-shaped Shield over it. There was a burst of Redfire that shook the room and rained stones down from the ceiling.

Elanor slumped to the floor.

Shatter moved to help her, but Titania was already there.

"They work in pairs!" she called to Shatter. "See to the guards at the door."

Shatter opened the door to chaos. A dark form darted around the room, moving so fast, all she could see was a blur. Two guards were down. EagleClaw and the sergeant were back-to-back, swords up. Another guard emerged from a Shadow in front of the dark form, but in a blur, she was hit, and fell down in a puddle of blood.

"Forgive me," Shatter said, as she scooped up some of the blood with her Power and flung it in the direction of the dark form. It passed through the blood cloud, and tried to turn toward Shatter and the door, but couldn't stop. It hit the wall with bone-breaking force and began to writhe in pain. EagleClaw's blade darted in and impaled it. Screaming, it tried to climb up the blade, but Shatter took its head off. EagleClaw dropped his blade in shock as the mangled body of a young man emerged from the Shadow.

"Goddess's mercy," the sergeant breathed.

Shatter looked up the corridor, toward more yelling and clashing of arms.

"Shatter, Eagle, see what's going on," Titania commanded from the door. She supported Elanor under one arm.

Shatter nodded, and ran up the corridor. EagleClaw looked at his sword, covered in blood and gore on the floor.

"Take mine," Elanor offered, tossing him her sword. He caught it, and gave her a nod of thanks before following Shatter.

"He was admiring it earlier," Elanor explained. "I can stand," she told Titania after he left.

"See to them," Titania ordered, gesturing to the fallen guards on the floor as she went to the downed female Leather-wing.

Elanor stumbled to the two guards. She found them hamstrung, their throats cut. She looked across the room, knowing there was nothing to do. Titania was rising with a similar shake of her head.

"Sergeant," she called. "Are you hurt? Any cuts?"

"No, Ma'am," he called back. He held up his arms. "The ringmail held." He looked at Elanor. "Thank you, My Lady. You and your partner added a strong Weave to this." He helped her up.

"Don't call me that," she muttered. At his confused face, she clarified, "I am not a lady. I'm told that all the time. But I will take your thanks to her. She'll be very happy it saved you."

"My own partner will be happy, too," he told her. "Foul thing," he cursed, looking at the body. "What is it, Regent?"

"I don't know," Titania replied, prodding the body with EagleClaw's sword. "I can't see the eyes, but it has no wings. Either a wingless, or an Elenite."

"Who would do such a thing to someone?" the sergeant asked with a shudder.

Titania and Elanor shared a glance. They suspected they knew who.

A strong Send from Shatter hit them. *"Regent! The stronghold has been attacked by a squad of Air soldiers. They've all been killed. EagleClaw is taking a group to find their Ephemeral Ring, but this place is no longer secret."*

"And I was just getting to like it here," Titania replied. *"Begin the evacuation. I will go with Elanor to the Exile Queen's mountain. Split the others between the second and third sites."*

"Yes, Regent."

"And come to the mountain when you're done."

"I would stay, to make sure the Rings are destroyed. Then I will fly to another Ring," Shatter countered.

Elanor's fear surged.

"No, Captain," Titania told her. *"I need you. EagleClaw will stay with this group and destroy the Rings. Unless you don't trust him?"*

"No, Regent. He's a good soldier. I'll tell him. *Elanor, keep her safe.*"

"I will, Captain," Elanor replied. Then Shatter was gone.

"Sergeant," Titania said. "Please fetch a chest. I want to take this horrible thing with me." She gestured to the body.

"Yes, Regent," he replied, but he hesitated.

"Elanor will keep me safe," Titania assured him, wiping the sword she had been using on her skirts. She handed it to Elanor.

She hefted it. It was heavier than she was used to, but still a good blade. "A fair trade," Elanor said.

The sergeant grinned and ran up the corridor.

Titania slumped back against the wall, hit by a sudden weariness after all the fighting. "I really was beginning to like this place," she mused to Elanor.

"Too cold," Elanor commented.

Titania tried to smile, but the dead bodies at her feet blocked the effort. "More blood on their hands," she finally said.

Elanor could only nod.

Chapter Four
Between Storms

Elanor stepped out of the Ring into Min's embrace. They wrapped their wings around each other and held on. Elanor finally let herself relax, allowing the tension to float away as she drew a deep breath from Min's hair. Elanor would have stayed in her embrace longer, but Min pulled away, kissed her quickly, and then broke the hug completely as the twins began to kick. Then she hit Elanor on the shoulder.

"You had me worried."

"Next time you can go," Elanor said as Flora embraced her.

"No!" Flora said emphatically. "None of you are putting yourself in danger again. I forbid it." She squeezed Elanor until she was short of breath.

"You'll have to tell the False Sisters that," Merry-Weather replied tartly. "Oh, let her go, she's turning blue."

"It's all right, Mum," Elanor said, kissing Flora on the top of her head. "It wasn't your fault."

Flora nodded, and went to embrace her twin. Luna hugged her sister, her hands still wrapped in purple cloth.

Hesitantly, Min returned to Elanor's side and slipped her arm around her waist. "Your mother is here," she whispered.

"Goddess's mercy," Elanor whispered back.

"That's not the sword you left with," Merry-Weather noted.

"One of the soldiers, EagleClaw, needed the other one more than I did," Elanor explained.

"How is he?" Min asked. "I feel bad that we got him detained."

"He's well. He's coordinating the last of the evacuation and the destruction of the Rings," Elanor replied, her eyes sweeping the crowd in the library. "Shatter should be coming through soon."

"Good," Min said. "When news of the attack came, Merry-Weather Sent for Steel and Shield. They should be here in the morning."

Elanor raised her eyes at Min.

"Titania wants a full council," Min explained.

Elanor took a deep breath.

"Yes," Min said with understanding. "She'll be here." In a Send, she added, *"Keep her away from me. I can't take any more of her questions and accusations."*

"I'll try. If you'll keep my mother away," Elanor countered.

"I would rather go back to digging privies," Min replied with a shiver.

Elanor smiled, and then lost it as she saw Celia coming up the hallway from below. Her mother's quick eyes found her, too, and she came striding over. The staff of the Queen's Justice thumped impatiently on the floor as she stared at Min and Elanor. Min tried to pull away, but Elanor held her tight.

Elanor could read her mother's eyes: 'What are you doing with my daughter?' they demanded. Her dislike of Min and her unborn children — fathered by a non-Fairy! — had become yet another source of friction between mother and daughter. But Elanor refused to be cowed, and kept Min firmly by her side. Despite Min stepping on her foot and singing loudly in a widely-broadcast Send.

"So, what happened?" Celia demanded, holding out her hand.

Elanor kept her own hands at her sides. "The Ward I set up. . . ."

"Show me," Celia interrupted, shaking her hand at Elanor. She looked at Min. "This is a private conversation. You can seduce my daughter later."

Min narrowed her eyes, all thought of leaving now gone. She tightened her grip on Elanor's waist.

"Mother," Elanor said with barely contained anger, "you will not speak to her that way. She stays by my side until. . . ."

"Fine, fine," Celia said, waving her hand, and dismissing Min from her thoughts, "but stop singing. It's causing interference." She looked back at Elanor. "Lady Elanor," she said formally. "I must know everything that happened. I am the Queen's Justice."

"I had forgotten," Elanor said sarcastically. She held out her hand. "Here. I'll Show you."

Celia grabbed her wrist roughly and was in Elanor's head before she could take another breath. Elanor winced as Celia riffled through her memories. As her mother got close to her fights, first with Min and then Flora, Elanor summoned all her Power — and the strength of a Warding Min and Goldberry had added to her amulet after removing Talia's controls from her mind — and Pushed Celia out.

"That's enough," Elanor declared. She twisted her arm out of Celia's grip.

"Foolish child," Celia said, shaking her head. "It was a risk to push the Ward into the Ephemeral Ring. The whole Weave could have collapsed, and the backlash would have been monumental."

Elanor defended herself. "So was the blast of Redfire. And it was blood-fueled. I did the best I could. Most of it went through the open Ring. It was a risk, but a calculated one. You would have made the same decision to protect the Regent and our soldiers."

Celia looked like she wanted to debate the matter further, but instead she folded her arms. "Maybe. Maybe not. Next time, take a breath and examine all your options."

"If I she had done that," Min interjected, jumping to Elanor's defense, "then the Ward would have broken, and all of them would have been killed or severely burned."

"Who are you to speak to me so?" Celia responded with wounded contempt.

"I am a daughter of Paramounts going back to the First Fairies," Min proclaimed proudly. "I'm the one who created the Weaves that protect this place. My modifications to our soldiers' armor save lives. You may be older and more experienced in creating Weaves, but we've actually used them to defend our Sisters."

"You are nothing but an Elenite's. . . ."

"Mother," Elanor interrupted sharply, before the woman could insult Min further. "I'm tired." She turned to Flora, who had been watching the whole time. "Mum, would you wake me when the council is fully assembled?"

"Yes, Lady Elanor, I will," Flora replied with courtesy, ignoring Celia's dark stare.

Elanor and Min walked away. They went to Min's room and shut the door.

"Is there something I can help you with, Lady Celia?" Flora asked, her face neutral. "I think Regent Titania went below to see to the defenses."

'Why my daughter shows you all respect and none to me,' she thought, 'I will never understand.' Out loud, she asked, "Do you know when Lady Conwenne will be here?"

"No, My Lady. Merry-Weather might." She gestured to where her mother was standing under the crystal dome.

"Thank you," Celia said, with a stiff politeness that did not reach her eyes. She walked off toward Merry-Weather.

"You stand between storms," Luna observed. "I don't know how you manage it."

"Strong hair pins," Flora told her tartly. "And lots of tea, sister."

"Well, let us brew some then. The Regent will want her cup before long, too."

$$\left(\smallsmile \thickapprox \dot{\varnothing} \right.$$

"I thought you wanted to sleep," Min said, turning her head from Elanor's kiss.

"I just want to thank you for that."

"You can do that with words, not your lips." A pause. "And not your hands. Stop that. They get irritated when you do that." She pushed Elanor's hands away. "And I want to sleep, too."

Elanor moved back, but remained in Min's arms.

"I'm sorry. I just found it exciting: you standing up to my mother."

"Everything I do makes you excited," Min noted, with a touch of admiration, but mostly irritation. "I just want to sleep, now that I know you're safe."

"Yes, Beautiful." Elanor snuggled closer and sighed contentedly.

"Did you see her eyes?" Min joked, closing her own.

46

"I thought they were going to pop out and roll down the stairs," Elanor replied, laughing, and pulling Min closer.

"Maybe in the morning," Min muttered into Elanor's shoulder.

Elanor kissed her cheek, and drifted off to sleep.

Chapter Five
The Council

In the morning, Elanor and Min emerged from Min's room arm in arm. A large crowd was forming in the library. Under the dome, a large table had been brought in for the council. Flora and Luna stood in front of it, flanked by Merry-Weather.

"We thought you would never get up," Flora called. "Come, we have guests."

Min looked uncomfortable under so many eyes and tried to pull away from Elanor, but she held her close and walked proudly toward the gathering.

The crowd parted, revealing Shatter, who had returned during the night, and Steeltrap and Shieldbreaker, both looking tired and dusty from the road. Steel had her purple breastplate on, and held her dragon helm under her arm. She bore a Captain's sigil on her chest now. Shield wore a well-worn Healer's tunic over her ringmail. Her brown hair was getting longer, and she had tied it back in a short queue at the back of her head. She noticed Min's eyes on it and gripped it, slightly embarrassed.

"It's hard to get used to," she admitted as Min hugged her.

"It's beautiful," Min disagreed. "Suits you."

Steel snorted, setting down her helm to hug Elanor. "You two?" she asked, confused and slightly jealous. "I. . . . I don't know what to think."

"Then be wise and say nothing," Shatter advised from the side.

"You know you'll always be my soldier," Elanor assured Steel, kissing her on the cheek.

"You'll have to be careful about that now. My wives are here. Belladonna can be very jealous," Steel warned her, kissing her on the cheek as well.

Elanor raised her eyes.

"Not here now, but close," Steel amended.

"How are you feeling?" Shield asked Min, gently touching her belly.

"Tired, but that's to be expected. They keep me up, kicking and fussing," Min admitted.

"She works too hard," Elanor complained.

"I'll speak to Flora," Shield said. "See what can be done."

"Let the little mother go," Steel said, breaking away from Elanor and hugging Min. "It's my turn." She picked her up, and gently spun her around. "I've missed you, White Lady." She set her down and kissed her cheek.

"What about your wives?" Min needled her, not pulling out of her arms.

"They understand," Steel said, presenting her cheek to be kissed. Min complied.

Shield and Elanor hugged, not as emotionally, but as two Sisters reunited.

"And now it's my turn," Shatter pronounced, pulling Min into her arms and wings. "I, too, have missed you." Min rested her head on the Captain's strong chest and tried not to cry.

"Why do I make all of you cry?" Shatter asked with exasperation, letting Min go.

"We are foolish, emotional court flowers," Min replied, wiping her eyes. "You told us so."

"Flowers yes, but ones made of silksteel, with diamond thorns," Shatter countered. "I'm proud of both of you. All of you," she said, taking in Steel and Shield as well. She held out her hands. "Join with me, Sisters."

They all joined hands. *"Goddess be thanked that we are all safe and together again,"* Shield intoned.

"If only Gold and Raven were here," Min said.

"They're with us," Shatter swore. *"In our hearts."*

"We are the survivors," Elanor said.

"And we hope our Sisters will Return swiftly," Shield entreated.

They stayed in the Circle a few moments more, safe in each others' presence. Alone understanding all they had seen and done.

Finally, Shatter broke the Circle, and they all let go and bowed to one another.

"Now," Shatter said, clearing her throat. "I must introduce my wife and husband."

She turned, and presented two Leather-wings. "Stiletto, my wife." The woman bowed in respect to Min and Elanor, and nodded to Steel and Shield. She kept one hand protectively over her large, pregnant belly, while the other absently tapped the pommel of a dagger at her side. "And Saber, my husband." He smiled, and gracefully bowed to the Ladies and nodded to the soldiers. A narrow, curved, matched set of dueling sword and dagger rode easily on his hips.

"They were trapped on the north side of Fae-Treval when the Three Sisters struck," Shatter explained. "They were unable to hold the farm, and had to flee. Finally found Steel's wives, and made their way here. I'm happy to have them home again."

"That's why your aura was different," Elanor realized. "I'm happy for you."

"This is not home," Stiletto argued. "I don't understand why you wanted us here, Staff. There is much work to be done at the new stronghold."

"Now, dear," Saber said, trying to quell   the   coming argument.

"How soon will you give birth?" Min asked, also trying to ease the tension.

"Another moon," she replied politely to Min, then turned her intense eyes back to Shatter. "I am capable of doing anything needed. I am not to be coddled."

"I'm sure Staff doesn't think that," Saber said.

"I wanted the best midwives I know for your birth," Shatter explained. "Flora and Luna. I trust them with my life. And Shield, too. I will not allow anything to happen to you."

"This may be my first child, but I know what to do," Stiletto replied. "I could give birth in the middle of a battle, hand her a sword, and keep fighting."

"The point is, you don't have to," Flora said, stepping up. "I have delivered countless babies. I would be honored to assist you."

Stiletto seemed torn between her anger at Shatter and her respect for Flora. She finally nodded. "You said you had quarters ready?" she reminded Shatter.

"Yes." She turned to a passing soldier. "Tiger, could you take my wife and husband down to the storeroom barracks? The Quartermaster is expecting them."

Tiger nodded. "Yes, Captain."

"I will see you later," Shatter said, moving to kiss Stiletto. She turned her head, and only let Shatter kiss her cheek.

"Lead the way, soldier," Stiletto commanded, setting off. Tiger stumbled and followed at her heels.

Shatter gripped Saber's arm and kissed him.

"It will take time," he said, patting her arm. "You have been gone so long." Then he followed their wife.

Steel spoke into the sudden silence. "I will bring my wives here, too. Flora is good." She nodded at her. "But sometimes the teeth can be tricky. Best to have someone with experience there, too."

Flora smiled, not taking offense, and walked away.

"Teeth?" Min asked, not sure she wanted to know.

"Yes," Steel said proudly. "Some Leather-wings have teeth down there." She gestured down. "Nightshade doesn't, but Belladonna does. Almost lost a finger the first time. Well, not really teeth, more like fangs or barbs."

Min covered her mouth. Elanor had gone white.

"You're joking?" Min asked, looking from Steel to Shatter. "She is joking, right?"

Shatter shook her head, confirming that Steel was indeed not joking.

"I guess I should have mentioned that before we went off to the lake that night," Steel said to a still speechless Elanor. "I wanted to be called Fangtrap, but mother wouldn't allow it."

"Come on," Min said, pulling Elanor away. "I'm hungry."

"You can be a cursed bastard sometimes," Shield remarked, and followed them.

"I thought she knew," Steel said with a shrug.

Shatter contemplated hitting Steel, but she said, "So, Captain now," instead.

Steel grinned. "I hope I can do as good a job as you have."

"So, how is it?

"Silverfire and Riverbend are holding well. For a bunch of farmers and laborers, they can fight," Steel said with admiration. "And we've been reinforced with a few groups of Grass and Air defectors."

"Keep an eye on them," Shatter counseled.

"We do. What really worries me is Bell-Oak. Lord Arabore hasn't picked a side. He keeps his garrison tight to the castle and town." She frowned. "He lets us use the Ring in the Shrine, and he sells us supplies, but nothing more."

"He's waiting. Playing both sides. I knew him as a careful commander when he was known as Scimitar. These last years have made him more cynical." Shatter sighed. "I wouldn't count on anything from him, and be ready in case he turns."

"We are."

"Maybe I should send him a message. We do have a history," Shatter mused, half to herself. Steel shrugged.

"What about Paramount Holly?"

Steel snorted. "She's been a help, but I don't trust her either, and I don't think she's reliable. Shield is helping her with her addictions, but. . . ." She stopped. "We used her Ring to get here. I just. . . . As Gold said, she sets my teeth on edge. And that room of hers." She shuddered. "I get a bad feeling every time I'm there."

Shatter smiled in sympathy. "Let's get something to eat before the council."

She turned, and almost tripped over Obsidian, who was holding a tray. She stepped back, and offered it to them.

"Thank you," Steel said, grabbing several bacon-stuffed rolls. With a nod to Shatter, she moved off.

52

"Did you speak to her?" Shatter asked, taking some rolls for herself.

Obsidian nodded.

"Good. It will take time, but she'll help you."

Obsidian Sent a question.

"Because that's all I am willing to give you." Her voice softened. "She has the most memories. All of ours. It's best for you to See everything. But you must have patience. This is hard for all of us."

Obsidian frowned.

"I know it's hard for you, too. But she was my Sister. And you didn't know her as long I as I did. You must earn this."

Obsidian narrowed her eyes and frowned more deeply.

"Then find another place," Shatter said harshly. "Merry-Weather can take you elsewhere. Forget about her. Do you think I walked into the garrison, and they handed me a Captain's badge? You have potential, but you must earn your place. Especially now." Shatter took another roll from Obsidian's tray and walked off.

Obsidian remained rooted to the spot, radiating frustration. Her hands clenched on the sides of the tray, denting the metal.

"There you are, child," Merry-Weather said. "Where's all your food?" She paused. "Well, you know soldiers. Go, get some more. Titania and Conwenne want to start soon. And they can't do that if people are still hungry." Obsidian didn't move. "Go. Shatter is right: you need to earn your place."

Obsidian finally strode away.

"Children," Merry-Weather swore, taking in the whole of the room.

Titania sat in her normal place of honor at the table. To her left was an empty chair, reserved for the Queen. To the Queen's left sat Shatter and the other survivors. Celia and Lady Conwenne sat to the right, with Merry-Weather and a grim, scarred Leather-wing lieutenant.

Lady Conwenne was a tall, commanding Iridescent who had risen to the rank of High Paramount after the death of Miranda. Her head was shaved, except for 3 small braids: one — dyed blue — lay behind her left ear, while a red one lay behind the right, and the third — a bit longer and dyed black — ran down from the crown of her head to her shoulder. She smiled humorlessly as she talked to Celia.

"That is Lady Conwenne," Min whispered in explanation to Shield. "High Paramount. She's been studying the blackblades. She'll want to talk to you."

"What's with the braids?" Shield asked. "Iridescents rarely shave their heads."

"One for each remaining False Sister, and one for Wingless," Min explained quietly. "She's also the Twins' mother." Min made the Sign of the Three.

Shield repeated it. "I'm sorry," she said. She started to ask a question, but stopped.

Min answered the unasked query. "Nova's parents and family aren't here. I don't know where they are. They escaped the Night of Black Wings, but I haven't heard from them since. Maybe Titania or Merry-Weather will know."

"And the lieutenant?" Shield asked, putting her inner torment aside for the moment.

"I don't know," Min admitted. "He wears the symbol of the Queen's Guard. I expect the Regent will tell us."

Titania stood. The murmur of conversation stilled. "Thanks to the Goddess, the Mother of Waves, for keeping her people safe through these hard times. Since our Keeper and her Shrinekeepers are still missing, I would ask each of you to silently call to Her in your own way." She bent her head. All through the library, silence fell, as everyone entreated the Goddess.

Titania raised her head. "To the Queen," she said, raising her cup to the empty chair to her left.

"The Queen," came the response, echoing through the mountain.

"Now," Titania said, sitting down. "I know you have heard rumors and stories about what happened yesterday. I will speak to that later. Suffice it to say, my stronghold has moved. All who need the information will be given its location. Now." She turned to the lieutenant. "Breach, I know you are eager to return. Please report."

He stood. "Regent, I bring word from Lord Oberon and Captain Shattersteel. We hold the Embassy in Elen, between the towns of Ford and Bend. The False Sisters' forces press us hard, but we have managed to procure or improvise enough defenses for now. The bridge at Elen-Ford has been blocked since the Queen's death and the open hostilities with the Humans. Many are just caught in the middle. There are so many factions among the Elenites, and they seem to fight each other more than they do us, the False Sisters, or the Humans."

"What kind of factions?" Celia asked.

"Some want independence, while others want the Humans to leave, and others want the Fairies to leave. Then there are those who just want to kill. We've found Blood Cult agents in all of these groups." He shrugged. "It's chaos. I feel sorry for those who are just trying to feed their children."

Shatter spoke up. "The False Sisters are stirring the pot."

"Yes, Ma'am, but some groups are interfering with their troops, too."

Elanor noted, "Wingless is allied with the False Sisters, but he has his own plans. Or so the Heir — excuse me, the Queen — thought." Min squeezed her hand, sending her support.

Conwenne said what they were all thinking. "That brutal bastard must be stopped. What information do we have on him?"

Breach looked around the table, waiting for others to speak. When no one did, he replied, "We have only rumors. Some say he's fled to the north, to the mountains. Others say south. Even the Human Realm and the Exile Forest have been suggested."

"That's impossible," Min said with heat. "Those in the Forest would never support such a cruel man."

"I only know what I have heard," Breach replied with a bow of courtesy. "Several sources have said he's recruiting from the Elenites. And we know there's a large Elenite population there."

Min moved to speak, but Titania waved her to silence.

"This is something we must look into. All elements," she stressed, looking around the table. "We all know how easy it is to seduce those dissatisfied with their lives. Easy to lure them in, and get them to do horrible things." Silence filled the room. "Now, Lieutenant, what contact do you have with the Mistress of Shadows?"

A murmur went around the table.

"Her Agents come and go," Breech replied with a shrug. "They bring us information. But Oberon doesn't trust them, and her information is always treated as suspect."

"And is it always good?" Celia asked.

"As much as any information could be in a battle. Some is good, some's bad. Some is too old to be useful, and some is lies put forth by the enemy." Breach shrugged again.

"But Oberon doesn't trust her," Titania stressed.

"No, Regent. He does not."

Titania looked around the room. "Does anyone else have anything for Oberon and his soldiers?"

Shatter jumped in. "You say you're holding. Can you advance, or break the False Sisters' lines?"

"No," Breach replied. "We need more soldiers. But they can't defeat us, either. We're at a stalemate. Unless something changes, we'll still be there next year. And winter is near. That will slow things further."

"Is there anything you need from us?" Titania asked.

"More troops, more food. Oberon would like to see his wife and children," Breech noted with a smile. A light laugh rolled around the table.

"I would, too," Titania conceded. "I can give you more supplies. Lieutenant Breach, please take our best wishes to your soldiers and those helping you. You have the private letters?"

He touched his breast.

"Good," Titania said. "I know you need to return. If anything else comes up, I will relay it. And if more soldiers become free, we'll send them, too."

"That would be of great help," he commented with a bow. "Thank you, Regent."

"The supplies and the Ephemeral Ring to take you back are below," she replied, waving for a soldier to escort him.

Breach left, with another bow to the Regent and to the council as a whole.

"We must know more about Wingless and what his plans are," Conwenne said, banging her fist on the table. "If he's getting men from the Exile Forest. . . ."

"He isn't," Min argued.

"How can you know for sure?" Conwenne shot back. "Just because that one Elenite was a good man and said he was from there, doesn't make the rest of them good. Wingless could be breeding a whole army of foul blood users to overwhelm us."

Min banged her own fist on the table and stood. Shatter, beside her, stood as well. She put her hand on Min's arm and stopped her angry retort. "I can vouch for the young man. Unless he was even more naive than we knew, I do not think the Exile Forest is a danger to us."

"But," Merry-Weather added, also stopping Conwenne from shouting back, "there are many disaffected youths there. He could be exploiting them."

Titania stood. She motioned everyone else to sit back down, then turned to Min. "Lady Min, I know this strikes at your heart." She turned to Conwenne. "I understand your grief and desire to strike back. But." She addressed both of them, and all the others sitting and standing around the room. "You must remember we are all Sisters and Brothers here. We fight a common enemy. Things are confusing when we do not know all the details. We must be careful not to see enemies where there might be friends. Or friends where there are enemies." She paused, letting her words sink in. "Now." Conwenne and her research were next on the agenda, but she wanted the woman to cool down first. Turning to Merry-Weather, she asked, "What can you tell me about the state of our people and supplies?"

"Regent, winter is close, and game is scarce. But, as my daughter counseled me, there was much when we first arrived. We have stored and preserved what we could. It should be enough for us to get through the cold. The lower cavern that was overrun by fungus has been completely cleaned out now. It was damaged by a cave-in, but with some work, it should be suitable as a garden again." She looked at Conwenne. "I'll need the help of a few Paramounts to repair the sun shafts. Or, if they're damaged beyond fixing, to build Lamps to simulate the light."

"I'm sure Lady Elanor and Lady Min can help with that," Conwenne responded, casting a side eye in their direction. "My people are stretched very thin with providing security to the stronghold and the other refuges."

Elanor moved to speak, but Titania cut her off. "Min and Elanor are finishing the defenses for the mountain. That takes priority. I'm sure some of your students and staff have enough Power to do what Dame Merry-Weather needs. Some of the young people, perhaps. Many are very strong, or so I've been told."

"Getting them here is the issue," Conwenne objected. "When we have to go through multiple Rings and other security measures, it takes a great deal of time."

"You are High Paramount," Titania stressed. "This is your duty. This mountain supports all our other strongholds." She then turned to Elanor and Min. "Any time you can spare would be helpful."

"Yes, Regent," Elanor muttered.

"Anything else, Dame?" Titania asked.

"Of course, Regent, but I think we have limited time."

"Anything that all of us need to hear, then," Titania said with a smile.

"Just that we must be vigilant. There are enemies all around us. Some of those enemies are within our own groups. If you see anyone in need, it is your duty as a Servant of the Moon and Sun to help. My daughters say tea can heal anything. I usually need a shot of fireberry."

"Well said," Titania praised, to smiles and laughter all around. "We must never forget that we are Servants of the Moon and Sun. We bring light to the dark. The False Sisters have forgotten that."

She looked around the room again. "Paramount Conwenne, what do you have to tell us about these horrible weapons?"

Paramount Conwenne pulled a book from a bag at her side. She thumped it on the table and opened it. "They are very hard to study, which I think was by design. The fact that they function similarly to the Geodes — and allow communication and tracking — inhibits us. We have to be very careful, and maintain strong Wards. These foul things are almost alive, and try to escape. They can be destroyed by Silverfire." She nodded in grudging respect to Min. "And Lady Min has Shared her enhancements to our armor, which have saved many lives."

"But what are they made of?" Steel asked.

"We don't know exactly," Conwenne admitted. "It's some form of corrupted silksteel, but we cannot break it down. Something has either been added or removed to produce the killing effect."

"Have we consulted with the spinners or the silksteel smiths?" one of the soldiers standing behind Shatter asked. "Maybe they would have some insight."

"Of course I have," Conwenne snapped. "From the moment these things appeared, I have done everything I can to find out why they kill so quickly. The Crafthouses of the Human King were abandoned after his first attack on the Realm. We found nothing there." She paused, considering. "The Mistress of Shadows did lead that investigation, however." She looked up at Titania.

Titania sighed. "It seems we must discuss her now." She gathered herself. "During an attempt to gain access to Fae-Treval through a Ring, I was attacked by the Agent of Shadow who brought us the information about that Ring. He also smuggled in another Agent, who killed three soldiers before being killed himself. An Ephemeral Ring was planted outside, allowing a squad of Air to attack as well. They were all fought off and killed."

"What does the Mistress have to say about this?" Celia asked pointedly.

"I haven't contacted her yet, but I can imagine it will be the same thing she always says: These were rogue Agents, or ones corrupted by them, or some such thing." Titania's frown deepened.

"The same thing she said when those assassins attacked you on the road from Silverfire," Elanor said.

"And when they broke into the Tower of Learning at Fae-Kahani, thinking you were there," Steel supplied.

"Or after the attacks on Oberon," Merry-Weather added.

Titania held up her hands. "I understand. And I am furious at her lack of control over her people. Or her desire to kill me."

"But she has provided us good information, too," Shatter said. "We were warned about both attacks on Silverfire. Oberon's attackers were betrayed by their own Tether."

Celia sighed. "Then she is playing both sides."

"And she could be telling the truth," Min commented.

"In what way?" Titania asked.

"Her Shadow Agents operate mostly as teams, with only their Tether knowing what they're doing or why. It is possible she doesn't know, and these Tethers are the corrupted ones."

"Then she is either corrupt or incompetent," Conwenne declared. "How do you know this?"

"Raven was a teacher at the Shadow School before she joined the Queen's Guard," Min explained. "She told me certain things."

"And we don't even know where she is," Celia said with frustration. "She only communicates via Geode, and hasn't met with any of us in person since the death of the Queen."

"She's probably in the Shadow School," Min told her. "According to Raven, it's so wrapped in Shadows and Wards that it's not even really part of the Realm anymore. It exists in a place all its own." A murmur of amazement and frustration moved around the room.

"All of these are good points, and we could debate all day about what to do about her," Titania said. "There are two more things related to this recent attack. Lady Celia, have you studied the body I brought back?"

"Yes, but not as deeply as I would like. It was a foul thing. Definitely Fairy. Maybe Feather-wing, but I cannot be sure." She shuddered. "Young. I could see evidence of torture and corruption in the body. Definitely a blood user."

A shocked silence fell over the table. "How could anyone do such a thing?" Luna asked from behind Merry-Weather. "Goddess have mercy!"

"It has to be Wingless," Conwenne said, slamming her book closed. "There is little that murderous bastard would not do. This is evidence of the Mistress's collusion with the False Sisters. We must strike at her!"

"No, it is not," Celia countered. "The False Sisters are as corrupt and foul as him. Look at the things they do: use these blades, deny our dead a Return. There are rumors of mass graves outside Fae-Treval and other Sister strongholds."

Shield added, "And we do not know the fates of the Keeper and her people."

A murmur of voices rose around the table. Everyone had an opinion and was talking at once. After a moment, Titania nodded to Shatter, who stood up and called, "Quiet!" The room fell silent.

Titania also stood, and looked over all the faces before her. "I understand your anger and frustration. I cannot put into words the horror I feel after all the False Sisters have done. And something, I swear, will be done about it."

"You said there was a second thing?" Celia reminded her.

"Yes," Titania said, with a grim smile. She motioned for a soldier to come forth. She carried a steel-bound chest glowing with Wards. She placed it in front of Titania and stepped back with a bow.

The Regent laid her hand on the chest. "We captured the Ephemeral Ring used to attack my stronghold."

Another burst of commotion ensued, this time brighter, and more excited. Titania let it go on a bit longer, then waved to Shatter.

"Quiet!" she called again.

"I can see your excitement. But we must be careful. This might be another one of their traps," Titania warned, with a glance at Celia.

61

"We will not know until we examine it," the Queen's Justice said with excitement.

"Yes. Now." Titania gestured to the whole room. "We have plans to make, and tasks to finish. If there are no more questions or comments?" She paused. "Good. Go with the Goddess, and let her guide your steps."

Chapter Six
Mothers and Daughters

The crowd around the table began to disperse. The survivors, led by Shatter, joined hands for another quick moment of togetherness. Then they scattered, too. Shatter strode purposefully to the stairs, headed toward her wife and husband. Steel gave a wave, and made a beeline for the Ring, disappearing to wherever her wives were.

"I just need some sleep," Shield declared. "But first I need to examine you," she said to Min.

"No, you need to sleep first," Min disagreed. "The pain is gone for now. It was probably just overwork."

"You can take my room," Elanor told Shield. "I won't need it."

"So sure, are we?" Min asked, with a raised eyebrow.

Shield looked uncomfortably back and forth between the two. Elanor smiled, and Min sighed. "Go ahead. Last door on the left. I have work to do." She poked Elanor in the chest. "As do you!"

"Yes, Beautiful, I do," she replied with an even wider smile.

Not wishing to get caught in the middle, Shield left quickly, heading for Elanor's room.

Min was going to say something, but Elanor's face suddenly became grim, and Min felt someone behind her.

"Lady Min," Conwenne asked, "may I speak with you? Privately," she added at Elanor's frown.

"What is it, Paramount?" Min asked, with barely veiled anger. Elanor folded her arms.

"It is a private matter," Conwenne stressed. "I am the High Paramount, and you owe me your respect."

Elanor started to speak, but Min cut her off. "It's all right." She gave Elanor a quick peck on the cheek. "Would you come to my room, Paramount?" Min asked, leading the Paramount in that direction. Behind her, she heard Celia call out, "Elanor, I need you."

Once they reached her room, Min took her time getting settled in her chair, shifting this way and that. The twins kept moving in the opposite direction. After removing the books from the other chair, Conwenne sat and watched her.

"Twins are a chore," she finally said. "And wait till they start fighting for space. I got little sleep my last few moons."

Min smiled indulgently. "I get little sleep now."

"I could help you. Flora and Luna are superb midwives, but there are things that only another mother of twins knows," Conwenne continued. "Let me tell you. . . ."

"Paramount," Min interrupted. "What do you want? I have work to do. These Wards need to be ready before the next moon."

Conwenne visibly reined in her annoyance at being interrupted. "Your partner is very protective of you. I hope she isn't stepping on your toes too much. Mine didn't let me breathe for most of my pregnancy."

Min frowned. "I don't know if partner is the right word for her. This is all too new and confusing."

"Then paramour, lover, convenient bed partner."

"If you've just come into my room to insult me further, you can leave," Min told her coldly. "I have work to do." She shifted again, and glared at the older woman.

Conwenne swallowed a retort. "I just wanted to apologize for insinuating that he, your. . . ." She stopped.

"The father of my children. The man that I love," Min supplied, her anger rising again.

Conwenne nodded. "Might be in league with Wingless. I'm sorry. He seemed a good man, by all that I've been told."

"He is," Min stressed.

"But I do not apologize for being concerned about the Blood Cult and Wingless recruiting from the Exile Forest. There is a danger there. I'm right to worry." She pointed at Min. "And you should, too."

"He is not to blame for your daughters' deaths," Min told her, cruelly.

"Then who is to blame?" Conwenne snapped. "Our beloved and absent Queen? She, who could not contain her passion, and took all of you on her foolish quest? All of you who went with her? That bastard King who ordered the death of his own child? Wingless, who planned the attack, or those Elenites who killed them? Captain Shatterstaff, for not defending them?" She fixed Min under her gaze. "You, for still being alive?"

"Their faces haunt my dreams. I see them in every blond Fairy. Why did I live, and others die?" Min made the Sign of the Three. "I cannot answer that. No one can. Do you need my tears? I have them. More than I can count. Ask Shatter. She'll give you even more. The dead haunt us all."

Conwenne swallowed, her anger warring with her grief. "It is a horrible thing to outlive your children. I hope you never have to learn that." She took a deep breath. "And we can never be sure about the men who attacked you, since they were burned."

Min wanted to shout at her, order her out of her room, but instead she took a deep breath. "You know I do not have any memories of the attack. All I know I learned from others. If you need more, you must go to Captain Shatterstaff or Steeltrap. They disposed of the bodies."

"But they did come from the Human Realm. Under the orders of the King," Conwenne pressed.

"And they could have come from the Exile Forest," Min snapped. "Or they could have been some of the countless children our soldiers left behind. I do not understand your obsession with blaming the people of the Exile Forest. I didn't know such a place existed until I met him. You didn't either until very recently. It does them a disservice. To see enemies where there might be friends."

"And blind to see friends when they might be enemies," Conwenne quoted back.

"I love him," Min said through gritted teeth. "It kills me that I do not know if he is alive or dead. I cry every night that I will never see him again. Cry that my children might never know their father, as he never knew his. Paramount, what is the point of this? We are surrounded by real enemies. Why make others out of shadows? You didn't hear his story. You didn't see the pain on his face when he told us of his life. How he and others like him are tasked to rescue abused women and their children. Help them, or lead them to safety in the Exile Forest. I understand there may be cruel men there, too, but not in the numbers you worry about. There are plenty of enemies at our door already. The Forest is far away. Across the Realm. Let it be." Tears came to Min's eyes. "Across the Realm. Beyond the Diamond River." Min bowed her head, overwhelmed by her loss.

Conwenne stared at the young woman. She felt a prick of guilt for drawing her into such a painful discussion, but her own pain — her own desire for justice — drove her on.

"We all have pain and loss. All we can do — what we must do — is find ways to go on and fight." She stood and walked to Min, kneeling, and laying her hand on Min's leg. Min started and raised her head.

"I need your help," Conwenne said with effort. If Min's mind had been clearer, she would have smiled at the difficulty the Paramount had in asking. "The disk blades the Regent brought back are different. You've created defenses. I need your insight. I need to find a way to defeat these foul weapons. The spirits of my daughters insist on it. I demand it."

"Are you ordering me to help?" Min asked in surprise, wiping her tears away. "I would have given my assistance freely. They were your daughters, but they were also my Sisters. I cannot think of their sweet voices without crying. All I can see is their blood-soaked blankets. I don't need you to guilt me into grief. I have a whole store of it already. My convenient bed partner helps me carry it, as I help her carry her own."

"Then help me," Conwenne said, sitting back. "Help me, so no other mothers and Sisters have to carry the grief we do."

"Yes, Paramount," Min agreed, anger burning in her eyes. "I will help you." She stood, and waited for Conwenne to join her. The Paramount struggled to her feet, but Min did not offer to help her. Once she had risen, the Paramount went to the door. Outside, a Fairy waited, a steel Ward-bound chest at her feet. Min noted her beauty; she had a round face and wavy golden brown hair.

"We shall go to the Warded room in the armory," Conwenne announced. "Sunserri, take the chest ahead of us." The Fairy nodded, touched her Torc, and disappeared. "You know the Frequency of the Ephemeral Ring there?" Conwenne asked.

"I do," Min confirmed.

Conwenne nodded, and disappeared. Min looked around. There was no sign of Elanor. With a sigh, she touched her Torc and followed Conwenne and the young Paramount.

☾ ⌒⌒ ☼

"Elanor, I need you!"

Elanor frowned, as Celia strode across the floor to stop in front of her.

"Yes, Mother?" Elanor asked, with a glance at Min and Conwenne as they disappeared into Min's room.

"You can play later," Celia stressed. "I have need of you now. Come." She grabbed Elanor's arm, and started toward the hallway. Elanor did not move.

"We do more than play," Elanor told her mother harshly. "We're building the mountain's defenses."

Annoyed, Celia turned on her. "I need your help. We must study this Ephemeral Ring. The Regent commands it." She gestured to the chest that floated at her side.

"Why, when you need something, must I come? You're always too busy when I need you!" Elanor exclaimed, holding her ground.

Out of the corner of her eye, Elanor spied Flora and Luna. Flora moved closer, but Luna pulled her away. Other Fairies milled around, trying to ignore the spectacle.

"This is not the place to discuss this," Celia whispered harshly. She grabbed Elanor's arm, enfolded her with her Power, and transported them to an Ephemeral Ring.

As soon as their feet touched the floor, Elanor broke her mother's grip and stepped back, raising her hands defensively. "Never do that again! I don't care if you are my mother! Do that again and you will regret it!"

"Foolish girl," Celia said, ignoring Elanor's anger. "You made me leave the chest behind." She entered a Send. *"Sunserri. Please bring the chest to the Warded armory room."*

"I'm waiting for the High Paramount," Sunserri replied. *"She's speaking with Lady Min."*

"You can bring me the chest and return to your post. Go now," Celia commanded.

Elanor caught the edge of Sunserri's annoyance and wondered if she would disobey the order. But the young woman appeared quickly in the Ephemeral Ring, passed the chest to Celia, and disappeared again.

"Now we can go into the Warded room," Celia said, heading to the rear of the vast armory. With the conflict raging, the large cache of weapons left by the Exile Queen had been greatly reduced, so the space had been put to other uses. Elanor could hear armorers forming and fixing weapons. Her eyes were drawn to a corner, where seven suits of armor stood as silent guards on their wooden frames. The helms snarled.

Elanor approached them. Two empty frames stood in the middle. She ran her hand over the green and purple silksteel of a helm, muttering the names of the suits' owners.

"Honor, Helm, Talon, Harpoon." She stopped, making the Sign of the Three. "Spearhead, wherever you are, I hope you're keeping him safe. Shieldbreaker, I wish you would wear this, or at least the breastplate. Raven, may the Goddess keep you safe." She brushed the faceplate of Raven's helm and turned back around. Celia was standing before the door to the Warded room, her foot tapping impatiently.

"Are you done?" she asked.

"I was paying tribute to my fallen Sisters," Elanor informed her. "I don't come down here much. You should have more respect."

"That armor shouldn't sit here, gathering dust. Regent Titania should have a Guard. I will speak to her."

"No!" Elanor yelled back. "That is the armor of The Nine. No one else will wear it!"

Her shouting drew the eyes of the armorers. At Celia's glare, they returned to their work.

"Don't you have any self-control?" she said angrily. "Restrain yourself. It's just armor, meant to protect our brave soldiers. Would you have more die because of your foolish attachment? They're dead. Honor, Helm. . . ."

"Don't say their names," Elanor snarled, striding to stand right in front of Celia. "You dishonor them with your flippant words. They were my Sisters. You will respect their memory."

"They have Returned to the Cycle," Celia replied, not backing down. "They will have new lives, and a new purpose. By clinging to their old forms, you inhibit their growth. You must let go of them, and let their spirits move on."

"Are you the Keeper now, too?" Elanor mocked. "Oh, yes, nothing is beyond the great Paramount Celia. Queen's Justice. Confidant of the Regent. It must stick in your throat that Conwenne is High Paramount. You have two hands. You could hold both staffs." Elanor folded her arms. "Is there anything you can't do?" She glanced around the room, as if looking for answers. "Oh, yes — be a mother to your daughter."

Celia angrily gestured the door to the Warded room open. The chest flew in, landing with a thump in the middle of the room.

"Get in there," she ordered Elanor. "I will not be a spectacle. If you have things to say, you will say them to me in private."

Elanor gestured for her to go first. Celia went in. Elanor waited a breath, then followed.

The door slammed shut. The other Fairies returned to their tasks, smiling.

Chapter Seven
Bad Judgment

When Min appeared in the armory, Conwenne was standing by the door of the Warded room. Sunserri was by her side, still holding the chest.

"I'm sorry, Paramount," one of the armorers was telling Conwenne. "Paramount Celia and Lady Elanor went in there a while ago. They were having quite an argument. She Locked and Warded the door."

Min stepped up to the door. "Something's wrong." She opened her Sight, and Looked at the door and its Locking Weave.

"They probably wanted privacy," Conwenne disagreed.

"This was more than their normal mother and daughter fights. Can't you feel it?" Min stepped closer to the door, and began examining the Locking Ward with her Sight. Then she began to manipulate it.

Conwenne opened her Sight, too, and began Watching what Min was doing. "You won't be able to get through."

"Celia is strong," Min disagreed, her face contorting, "but she does things in a very rigid way. If you know that, you can usually get around or through." She pulled her hand back. "Curse!" She held her hand out to Conwenne. "Paramount, I need your help."

Conwenne stared at the hand. 'It's just an argument,' she thought. She opened her mouth to refuse, when a dual voice spoke in her mind. 'Mother,' it said in the most annoyed adult child voice possible. She also felt a mental prod.

"What do you need?" Conwenne said, taking Min's hand.

"Keep this line of force in a loop. No, in the other direction."

"But that's the opposite of the way it flows," Conwenne complained.

"Exactly."

Conwenne complied. The line moved like a wet cat in her mind, but she held it in a loop.

"Good," Min Sent. *"And I will do this."* Then, after a short pause, the Locking Ward fell away.

Conwenne let go of Min's hand and looked at her in shock. This young Fairy had removed the Weave of a Paramount — one with twice her age and experience — without a touch of feedback. What Conwenne had initially taken for arrogance now looked more like justified confidence.

Shaking her hand, Min said, "More like three times the age. And there was a small bit of feedback. I just Shielded you."

"You didn't have to do that," Conwenne protested, looking at her with new eyes.

"I understand pain, Paramount," Min replied. She began to conjure a Shield. "There is nothing I would not go through to defend my Sisters." She shaped the Shield to fit the door. "If you could open the door," Min prompted.

Conwenne began to feel uneasy. "Step back, all of you," she warned the onlookers. "Sunserri, set the chest down, and be ready with a Shield."

As Min raised her hands and Conwenne prepared to open the door, the forgotten chest began to glow like the red sky before a storm.

☾ ♒ ☼

As soon as Elanor crossed the threshold into the room, Celia gestured the door closed and reactivated the Wards. The edge of the door caught Elanor's skirt, ripping the cloth as it slammed shut. Elanor jerked the torn hem out of the door.

Shaking the cloth at her mother, she said, "Look what you did! This was the last decent thing I had. Now you've ruined that, too."

"Did you act that way with Talia?" Celia questioned. "No wonder she found other lovers and left you behind."

Before she knew what she was doing, Elanor crossed the space between them and slapped her mother. The sound echoed through the closed room.

"How dare you!" Celia raged. "I am your mother, and a Paramount. You will apologize. If you were anyone else, I would throw you into a Warded cell!"

"Mother?" Elanor raged. "You were never my mother. I may have come out of you, but that's it. You gave me up to Flora. Expected her to raise me. Left me, so you could study and become a Paramount. Why did you even have me? You never cared about me. I just got in your way. Prevented you from rising through the ranks. I saw you, maybe for the full moon, but most times not. I went to you with questions. I wanted your love. You turned me away."

"I did it all for you," Celia argued back. "I wanted a good place in the court for us. As a Paramount, we would have access to the Queen, to the nobles. Our status would be assured."

"I never cared about all that. I wanted my mother. Wanted you. You taught me I was a fool to try and get anything from you." Elanor clenched her fists. "Then he. . . ." She stopped, unable to go on.

"You can't blame me for him. That was your own bad judgment. And it seems to go on and on."

"My bad judgment?!" Elanor said, aghast. "Bad judgment. He raped me, Mother. Body and mind. I'm sorry my violation upset your ambitions."

"I didn't mean that," Celia responded, but Elanor interrupted.

"No, you meant it," Elanor stressed. "You mean everything you say. I saw your eyes that morning. It took ages for Luna to find you, and you were annoyed. Annoyed! You had been deep in contemplation, and my attack disrupted that."

Celia tried to explain. "That's not the way it was. She didn't tell me what had happened, but just dragged me away. No one told me till after I saw you. Your father wasn't there, either," she said, trying to shift the blame.

"He was hunting the bastard. Him, Oberon, and the Queen's Guard. Shatter's mother brought him back in chains." Elanor wanted to scream, but she took a deep breath instead. "And where were you? Flora never left my side. Tal. . . ." Elanor's voice broke. "She never left my side. And even the Queen: she was there, too." Elanor pointed at Celia. "But where were you? Back at the Tower. 'A delicate Weave,'" Elanor mocked. "Your work was more important than your daughter."

"Well, maybe it was," Celia shot back. "I provided you and your father a life of luxury. Where would he have been without me? Always telling the stories of that cursed spear. Living off the deeds of his ancestors. He would have starved without me. He would have dragged you down. You would've been living outside the walls, scraping by on the generosity of others." Celia pounded her chest. "I gave you a home in the palace. A seat beside the Heir. You even shared her bed." Celia sneered. "And you managed to mess that up, too. Just like your father."

"My father," Elanor snapped. "You never even came to his Pyre. I had to stand his Vigil alone." Tears began to flow. "I was just a girl, still in pain, and I had to tell my father's dead body about my life. Had to stand there all night. Curse you! You should have been there. Didn't you love him? Why did you leave us like that?"

"He always loved you — and the idea of you — more than me," Celia admitted, taking a deep breath. "He desperately wanted a child. Pestered, pressed, bribed, and cajoled me, until I just gave in. I never wanted to be pregnant. It just got in the way."

"Then why?" Elanor asked. She felt dizzy. She had always suspected, but to hear Celia say it out loud was still a blow. "Why not leave him? Let him find someone else, someone who would love his child? I don't understand. Why be that cruel?"

"I had to marry him," Celia shot back. "Him and that cursed spear. My mother and grandmother were waiting for a male from his line. All his brothers died. He was the only one left, so it had to be him."

"What are you talking about?" Elanor asked with confusion. "He never told me anything like that. You're lying. You're just covering up your neglect. Your weakness."

"I am not weak!" Celia finally shouted. "You're the weak one. You cannot live without your Talia, and now without your Min. You can't stand on your own two feet. I thought I taught you better. You're the weak one. Whatever strength you inherited from me, you use to grip tight to someone else. You never use it to be your own Fairy." She gestured around the room. "You blame me. You blame Talia. You blame Puck. Everyone but yourself. You should have been stronger! No true daughter of mine would have allowed herself to be used as you were."

Elanor saw only red. Fire bloomed from her hands, and she lunged at Celia. No Weave, just rage. Celia caught her daughter's hands in her own, wreathed in her own fire.

"Used?!" Elanor raged, as they pushed and pulled against each other. "Used?! I hated it, and struggled every moment." Celia pushed her back. Elanor went to one knee, Celia's Power Pushing to keep her down. "I fought him!"

"Not hard enough, apparently," Celia said dismissively, Pushing at Elanor's arms, trying to dampen her fire. But Elanor was too strong. "Release your fire!" Celia commanded. "Stop this!"

"I will release it," Elanor snarled. With supreme will, she surged to her feet and cast the Redfire at her mother. She poured all her rage into the flames. All the long years of pain and neglect. All her hate.

"Elanor! No!" Min yelled from the opening door, as a Shield appeared between Elanor and Celia. The fire rebounded, and Elanor gathered it back, forming a spinning circle of light. The whole room glowed red. Red light poured out of Elanor's flames and from the forgotten chest Celia had brought. Light shone from under the lid, which was struggling to remain shut. Red light also emanated from the other chest, now floating into the room on its own, unnoticed by the four women.

"Elanor!" Min yelled again, striding into the room. She held the Shield and Sent desperately to Elanor, trying to penetrate her rage-filled mind, seeking to calm her. Conwenne tried to hold her back, but Min shook off her hand. "Get Celia out of here," she ordered the Paramount.

"Stay out of this!" Elanor yelled, as she pushed Min's Send away. Rage fed her Fire, and the whirling circle became too bright to look at. "You, too," she snarled, casting a line of Fire to keep Conwenne back.

"Elanor, stop this!" Celia ordered. She began to form her own Shield. She intended to entrap Elanor with it and smother her Fire. She felt something fraying her Weave, pulling the lines askew. She pressed more energy into it.

"Elanor, stop!" Conwenne called. "I command it!"

Elanor only pressed the circle of Fire into Min's Shield. Sparks and red lightning filled the space between mother and daughter. Snarling, Elanor pressed harder, trying to overwhelm the Shield.

"Elanor, stop!" Min yelled again. Something was wrong. Elanor seemed to be wrapped in a red light, but it wasn't coming from her Fire. It ate into her aura and wreathed her like a cage.

"I don't want to hurt her!" Conwenne warned. She raised her hands, and Silverfire bloomed. "Elanor!" she yelled. "Stop, or I will stop you!"

But Elanor was lost in her rage. More Fire surged, beginning to eat away at the Shield. Min desperately poured more Power into it. She tried to reach Elanor, but the red light around her deflected the Send. She looked around the room, searching for something to use to stop Elanor. Conwenne was poised to cast, with killing intent.

Then Min saw the chests. They sat like two snarling dogs, lids opening, facing each other. The Wards had disappeared, and red light poured out of them, eating at Celia's Shield, feeding Elanor's rage, and sucking Power from the room to feed something growing in them.

'Forgive me,' Min thought. "Celia!" she both yelled and Sent with all her Power. "Down!"

Celia dropped. Min released her Shield, allowing Elanor's Fire to surge across the room, flying just over Celia's back. Then Min Pushed Elanor with all her strength, flinging her across the room to pin her against the wall. Elanor snarled and clawed at the Power holding her, ignoring the pain of her back against the rough stone. Her rage fought back, sending painful sparks up and down Min's arms.

"Conwenne," Min gasped, the effort of holding Elanor driving her to her knees. "The chests. Something's building! Get them out of here!" She struggled to her feet. The Power coming out of the chests began to eat at her. She screamed in pain as it cut into her. 'My children,' she thought, panicking, but she did not have any more strength for defense: she was using all of it to keep Elanor pinned to the wall. She was caught between a storm of rage and blood-red daggers. Min screamed again, unable to free herself.

Then there was a thump, and the pressure she had been feeling from Elanor's rage ceased. Fear added to the pain as Min looked in that direction, fearing that Elanor was dead. Conwenne stood beside her, her fist still balled. Elanor's head hung limply against her chest, but she was still breathing.

"Unconscious," Conwenne reported. "Release her!"

Min did so, and redirected all her Power into containing whatever evil was coming from the chests. Screaming in rage, she focused all her Light — as white as the sun — on them, their lids now open. More red light formed around them, eating into Min's white Light, dimming it and forcing her back.

"Get out!" Min called. She saw Conwenne drag Elanor toward the door. The light was too bright for her to see where Celia was. Min took a step back, then set her feet. "You will not win!" she swore. She pulled all her strength and formed a Shield. Min pushed it over the chests, seeking to contain their rising Power. The red light fought back, eating at her, and her Shield began to fray, bending under the assault.

Behind her, Conwenne dragged Elanor through the door. Min took a few more steps back. She still could not see Celia. Her store of strength was almost gone, and the red light seemed to sense it and prepared to surge. Min knew she had too far to go to make the door before she would be overwhelmed. She said a silent goodbye.

Then Light was offered to her hands. Blue Light from her left, and green from her right. 'Mother,' a voice boomed in her mind, 'stand." She tried to push away the offered potential, fearing harm to her unborn children, but the Light was pressed into her hands, and woven into her Shield. With a surge, Min pushed the red light back. A harsh gold Light wrapped around her and began to pull her back.

A silver Light, as strong as starlight on a moonless night, joined hers and pressed at the lids of the chests, struggling to close them.

Min took a few more steps back, and finally felt the threshold under her feet.

"Min," Celia commanded, *"when I say, pull your Power back completely. Conwenne: are you ready?"*

"Yes," Conwenne replied.

Min didn't have the energy to form words, just understanding. It was enough.

More Power surged from her allies, and Min screamed again, pushing at the red light. It fought and twisted, ripping tiles from the floor and stones from the wall.

"Now," came Celia's command.

Min pulled her Power back into herself. She wrapped her arms and wings tight around her belly as she was jerked back, like a puppet on a string. There was a thunderous boom as the door to the Warded room slammed shut, and Min skidded backwards on the smooth floor.

"Shield the door!" Conwenne yelled. "All your Power! Hold that door!"

Min Looked up from the floor and Saw the riot of colors as all the Fairies in the room, both trained and untrained, threw their Power into holding the door. Min had to drop her Sight or be blinded. Iridescent sparks flew all around the room. Rainbows of Power exploded and reformed, holding the red light behind the door. Then, there was a boom like a giant hammer hitting the entire mountain. Fairies fell to the ground, clutching their ears, as everything standing was knocked to the floor. With a great intake of air, the doors of the Warded room imploded. Chunks of door and stone flew around the room.

A piece of the door — a hinge, she noted — flew in Min's direction. She was too spent to use her Power, and simply watched it as it tumbled through the air, sharp edges ready to cut her down. She said goodbye again.

Then Celia appeared in front of her. The flying metal hit her in the back and drove her across the room. Min watched her fly, her body limp, to hit the floor on the far side of the room. Then a large rock hit Min's head, and she fell into darkness.

☾ ♒ ☼

"Did it work?" Dina asked eagerly, leaning over Tra.

Tra, her eyes still covered by a blue cloth, looked up from the black Geode. "No, it did not. There was a large explosion, but only a few deaths." She struck the table. "You were supposed to include an undeniable desire to examine them in the Wards on the chests. It should have gotten the whole council."

"It's not my fault," Dina said defensively, rubbing the stump of her right hand. "They must have been more careful than I expected."

"You should have planned for any eventuality." Tra wanted to sweep the Geode from the table, but settled for throwing a cup at the wall instead.

"And you should have put more Power into them," Dina accused back. "If the explosion had been larger, it might have cracked that mountain of theirs."

"If I had put more Power in, they would have been suspicious," Tra countered. She took a deep breath. "Send to Hooklance. Tell him to put the next step in motion."

Dina grinned. "I hope we have enough prisoners."

Tra smiled. "If we don't, we can bring more from Elen. No one will miss them."

Chapter Eight
Paramount

Min sat bolt upright in bed.

"My babies," she gasped.

"Are both fine," Flora reassured her, holding her left arm, or else Min would have darted right out of the bed. Luna held her other arm.

"Elanor?"

"She is also fine," Luna confirmed, with a glance over Min's head at Flora, who nodded slightly.

"Your babies protected you," Flora continued as she pushed Min, gently but firmly, back into the pillows she had piled up behind her. Min settled back, sitting up. Her hands covered her belly, feeling the twins move and kick. Their minds reached out and gripped hers. Min pushed back tears of relief as Luna passed her a cup of soothing tea.

Min drank, then turned to Flora. "What do you mean, Mum?"

"Conwenne swears she saw a Shield form — slight, and very much like a student's first try — and deflect some of the flying stones. The Shield looked like yours, but different, colored green and blue. The rock that got you was too big to be deflected," Flora told her, shaking her head in amazement. She made the Sign of the Three. "Goddess be thanked you're in one piece."

"And Elanor?" Min asked, looking around. "Where is she?"

Luna and Flora glanced furtively at each other, and Min felt a surge of worry.

"You said she was okay," she demanded. "Where is she?"

"She is safe," Flora said calmly, holding tight to Min's arm. "But Titania wants her kept asleep until she can be fully examined. Everyone was waiting for you to awaken."

"Then bring Titania here," Min demanded, trying to swing her legs out of the bed. There was a sudden rush of dizziness, and pain blossomed behind her left eye. Min let Flora pull her back into the bed.

"You do not command the Regent, Paramount," Luna chided her. "But she did leave orders for me to find her when you woke up." She patted Min's arm. "If you stay in bed, and listen to Flora, I will go and find her." Luna gave Min a peck on the cheek and left the room.

Min closed her eyes, taking deep breaths, and fighting back the pain. She felt Flora's warm, familiar Healing wash over her. The touch of it almost made her cry. "Mum," she muttered, and Flora gathered her into her arms. Then she did cry, pouring out all the worry and pain of these last many days. Flora held her, stroking her back.

After her sobs subsided, Flora sat up and admonished her. "You are scaring your children, Paramount. You must be strong."

Min sat up, wiping her eyes. "Yes, Mum. I'll try." Then Min looked at Flora. "What did you call me? Paramount?"

Flora smiled. "Yes. Conwenne pronounced it. 'She has the skills and knowledge. She just lacks the title,' she said."

"But I haven't taken the test, or walked the circle, or. . . ."

"Well," Flora said, pressing another cup into her hand, "she is the High Paramount, and with the Tower of Learning denied us, she can do as she wishes."

Min sipped her tea. Her headache was receding. "I don't know what to say."

"Then thank the Goddess, and your Sisters," Flora said with a shake of her wings. "You young people. When will you stop putting yourselves in danger?"

"I don't know, Mum," Min said, while swishing her tea around in its cup. "I guess when there's no danger left."

"And when will that be?" Flora asked, sitting down. Shifting topics, she asked, "How's your head? Shield told me you've been getting headaches. She hasn't had time yet, but you will make time for her to do a deep scan of you." Flora shook her hand at her patient. "You will not endanger these children with your stubbornness."

"Yes, Mum," Min agreed sheepishly, before taking another drink. Then she coughed, remembering. "Celia!" she exclaimed. "How is she?"

Flora was grim. "She's alive, but she won't be on her feet for a while. That cursed piece of the door just missed her spine, and it did major damage. It was a good thing," Flora made the Sign of the Three again, "that Longstride was below, and Sent to Shield right away. She might have died otherwise. As it is, she won't be able to walk or fly for a long time. But she can talk. She was demanding that Elanor be brought to her as soon as she woke up."

Min's stomach clenched. "After what she did? Celia must be furious."

Flora shook her head. "No. Celia knows something was affecting her. That it wasn't really Elanor."

"What happened?" Min asked.

"Beyond the False Sisters attacking us again," Titania answered breezily, as she strode into the room, "we don't know. Conwenne has some theories, but she wanted to wait until you were up before sharing them more widely. She wants your memories of the event."

"Regent," Flora said reverently, standing. "If you would excuse me." She moved toward the door.

"No, stay," Titania said, waving the maid back to a chair. Luna appeared behind her and offered Titania a chair as well. The Regent sat, and fixed Min with a stern eye. "So, you saved us again. I fully support your elevation to Paramount. It is long overdue."

"You're too kind, Regent," Min said, blushing. "But I don't know if I'm worthy."

"Then you most definitely are," Titania declared. "I felt the same way when the Queen" — she made the Sign of the Three, which was repeated by the others — "gave me the Staff of the Queen's Justice. You deserve it. You make all your teachers proud."

"Miranda," Min said in remembrance, touching her belly. "May she Return swiftly."

"Goddess grant," Luna echoed.

Titania hid her personal surge of grief by folding her arms and squeezing her chest. "Conwenne thinks the weapon and the Ephemeral Ring were linked somehow, and when they came together...." She clapped her hands. Luna jumped, then laughed nervously.

Min frowned. "You were the only one to handle the Ephemeral Ring chest," she reasoned. "I don't know who had the one with the weapon. . . ."

Titania made a slicing gesture. "We will not speculate more until you are better, and we are more secure. There might be prying eyes and ears about."

Min nodded, but her mind was racing. "What about Elanor?"

Titania sighed. "We think she was influenced somehow, but we don't know how, or to what extent."

"I felt something, even through the Warded door. Something evil."

"Conwenne told me," Titania agreed. "It might have been your link to Elanor. You two have become very close."

"Touching the Goddess so much," Flora said tartly, "will do that."

"Jealous, sister?" Luna asked, as she handed Titania a cup of tea.

"Of course I am," Flora said boldly, standing. "Who doesn't want the touch of a loved one? To lose yourself in their eyes, and their hands? I may be old, but I still yearn." She turned to Titania. "If you will excuse me, Regent, I have other patients. You." She pointed at Min. "Stay in bed, or Paramount or not. . . ." She left the threat hanging.

"Yes, Mum," Min promised. "I will."

Flora left, brushing Luna with her wings as she did so.

"I must go as well," Titania announced. "Conwenne is resting, but will see you soon." She glanced at Luna. "Do you need anyone to stay with you?"

"No. I think I'll sleep some more. Where are the others?" Min asked.

Titania filled her in. "Steeltrap has gone back to Paramount Holly's tower. We're sending more soldiers there. Shatter is on patrol, looking for spies and watchers. If it was their plan to destroy the mountain, then they may have scouts nearby." Titania looked to Luna.

"Shield is tending to the wounded with the other Healers. I will tell her you would like to see her," Luna offered.

Min yawned. "Thank you."

"Goddess guard your sleep, Paramount," Titania said, and left, followed by Luna.

"Paramount," Min whispered, awed. She touched her belly. "Your mother is a Paramount," she told the twins. Min smiled as their bright colors responded with happiness.

Min woke hungry.

She glanced around the room. Shield was lying on the floor, her head in the lap of a Leather-wing soldier. His eyes were open, staring at the ceiling. He was gently stroking Shield's hair. Min couldn't tell if Shield was asleep or not. After a moment, the soldier sensed Min's gaze on him.

"She's awake," he announced.

Shield shifted, and sat up.

"Don't move on my account," Min said cheekily. Shield looked tired. She always looked tired lately. Min wanted to order her into bed, or put her out with a Sleep Spell. But that would be too much, so she settled on teasing her instead. "So, he seems comfortable."

Shield only smiled. The soldier grinned and stood, then offered Shield a hand up. "Her head is padded now," he said to Min, batting at the knot of hair at the back of her skull. "I will fetch you both some food." He tried to kiss Shield, but she avoided him and went to stand by Min's bed. He smiled again and left.

"Who is that?" Min asked, adjusting her pillows so she could sit up. She tried to keep the grin off her face.

"Longstride," Shield answered, laying a hand on Min's arm.

"The one who you Healed." She motioned down with her chin.

Shield smiled despite herself. "Kind of takes away the mystery."

"And you and he?" Min let the question hang. She felt Shield's Power flowing through her, felt the twins grab at it with slow hands. Shield grinned, giving them each a pat.

"He wants to," Shield conceded. "He was one of the few who accepted my change in vocation and didn't shun me for leaving. But." She shrugged. "He could be dead tomorrow. Or I could be. Why make plans?"

"All the more reason to take what you can," Min argued. "If he's willing, and so are you. Why wait? If I had waited — if I had thought about the future — I would never have taken him to my room. Never. . . ." Min leaned back, fighting back tears. "Curses," she said. "I'm getting tired of crying."

Shield tried to think of something comforting to say, but she failed. "If you hadn't," she joked, "one of us would have. Who knows, it might have been me, with his child."

Min managed to smile. "Maybe. Maybe not. He liked my hair, all over him."

"Then I would have grown it," Shield said, shaking her hair out of its knot. She grinned. "I see the appeal," she said, brushing it out of her face.

Min laughed. But then she sighed. "I hate this. Not knowing."

"He's alive," Shield declared firmly, taking her hand. "I know it. The Goddess would not be so cruel as to take him away from you again."

"But she did," Min snapped. "He's not here. I'm alone."

"Don't talk like that," Shield said. "You're not alone. You'll see him again."

Min tried to pull away, but Shield held her tight. "You are not alone," she stressed. "They have a father. They will meet him one day."

"Don't argue with her," Longstride advised Min from the door. "She can be very positive when she wants to be." He set down a tray. Min's stomach jumped at the smell. "I have to go. Will I see you later?"

84

"I'll be here," Min told him.

He paused, waiting for more, but when Shield neither moved nor spoke, he smiled at Min. "Make sure she eats."

Min nodded, and Longstride left.

"Sister," Min admonished, batting Shield's arm.

"Sister," Shield shot back. "He's always doing that. It annoys me."

"What, caring about you? Making sure you eat and sleep?"

"Thinking I can't take care of myself. That others around me need to be told to feed me and make sure I take a nap." She went to the door, and made sure it was shut. "I am not a child."

"Well, you're acting like one now," Min said, lifting the lid on her tray. "He cares about you. Wants you to be safe. I can see the exhaustion in your eyes. He's right to worry."

"We're all exhausted. All of us," Shield stressed, sitting down. "First, I take Wake to get through the long days, then herbs to sleep. Then more Wake. Do you know how many arms and legs I've taken off? I don't, but her face hovers over all of them."

"Shieldbreaker," Min commanded, pulling the tray into her lap. "Come here and eat."

Shield looked to defy her at first, but then slid the chair over closer to the bed. She took a piece of bread, and dipped it in the herb spread. She chewed deliberately, then swallowed.

"Thank you," Min said, offering her a chicken leg.

"I don't eat meat anymore," Shield informed her, but she took the whole bowl of moonstems into her lap and dove in. Min took a bite of the chicken, and felt slightly guilty, but continued eating. They mock fought over the herb spread for a while. When the tray had been emptied, Shield looked much better.

"Now," Min said, sliding over to the edge of the bed. "You will sleep while I meditate."

"Min," Shield protested. "I have duties."

"A Paramount has given you a command." Min patted the side of the bed. "If there's another crisis, I'll know, and I will wake you. Now, get in this bed and sleep."

"Just another freshly promoted Fairy, abusing her new authority," Shield commented, but she climbed into the bed. She had to tighten her wings in the narrow space, but she got comfortable after a few moments of adjustment. "Is that how you ordered him?" she asked, closing her eyes.

"No," Min said wistfully, but also playfully. "I never had to say anything to him. He just joined me."

Shield chuckled, but there was a surge of grief and pain with it.

"It's all right, Sister," Min said soothingly, draping Shield's arm gently over her belly. "Listen to their heartbeats. They calm me. The others aren't really gone. We remember them."

"May they Return swiftly," Shield murmured, feeling the bright colors of Min and her children enfold her. For the first time since the cliffs, she drifted off into a dreamless sleep.

Chapter Nine
Stars of the Fallen

It was dark. Shatter opened the door carefully.

"It's all right," Min Sent. *"There's a Silence Weave over us. Did you bring it?"*

Shatter held up her right arm, and let a silver disk on a chain fall, spinning, from her hand.

Shield was still snuggled up to Min's right side, so Min could only reach out with her left hand. Shatter laid the disc in her palm. She ran her fingers over it, feeling the etching on it. In the center was a three-pointed star. In the spaces opposite the points were three nine-pointed stars. Around those was a border of seven more nine-pointed stars. On the back, Shield's name was engraved in Old Fairy.

"It's beautiful," Min marveled. *"You said Obsidian made these?"*

"Yes. One for each of us," Shatter Sent. *"When you Sent to me about needing something, I went to her. They're not all ready, but I persuaded her to finish this one. It should be perfect for what you need."*

"Yes, it is perfect." Min offered it back to her. *"Hold it up for me."*

Shatter did, and Min flexed her hand. A Weave — shining green and blue — appeared. She made a small adjustment, then let it float across the air to merge with the disk. There was a burst of light, and the scent of Flora's tea filled the air.

Shield sat up, blinking in the dim light. She said something, then realized there was a Silence over them, and glared at Min.

Min freed her right arm, and shook it back to feeling. She then brushed her palms together twice, and made a wide motion, dispelling the Silence.

"You let me sleep too long," Shield accused, getting out of the bed.

"You needed it," Shatter said. She presented the disk to her. Shield took it, confused. She sensed the Weave, and examined the etching.

"The Weave is the feeling of my twins' heartbeats. You slept so peacefully and for so long, I decided you needed some way to take them with you. And." She looked to Shatter.

"We needed something to put the Weave into, and Obsidian.. . ." Shatter looked questioningly at Shield. "Remember her?"

"No, I don't," she replied.

"The little girl Honor helped rescue at Riverbend," Min reminded her.

Shield nodded. "I remember her now. She couldn't talk."

"Still can't, or won't," Shatter noted. "She's obsessed with the story of Honor and the others. She's been pestering me ever since she arrived here. And Min has spoken with her, too."

"Well, so to speak," Min said with a grin.

"Yes," Shatter said, annoyed at her story being interrupted. "She's been making these for all of us. A gift, or tribute. I had to get her to add the other three stars."

Shield looked more closely at the disk. She rubbed her finger over the center star. "Sunrise," she breathed. She staggered back, and would have fallen if Shatter hadn't pushed a chair under her.

Min nodded. "Three stars, for Eagle, Macemother, and Silvermane."

"And seven for those who died at the cliffs." Shield looked up at Shatter. "What about Willow and Nova?" she asked, her voice catching.

"That was another argument," Shatter said. "That girl is more stubborn than any of you." Min smiled brightly, but Shield still frowned. "She'll add them to the back, with our names. That's why they're not all done."

Shield moved to hand the disc back to Shatter. "I will not accept it without them included."

Shatter held up her hands. "I'll take it back to her."

"But you need to put it on first," Min told her. "Make sure the Weave works."

"I'm sure it does," Shield said, hesitating.

"That's an order," Shatter said, folding her arms.

"Everyone is ordering me around today," Shield groused, but she reverently hung the disk around her neck. She took the silver in her hand, and closed her eyes. Wonder spread across her face. "Thank you," she said to Min. "This will help." Then she took it off, and handed it back to Shatter. This time she took it.

"If you Look with your Power," Shatter said, "within the stars are their names. Their full names."

Min snatched the disc out of Shatter's hand with a gesture. After examining it more closely, she said, "That girl is a wonder," and propelled it back to Shatter.

"Well, a Paramount needs an apprentice," Shield suggested with a shrug. Min muttered, not appearing to hear her.

"Conwenne should be here soon," Shatter announced. "Come on, Sister." She held out her hand, and pulled Shield from the chair. "We have duties."

"Yes, Captain," Shield said with good nature. She pointed at Min. "I'll see you later. Get some rest."

"Oh, yes," Min muttered, caught up in her own thoughts. "I might."

Shatter shook her head, and pulled Shield out of the room.

"An apprentice," Min muttered.

☾ ⌇ ☼

Min was sitting up and resting her feet on the floor when Conwenne knocked at the door.

"Feeling better?" she inquired when Min answered.

"Yes, Paramount, I am." Min swayed a little, and sat back down. "But I might still need a little more time."

Conwenne rushed into the room, but stopped short of touching Min. "I was worried," she said, standing awkwardly at Min's side.

"I'm getting better," she said with confidence. "I hope you've come about Elanor."

"I have," Conwenne replied, sitting down. "I came by earlier, but you were asleep with Healer Shield."

"She needed her sleep," Min said defensively.

"I understand," Conwenne said, raising her hands in a placating gesture. "I saw her save many lives. Celia wasn't the only one." Conwenne smiled. "She did rush to you first, though. And only after she was assured you were safe, did she go to the others."

Min narrowed her eyes, wondering if there was a rebuke there.

Conwenne sighed. "We had a rocky start, and there is much we disagree on, but you are powerful, and your Sisters are, too. Your loyalty and dedication to one another is admirable."

Min continued to frown. "I keep waiting for a but."

It was Conwenne's turn to frown. "I worry you might save one of your Sisters first, and let others come to harm."

"That is a concern I cannot allay," Min said. "I will defend all to the best of my ability. But I will not let one of them die when I can save them."

"If it was a choice between Elanor and me, who would you choose?" Conwenne asked.

"Right now, Paramount," Min said, pausing, then looking right at Conwenne. "I would die to save both of you. I almost did."

The two women stared at each other. Min's stubbornness clashed with Conwenne's. The air between them was filled with the unsaid.

Finally, Conwenne sat back, not breaking eye contact, but relaxing. "I would do the same for my partner or my children," she admitted. "We have our differences, but as you said, we have enemies at the door. We must work together. I gave you the title because I believe you deserve it. Do not make me regret that decision."

"You won't, Paramount," Min assured her, also relaxing.

"Good," Conwenne said. "I wanted to talk to you before we go to see Elanor. You sensed the evil in the chests. How, why? I felt nothing."

Min sighed. "It's hard to explain. It was just a feeling. I got nothing from the chest that was with us — not till it opened, at least. But I detected something inside the room. Maybe it was our connection. Elanor and I have worked mind in mind so much, and for so long now." Despite herself, Min blushed. "And we've been physically close lately as well."

"So I have heard," Conwenne teased. "So others have heard."

"Are you going to shame me like her mother does?" Min asked, slightly annoyed.

"No," Conwenne said. "But you must stop being so sensitive. If a simple teasing response makes you angry, then there might be something more. Something the two of you need to talk about."

"You sound like my mother," Min said. "But I'm sorry. I have been overly emotional." She gestured wryly to her belly. "I don't understand why."

Conwenne smiled honestly. "I remember that feeling. It was like I was walking a knife's edge. Stray one way, and I was ready to rip someone's eyes out, and the other way, cry and beg to be held. It's good that you have someone. I needed physical and emotional intimacy. A lot of it," she said with a twinkle.

"Elanor is never one to turn down intimacy," Min admitted. "And she's always asking for it, even begging sometimes. It's annoying when I just want to sleep and she's got her hands. . . ." She stopped, noticing Conwenne's wide grin. "I don't know why I'm telling you all this. It's personal."

"You need to talk to someone who's not one of the survivors or Flora. Your mother isn't here. You're still young, despite all you've been through." There was an invitation in Conwenne's voice.

Min shook her head. "Maybe. My mother has been busy. She's supporting Oberon, and trying to keep the north from falling into chaos."

"I'm here if you need me," Conwenne offered simply.

"I will remember that," Min said. "Now, about Elanor."

"Yes. Flora told you I kept her asleep after her minor wounds were Healed. I wanted to go deeper into her mind and make sure there was nothing implanted or left behind by the evil the False Sisters hid in those chests."

"And her defenses are too strong for you," Min reasoned, "even when she's asleep."

Conwenne nodded. "The Queen taught you all well."

"She did," Min affirmed. "And we strengthened them after as well."

"There is a wall in her mind, hard and impenetrable." Conwenne was troubled. "What's behind it, none of my people can See."

Min paused before replying. She worried about revealing too much about Elanor that was private: things that were just between the two of them. Even emotions unknown to her. "She keeps her darkness behind that wall. Everything that happened to her with Puck. Everything that happened between her and Talia. Even things about her mother." Min sighed. "I do not know all of it, but I know enough. She keeps it locked away. Otherwise, it would overwhelm her."

Conwenne also paused before responding. "As a mother and a daughter, I understand, but as High Paramount, there are bigger issues at play. What if this evil found its way behind her wall? What if it's influencing her, maybe without her knowledge? She could become a danger. More than a danger: she could destroy us all."

"I don't think anyone can truly understand her and her pain. It's personal. I've Shared some of it. I still have nightmares about removing the controls Talia put in her mind." Min looked straight at Conwenne. "What will we do? Leave her asleep forever? Put her in a Warded cell? She couldn't bear either. I cannot bear either."

Conwenne nodded in understanding. "That's why I came to you. You know her better than anyone else. You've been in her mind the most. And you're close in other ways that might help."

"You want me to exploit my relationship with her to make sure she isn't infected with this evil?" Min asked harshly.

"In a word, yes." Conwenne held up her hand to stop Min's angry retort. "There are paths only an intimate partner may trod. Your relationship may allow you to see beyond her wall. Might allow you clear Sight to make sure she's free of any influence. That is what I want. I don't want to keep her asleep forever. I can't hold her in a cell. She's too valuable to the Regent, and to you." She smiled. "It would take many Fairies to keep her secure and defend against your attempts to free her."

"I would never. . . ," Min began, but Conwenne smiled and raised an eyebrow. "Well, I would," Min amended. "And Steel would definitely help."

"All of you would help," Conwenne said with a grin. "You keep forgetting. I was young once, too, and had passionate lovers and dedicated friends. We would have done anything for each other. And we did."

"This feels like a betrayal, but sometimes love demands the hard things." 'Especially with Elanor,' Min thought. "So, what do you want me to do?" Min asked, trying to stand again. She rose with only a slight sway, and pushed down the lightheadedness.

Conwenne got up and offered her chair. "First, I want you to sit." Min did so with gratitude. "Then, are you hungry?"

Min started to say no, but her stomach growled. Conwenne smiled.

"I will get us some food." Her eyes unfocused as she Sent. "Then we will Ward this room till our hair stands on end, and we will discuss and Share all we saw and experienced."

"Then you will need wine," Min said.

Conwenne smiled. "It's on the way." Min smiled back, feeling the beginnings of not friendship, but camaraderie, with this woman.

'What do you think?' she asked her children. A mix of positive thoughts and worry flowed from them both. 'I agree,' Min thought back, enfolding them in her love.

☾ ⌇⌇⌇ ☼

Shatter and Shield carried Elanor's stretcher into the room, stepping carefully over the chalk lines around the door and the bed.

Though she was prepared, the sight of Elanor, still in sleep, triggered memories of that long ago morning in the Heir's Garden when Elanor had been found Magicked asleep on a bench. Min had to turn away as Shatter and Shield laid Elanor gently on the bed.

"She'll be fine," Titania reassured her, gripping Min's arm. "And you are strong. The Goddess is merciful."

'She hasn't been so far,' Min thought, then asked forgiveness for her irreverence. "I will do my best, Regent," she said, turning back.

There was a stone — a piece of the cavern — on Elanor's chest, clutched in her hands. In Min's Sight, she could See the lines of the Weave holding Elanor in sleep wrapped around her like a cage of hard silver light.

"I used what was available," Conwenne explained, handing Min Elanor's amulet. "I had to remove this. The Weave protecting her was too strong. I feel Celia's touch, but also yours, and that of another."

"Goldberry," Min supplied, taking the amulet, and worrying it in her palm. "That was its purpose."

Shatter and Shield stepped back, careful in the now cramped room. "Flora is outside. She couldn't bear to come in," Shatter explained.

Min nodded, her eyes fixed on Elanor.

"Regent," Conwenne asked. "Are you ready for your part?"

Titania nodded. "Goddess grant you strength," she said to Min. "Come, Captain." She motioned to Shatter. "We have a trip to plan for."

"I'll be right there, Regent," Shatter replied. Titania smiled knowingly, and left the room.

"I don't like you doing this alone," Shatter said as the door closed.

"I have to," Min replied. "It might be the only way to reach her. And another mind might scare her, or make her fight back."

"You should have someone to monitor you," Conwenne advised. "I could do it. Pull you out if there's a risk of being mindlost."

Min shook her head.

"I could do it," Shield offered. "She knows my mind, and I would be far enough back. Just linked with Min. She wouldn't sense me."

"That's a good idea," Conwenne agreed.

"No," Min said emphatically. "It must be just me. She won't trust anyone else. What's behind that wall is the core of her trauma." She shook her head. "To share it with another would be more of a betrayal than this already is."

"Even her Sister?" Shield asked, perplexed, and slightly hurt. "My Healer's Oath prevents me from revealing anything."

"It's not just that," Min said, trying to explain. "I don't know what state I'll find her mind in. Calm and free of influence, or hurt and striking back. Or so guilt ridden she'll lash out. I will not risk another."

"But you already are," Shatter argued. "Your children. Any backlash could harm them." She looked at Conwenne. "What would happen to them if she were mindlost?"

Conwenne looked down.

"Paramount?" Shatter pressed, her voice rising.

"There have been few cases of pregnant mothers being mindlost. Most of the babies died. Others were born, but were so scarred by the experience, they were feebleminded, or grew up violent and twisted." She looked at Min. "It would have been better for them to have died."

"That settles it," Shatter declared. "You will take Shield with you. And she will pull you out at the first sign of trouble."

"I am no longer your Lady to protect," Min protested.

"You will always be my Lady to protect," Shatter returned. "And your children are my niece and nephew. I will not have them come to harm." Shatter's voice dropped. "I loved him, too."

Min almost broke down, hearing Shatter's confession. Conwenne stepped in, allowing her to compose herself.

"And as your High Paramount, I order you to take Shieldbreaker with you. You are my two best and brightest young Paramounts. With her with you, you will have a much better chance of success." Conwenne folded her arms and glared at Min.

"And I will not leave," Shield declared. "I will prevent you from entering her mind."

"And just how will you do that?" Min asked, glaring around the room.

"I will tickle your right wing joint," Shield said simply. She produced a feather. "From Flora."

Min shifted, uncomfortable at even the thought. "It seems I have no choice."

"No," Shatter said. "You don't."

Min smiled. She was relieved that she wouldn't be going in alone, despite her protests. "Then get out of here, you two. I must get into the right frame of mind, and I can't do that with you mother hens hovering over me!" She made a shooing motion. "Go."

Conwenne bowed her head. "Come on, Mother Shatter," she said, moving to the door and taking the soldier's arm. "Let us leave the children." She then turned and directed a private Send to Min. *"If she is infected. . . ."*

"I know what to do," Min replied.

"But can you?"

"If she is, I would rather she be dead," Min replied, her tone as hard and cold as she could make it. *"Elanor wouldn't want to live like that either."*

"Min. . . .." Conwenne started, sending motherly emotions at her.

"Go!" Min practically shouted. *"Or I will lose my nerve."*

Conwenne nodded, and let Shatter escort her out.

"I heard some of that," Shield admitted, taking up a position behind Min's chair. "I've given a mercy stroke before." She made the Sign of the Three. "I hope I will never have to again, but. . . ."

"No," Min told her. "If it must be done, I will do it."

"Min. . .," Shield started, but a swift motion from Min cut her off.

"No more talk. I must prepare myself." Min settled into the chair, Elanor's amulet in her right hand. She took several deep breaths, and pushed all her doubt and worry away. She pushed her love and desire away, too. She needed to be calm and cold. Her eyes needed to be clear.

"Now the Wards," Min said, and raised her left hand. The Wards around the perimeter of the room lit up, and covered them in a dome of silver light. "Could you slide me closer?" Min asked Shield. "Mind the chalk."

Shield muttered, and pushed Min's chair closer to the bed. She stepped over the line that formed more of an oblong circle around Elanor. Behind them, the Wards snapped into place. Shield's skin tingled.

"Now link with me," Min instructed. Shield put her hands on Min's shoulders. "You will monitor me, ensuring I continue to breath, and that my heart keeps pumping. Don't do anything else. Even a twitch from you might disrupt what I'm trying to do."

"How will I know if you need me?" Shield asked.

A red-gold star appeared in Shield's mind. "Sunrise's star. If you see that, pull me out."

Shield nodded. "Goddess keep you safe, Sister," Shield said, and kissed the top of her head.

"I will need all She can give me," Min replied. She took a deep breath, and placed her left hand on Elanor's forehead. Then she placed her right hand, still holding the amulet, on top.

"Elanor, love," Min muttered. "I'm coming."

Chapter Ten
A Field of Fire

Min found herself in a field, burnt black and still smoking. The weak sun overhead was filtered by grey smoke. Ash fell like slow, dirty snow.

Min remembered this. They had been resting in a played-out field. They had collapsed among the stripped fireberry bushes, looking for shade and a moment's rest from the relentless push of Summerwind's Supervisors. Elanor was smiling, teasing Willow and passing out water. Suddenly, smoke had rolled over them. One of the Supervisors had set fire to the field. It had been scheduled for later in the week — to prepare the field for tilling and replanting — but he had done it early. Without a shout or even a Send of warning. Min remembered the terror as the flames chased them, as they coughed in the smoke and heat. Willow fell, and was dragged up by Goldberry and Elanor. The Twins screamed as cinders burned their backs. The Supervisor yelled at them to run, laughing at their fear and pain.

Talia, Gil, and Nova had finally conjured wind and blew the fire back into his face, clearing a path for them all to escape. After, Talia had threatened to drive a still-burning branch down the man's pants. They had been denied dinner that night, but Min still smiled at the memory.

Min looked down, remembering charred feet and the foul-smelling mud of the drainage ditch they had huddled in until the fire had passed. The yells and blows of the Supervisor, forcing them back to work, seemed as though they were happening all over again.

"It's not real," Min reminded herself. "Just a memory." But the ash clogged her nose, and cinders singed her legs. She looked around, and saw the stone-topped well they had been allowed to drink from.

She set her eyes on the stone, and walked confidently across the scorched field. The pain in her feet faded as she got closer to the well.

Min reached into the bucket, taking a handful of water. Elanor's face appeared in the ripples.

It was raining.

Lightning made Min jump. She looked around, but there was no shelter, just the flattened grass, pounded by the rain. She was soaked, drowning in the water, standing ankle deep. Wind buffeted her wings, pulling her off her feet and flinging her into the air. She struggled against the crosswinds, trying to keep from being pulled apart. Finally, she folded her wings and let herself fall, the wind whistling by her ears. Down she plunged, grey clouds and rain whipping past her. She saw something like ground below. Desperate, she spread her wings and tried to halt her descent. Min screamed as the wind almost wrenched her wings from her back, but she eventually slowed. With the sky full of lightning, she rolled, spraying water and mud all around her. Dark forms appeared in front of her, looming over her.

"Stop!" Min shouted, pushing forward with her Power and back with her wings. Sliding, she bumped into the rough bark of a tree, sending red leaves falling, covering the ground.

"Stop!" she shouted again. Only lightning answered. She clenched her hands, as the deep fear its crackles brought cut her and almost made her heart stop.

"Elanor!" she cried, her back still to the tree. "I want to help you! Let me through!"

More lightning flashed and thunder crashed, but Min could make out a distant flicker through the rain and darkness. The iridescent glow of a Shield. Coughing in the rain, she dragged her feet through the mud in that direction.

"Elanor!" she called with every step. "It's me. Love, it's me! Let me help you."

As she got closer, she could make out a form, wings spread, standing at the edge of a Shield. Min began to run, tripping over her sodden skirts and dodging branches. She groaned. "Even in a dream, you dress me like this." The Shield was before her, Elanor behind it, her wings glowing red. As Min reached out, Elanor turned.

They were before the door of the Tower of Learning, the mid-day sun beating down on them, turning the grey stone of the tower red. Elanor, now a child — and looking a lot like Obsidian — stood in front of the door. She beat on it, yelling. Suddenly, the child Elanor was thrown back into Min, who wrapped her arms around the child to keep her upright. The door flew open.

A younger Celia stood in the door, rage flashing in her eyes. "Stop making so much noise. What do you want, foolish child? I'm busy."

"Mama," Elanor called, pulling out of Min's grasp. "I want you to see. I can glide." She spread her wings. "Flora showed me," Elanor said proudly, gesturing back at Min. "She made sure I didn't fall, but I didn't need her. I glided from the roof of the library to the courtyard." The earnestness in Elanor's voice almost made Min cry.

Celia looked at Min with rage. "I told you not to let her come here. I have delicate work to do. Take her away." She looked expectantly at Elanor. "Well, you heard me. Go!"

Elanor, holding in tears, turned and ran, disappearing after a few steps.

Min stepped back and saw a younger Flora glaring at Celia. "That was cruel. All she wanted was your time."

"Don't speak to me with such disrespect. I don't care who your mother is. Do that again, and you will feel my wrath." She looked around the courtyard. "Well, you'd better find her." Celia slammed the door in Flora's face.

"Shouldn't have given her a Torc," Flora muttered, her voice low. She turned, yelling for Elanor and Luna. Getting no response, she ran to the nearest door and disappeared through it.

Min looked around, wondering aloud, "Where would you go?" Then she stopped, and smiled. "Not far. You saw this, so." She pricked up her ears and opened her Sight. After a moment, she heard sniffling. It was coming from behind a large pot of flowers by the door. Min walked around it, and there, in the shadows, sat Elanor. Her knees were drawn up to her chest. "Clever girl," Min whispered, kneeling down. "Elanor," she called gently. "Elanor, it's me."

Her eyes came up, and she looked at Min with fear. "I'm sorry," she cried, cringing back from Min. "I didn't mean it. Don't punish me."

"It's all right," Min said softly. "No harm done."

Elanor shook her head. "You said if I hit you again, you would take my Power away."

"No, I won't," Min contradicted gently. "I love you. I would never do that." Min thought, 'She thinks I'm Celia.'

"Yes, you would," Elanor cried. "You said so. You never lie."

"Elanor, I love you," Min said, her heart breaking both for this little girl and for the woman she had become.

"No, you don't!" Elanor shouted. "You hate me! I heard you. You hate me. I just get in the way." Elanor stood up in the cramped space. She pushed, using all her strength, and toppled the pot over. "I hate you!" she screamed.

Min jumped back, avoiding the falling dirt and flowers. "No!" she cried, but Elanor was running, away from the direction in which Flora had gone. Min tripped over the fallen greenery, but the little girl was faster, and was at the door before Min could call out again.

"Goddess," Min swore. "Elanor, stop!" she called, but Elanor was already through the door and slamming it closed. Min forced the door open and entered.

She found herself in the middle of another hall. It was night, and quiet, except for the sound of running feet behind her. She turned, and saw an older, mostly grown Elanor. She was fleeing, clutching a rent and bloodstained dress to her chest. Her eyes were full of terror, but her mind called out, *"Fire! Fire! Danger! Fire!"* remembering Halfwing's teaching that the fear of fire would bring help faster than anything else she could Send. Elanor raced past, leaving bloody footprints in her wake. Min saw cuts — some shallow, and some deep — all along her back and legs. Elanor turned down a hallway and disappeared, leaving the sounds of the castle stirring in her wake.

Min moved to follow her, but a dark form — wings spread, with glowing red eyes — materialized from the direction in which

Elanor had first appeared. Min couldn't see its face, but knew it was smiling cruelly just the same.

"Stop!" she commanded, holding up her hands, Whitefire blooming in her fists. "You cannot have her!"

"I don't have to," a voice heckled, bright and evil. "She carries me everywhere she goes. She needs me. What would she be without me? Just another pathetic woman."

"I will not let you hurt her!"

"You have no choice," the dark form taunted. "She keeps me close, even closer than you. When she's with you, she sees me."

"Begone, bastard!" Min yelled, as she cast Whitefire into the heart of the shadow. With a laugh, he sprang into the air and disappeared.

"Enjoy those wings," Min said to the vanishing form. She turned. The hall was empty again. The blood was gone from the stones. "Where would she go?" Min said out loud. "Talia," Min realized. "She would run to her. But she didn't have her own quarters yet." She snapped her fingers. "The Queen's rooms." Min moved to touch her Torc, but hesitated. "Will this work?" she wondered aloud, but then shrugged, and touched the Torc, conjuring the Frequency of the Queen's Ring in her mind. The ground dropped away.

Min stood again in the burnt field, but now there was a wall before her. It looked like lashed-together wood, reminding her of the cabins at the cliffs. Movement to her right made her turn. There was a door in the wall there. Elanor stood on the threshold, looking back.

"Elanor!" Min called, but Elanor darted in and shut the door. It disappeared into the wall as if it had never existed. Min started toward where it had been, but the shadow form blocked her way. Its wings were gone, but its eyes were brighter.

"You don't want to go in there," it warned her. "She keeps all of me in there."

"Then what are you doing out here, foul thing?" Min challenged, raising her hands. Whitefire bloomed.

"I am not him. I'm what you brought with you," it taunted. "I'm the fear you carry. I am everything you worry about when she's asleep and dreaming. I'm the thing that lies between you, no matter how close you get." Shadow arms waved in dramatic moves. Min thought she saw a smirk.

"Then why did she go in there?" Min asked, not lowering her hands.

"She goes in there all the time," he said. "She needs to make sure it still hurts."

"Curse you!" she swore, and cast two lines of Fire at him. She raked the lines across his body, but received only a puff of smoke and a cruel laugh in response.

"I am already cursed," the voice said, fading away. "You cannot kill me. I am everywhere. In her hair, her kisses. Everything she gives you, I took first. She will never be free."

Min gathered her Fire back and held it within the core of her being. She fed it with her love and determination. She gave it every good thing between them, every smile and look. Every time Elanor had touched her, every brush of her shoulder or fierce grip of her arms. Every leisurely kiss to promise pleasure, or quick brush of her lips to swear she'd be back. She fed a furnace of Whitefire within herself. Fed it until her entire form glowed white with passion and purpose.

With a cry, she let it all go. A wave of Whitefire burst forth from her, expanding in an ever-growing ring. The last of the shadow disappeared, consumed in the blast. She felt the ring strike the red tower and the rain-soaked red trees. Felt her love consume these places of hurt and pain. The blood-soaked hall resisted, but Min poured her promise to help her Sister, spoken in the storeroom of the mountain, into her flame. "I'm here, Sister," Min called. "I'm here!"

With a whining cry, the hallway vanished.

Exhausted, Min fell to her knees, and dug her hands into the dirt. She felt the soil and ash fade away, leaving her hands empty.

Min looked up. She was in a place of nothingness. Everything was grey, except for the wall in front of her. The brown of the wood seemed to glow in this place otherwise devoid of color. The planks were thick, and bound together with cords of black. The wall stretched to the limits of Min's vision in both directions. She looked up. The wall rose, straight into the nothingness. At the very limit of her sight, Min thought she saw a glint.

She stood and went to the wall. She brushed her right hand over the wood. It felt smooth, worn by many hands. As she ran her hand up it, something caught her first finger, and she pulled it away in sudden pain. Trying to focus on her hand, Min saw a splinter of wood in her finger. Mumbling, she pulled it out.

"What are you?" Min muttered, sucking the blood away. Then, with a sudden revelation, she looked up again. She opened her Sight, and strained to See the top of the wall. It took a moment for her eyes to focus, but then the glint became the shine of metal. Min smiled, as she realized that the wall before her was made of spears. Elanor's father's spear. The one she had carried all through their adventures, and that was now with Goldberry on her quest. The first time Min had held it, a splinter had pierced her right hand.

"It only likes some people," Elanor had said, taking it back.

"Elanor," Min said with loving exasperation, unsure whether to laugh or cry. "You made your wall of the only thing you have of your father. What protects you is him."

Now Min did cry. Hot tears ran down her face as she laid her forehead against the wall. "Elanor," she begged. "I need you. We need you. Come out. I cannot continue without you. I can't have these children without you." She pressed her hands to the wall, feeling the sharp pricks as more splinters drove into her palms. She endured the pain. Min remembered standing, looking down at the sea, singing to the full moon, Elanor's hand in hers. Just days ago, Elanor had held her when the weight of everything had been too much.

"I will not go," Min swore. "If you won't come out, I'll stay here. I will not leave you." Min brushed her hands off and settled, cross-legged, on the non-ground. She gripped Elanor's amulet to her chest and began to remember. She started with her earliest memory of Elanor. Her parents had brought her to court. . . .

"How are they?" Flora asked from the door.

"There was a lot of pain and terror earlier, but now she seems to have settled down. Min is going through her memories of Elanor." Shield reached up — first with one arm, then the other — stretching. "If I had known this would take so long, I would have brought a chair."

"I can bring one," Flora offered. "And food."

"I can stand a little longer," Shield said. "It would be difficult to open the Wards. As to food." She shook her head. "I must abstain."

Flora started to call her a dramatic soldier, but stopped. "I'll be right outside."

"Thank you, Mum," Shield said, then returned all her concentration to Min.

Flora looked at the three of them for a long moment. Elanor, asleep on the bed. Min, sitting beside the bed, hunched over, her hands on Elanor's forehead. Shield, a pillar of strength, standing tall behind them. Flora felt a surge of fear for all of them. But there was also pride. Pride for all they had become.

"My children are growing up," she muttered tearfully, shutting the door. Flora settled back into her own chair in the hall. Her wings cramped, but she pushed away the pain. Then her legs began to hurt. Now frustrated, she pushed that pain away as well, along with all it carried with it. "The past is the past," she muttered. "I cannot help them now. Goddess's mercy, let them all wake up."

A little while later, Flora was considering calling for Luna to bring her food when a strong Send hit her.

"Is she awake yet?" Celia demanded.

Flora took a moment to put all of her emotions in a box before replying. *"No, Paramount. Shieldbreaker says there was a lot of activity before, but now they're calm. She has no idea what's happening in Elanor's mind, or how long it will take."*

"I should come down there," Celia said. *"I might be able to help."*

"No!" Flora shouted, in spite of herself. *"No,"* she corrected, at Celia's surge of annoyance. *"We have it well in hand. You must rest. When she wakes up, I will Send to you."*

"She is my daughter," Celia Sent back. *"I have a responsibility to her."*

"Daughter," Flora replied, no longer able to contain Elanor's lifetime of emotions. *"She is only your daughter when you need something from her. Or want to criticize her. If she is anyone's daughter, she's mine. You gave her to me. Told me to raise her alongside Talia. 'As the Queen has done,'"* Flora mocked. *"But you never cared, beyond how she was progressing in her studies. Or if she might embarrass you at court. I've seen choras who were cared for more."*

"Now see here," Celia started. *"You have no right."*

"I have every right, Paramount," Flora shot back. *"You provided her with a home and status, but that wasn't what she needed. She needed her mother."*

"I thought you provided that," Celia taunted.

"I did my Goddess's merciful best. But I was not her mother. You were. I did my best," Flora said again, almost breaking. *"But she needed more."*

"I gave her everything I had," Celia protested. *"She never wanted for anything. I worked so hard to give her that."*

"She needed a mother at her side, or at least interested. Do you know when she first conjured Light?"

"Yes," Celia replied smugly. *"I can see the day clearly. I was so proud."*

"But do you know when she lost her first tooth, or could finally fly without falling? Could you tell me anything about your daughter that isn't related to Magic?" Flora stood, gesturing to the air. Celia was silent. *"No, you can't. I can. I know all those things. Things a mother should know."*

"I haven't been the perfect mother," Celia started, but Flora cut her off.

"You will do one of two things," Flora informed her. *"Either you will be the mother she needs you to be, giving her unconditional love, refraining from cruelly criticizing her, and teaching her the things she still has to learn."*

"I have," Celia tried to interrupt.

"I am speaking, Paramount," Flora said, with all the steel she possessed. *"You will be that mother to her. You will be happy for her, and support her. You will be there for her when she wants you, and you will step away when she asks. And you will never even look at Min with anything like that dishonorable disrespect you showed her when Elanor returned from the stronghold with her. If you ever insult either of them like that again, I will rip your eyes out myself. They are my daughters, and I will defend them."*

"You'll try," Celia blustered.

"You forget, Paramount: I am a survivor, too." Flora considered. *"Maybe I'll ask Shatter's husband, the famous duelist, to be my champion."*

"You mentioned two choices, Flora," Celia said coldly, putting all the contempt she could muster — with the image of Saber in her mind — into her Send.

"Or, you will go before the Regent and all the Fairies here and announce that you are no longer Elanor's mother."

There was shocked silence from Celia.

"You will formally sever all links between the two of you," Flora said simply. *"You will free her from your presence, and allow her to move on. Those who truly love her will step into the vacancy. It won't be a big step. I've been there all along."*

"You go too far," Celia stuttered. *"The Regent. . . ."*

"The Regent knows you," Flora interrupted. *"She knows who you are. One of the most powerful Paramounts, yes. Queen's Justice, yes. But lacking completely as a mother. She will say nothing."*

Celia was silent — seething, and radiating hatred and fear.

"The proper response, Paramount, is, 'I will tell you my decision before the sun rises.'"

"I will give you my answer before the sun rises," Celia responded crisply, and broke the connection.

Flora sat down, shaking and lightheaded. She put her head in her hands.

"You went too far this time," Luna commented from her side.

"I know. But I couldn't hold it in any longer." Flora looked up. "I couldn't take another moment of her arrogance."

"Well," Luna said, putting down the tray of food she carried, "it is never simple. I will tell the Regent. Should I find you a good sword?"

"No," Flora replied, blowing out a long breath. "Do ask Saber to join me, though. I was serious about that."

"Sister," Luna said with a smile. "I Sent to him even before you threatened Celia. Stiletto is coming, too." She gestured to the tray. "Why do you think I brought so much?" She kissed Flora's cheek. "I'll be back." She touched her neck and disappeared.

Flora sat back in her chair. She hoped Celia would make the right decision. But what that was, she wasn't sure.

Chapter Eleven
Before A Wall of Spears

"And do you remember that time when I wanted to bed that son of the Elen-Gold Ambassador, but he only liked redheads, and you wouldn't have anything to do with him? So we tried to dye my hair." Min shook her head. "And it turned this weird color. Like a cursed rainbow, Gil said." Min smiled. "And I did get him to sleep with me, but he wasn't that good. Wasted effort, I guess."

"Why are all your stories about the men and women you sleep with?" Celia's voice came from her left side. "You. . . ."

"Call me slut or whore again," Min warned, raising her hands, which were glowing with Whitefire, "and I will pull you apart. I don't care if you're just a memory, or the projection of my own thoughts. It will still feel good."

Celia vanished with a huff.

"And I didn't sleep with all of them," Min commented to the air. "Most of the time, I never stayed the night." She looked up at the wall. "Where was I? Oh, the forest twins. Or was it triplets? I could never remember. They were so fast, I could never get a good count."

"Only Min would think talking her friend and Sister out from behind her wall of emotional protection could best be accomplished via a recitation of her conquests."

"Well, hello, Shatter," Min said brightly. "What are you doing here?"

"Just wondering when you'll give up and come home. She's gone."

Min frowned, and cast Whitefire into Shatter's face.

Puck disappeared with a laugh.

"Come back!" Min cried. "I want to keep killing you!"

There was only an echo of mocking amusement.

"Bastard," Min said, adjusting her legs. "Only about half are conquests. I've been pursued a few times as well. That's fun, too."

She looked around. "How long will I sit here?" she asked the wall. Answering herself, she declared, "I will stay here as long as I have to. You can send an army of their memories at me, but I will not leave. I will only leave with her."

Min listened to the silence. "Well," she said after a while, "that about covers the first year I was a Lady. Oh, I remember! The next year was when Glaive and his squad were stationed in the palace. They were a very handsome bunch. Pity, given what we now know about Air. We should have seen it. They were always a little rough and dismissive. Except him: Glaive was always a gentlefairy. Too bad Talia claimed him for herself. I did like the Sergeant, but I can't remember his name."

"I don't either," Elanor said.

Min looked up in surprise. Elanor was standing at her side. She was pale, almost translucent. The only point of color was her red wing. She raised her hand as Min tried to get up. "Stay there," she commanded. "This is just a projection. I'm still safely behind the wall."

"You aren't safe," Min disagreed, but Elanor shook her head.

"I am. No one can hurt me there."

"How can you live there with all that is him?" Min asked, wanting to run to her.

"I've pushed him back, and exist in a bubble of memory." Elanor looked up. "Above the timberline. I didn't know it then, but that was the last moment of happiness for us."

"There can be more happiness for you," Min pleaded, hot tears falling. "For us. Please, love, I need you. Come home."

Elanor opened her mouth to speak, but then her eyes widened. Min heard footsteps running toward them. Without looking, Min raised her arm and cast Whitefire. It devoured Puck, leaving a greasy stain in the air.

"Don't worry," Min said. "He keeps coming, but I keep killing him. Feels good, but gets tedious."

Elanor dropped her hands. The red light coming off her wing dimmed, but did not disappear. "I attacked my mother. Hit her, and tried to kill her. She'll never forgive me."

"That threat was to a child," Min countered. She ached to run to Elanor, but forced herself to stay still. "Even as a Paramount, she can't take away your Power. You were under the influence of evil Magic. It's been destroyed. She understands. Celia even saved my life, and the lives of my children."

Elanor shook her head. She focused on a point behind Min.

Min sighed. "She's watching us." She turned. Younger Celia was standing behind her, hands on her hips.

"I promised I would punish you," she said, shaking her fist. "Your little trollop is lying. I will bring you before the Regent as a naughty girl. She will cast you out."

"Quiet!" Min yelled, bounding to her feet. "You're nothing but a memory. You have no power here!" She raised her hands. "You know nothing of your daughter, never wanted to know anything. Go away, and leave us in peace."

Celia vanished with another shake of her finger at Elanor.

Min turned back to Elanor. "She's been bothering me, too."

"You've been talking a lot," Elanor said. "She hates stories of your adventures."

Min took a step closer, but Elanor matched it with a step back. The red in her wing increased.

"I just want you to come home," Min begged. "You're in an enforced sleep. Everyone is worried that you've been infected by this evil. I cleansed the rest of your mind. But you might still be carrying some of it with you." She gestured to Elanor's red wing. "There might be a crack in your wall, letting more evil in. Let me touch you to make sure there isn't."

Elanor stepped back again. "You hit me. How can I trust you? You might be a memory, too. How can I know?"

"Would a memory of me talk about all my conquests? You didn't know about all of them," Min reasoned. "It's me, love. Please come home. Everyone is worried about you."

"You threw me out the other day, and now you want me back." Elanor shook her head. "You're confusing."

"I was angry at you." Min gestured to her belly. "I'm pregnant by a Human I may never see again. I don't know what my children will look like, or if they'll even be accepted by our people. I have a right to be angry at you once in a while."

111

"They'll be beautiful," Elanor said in a low voice. "They'll have your eyes, and his sweet, caring disposition. They'll be a wonder to the Realm, no matter if they have wings or not."

"My mother hopes they do," Min said under her breath. "I can't get my father to look at me."

Elanor gestured angrily. "Then tell them to leave, get out of your life. They're your children, and they will be loved, no matter what. We will love them. All of us. You're our Sister. Shatter will challenge anyone who says a bad thing about them to a duel."

Min shook her head, but was smiling inside. "And then there's your mother. The memory of her keeps insulting me. What will the real one do? You saw her after the council meeting. She was ready to call me a whore." She tapped her chest indignantly. "I am no whore. I rarely ask for silver."

"Most of them couldn't afford you if you did," Elanor said, beginning to smile.

"They pay me in other ways," Min said with a twinkle.

"If she will not accept you, then that is her failing. I love you, and I will love your children," Elanor declared, and the red of her wing began to dim as she herself became more solid.

"Then come out from behind that wall," Min implored, stepping closer. "I don't know completely how I feel about you, but I know I cannot do this," she gestured to her belly, and then the whole of the empty world, "without you. The gap he left in my heart hurts so much. I don't want to use you, but I don't know what else to do."

"She left a black pit in my heart," Elanor admitted. "I couldn't go on without you at my side." She frowned, looking at Min's outstretched hand. "You're trying to trick me. You got me angry about Celia's treatment of you."

"Is it working?" Min asked, half smiling and half ready to cry again.

"Yes," Elanor admitted, taking Min's hands. She became solid. Min felt Elanor's familiar weight in her hands and squeezed them tightly. Tears began to flow.

"I cannot promise anything," Min began. "I don't know where my path will take me. I don't know if I can always walk beside you."

"Then I will walk in front, or behind, or wherever you want me to," Elanor replied, smiling through her own tears. "You're being honest with me, something she never was until I forced her to be. I had my eyes closed then, but now they're open." Elanor pulled Min into a hug. "As long as this path goes — once in a while — to your bed," she whispered in Min's ear.

Min playfully pushed her back, then pulled her into a passionate kiss. "Who's being a trollop now?" she asked breathlessly, breaking the kiss, but staying in Elanor's arms.

"I am," Elanor said proudly. "They keep telling me so."

Min took a breath. "I need to see you, all of you," she said, looking deep into Elanor's eyes. "I need to be sure. Titania needs to be sure."

"I understand," Elanor said. She rolled back her Wards. "I am fully outside my wall. I left nothing behind."

"I must see beyond your wall," Min pushed gently. "You might have taken something in with you."

Elanor began to tremble. "I don't want you to see that. I don't want you to know what he did to me. It was horrible, and I don't want to have to look at you and know that you've seen it, too."

"Nothing will change how I feel about you," Min reassured her. She hugged Elanor tighter. "I told you I would be there for you when you were ready to heal. I meant it. I still mean it. Nothing will drive me away. Nothing will change how I see you."

Elanor shook her head again, and Min felt her begin to withdraw. She gripped Elanor tighter with both her arms and her mind. "It wasn't your fault," Min pressed. Elanor struggled against the sudden constriction, but Min raised her hands, showing her that she was free to go.

"It's not your fault," Min repeated. "Go if you wish, but I will stay here until you come out again. I will not leave you."

"But your body, your children. What will become of them?" Elanor asked.

"I will not leave you," Min repeated.

"Then neither will I," Elanor said. She took Min's hand and led her up to the wall. Elanor made an opening gesture, and a portion of the wall swung open. "Look inside," she urged. "I won't let you in, but you may Look."

Min — through hot, stinging tears — opened her Sight and Looked in. There was the dark figure she had fought and burned so many times. His wings filled the space, blotting out the sun and moon. Then, the wings disappeared, and his whole body rose to loom over them. Min heard his mocking laughter.

"Tell her," he said. "Tell her what you know. Will she trust you then?" He laughed, and reached out his hand. Dark fingers grabbed the edge of the door. "Let me out, and I will tell you all my secrets. Secrets you can use. You know what it feels like," he said, his voice low and suggestive. "I can give that to you."

Elanor began to tremble. The memory of the seductive warmth of Talia's blood-fueled Power as it regrew her wing was strong. She felt her defenses crumble.

A grin emerged from the darkness. "Good. You remember. I can give that to you always. You will never hurt again. Never know pain or heartache. You will have your revenge on all those who hurt you."

Elanor took a deep breath. "Those like you?" she asked, and held up the hand that was still clasped with Min's. "Go back. I need nothing from you. I have my Sister." Together, they Wove a bolt of White- and Silverfire that smote him, and drove the darkness back from the door. There was a horrible scream, but the mangled form began to advance, fighting back the bright Power with his own Darkfire.

Min and Elanor gripped each other more tightly and summoned all their combined strength. The glare of their Fire illuminated the whole area, but Puck's darkness still advanced upon them.

"You cannot have her!" Min growled. She pulled her hand away from Elanor's and focused all her Power into driving him back. "Close the door!" she called.

"She doesn't have the strength," Puck taunted, taking another staggering step under the pressure of Min's fire. "She knows. Knows who I am."

"I do!" Elanor shouted. She summoned everything she was, and everything all the Ladies and The Nine had given her. All their strength and support. Even Talia's love — however colored with betrayal it had become — allowed her to slam the door of her wall in Puck's face.

Min and Elanor staggered back, clinging to each other, standing each other up.

After a few moments, they could each stand on their own. Elanor took Min's hand again.

"Have you seen enough?" she asked.

"More than enough," Min said with wonder. "I don't know how you do it."

"I have the help of my Sisters," Elanor replied simply. She kissed Min's cheek. "Let's go home."

Chapter Twelve
Meeting the Wives

Min raised her head and reached back with her right hand to touch Shield's wrist.

"She's all right," Min announced.

"Thank the Goddess," Shield replied, dropping her hands from Min's shoulders. "I don't know if I could bear it otherwise."

Min smiled. "Help me dismantle the Wards around the bed." She gently placed the amulet on Elanor's chest.

Despite her exhaustion, Shield was right at her side, undoing the Ward. Quickly, they released the Power back into the Realm. "The Sleep one next?" Shield asked, reaching for the stone.

"Just a moment," Min interrupted, standing. She stretched her arms and wings. "First, sit down."

Shield didn't argue, and sat in the chair. She sighed, and rubbed her legs. "I think that's the longest I've stood since my training days. If I'd known how long you were going to be in there, I would have brought a chair for myself."

"How long was I in?" Min asked.

"About a day," Shield replied. "It's getting dark now. Flora and Luna are outside," she replied to Min's unasked question. "Saber and Stiletto are with them. And I think Steel's wives are there, too. They're hard to see." To Min's raised eyes, she elaborated. "Assassins and former Shadow Agents."

"Of course they are," Min said, amused. "I thought it was quite difficult to leave the Shadows, except by Pyre? Raven did, but she was mostly just a teacher."

"Nightshade is a special case," Shield said. "Very special. You'll have to see for yourself. They scare me, but in a good way."

"Should Elanor be worried?" Min continued with amusement.

"Only if she pulls another lake stunt."

"I'll warn her," Min promised. "Now, before we wake her, what did you see?"

Shield sat back. "Only a little. I felt a lot of pain and terror at first, but then you settled down. I felt moments of satisfaction." Shield frowned, not sure that was the right word. "And other moments of joy. Then there was a lot of joy and fear. Then you woke up."

"And you saw nothing clearly?"

"No, just felt." Shield looked at her strangely. "What were you doing in there?"

"Practicing," Min said simply. "Now, let's remove this Ward and get her up."

The Sleeping Ward was more complex. Many hands had been part of its Weaving, so Min and Shield had to take it apart one bit at a time. Min felt the touch of both Conwenne and Titania. One part, Min took all for herself, memorizing all the twists of the Weaver's Power. She stored it away for later.

"Now," Shield pronounced, sitting back, "the last part is for you."

"Should I?" Min asked, unsure of herself.

Shield smiled. "I think it would be proper."

Min leaned in and kissed Elanor. Under her hands, the last strand of the Ward dissipated. Elanor took a breath, and opened her eyes. It took a moment for her to focus, but then she smiled.

"If I can wake up like that for the rest of my life, I'll be happy." She reached up, trying to pull Min into another kiss.

"No time for that," Min said, moving back. "Our family is waiting, and getting impatient."

Elanor frowned, but sat up with Min and Shield's help. "I guess I must," she said with a grin. "Later."

Min only nodded.

Elanor's legs were shaky, but she stood. "How long have I been out?"

"Only a few days," Shield said. She sat down on the bed. "The Ward suppressed your appetite and sustained you. By nightfall, you'll feel hungry again. Keep your arms away from her then," she joked, looking at Min.

"I will," Min said. Then, with a quick motion, she grabbed Shield's legs and levered her into the bed.

Not fighting, Shield settled down quickly. "Good idea," she said, her eyes closing. "If you could, put a Sleep Spell on me."

"Of course," Min agreed. "When do you want to wake up?"

"In the morning," Shield said. "Have Longstride wake me. We have some things to talk about." She paused. "And do."

Grinning wider, Min wrapped her in a Sleep Spell. She debated giving her dreams, but then decided it would be better for her to just sleep. "Rest, Sister," Min said earnestly, brushing her lips on Shield's cheek. "You deserve it."

Elanor was staring at the door. The Wards around the room still glowed. "Who's waiting?" she asked nervously.

"Flora and Luna, with Shatter's wife and husband. Steel's wives are there, too."

Elanor smiled ruefully. "Not exactly the best time to meet them."

"There is no best time," Min said wisely. She took Elanor's arm. "I will be by your side."

"Then we'd better go," Elanor said, but she didn't move.

"What did he mean?" Min asked.

"What do you mean?" Elanor asked back, suspicious.

"Puck," Min said, having trouble saying his name. "He said, 'You know?' I thought you told me he was dead. That your father died killing him."

Elanor became very still. Min could feel her pushing something down, but it happened too quickly and was too complex for her to understand.

"He was just taunting me," Elanor finally said. "He always taunts me. Wants to make me believe I wanted it. Wanted everything he did to me. That I'm like him." She looked desperately at Min. "But I'm not. I never will be."

Min hugged Elanor fiercely, while pushing to the back of her mind the fact that while Elanor hadn't lied, she hadn't told the complete truth, either. Min kissed her again. "You're right. You are not him. He can't hurt you anymore. All that's left is memories." She touched the amulet that was back around Elanor's neck. "And we have him safely walled off. Until you're ready."

"Yes. He's gone," Elanor agreed lightly. "Now, let's go meet the wives of the woman I tried to seduce."

Min smiled. "It's easy. Just walk up to them and say, 'So you're the ones she chose over me.' Works for me every time."

"No one chooses someone else over you."

"One did." Min frowned, but quickly recovered. "Now help me with the Wards. A Paramount must be sharp. And you're a few days behind me. You must show your skills."

"Wait," Elanor said, turning to Min. "Paramount?"

"Wake up," Luna said, prodding her sister in the shoulder. "They're about ready to come out."

Flora sat up straighter in the chair. "I wasn't asleep," she lied, wiping the sleep out of her eyes. "Let Conwenne and Celia know."

"Already done," Luna told her. "Conwenne said to take our time, and send them up when they're ready."

"You told them before me," Flora griped. "How could you?"

"I wanted you to sleep a little more," Luna returned saucily.

"The Wards are coming down," Saber reported from his spot on the floor, interrupting Flora's reply. He stood up, and offered Stiletto a hand out of her chair. She shook her head, intending to stay seated. He went over and offered Flora his hand instead. She stood, and brushed nervously at her skirts. Further down the hall, Nightshade and Belladonna stood, putting away the knives they been passing the time sharpening and juggling. Belladonna glanced down, ensuring the child at her side was still asleep.

"Don't overwhelm them," Luna chided.

Flora turned to say something, but the door opened, and Min and Elanor stepped out together.

"Children," Flora cried, pulling them both into a hug. "I was so worried."

"It's all right, Mum," Elanor muttered into Flora's wing. "I'm safe."

"I was sure of that," Flora said, stepping back. "You have to stop putting yourselves in danger. I can't take it."

"You'll have to tell the False Sisters that," Min said. "I would rather be home at Fae-Treval, watching the sun set and wondering what's for dinner."

"All of us would rather be doing that," Luna commented.

"Are you sure?" Flora sent to Min. *"Conwenne was very worried."*

"I'm sure, Mum," Min replied. *"All traces of the evil have been removed. Only that which we all carry with us remains."*

"More's the pity," Flora replied.

"I'm glad, too," Saber said, stepping up and gripping the arms of Elanor and Min in quick succession. "I would hate to break the news of a tragedy to Staff."

"We are strong," Stiletto said from her chair.

"Yes, we are," Min agreed, gripping her arm. "We fight for the ones we love."

Elanor turned — hesitantly — to address Steel's wives. They were both, unsurprising to her, shorter and slighter than Steel. Belladonna, however, had surprisingly long black hair, shot through with white. Nightshade had short hair, but hers was black as night. Both had swords on their backs and bandoleers of throwing knives across their chests. Nightshade stood back, while Belladonna walked up to Elanor and gripped her arm.

"You must be Elanor. Steel has told us so much about you," she said with a friendly tone.

"Not everything, I hope," Elanor said lightly, truly hoping.

"Yes, everything," Nightshade replied grimly. Then she smiled. "But you aren't her type. Too bright. She likes the dark ones."

"Steel tells me you're a good archer. We must go shooting sometime," Belladonna said, her light tone dropping away. Her hand tightened on Elanor's wrist. "I've been practicing."

"And I am out of practice," Elanor admitted. She reached back and found Min's hand. "I've been busy."

Belladonna smiled again, releasing Elanor's arm. "Then we must work with you. I've been training the young ones. It would be good to work with someone who can hit a target."

"The right target," Nightshade put in. She stepped up — Belladonna sliding gracefully out of her way — and took Elanor's arm. "I understand you swore to keep each other safe."

"We did," Elanor confirmed, not breaking eye contact.

"Good. Keep doing that. She can be reckless sometimes." She glanced at Min and the knife on her belt. "Can you use that?"

"Raven taught me," Min replied. "I'm not as good as she is, but show me a Blood Cultist, and I can hit them."

"No one is as good as Raven," Nightshade conceded. "I'm glad both of you are well." She stepped back. Unconsciously, she linked arms with Belladonna. "We must take our child back to bed. It was good to meet all of you."

"For once, Steel did not exaggerate," Belladonna said. "I meant what I said. I would be honored to work with you, Lady Elanor. Excuse me, Paramount. We will be staying a while."

"Come on, little one," Nightshade said, picking up the sleeping child. "Back to bed." The two Leather-wing women disappeared up the hallway to a chorus of cheerful farewells.

"Well," Elanor said, letting go of her tightly contained nervousness, "they didn't kill me."

"Still might," Stiletto said, standing with Saber's help. "Those two are deadly. Don't take anything with them for granted. Nightshade used to be a Shadow Agent, and Belladonna — well, she's a legend. Killed half the Human King's bodyguards at Brine Hill. If Hooklance had gotten his flyers in faster. . . ." She let the thought drop. "Well, I must go, too. Saber, make sure they get safely to Celia's rooms." She held out her hand to Luna. "Mum, if you would walk me back?"

"I will," Saber agreed, giving her a quick kiss. Luna kissed Min and Elanor before taking the hand of the now-impatient Stiletto. They followed Steel's wives up the hallway. Saber smiled and shrugged at the looks from Flora and Min. Then he bowed and stepped away to give Flora a moment's privacy with her Ladies.

Elanor hugged Flora again, holding on to her tightly. "I love you, Mum. I'm sorry I scared you."

121

"You should be," Flora said. "I'm getting too old to worry about all of you. First Min's babies, and now you. If I didn't already have grey hair, you lot would have given it to me."

"But you love us," Min reminded her, joining the hug. "Your life would be boring without us."

Flora sniffed. "Sometimes I wish for boring! But your mother is waiting for you."

Elanor pulled away, her anxiety spiking.

Flora patted her hand. "Don't worry. I think she has something important to tell you."

"So, I won't need my blade then," Saber commented from the side. He patted the slender sword on his hip.

"You always need your blade," Flora quipped back. "But for that, no."

Min and Elanor looked at each other, then back at Flora, confused.

"You will see," Flora promised. She kissed them both again. "Now, I will go, too. And make sure they both eat," she ordered, directing her gaze to Saber.

"Yes, Mum," Saber said with a bow. "Celia has food ready."

"I'm not hungry," Elanor said, her stomach in knots just thinking about facing her mother.

"I think it will be all right," Min said, putting her arm around Elanor's waist. "Something feels different."

Saber started up the hallway in the opposite direction from which everyone else had gone. "Well, come on," he called. "We can't keep them waiting."

Flora shooed them off. "Yes. The two newest Paramounts must not be late."

"Paramount," Elanor said with awe as they followed Saber. Her anxiety dwindled at the sound of her new title.

"Yes, Paramount," Min said in the same tone.

Chapter Thirteen
Who Carries the Shield?

They wound through the corridors, passing closed doors and open rooms. Without Saber to guide them, they would have been lost. Min had only come down here once after returning to the Exile Queen's mountain. With the influx of refugees fleeing the False Sisters, Titania had decided to open the area that Steel and Nova had found at the base of the mountain. There, they found a warren of musty rooms and corridors. Nothing like the library and storerooms, but once cleaned, they were suitable for habitation. Conwenne had claimed a group of rooms for her research, and of course Celia had needed a similar set for her use as Queen's Justice.

A large portion was dedicated as an infirmary and recovery area for the wounded. They passed one large room where the ceremonial regrowth of an arm was in process. Min and Elanor looked at each other, memories of the smell of the sea and gentle waves strong between them. In another room, a smaller group was working on a Weave like the one on Shatter's right arm. They stopped and watched a Healer and Paramount fit a soldier with a new leg. She stood up and fell, but got right up and tried again. The Paramount felt their eyes on her and looked up. She smiled brightly at Min and waved. Min waved back.

"When your project is done," the Paramount called, "I could use your help."

"When I get a moment, Goldenmane," Min called back, then waved in apology as Saber called them on.

"Staff's arm has been a Goddess-send for us," he said as they continued. "So many will be back to fighting shape. I want to thank you for what you did."

"We didn't do much," Min admitted. "Shatter did most of the work. We just smoothed out the edges of her Weave."

"Then you are double thanked. She could barely create a Weave when she left us," Saber said with a bow.

"Why do you call her Staff?" Elanor asked.

"I served with her brother, Captain Shattersteel. He was Shatter to me, and when she and Stiletto propositioned me, I couldn't call her Shatter, so she became Staff. Stiletto quickly followed in using the nickname. Just works for us."

"How do you do it?" Min asked. "Love them both, I mean. It was always quick affairs for me, never a long-term relationship."

"We have an infinite amount of love within us," Saber explained, making the Sign of the Three. "The Mother of Waves saw to that. I just have to figure out what part of me they each need. You know the Shield and Sword formation?" he asked.

"A little," Elanor admitted. "One carries a large shield, and another a two-handed sword."

"Yes," Saber said. "It's just a matter of who uses the shield, and who has the sword." He took a moment to contemplate. "Stiletto is usually the sword. But there are times when I must lead, and she defends my back."

"What about Shatter?" Min asked.

"She's been gone so long, it's taking longer than usual to fit her back into our dance," Saber admitted with some sorrow. "But we will endure. We are soldiers, and sometimes our paths take us away from the ones we love." He looked at Min with compassion. "But they always return, one way or another."

Min put a hand over her belly. "Always?" she asked.

"Always," Saber said with authority. "When we heard what had happened, when the families of the Ladies and The Nine were called back to the palace, Stiletto was scared: fearful for Staff, and what she might have become. I never was. I've always been sure she would come back to us. Always sure she will be there to raise our child."

Min squeezed Elanor's hand. "I wish I had your certainty."

"I get it from Staff. She swore to us on our wedding day, she would always be there." He smiled and touched Min's arm. "She never breaks her promises."

"I will never . . .," Elanor Sent, but Min cut her off.

"Do not make that promise," she said fiercely. *"You made that promise to her, and he made the same vow."* Her emotions settled. *"Just be here for me now."*

"I will," Elanor replied, slightly hurt, but understanding.

Saber, sensing their inner conversation, led them on in silence.

☾ ∼∼∼ ☼

At the top of a gradual rise in the corridor, they met Conwenne at a fork in the path.

"Greetings," she said. "Flora notified me via Send that you both were awake." She looked to Min. "It was as you said?"

"Yes," Min confirmed.

"May I see?" she asked Elanor, holding out her hands.

Elanor only held back for a moment before taking Conwenne's hands. Her probe was skillful and quick. "Yes," she agreed, releasing Elanor. "I sense nothing left from the False Sisters' attack. Though your wall does worry me."

Min and Elanor both rushed to explain, but Conwenne held up her hands. "And I understand. There are things in all our lives that we must keep hidden. Even from ourselves. It allows us to keep going. I know that better than many others."

Min looked at Elanor. "Paramount," she said gently. "We did not mean. . . ."

Conwenne waved her sympathy away. "We can huddle in a corner and cry over our losses another day." She looked at Elanor. "I know she'll be there for you when you're ready to face this trauma. I hope you will find your way to trusting me and the others. We are always here for our Sisters. We haven't faced what the two of you did, but we all have our tragedies. Too many." She took a deep breath, pushing her own emotions away. "I had hoped to have a ceremony, officially conferring your new titles on the two of you, but events are moving fast."

"That's all right," Elanor said. "Just to hear others call me Paramount." She smiled. "It is enough."

"But you should be praised before all of the Realm, or at least this part of it." Conwenne shrugged. "When this crisis is over."

"Of course, Paramount," Min agreed.

"Now." Conwenne gestured to the left fork. "I know you have some hard conversations to have with your mother, Elanor. Min, I know you need your rest, but please see me before you return to your rooms. I need your counsel." Then, with a nod to Saber, she headed up the right fork.

"It seems things have changed while I was asleep," Elanor commented.

"Yes," Min confirmed. "But I still don't trust her. She holds a deep hatred of Elenites. And a fear of the Exile Forest."

Saber spoke up. "That is understandable. After all, they did kill her daughters."

Elanor flinched at the brutal truth. Min glared at him. "We don't know that they were recruited from the Exile Forest."

"We don't know that they were not, either," Saber countered, standing firm.

"This is the same argument I had with her," Min said with exasperation. "And we came to no agreement." She sighed, and took Elanor's hand. "We must let the Goddess guide us to the truth." She looked pointedly at Saber. "Whatever that truth may be."

Saber nodded, then gestured them on. "I think she's waiting."

Now it was Elanor's turn to sigh. She gave Min's hand another shake and headed up the left fork, head high.

The corridor grew narrow and ended in a door, guarded by a Leather-wing soldier.

"Tiger-Claw," Saber greeted him. "Is she awake and ready?"

"Of course she is," Tiger-Claw replied. "She's been asking me every moment if I've seen you yet." He gestured to the door, and stepped back into a slight depression in the wall. Elanor opened the door and — without hesitation — entered, with Min at her side.

Inside was a large room, filled with desks, chairs, and glowing Fairy Lanterns. A sense of purpose and drive emanated from everything within. All the desks were piled with papers and books. Min sensed a powerful Ephemeral Ring in the corner. There was no one at any of the desks, but the room had the feeling of being recently cleared. Celia was in the center of the room.

She was standing, supported by a large board. Ropes secured her to it at her chest and waist. Her legs were securely bound with purple cloth. Min could feel the strong Weave keeping her upright, and the Healing ones working on her body.

Celia smiled at them. "How are you?" she asked.

"She's fine," Min replied. "All traces of the evil that attacked us are gone."

"I was speaking to my daughter," Celia began sharply, but stopped. "I apologize, Lady Min," she said with a nod. "It has been a long day." She held out her hand. "Elanor, how are you?"

"As she said," Elanor replied, suspicious, and not moving forward. "I've been Healed of the infection." She looked Celia up and down. "How are you, Mother? I'm told you saved Min's life. I cannot find the words to thank you for that," she said grudgingly.

Celia dropped her hand. "I merely repaid a debt. She saved you. I could do nothing less," she said, the words coming out with mixed emotions, "than defend the woman you care so much about." She cleared her throat. "The Healers tell me I must be in this contraption for a few moons. Bone and nerve damage take longer to Heal, and I cannot be moving around. I just got the feeling back in my legs, but I can't move them yet."

"I know that must be hard," Min said into Elanor's silence.

"It is," Celia admitted. "But it's a small price to pay for both of your lives." She looked down. "When Flora Sent to me that you both were whole. . . ." She stopped, blinking, and rubbing her eyes. "I was happy. I was so worried about you." She stopped again, overcome with emotions she did not know how to express.

Min and Elanor looked at each other, perplexed and surprised at Celia's intensity. She had never openly shown any emotions beyond disappointment or anger. From the door, Saber cleared his throat.

Celia looked up. "I would like to speak to my daughter. Alone," she stressed, the old Celia coming out.

Min bristled.

"Whatever you need to say to me," Elanor told her, "you can say with her in the room."

"What I have to say is not for your . . . friend, or for strangers." She gestured to Saber. He started to move back and shut the door, but Min gestured for him to stay where he was.

"You do not understand who your daughter is," Min informed her, folding her arms. "We're more than friends. We're Sisters. We've been through fire and blood and pain together. If she wants me to stay, I'll stay."

There was a sharp retort ready on Celia's tongue, but she swallowed it, with visible effort. "I'm sorry," she finally said. "I had been told that by another. It's hard to hear a truth when you deny it. I just want to speak to my daughter. We have things to talk about. Things just between us." She looked at Elanor. "Things about your father. But if you need her to stay, I will not dispute you."

Min felt complex emotions flowing between mother and daughter. "It's all right," Elanor finally said. "I'll meet you back at your rooms. If you want me to?" Elanor asked, suddenly unsure.

"Yes," Min assured her, kissing her on the cheek. "I don't think I could sleep without you tonight."

Celia frowned, but quickly hid it in a cough.

Min looked pointedly at Celia. "Paramount," she said with forced courtesy. She brushed Elanor's hand, and left.

With relief, Saber shut the door behind them. The strain of witnessing something so intensely private and beyond his understanding was evident on his face. Tiger-Claw chuckled in sympathy.

Min turned to Saber. "I must go speak with Conwenne. I know the way. You should go back and be with your wives."

"With all due respect, Paramount," he said, "I'm to stay with you." To Min's raised eyebrows, he explained, "Regent's orders. With all the possible Shadow Agents — excuse me, rogue Shadow Agents — or traitors about, you need protection." He held up his hands at her obvious denial. "You're the prime architect of the defenses for the mountain. You're a member of the Council of the

Regent. A Paramount. You are no longer just a Lady of the Heir. You are a valuable member of this court in exile. And a prime target."

"I can defend myself," Min argued. "There's no reason to put anyone else at risk."

"There is every reason," Saber countered. "You underestimate your worth. There is honor in your humility, but the reality is, if you die, or are disabled, it would be a bitter blow to the Regent and the resistance against the False Sisters. Plus." He smiled. "Staff would never forgive me if something happened to you or your children. She might never let me back into her bed."

"We can't have that," Min admitted with a smile. "Well, bodyguard, lead the way. The High Paramount wants to see me."

"Yes, My . . . Lady Min," he quickly corrected. "This way."

☾ ⌇⌇⌇ ☼

Elanor was eating. Despite her nervous eagerness to hear what Celia had to say, the moment she saw the food, Elanor fell on it like a large flock of starved birds.

"I had it brought up when I heard you were awake," Celia said, as Elanor filled a plate. "I was once put into an enforced sleep after a backlash. When I woke, I was ravenous."

"Thank you," Elanor said earnestly, plopping three thick slices of meat onto her plate. "I thought the last of the tarnegols had been eaten a few days ago." She grabbed a roll, then went back and grabbed another slice.

"This is from the Regent's supply," Celia said. She floated a roll to her hand. "It's your favorite, so I persuaded the Regent to give it up. There's a bowl of the herbed spread over there."

"That's Min favorite," Elanor said, but she still took a large spoonful. She moved to a desk close to Celia, pushing the papers and books aside. Celia made a noise, protesting the disruption of an absent Fairy's work, but did not speak. Elanor dug into her meal, not looking up. Celia watched her as she nibbled on the roll. She tried to speak a couple of times, but couldn't find the words.

Elanor finally finished. She put her plate back on the food tray. Then she straightened the area she had been using, putting everything back where it had been. With a cup of wine in her hand, she faced her mother.

"Well," she said. "What do you want to tell me?"

"I have been told," Celia started, "that I have not been the best of mothers."

Elanor snorted in laughter. "After much consideration of the facts, you've come to this conclusion. Jawan lizards — who regularly eat their young and leave their eggs to hatch alone — are better mothers than you. You are a horrible mother." She narrowed her eyes at Celia. "If it takes slapping you and casting Fire at you to make you see that, I should have done it years ago."

"I'm doing the best I can," Celia snapped. "Did you ever think that this was hard on me, too? I lost your father, and I almost lost you, too."

"Lost me?" Elanor sneered. "You never had me. You gave me up to Flora. She is my mother in all the ways that matter."

"Then in the name of the respect you give her, listen to me now," Celia snapped. Then she lowered her eyes. "Please, Elanor. Just listen."

Elanor put down her cup and folded her arms.

"I have been a horrible mother," Celia admitted. "I thought I was doing the right thing. I gave you a home, and status. A place to grow up with the nobles. I fought for everything I gained. I was the youngest Fairy ever to be named Paramount. Miranda brought me into her inner circle." She looked at Elanor, pleading. "I did it all for you."

"But you never asked me if that was what I wanted."

"You were a child: you didn't know what you wanted," she said dismissively. Then she put her head in her hands. "Goddess's mercy, you have to meet me somewhere," she pleaded. "I'm trying. Please say something."

"It has to be a longer walk for you," Elanor said. She sighed. "But I am willing. Answer my questions. Then we shall see." She pulled a chair over and sat down.

"What do you want to know?" Celia asked.

"My father," Elanor said. "You talked about him as if you had no choice but to marry him. That you didn't love him."

"I did love him. I did. He was a kind, gentle man. Flighty, and full of dreams. He loved you. Loved me." She bowed her head. "You asked why I didn't leave him. Maybe I should have been braver. I almost did once. But then you were attacked, and then he died. And I just couldn't. I couldn't face you." She begged, "Don't you understand? I knew I had failed. I couldn't find a way to make it up to you. So I didn't try. I left you to Flora. I knew she would be a better mother than I could ever be. I thought you were in good hands." She bowed her head. "I guess I was wrong."

"Yes, you were. Yes, you failed," Elanor told her. "You can stop justifying and explaining it. It's done." She made a chopping motion. "You made your decisions, and you have to live with them."

"I'm trying to make up for them," Celia said.

"Then tell me about my father," Elanor pressed. "And that 'damn spear,' as you called it. Explain, or I will leave." She moved to stand.

"It's an artifact of the far past," Celia quickly explained. "From the time before the Exile Queen. Her mother or grandmother, I think. It was forged for that great war with the Humans. Your ancestor bore it at the side of the Queen. Defended her and, if the rumors are to be believed, loved her." Her voice dropped. "As you did."

Elanor's fists clenched. "So you had me so I could walk those same footsteps? Is that all I am to you, some duty?"

"I never understood it either," Celia admitted. "But my mother and grandmother believed this ancient prophecy about a spear and a Queen born on the shore of the sea. They forced me to marry him and have a child."

"I don't believe it," Elanor said. "No one can force you to do anything."

"Yes, they can," Celia countered. "Apply the right pressure in the right place, and anyone will do anything."

Elanor started to disagree, but remembered Willow's eyes and remained silent.

Celia smiled ruefully. "It was supposed to be his older brother. But he and the other brothers all died. An accident, then a duel over something foolish." Celia frowned. "Now that I say it out loud, I wonder. Was it an accident? The duelist was a professional."

"Stay focused, Mother," Elanor snapped. "The spear. What does this all mean?"

"I don't know," Celia snapped back. "And you gave it away. Let that Keeper's brat take it on some foolish quest with the Queen."

Elanor defended Talia. "She's looking for her daughter, the one we thought was dead. And I don't know why I gave it to Goldberry." She stressed the name. "But I knew she needed to have it."

Celia took a moment to master herself. "I can only tell you it's important. It's a key, or a lever, to 'move the waves,' or so my grandmother said. I never saw the text; they wouldn't let me. 'It's too fragile,' they told me. It was stored in the Tower of Learning. I hope the False Sisters haven't destroyed it. Regardless, it's lost to us now."

"It's not lost," Elanor said. "She will return."

"The Queen always brings back fewer than she leaves with," Celia said offhandedly.

"You say you're trying to be better, but you keep insulting my Sisters," Elanor said, rising. "Whatever has caused this change of heart is insufficient to truly change you."

"Wait," Celia said, reaching out to Elanor. "This is hard for me, too. You can't expect me to change in one day."

"I've been waiting for you all my life," Elanor said dispassionately. "I cannot wait any longer." She went to the door.

As her hand touched the knob, Celia called out desperately, "I can help you."

Elanor paused. "How?" she asked without turning.

"Your wall. Conwenne Shared some of it with me. Not much," she reassured her when Elanor's shoulders tensed. "But enough. I cried at the trauma you've hidden from me, from all of us."

"You never cry," Elanor said, as she leaned her forehead on the door. "Never."

"I do," Celia told her. "You just never saw the tears."

"How can you help?" Elanor asked again.

"The same way you tried to help the Queen," Celia said simply.

Elanor turned. She had forgotten that she had told Celia about trying to break through the block to allow Talia to access her Power. "I don't understand."

"It's just a theory, but we can create a space, a Shield, in your mind that allows you to face the trauma and integrate those experiences back into yourself. You'll be free of him, and you can move on with your life." Celia — relieved that Elanor was listening to her — continued. "It will take time and courage to face the pain, but we can do it together. I'll help you. Your Sisters will help you."

Elanor looked down at the floor. The idea that she could be free of the pain she had carried for so long frightened her. She didn't know who she would be without it. Would she still be the same person?

Deciding, she went back to the chair. A cup floated to her hand. "Tell me more."

Celia smiled. She gathered her thoughts, and began to explain.

☾ ∭ ☼

The sound of the inner door sliding open woke Min. She looked up to see Elanor shedding her dress.

"That's the biggest Fairy I have ever seen," she commented, tossing her dress at the basket.

"Yes." Min giggled, despite her exhaustion. "Foxruff is that. Shatter trusts him, though. He's one of the cycle of bodyguards we have now."

"Yes. Tiger-Claw wouldn't leave my side after I left my mother's rooms. Do you think they're being overprotective? We can take care of ourselves." Elanor sniffed at her slip and, after a look from Min, removed it, too. She looked around for something to put on.

"No. Conwenne and Saber convinced me there's a real danger." She noticed Elanor's search. "Just come to bed," Min told her. "I need your warmth. It's getting cold."

Elanor raised her eyebrow.

"You have that kind of energy?" Min asked, amazed.

"I guess not," Elanor admitted, climbing under the covers and snuggling up to Min. She felt movement from Min's growing belly against her. "Yes, I'm back," she addressed the twins. "To stay this time."

Min kissed Elanor. "I want you to know," she said, going serious. "I don't know if I can be everything you need me to be."

"I don't even know anymore what that is," Elanor confessed. "This change in Celia has got me very confused and twisted."

"But," Min said, continuing her thought, "I will try." She looked Elanor in the eyes with intensity. "As long as you can try to be what I need you to be."

Elanor smiled while holding back a tear. "I will also try." She watched Min's face, watching her. "Do you want to make a vow before the Goddess on it?" she asked after a bit.

"No," Min said. "Just kiss me, you foolish girl."

Chapter Fourteen
Paramount Holly's Tower

In the morning, Min and Elanor made love: quickly, but passionately, exalting at being back in each other's arms. As Elanor tried to find something clean to wear, Min struggled through her own daily routine of trying to fit into her clothes.

Finally, Elanor, amused by Min's struggles, helped her tie the back of her dress, leaving most of her back exposed.

"Flora and the others can alter this to fit, you know," Elanor told her. "They've just been waiting."

"I know," Min admitted, frustrated. "It's just, everything I own is too small now. Others need clothes as well. Some came with nothing but what they were wearing. It's a full-time job just keeping them clothed. I hate to pull them away from that."

"Face it, little mother," Elanor joked. "Your body is changing, and you must change with it. Soon, Flora and Merry-Weather will be calling you a trollop. Too much back and chest, little lady." Elanor contemplated Min for a moment. "Not that I mind," she said slyly, kissing the back of Min's neck. "But it may not be the best look for the newest Paramount."

Min stepped forward, out of Elanor's reach. She bowed her head, shoulders and wings shaking. Elanor thought she was laughing, but then she heard her crying softly. She grabbed Min's shoulders and pulled her around to face her. Min buried her face in Elanor's chest.

"I can't get rid of these. They're all I have," she sobbed.

Elanor comforted her. "We'll find you new ones. It's not that difficult. I'm sure something can be found."

"No." Min pulled away. "These were all he saw me in. I can't lose them. I can't lose the last things he saw me in."

Elanor tried to pull Min back into her embrace, but she resisted. Finally, Elanor gave up. "Who's being a foolish girl now? They're just dresses," she told her. She knelt down, so her face was even with Min's belly. "Hear that?" she whispered to the children.

"Your mother is worried she'll have no link to C. . . him. What are you two?" she joked. "I don't know much about these things, but I'm pretty sure he helped bring you two into existence. Or." She looked up into Min's tear-streaked face. "Are they someone else's? You never know with Fairies. Tell Mama she's being overly emotional."

"I am allowed to be overly emotional," Min said haughtily, grabbing Elanor's hair and pulling her back up. "And they are most definitely his." She grabbed Elanor's face. "I just can't bear to put these clothes away."

"They'll still be here after," Elanor said gently. "He's out there. You and your children will see him again. I know it." She pulled Min's hands away from her face and gripped them. "I'll go to Flora. She'll find you new clothes. No alteration of these. I promise."

Min sighed. "And I have to go see Conwenne." She wiped at her eyes. Min took a deep breath to center herself. Elanor mirrored her, and after a few beats, they were both calm again.

"I just hope Conwenne and the other Paramounts haven't fouled up the defensive Weaves while I was gone," Min said, pulling away, but not before giving Elanor a quick kiss.

"Do you need me with you?"

Min smiled. "No. Should be simple. Unless they tangled something."

"Good," Elanor said, pulling on a shirt. "There was a note under the door. Belladonna expects me for archery practice this morning." Now it was her turn to sigh. "Not sure where I stand with them."

"If they wanted you dead," Min joked, "you would be."

"I guess," Elanor said, not quite believing it.

"It's just like the Twins used to do," Min said. "They're testing you. Just prove to them that you're the strong, capable woman you are. Then they'll accept you. Use everything Raven taught us."

"Steel won't make this easy. She'll flirt with me every chance she gets."

"I don't think so," Min disagreed. "I think she'll be different when they're around." Min winked. "She's afraid of them, too."

Elanor grinned, kissed her, and ran out the door. Min flexed her shoulders, feeling the ties of her dress pull. She spotted one of the wraps Flora had accidentally left behind. Draping it across her shoulders, she whispered, "I know. I'm being silly. Flora will be my first stop." She gestured the last Warded chest to her and left the room. Foxruff fell in beside her as she cleared the door.

"I hope you weren't out here all night," she commented, concerned. Min was used to looking up at people, but she felt her neck crack gazing up at her new bodyguard. She wondered how he fit through doors. Did he have to turn himself? With those broad shoulders. . . .

"No," he replied in a deep voice. "Longstride relieved me. I guess he had somewhere to be this morning. He took off like an arrow the moment I returned."

"Hope he won't be too tired," Min said, smiling knowingly.

"Don't worry, My . . . Lady Min." He grinned back. "I gave him a big cup of Luna's wake up tea. He'll be fine."

Min laughed. 'At least someone will be happy today,' she thought.

☾ ∼ ☼

"So, what did you want to show me?" Steel asked as she walked to the edge of the tower. The lookout passed her his spyglass.

"North," he directed. "There are flyers circling. They aren't ours."

"How long?" Steel asked, watching them.

"Since first light. They're far enough away to be out of arrow range. Should I signal Windrider to send scouts?"

"No," Steel decided, giving the glass back. "I don't like this. Air is usually a squad of four, and there are five of them. There's something in the wind." She walked to the other edge of the tower and looked down. *"Windrider, Sovnya! Get your soldiers back from the town. Something is coming. Get scouts out there, but keep them out of bow range. Make sure they're Shadowed."*

"Yes, Captain," both Lieutenants Sent back as they ran off in opposite directions.

Steel turned back to the lookout. "Falcon, keep an eye on them. The moment they do anything, let me know." Steel grimaced. "I have to make sure Holly is ready."

"Yes, Captain." Falcon returned his eyes to the circling flyers.

As Steel descended the stairs, she felt the Ring surge. She quickened her pace, turning the corner to see Paramount Holly dragging the last of her chests into the Ring.

"Where are you leaving them?" Steel asked, taking in the room. It was now bare, except for Holly's old chair and the other large furniture. All the books, scrolls, and other small objects were gone.

"In my own hiding place," Holly assured her. "I heard your Send, and I feel it, too. I dreamed of blood red hawks last night. Always a bad sign."

Before Steel could say anything else, Holly stepped into the Ring and disappeared.

Gritting her teeth, Steel took in the room. Empty, it felt different. It no longer pricked her skin as it had before. The only thing that did was the satchel on Holly's chair. She could feel uneasiness coming from it. Paramount Holly had been working with Shield, trying to ween herself from her sleeping herbs and deal with her mental issues. She had been mostly successful: the room no longer reeked of the herbs as it had before. But the whole place still set Steel's teeth on edge.

Another surge, and Holly was back. "I need the Geode," Steel said.

"It's where it always is," Holly replied, returning to her chair. She set the satchel carefully between her feet as she sat. "In the stove."

Steel growled, but went to the oven. She pulled out the Geode and cast herself into the Web.

"Regent," she called.

"Here," Titania answered.

"Something is happening. They may have taken the bait."

"Good. Make sure your soldiers are ready to move."

"Yes, Regent. They're already moving."

"And the town?"

"Evacuated as many as we could. Children and young wings were sent to Riverbend and Silverfire. Many of the adults wanted to stay, but your words persuaded them to keep their families together."

"Paramount Holly?"

"She's moved all her books and papers to her own hiding place. I assume you don't want her to come to the mountain?"

Titania replied with dark amusement. *"No. Her ties to the False Sisters make her dangerously untrustworthy, even after all she's done for us. Send her to the third site."*

"I will, Regent."

"And Captain: be careful."

"I always am," Steel replied with a jaunty thought. Titania broke the connection.

"Where am I to go?" Holly asked, as Steel returned the Geode to her. Holly wrapped it and put it in another satchel, which she gave to Steel. "You'll have better use for this."

"Thank you, Paramount," Steel said grudgingly. "The third site." She Sent the Frequency.

"Good," Holly said. Then she settled back into her chair. "I will also watch the enemy," she said. "My Wards go far in all directions. I will alert you if anything not us stirs."

Used to Holly's abruptness, Steel wove her own Ward around the satchel, then went to the stairs.

"Blood," Holly muttered. "I smell blood."

A shudder went through Steel, and she took the steps two at time to the top of the tower.

Anticipating her arrival from her footfalls, Falcon was turning to the stairs when she reached the top. "They just landed, Captain." He handed her the spyglass. "Four are walking off a circle, pouring black powder out. The fifth is in the middle. I think he has an Ephemeral Ring."

Steel Shared the information with her Lieutenants as she put the glass to her eye. The four were just finishing. They turned to the fifth Fairy. With a surge Steel could feel even at this distance, two hooded and bound Fairies appeared in the Ring. Gesturing, the fifth invader had two of the others each take one to the perimeter of the black circle.

Another surge, and two more captives appeared. They were given to the last two Fairies.

Steel's skin crawled. *"Windrider!"* she Sent. *"Pull your scouts back. Right now! I don't like this."*

"But we could rescue the prisoners," Windrider argued.

"No! Pull them back. Now!"

"Captain!" Falcon yelled.

Steel turned her eyes to see the prisoners falling, blood spraying from their slit throats and flowing into the black line. The fifth Fairy raised his arms and called out. His words were Old Fairy, but twisted and foul. They set Steel's ears ringing. There was a flash of lightning out of the sky, and red light surged from the now-boiling blood.

Steel heard the new corrupted Song. "Blood Ring!" she yelled. "Get everyone to the tower!" She repeated the call with a Send to all her soldiers.

Falcon was gazing upon the scene with horror as the bodies of the prisoners were pushed into the flowing Ring, disappearing with a ripple. With another surge, ten Fairies in black armor appeared. Together, they raised their hands and pointed at the distant tower.

"Down!" Steel yelled, pulling the frozen Falcon off his feet. There was a blinding flash and a deafening bang as a lightning bolt leapt from the Blood Ring to strike the Wards around Holly's tower. Sparks showered Steel and Falcon.

"Down the stairs!" Steel yelled over the sound of the stone around them settling.

Falcon half crawled and half fell down the stairs. Steel risked another look, and saw more Fairies inside the black circle, this time in blue and red armor. Five bearing shields and long spears formed a square, and the other five — carrying bows — took up positions inside the square and scanned the skies.

Steel stumbled down the stairs as another lightning bolt shook the tower.

Below, Holly was directing soldiers into the Ring. "Someone rang my doorbell," she commented to Steel. "Five at a time, hurry," she urged the soldiers. They disappeared.

Another bang, and mortar rained down from the ceiling. "And there it is again," she commented. "Next group."

"How long can your Ward hold?" Steel asked.

"Not long, with all the Power they're throwing at it," Holly admitted. "Should be enough to get all your soldiers out of here, though."

"I've never seen anything like it," Steel said. "I've seen Blood Rings, but that is beyond anything."

"The False Sisters are tapping into an ancient Power," Holly remarked, gesturing for the next group to enter the Ring. "There is much we don't know. This goes deeper than we had suspected."

"Windrider!" Steel called via Send. *"Are you near?"*

"Yes, Captain. All my soldiers are approaching the tower. There are five shield squares now. One is headed to the town. Two are headed your way. Should we try to delay them?" Steel looked at Holly.

"I need all the time you can give me," Holly said. "But against a shield wall, your flyers won't last long."

"Pull them all back," Steel told Windrider. *"Leave some Silverfire traps for them. But get clear."*

"Already done," Windrider told her. *"On the way."*

Sovnya appeared at the top of the stairs heading down. "I left a squad to guard the door," she told Steel. "One squad stayed in the town. They're going to delay them as much as they can." She smiled. "They have the heavy Human crossbows. Short range, but they'll punch right through those bastards."

"I told you to get them out!" Steel yelled. "They'll be cut off."

"They know that, Captain," Sovnya told her calmly, standing straight against her Captain's anger. "They'll take as many with them

141

as they can. Another squad is waiting to ambush the approaching shield walls."

Steel growled.

"We have to make it look good," Holly said from the floor. She had sat down; the Ring was draining her energy. "If all of us run without a fight, it will seem more like a diversion."

"They all volunteered," Sovnya stated. "They all escaped the Night of Black Wings and lost Sisters and Brothers in that fight. They will not fail us."

Steel's reply was lost in the thunder of another lightning strike. Holly fell over, whimpering in pain.

Steel pulled her to a sitting position. Holly waved to those waiting in the Ring. "Go! You know where you're going." The soldiers glanced at Steel, then disappeared.

"Another strike like that, and my Ward will collapse," Holly announced. "And then they'll take this tower apart like a cookie."

"Windrider's soldiers are all inside," Sovnya called. "My soldiers have engaged the shield walls." Then she screamed, and fell to her knees. "Lightning just took out half of them," she told Steel once she had recovered.

"That will give me time to add to the Ward," Holly said. She began to move her hands. In her Sight, Steel could See lines of force rising from below and spreading out above them.

Steel swallowed. "Tell your soldiers to make as much noise as possible. Throw Silverfire, rocks, anything to draw more fire." She looked at the line of soldiers waiting by the Ring. "We need more time."

"Yes, Captain," Sovnya confirmed, and went into a Send.

"I've reinforced the Ward," Holly announced. "You can let go of me now, Captain. I appreciate the strong arms, but we both have other duties."

Steel blinked, and let go of Holly. She helped her climb to her feet.

"Get me to the Ring," Holly requested. "I need to give it more Power."

Steel helped her to the edge of the Ring. Holly sat down, and put her hand on the metal. "Just a little more, old friend."

Sovnya had her head on the floor, speaking low. "All but one are gone. He's playing dead, waiting for them to find him." She jerked. "Gone." She sat up, and shook her head. "The squad in the town took out most of the first shield wall with the first volley. They're leading them a chase from house to house. Another group is headed their way."

Steel was relieved to hear that most of the town's Fairies had gotten out.

The tower shook again. An empty bookcase crashed to the floor. Windrider appeared at the back of his flyers. "All mine are here. Only the guards at the door are left."

"Tell them to trap the doors with enough Silverfire to be seen at Riverbend and get up here," Steel ordered. She pulled Sovnya to her feet. "Go."

"No," she said. "Not until I know the last of my soldiers are gone."

Windrider helped the last of his flyers into the Ring. He looked at Steel and Sovnya.

"Go," Steel ordered him. "Go to Silverfire and alert them. If we're being attacked, they might be, too."

Windrider nodded. "Goddess keep you safe," he beseeched, and disappeared.

Sovnya screamed, a gut-wrenching yell of pain and sorrow. When she could talk, she reported, "Multiple lightning strikes swept through the town. Everything is on fire. They're all gone."

"Goddess keep them," Steel implored. Holly bowed her head as another impact rocked the tower. Sparks danced over the ceiling, and more furniture fell.

"You'd better go," Holly said. "The Ward will break with the next hit."

"Go," Steel said, pushing Sovnya into the Ring. "I will destroy the Ring and follow you."

"Can't," Sovnya said. "Too drained. I gave everything I had to Silverfire for my soldiers."

"You must take her through," Holly said. She was standing now. "I must be the one to destroy this Ring. It is my responsibility."

Steel was torn between her duty to her soldiers and her distrust of Holly.

"I will not betray you," Holly swore. "I have wandered a dark path, but you and your Heir showed me a better way." She motioned Steel into the Ring. "Go, or I will send you through by force."

Steel knelt down beside Sovnya. "Goddess keep you safe," she told Holly.

"I guess someone has to," Holly quipped.

Steel smiled and disappeared.

Holly lost her feet again as the lightning took down her Ward.

"Curse you!" Getting up, she shook her fist in the direction of the enemy. "It took me years to construct that." She looked up, expecting the ceiling to vanish in another strike. When it did not, Holly sat down in the Ring. "Of course," she said. She gestured, and her satchel flew to her hand. "You want prisoners. Better for me." She closed her eyes. The traps the soldiers had left at the door were powerful, but crude. Any Power-user who could throw lightning like that would disarm them from across the room. Holly improved them, and added to her own countermeasures as well. "I'll never be back here," she muttered, resigned, and threw almost all her energy into them. She smiled. "This will truly be seen from Fae-Treval."

Then she turned her attention to the Ring. She was sinking down into its lines of Power when she felt a foul Song begin to wrap its arms around the Ring.

"Clever," Holly said. "Trying to keep me here. Well, you are not clever enough." Holly reached deeper than she ever thought she could and formed a bubble of Power around herself and the Ring. She threw in some Illusions pacing around the room for good measure. She laughed, eager to see the faces of the False Sisters.

"Now." She reached into the Ring, ready to rip it from the Realm. Something wrapped its arms around her.

"No!" she cried. "I must destroy you. I'm sorry, I must!"

Something nuzzled against her face. Emotions flooded her mind.

144

"All right," she relented. She released her hold on the Ring and on her own control. "I trust you."

Then, with a sound like the plucking of a flower, both Paramount Holly and the Ring were gone.

Chapter Fifteen
Defenses

A Fairy in black armor strode indifferently through the lightning-blasted town. Behind him, his soldiers gathered the bodies from both sides and threw them into waiting wagons.

"Swiftly, get them back through the Blood Ring," he yelled.

"Yes, Sir!"

"*What is your progress?*" demanded a harsh Send through the blackblade on his belt.

"*All the rebel troops have been eliminated. The tower is the only thing standing. My Power has blocked the Ring. You will have your prisoners.*"

"*Do not fail me,*" Tra Sent coldly. "*Lady Perrault and her son speak highly of you. I hope their confidence is not misplaced.*"

"*It is not, my Queen,*" he Sent with pride.

Stopping before the door of the tower, he smiled. "*You warned me this Paramount was tricky, but she left her door unlocked. She can entertain my men on the way back.*" His hand touched the door.

"*Wait!*" Tra's Send came too late.

Twisting like a cyclone, Silverfire erupted around the tower, spiraling upward, utterly destroying the building. Stone and earth were pulled up, splitting and burning as the Fire rose higher, reaching far into the sky. All eyes were drawn to the bright pillar as it burned, a beacon of silver light that spun for a three count. Then, with a deafening crash, the pillar descended, breaking into a wave of Fire spreading out in a circle from the remains of the tower. The other black-armored troops barely had time to stare at the oncoming wave before it broke over them, incinerating them in bursts of smoke and sparks.

The remaining Fairies at the Blood Ring desperately threw their Power into a defensive Shield and stopped the wave just shy of the circle of blood. Sparks and foul smoke rose as the Silverfire wave dissipated against their blood-fueled Wards.

The remaining four black-armored Fairies dropped to their knees, breathing hard and thanking the Dark Mother that they had survived.

They all looked at one another, none of them wanting to answer the furious Sends coming in from their Queens.

☾ ∭ ☼

Min and Conwenne appeared in the Ephemeral Ring at the top of the mountain. Coming here was always hard for Min. Memories of Queen Zellandine's Pyre were strong. The shock of Talia's refusal to accept the Queenship — and then her quick abandonment of all of them thereafter — had cut Min deeper than she knew. Then there was Elanor. She called this place the beginning of the end of her happiness. She used to look back on this mountaintop, above the timberline, as the location of the reaffirmation of her love for Talia. Now it was just a bitter reminder of who Talia had become.

The bowl in the rock, lined with soft moss, was still there, but Min and Elanor avoided it. It had become a place of contemplation for others. Merry-Weather, in a rare moment of openness, had called it a unique place close to the Goddess. Fairies would come to watch the sunrise and sunset from it. Titania had even stood there to lead them in a, muted, celebration of the full moon.

One night, after drinking too much wine, Elanor had complained, "We touched the Goddess there first," before trying to kiss Min, missing, and passing out. Min laughed till she cried, holding her belly, which had not yet begun to swell.

"I will check with the others," Conwenne declared. "I'll Send when we're ready to test."

Min nodded, and watched Conwenne fly off. Foxruff offered her his arm. Having the solid mountain of a Fairy beside her had quickly become a comfort, and Min took it easily.

"Where would you like to wait, Paramount?" he asked. He pointed to the wood and stone watchtower that had been constructed at the highest point on the mountain. Min could see the glint of the three steelsilk bands going around the tower. They were part of the mountain's defenses. Her plan, her construction. She hoped it would work.

Min was ready to head to the tower, but something behind her drew her attention. She heard bow strings and cheering. Turning, she saw — further across the stony mountaintop — Elanor, Tiger-Claw, and Belladonna. Elanor and Tiger-Claw raised bows and aimed at four floating targets.

"Fire till I say stop," Belladonna called. Min felt the tension as the two held their drawn bows.

"Fire!" Belladonna called.

Arrows leapt into the air, faster than Min could follow. At first, she heard the thunks of hits, but then the targets began to move, dipping and rising, as though actively avoiding the arrows. Tiger-Claw kept firing, missing more than he hit. Elanor paused, watched the pattern, and then let loose a barrage, hitting three of the targets and missing the fourth. She was drawing her last arrow when Belladonna called for a halt. Tiger-Claw had exhausted his quiver long before.

"Not bad, Elanor," Belladonna complimented her, floating the targets back toward them. "Your form needs improvement, but it's not bad for being out of practice." She fixed Tiger-Claw with a dark eye. "You need to focus more. A barrage of arrows might work against a mass of Humans, but you need precision to hit a flying target. Elanor took a breath, found the pattern, and then fired. Rushing and hoping will not kill a skillful enemy."

"Yes, Ma'am," Tiger-Claw agreed with chagrin. He went to the targets and began pulling out his arrows. His anger and frustration were clear even from behind.

Arriving to collect her own arrows, Elanor told him, "You did well. It took me a long time to master this exercise."

"Time is something we might not have," Belladonna interjected. Then she gave a piercing whistle. Bundles of arrows floated up and dropped in front of the two archers. Belladonna made a quick count. "You missed some!" she yelled.

Images of arrows — lower down the mountain, among the low trees and scrub — appeared in their minds.

"Well, go get them," Belladonna ordered. "We can't afford to waste any." A pause. "Well, hurry up, child. If you want a turn, I need all those arrows."

Min and Foxruff made their way carefully toward Elanor and the others. Belladonna turned and greeted them.

"Paramount Min, Soldier Foxruff. Would you like a turn, Lady?"

"No," Min replied, coming closer, but not touching Elanor. "I'm not that good with a bow."

"It never hurts to practice," Belladonna cajoled. "I have a shorter bow, easier on the belly. A simpler exercise, maybe?"

"No, thank you," Min said again.

"Then knives," Belladonna pressed. "Let's see what Raven taught you."

"I am here to test the defenses," Min said firmly. "Paramount Conwenne is below making the last checks. They should be ready any time now."

"As you say," Belladonna finally relented. "But your condition doesn't give you the excuse to forget your skills. Steel taught you the adaptive patterns. Have you been doing them?"

"She has," Elanor spoke up. She slung her bow over her shoulder. "Every morning," she fibbed.

"Not just the ones used in bed," Belladonna replied, seeing through the lie. "You have become soft," she shot back at both of them. "You dishonor the Fallen by not keeping up your skills. You'll need them. The False Sisters' troops are brutal. They give no quarter. Nothing about you — not your wings, your status, or your womanhood — will save you when you're under their blades. I'm here to make sure you survive."

"We understand that," Min said firmly. "We've seen their brutality. We're under no delusion: this is a fight to the death."

"Then act like it," Belladonna snapped. She picked up one of the targets and threw it into the air. Her hands blurred, and knives glittered in the sun. The target shivered under the impacts as it arced downward. Out of knives, Belladonna gestured, and the target flew back to them. It landed at her feet, and she knelt, pulling her blades out of it. When her scabbards were full, there were still three blades in the target. She turned, looking at the two women with a raised eyebrow.

Min gestured, and two of the blades leapt out of the target, returning to her hand, while the third floated back to Elanor.

"I didn't notice you throwing," Belladonna remarked. "I must be getting soft myself." She looked at Elanor's belt. "You missed."

Elanor blushed, clapping a hand to the empty sheath.

"I would go get it," Belladonna suggested.

Elanor frowned, but moved toward the edge of the cliff. The image of her knife in a hand appeared to her. Min covered a laugh, and Elanor smiled.

"Ma'am," Tiger-Claw spoke up. "Could you show me the proper motion for quick fire? I don't think I have it right."

Belladonna glared at Elanor and Min, but went to Tiger-Claw. "It's not your motion," she advised. "You have your quiver in the wrong place. Here, let me show you."

"Who's down there?" Min asked, moving away from Belladonna.

"Obsidian," Elanor replied.

"She's taking my apprentice," Min accused.

"She's not yours yet," Elanor replied. "And she seems to be the apprentice of everyone here. She was with Belladonna when I arrived. You're right: she is strong. And fast. But short-tempered."

"Belladonna will take care of that quick," Min told her. "I still owe her more information. Maybe later. We could both Share with her," she suggested.

Elanor drew a deep breath. "Maybe."

"It's part of the healing," Min stressed, but her own anxiety rose at the mere thought.

Elanor felt it and smiled knowingly. She looked back to make sure Belladonna was occupied with Tiger-Claw, and Foxruff, noticing, moved so his body was between them and her. Elanor smiled and kissed Min. Min was slipping an arm around Elanor's waist when Belladonna yelled.

"Foxruff! The Paramounts will be safe up here. I have a bow that needs your strength to pull."

Min sighed, and gestured for him to go. He bowed his head with a smile and turned to leave. Elanor noticed the large, two-handed blade on his back.

She gestured to it. "I don't think I could even lift that, without using my Power."

Min grinned. "I would have trouble even with my Power."

While Elanor watched Foxruff string a longbow that looked more like a roof support than any bow she had ever seen before, Min wandered toward the north edge of the mountain. Below her lay the lake, shining blue and clear. She remembered her first time seeing this place, barren of all signs of Fairy life. Now the shores of the lake were populated with dozens of tents and rough houses. On the eastern edge of the lake, she could see a group of chora-mounted Fairies returning from a hunting or scouting trip. She began to wonder what was keeping Conwenne, and if there were more problems to be dealt with.

She was about to Send, when a commotion from the Ephemeral Ring and the watchtower pulled her attention. Longstride was running across the rock toward her. He wasn't wearing his armor, but was carrying his sword and belt in his hands.

"Lady Min!" he called. "The Regent commands you to activate the mountain's defenses." He skidded to a stop in front of her, breathing hard.

"We were about to test them," she started.

He shook his head. "No. Fully. Regent Titania just received word of an attack."

"I just received the same message," Conwenne Sent. *"We will be up soon. Gather everyone you can, and start the ritual."*

"Where was the attack?" Belladonna demanded.

"Paramount Holly's tower and Silverflow," Longstride told her. "I don't know all the details, but it seems they're using some huge Blood Ring to bring troops in."

Only a moment of concern passed over Belladonna's face. "I must see to my archers and scouts. The three of you," she pointed to Longstride, Tiger-Claw and Foxruff, "stay with the Paramounts. Relay any sightings to Nightshade and me." She turned to Elanor. "Keep Obsidian with you. She'll be of more use up here. Whenever she gets back."

"She's on her way," Min put in.

Belladonna nodded. "Goddess keep you all safe," she implored, then strode to the Ephemeral Ring and disappeared.

"What do you need, Lady Min?" Longstride asked.

"I need you to go get fully armed and armored," Min responded with a smile. "Looks like you were interrupted."

"No, we were done," he said, then realized his words. He blushed. "There should be something in the tower." He turned and ran back.

"Bring signal and flame arrows!" Tiger-Claw shouted at his back.

"What do you need from us?" Foxruff asked. His eyes scanned their surroundings.

"I cannot Power the Wards without a full Circle of eighteen," Min explained. "But I can prepare the lines." She held out her hand to Elanor. "Just grant us some of your Power. Put your hands on our shoulders," she told the soldiers. "Open yourself, and let your light flow into us." The soldiers did so without hesitation.

"Remember," Elanor told them, "your hands will tingle, and a pressure will build in your head. That's normal. Pain and burning in your hands are not. Break the connection if either of those happen."

"We've been trained," Foxruff assured her. His Power flowed into Min like spring water, clear and strong. She shivered in joy. Elanor sent a hint of mock jealousy at her. Tiger-Claw's Power transfer was slower at first, but once he understood what to do, it became an avalanche of youthful energy.

"Not all at once," Elanor Sent to him. *"Save some for later. Slow and steady."* She winked at him over their link. He colored at the innuendo, but settled down and let his Power flow into her more smoothly.

"Now who should be jealous?" Min muttered. Elanor squeezed her hand.

Min could feel the lines of Power she had set up. There were three solid, concentric circles that would become domes over the mountain. She had taken Goldberry's designs for the eclipse Wards and modified and enlarged them. Nine guide stones had been set up around the mountain and lake to guide the Wards. Posts for the fence, Goldenmane had joked. Min reached out and tested the connections. With a snap, the energy circled the mountain. Smiling, she tested the middle ring. Pride bloomed in her as the second ring sprang to life. Then she tested the inner Ward. A whip crack of feedback jolted them out of the Circle. Both Foxruff and Tiger-Claw stepped back, wringing their hands.

"Something's wrong," Elanor said.

"It was the third stone," Min said. "Maybe a fallen tree, or a minor avalanche." She Sent to Conwenne.

"I felt it, too," she replied. *"We're on the other side of the mountain. Can you send someone to check it?"*

"I'll go," Min offered.

Conwenne's concern rose, but she replied, *"Be careful. The added weight will throw you off balance when flying."*

"I know," Min replied. She broke the connection.

"I should go," Elanor declared.

"No," Min disagreed. She flexed her wings. "I set all the posts. It will be quicker for me to do it."

"Take Longstride, then," Elanor said, knowing nothing would turn her. The soldier was running back from the tower, multiple quivers balanced in his arms.

"I will." Min kissed Elanor quickly and motioned for Longstride to follow her. He tossed the quivers to Tiger-Claw and obeyed.

"It's in the little valley." She pointed. "It would be easier to swoop around to the left and approach that way."

"But faster to drop and pull out at the bottom," Longstride said, guessing her thoughts.

Min nodded. She regretted the dress, but there was no time to change.

"As long as you're confident," he said, "I'll follow you."

"As long as I'm not too fat to pull out in time, you mean," Min replied. She put her hand on her belly, feeling her twins. They were worried, but trusted her.

"I would never say that," Longstride said. He looked at her dress.

"I'll use the Queen's old trick to keep the dress from flying up," Min said with a frown of concentration.

"If you're sure," he said, not sure himself. "That's something I'm unfamiliar with. My daughter never wears dresses." He moved to the edge. "Ready?"

Min nodded, and stepped up beside him. The wind hit them hard. Min tightened her wings, and called to the Goddess to help them.

They stepped off the cliff and plummeted down. The wind whistled past her ears, igniting joy in her blood. She hadn't flown like this since before the cliffs. She'd missed it. Her Power reached down, sensing the spot where the guide stone sat. It was getting closer. She knew exactly where she would normally extend her wings, but she was heavier now. Too late, and she would smash into the rocks. Too soon, and she would feel the fool. Best flyer of the Ladies. Hah.

"Fool," she berated herself, extending her wings and slowing her descent. Longstride opened his wings a moment later, staying beside her. Gliding on the currents, they touched down beside the guide stone.

"Well done," Longstride said. "I shouldn't have been worried, but I was."

"I was, too," Min admitted. She approached the stone. There were no rocks or trees around it. No obvious problems evident. She got closer.

"Wait!" Longstride yelled. She stopped.

"There's a small Weave at the base. Just hidden by the rocks and a Shadow." He pointed. "See the white stone?"

"Yes," Min said, squinting. "I see it. The testing must have degraded the Shadow." She reached out. "It's complex. I feel Fire, and some sort of blocker." She shook her head. "I'm afraid to move it. Might trigger the Fire."

"Then what do we do?"

Min contemplated. The best thing to do would be to bring more Paramounts down and unweave it a strand at a time. Any explosion might destroy the guidepost, and they were difficult to make.

Longstride scanned the area. "I sense nothing else. Whoever put this here is gone."

"It's been here a while," Min commented. "I can see the buildup of dirt from the rain. Curse. We can't Power the Wards with that blocker in place, and if we move it, it might explode." Min reached out again with her Power. There must be a flaw in the Weave. There always was. "I will bring others down."

"Don't," Longstride said, his voice suddenly dead. "It will explode when you try to Power the Ward. We didn't think you would test it first."

Min turned, and saw that Longstride had a Silverfire stone gripped tightly in his fist. "I'm sorry, but they have her. Send, and I will kill us both." He frowned, stepping closer. "I'm sorry, but there's nothing I can do. They'll kill her if I don't disable your Wards."

Min's mind churned. She saw the ghost of Willow in his eyes. The same desperation. The same resignation.

"She's already dead," Min told him sadly. "They never keep their promises."

"I spoke to her the other day," he disagreed. "They warned me this was coming. Now just sit down, and it will all be over soon."

"Illusion," Min argued. "You've been fooled and manipulated. Put that stone down, and help me remove that Weave. Then, we'll help you find her."

"If she's already dead, there's no point." He ran his fingers over the stone. "Then I will have betrayed all of you for nothing. Better to die, and meet her again." He began to manipulate the Weave.

"Wait," Min called. "She might be alive. We can find her. You can help us. We can track where their Send came from. Send Fairies to rescue her. Nightshade will be able to help. Please," she begged. "Let us help you. I lost a Sister to them before. I will not lose you, too."

"I have no choice," he said dully. "All I have to do is open my hand."

"Enemy fliers on the horizon! Min," Elanor Sent desperately. *"What's wrong? Can you fix the stone?"*

Longstride looked at her. "I'm sorry. Forgive me."

"No," Min said. Her Power struck like a blade, severing his hand. Then it grabbed the stone and the soldier's cleaved hand, flinging them high into the air. The stone detonated with a bang. Shock and pain bulged Longstride's eyes, but he took a step forward. Min's Power pulled his legs out from under him, and she hammered him to the stone. Stunned, but not yet unconscious, he struggled to get up. Min leapt on him, grabbing the stump of his arm, and striking it against a stone. Longstride screamed, his defenses failing due to the intense pain. Min forced a Sleep Spell into his mind, and he went limp.

Min Healed the wound enough to ensure that he wouldn't bleed to death, then tightened the Sleep Spell and tied his arms with his own belt.

Finally, she answered the increasingly panicked Send from Elanor.

"I'm okay. Longstride betrayed us. He set a trap on the post."

"I'm coming down," Elanor declared.

"No," Min replied. *"Power up the first two Wards. I'll remove the trap."* She mentally grabbed Elanor's face. *"I'm okay. But the Wards must be activated."*

Conwenne cut in. *"We're doing it. Tiger-Claw is on his way. Min,"* she stressed. *"Can you do it? Any damage to the post. . . ."* She trailed off.

"I know. I'll be careful, but we must have the defenses up."

"Goddess guide you," Conwenne said, and broke the connection.

Min looked down at Longstride. "I forgive you," she said. "But I must do this." She Projected her mind into his. His defenses were returning, but she held them at bay. 'I just need to know who. You couldn't have done this alone.' She looked through his recent memories, mourning for Shield as she saw their passion. Further back, Min sifted through his mind, Looking. Then she felt the touch of another's Power. 'Yes,' she thought, and withdrew.

Min returned to the guide stone. She could feel the energy of the two Wards building. The trap Weave began to pulse in sympathy. But Min knew who had made it now, and knew where to look for a flaw.

The Weave fought back, but Min was stronger. Given time, she could have gracefully unwoven it and channeled the energy harmlessly away. Instead, she severed the lines of Power and channeled their energy into the guide stone. The stone rang as the lines tested true. There was no other damage.

"The guidepost is clear," Min Sent to Conwenne. *"Activate the third Ward."*

Confirmation came as the energy of the third Ward washed over her. Min Reached into it, testing. It was solid, and charged with the strength of all the mountain's Fairies.

Min sat back, exhausted. She picked up the stone that had once held the trap and bounced it in her hand. Then, with anger, she pushed it into Longstride's forehead. She bound it there, attached to his skin and bone. He grunted in his sleep.

"I can forgive you, but I cannot forget," Min declared, sitting back down heavily. She looked up, and saw Tiger-Claw slowly descending toward her. She waved. He waved back.

"Is he alive?" he Sent.

"Yes, but bound."

By his emotions, she could tell her bodyguard wasn't sure if that was a good thing. *"Elanor has Sent for Shield,"* he Sent instead of commenting.

"*Then I must be the one to tell her*," Min replied, standing. He landed beside her and pulled out a pair of Power-nullifying cuffs. Min recoiled at the sight. Surprised at her reaction, but doing his duty, Tiger-Claw bound Longstride's remaining hand and arm.

"Now," he said. "How do we get him back up?"

Chapter Sixteen
Hammer of Lightning

Steel appeared in the library Ring. The room was oddly empty and quiet. She stepped forward, but ran into the Ward around the Ring. She traced the day's symbol in the air, but nothing happened.

Suppressing her fear, she Sent first to her wives, then to Elanor and Min. There was no response.

"You'll get none," said a voice from behind her. Steel whirled, and saw the young Paramount Sunserri. "I had hoped to catch Titania, but you'll do." She raised her right hand, and began to tighten her fist. Steel felt the Ward begin to close in on her. She tried to use the Ring, but its Power was blocked.

"No use," Sunserri taunted. "I've Warded it against all travel. I'll crush you inside like Queen Zellandine crushed my family. She drove them from our home, just so she could plant her precious flowers." She walked around the Ring. "I can feel them trying to activate the defensive Wards." She closed her fist a little more. "I would love to see Conwenne's face when it all blows up. Including that little slut you're so fond of."

"If you hurt them," Steel threatened, folding her wings to keep them out of the way of the constricting Ward. "You'll pay for this."

"Yes, I will," Sunserri crowed. "I will be paid very well by the True Queens. Anything I want, just for delivering this mountain." She waved her left hand. "This fortress of the Regent. I took it down with just one other Fairy."

"I don't believe you," Steel said. "An attempt this big would take more traitors than just you. Where's everyone else? This Ring should be guarded."

Sunserri smiled. "It was." She held up a bloody knife. "I took care of him. He was so easy to fool. All of you were so easy to fool." She rubbed the blood on her arm. "They wanted to send more, but I told them just one pretty face and a soldier would be enough." She waved her arm around the empty library. "And I was right."

Steel began to struggle against the tightening Ward. It was becoming hard to draw breath.

"Curse you," she said, using up more of what little air she had. "Curse you and your False Sisters. They will betray you, too. As they betray everyone."

"I'm prepared for that," Sunserri said. "I have information they need. The locations of your Regent's other strongholds. Soon they will be rubble, as this place will be."

"Goddess curse you!" Steel yelled.

A deep thrum of Power permeated the mountain. The air in the library crackled with energy. Even through the Wards, Steel could smell the sharp tang of a coming storm.

Sunserri whirled. "What!" she cried in surprise. "The Wards! That fool Longstride must have failed." She turned back to Steel. "I guess I have to do everything myself." She raised her right hand, closing the fist.

Nothing happened. Steel made a pushing gesture, and the Wards sprang back. She adjusted her tabard and pulled an amulet out from around her neck. The Weave contained within it flared, breaking the Ward around the Ring.

Sunserri gestured again at the Ring, backing up as Steel walked toward her.

With a smile, Steel looked over Sunserri's shoulder. "We need her alive," she called.

"If you insist," a voice returned. The knives tumbling toward Sunserri altered their flight and struck her with their hilts instead of their tips. One hit the back of her head, and the other the middle of her spine. She went down, and Steel was on her in an instant, pulling her arms roughly behind her back. Steel held out her left hand, and Nightshade slapped a pair of Power-nullifying cuffs into it.

"How?" Sunserri muttered, as Steel bound her hands tightly.

"Once you know who your target is," Steel growled into her ear, "you can find their weakness. The little slut taught me that." She yanked Sunserri to her feet. "Now off with you." She shoved the traitor into the arms of two waiting soldiers. "Take her below."

"You won't win!" she yelled as they dragged her off. "Too many are coming."

"Gag her," Nightshade called to the soldiers. She turned to Steel. "Well played, wife." She kissed her with intense passion.

"I did my best," Steel said after. "But she's right. Many more are coming." She turned back to the Ring. "I have to leave and see how things are going elsewhere. And deal with another traitor."

"Belladonna is about to take her squad out," Nightshade called. "I'll lurk around and ensure Sunserri left no further traps. And that she wasn't lying about them being alone."

Steel waved to her wife as she disappeared into a Shadow. With a sigh, she traveled to the Ephemeral Ring at the top of the mountain.

☾ ⁓ ☼

The sky lit up red as another lightning bolt hit the Wards.

"How long can we hold?" Titania asked.

"I don't know," Conwenne admitted. "This has never happened before." She looked toward Min, who was Joined in a Circle with the other Paramounts. "Min might know, but it would only be a guess."

"We have to send out soldiers," Shatter argued. "They keep bringing in more and more. Soon, there'll be too many to push back." She clenched her fists. "We have to destroy that Blood Ring."

Steel came storming out of the Ring. "Where is he?" she demanded, looking around for Longstride.

"He's in custody," Titania informed her. "He was manipulated by the False Sisters. Min says they hold his daughter."

"That's no excuse for betrayal." Steel spotted Longstride, splayed out on the stone, surrounded by soldiers. Elanor and Shield stood nearby. Steel moved toward them, but Titania's voice stopped her.

"Captain! There are bigger issues now. We'll deal with him after this crisis is over." Steel turned back to her slowly. "Now. I assume our trap was sprung?"

160

"Yes, Regent," Steel confirmed, mastering herself with effort. "Sunserri has been captured. I sent her below under guard."

"What of Holly's tower, and Holly herself?"

"The tower and the town are both probably destroyed." Gasps went up all around. "They hit us hard. I just barely got out before her Wards broke. Holly was the last out. She said she was the only one who could destroy her Ring."

"And you believed her?" Shatter asked incredulously.

"I had no choice. I went to the stronghold first, then came here. I don't know where Holly went. She said she had her own hiding place."

Titania sighed. "I'm sure she does. Only the Goddess knows what goes on in her shattered mind. She'll be back, or she won't. Now, we need to deal with this." She walked to the edge of the mountain. "They're bringing in troops, about ten at a time."

"That was what we saw, too," Steel confirmed. "Flyers?" she offered. "Drop Silverfire on it?"

"They have a line of archers," Shatter informed her, giving Steel the spyglass. "Not enough would get through."

"Belladonna is taking her scouts out," Steel reported. "With enough archers, we could thin their line and get our flyers through."

"They have a strong shield wall," Shatter countered. "And they'll put up Shields." She shook her head.

"Something must be done," Titania snapped. "If this mountain falls, then the best line of defense against the False Sisters goes with it."

"They're cruel and arrogant," Conwenne remarked. "We must find a way to use that against them."

"I see Hooklance," Steel called in surprise. "I thought I killed that bastard."

Shatter smiled. "I think I have an idea."

(☽ ∿ ☼

"I must go," Shield said, standing. "There will be wounded soon."

Elanor gripped her hand. "I. . . ."

"I will deal with it later," Shield said firmly. "Now, I must do my duty."

She headed to the Ring. Steel ran up behind her. "I'll go with you."

Shield turned on her. "If you say one word, I will rip your tongue out."

Steel stepped back, awed at the force of her Sister's fury. "I didn't say anything. I just want to go below and coordinate the defense."

"Don't," she warned. Steel raised her hands again in tacit agreement. They stepped into the Ring and disappeared.

Elanor approached the Circle of Paramounts monitoring the Wards as another bolt of lightning hit the Shield. She clenched her fists, fighting off the panic that attempted to overtake her.

Min turned as she got closer. "How is she?"

"As you might expect," Elanor replied. "I can't put into words what she's feeling."

"I understand," Min said. Another bolt hit, and the two gripped each other tight.

"Curse them!" Min yelled. "Why lightning?"

Running up, Conwenne asked, "How long can we hold?"

"I don't know," Min replied. "The Power from those bolts is immense. Soon, the first Ward will collapse under the strain."

"We have to do something," Conwenne urged. "This place cannot fall."

"I know," Min said. "I just don't know how." She looked to her side, where Obsidian was pulling on her sleeve. The girl made a fist with each hand and brought them together, leaving the left hand pushed back. She hit them together again and again, till her left hand dropped.

"I know. We can only take so much," Min said.

Obsidian nodded, then held up her hands again. Now, the left hand was open, and she hit her fist into the palm. This time the left arm moved back, but then returned to where it had started. She hit it again. Each time, the left arm moved back, but rebounded.

"I don't know what you mean!" Min said with exasperation.

Elanor watched the girl hit her hands together again, and her eyes came up. "Use the energy of the bolt to shore up our Ward. Use their own Power against them."

Obsidian nodded, smiling widely.

"I wish you would have just Sent it," Min told the girl with a bit of pique. "I guess it's possible. It would be a fundamental change to how the Wards work, but. . . ."

"Can you do it?" Conwenne asked. "And will it work?"

"Yes, and I don't know," Min admitted. "We'll have to run a physical line from the first Ward's guide stone to its mate in the second. Fairysilk rope. . . ."

Obsidian was off, running toward the watchtower.

"Elanor." Min grabbed her arm. "We need to Join and work out the Weave." Elanor nodded, and the two of them sat on the rock and Joined.

Conwenne called to Shatter. "We have a plan. But I'll need soldiers to guard my Paramounts."

"How many?" Shatter asked, striding over.

"Two for each Paramount going to the nine guide stones."

Shatter nodded. "Tiger-Claw, Foxruff, you two go with Elanor. I'll get you the others." She entered a Send.

"Conwenne," Celia Sent. After the trap had been sprung, she had returned to her place under the dome and had been following everything that was happening from there.

"Yes?"

"If this works, we might be able to use it as a weapon."

"What do you mean?"

As Celia explained her plan, Conwenne's smile grew larger. When she was done, Conwenne turned and ran to Titania.

"Regent," she said. "I think we have a way to strike back."

Before Conwenne could elaborate, Goldenmane came running from the Ring. "Regent, Paramount, I think I have a way to destroy or at least neutralize the Blood Ring. But it will be dangerous."

"What isn't dangerous?" Titania asked. "Captain!" she called. Shatter put down the spyglass and joined them. She held out her hands. "All of you, Join with me."

They all joined hands and entered a Circle.

"With your indulgence, Celia, I would hear Goldenmane's idea first. Stopping the flow of troops needs to be our first priority."

"Agreed," Celia replied.

Goldenmane took a moment's breath, then plunged into her idea. *"We know the Rings are connected across the Realm in a way we do not fully understand. The Blood Rings must act in the same way. I believe they use the spirits of the Fairies they kill as their Power."* All of them mentally made the Sign of the Three for the dead. *"If we can get Silverfire stones into the Ring, then we can disrupt the connection. If we can destroy the bodies that are in there, and free them from their horrible bondage, it should stop the Blood Ring."*

"Shatter?" Titania asked. *"You're the only one with experience destroying a Blood Ring. What do you think?"*

"It took a whole plantation of Fairies to destroy the Blood Ring at Silverfire," Shatter disagreed. *"I don't see how a few Silverfire stones would do anything. And it would cost lives to get that close."*

"The one you destroyed was old," Goldenmane argued. *"It was powered by generations of Fairies trapped in their bodies. This one is new. It only has five to Power it. I've been watching them. Five of the black-armored ones are casting lightning. Five more are not. They must be giving their own Power to the Ring."*

"Then we kill them," Shatter snapped. *"Any attack on the Ring will be costly. I might be able to lure Hooklance out, but maybe not. He might not fall for this again."*

"Hooklance is a bastard," Celia put in. *"I've heard complaints about him and his officers going back years. He's always resented any woman in power."* Titania nodded in agreement. *"I think you're the best chance we have to get him out and distracted enough to allow us to send in a group under Shadow. Nightshade can lead them, with Belladonna and her scouts as backup and cover."*

164

Shatter looked at Titania. *"If they fail, they'll leave a large group out in the open. We could lose a significant portion of our forces."*

After a few moments of silence, Titania declared, *"I think this is the time to take risks. I don't want to lose any of you. But if you can distract him long enough to get the Blood Ring disabled or destroyed, and Celia's plan to use the Wards as a weapon works, I think we have a good chance to win this battle."* Titania broke the Circle.

"Captain, take Goldenmane with you. Are the Silverfire stones ready?" she asked Goldenmane.

"I have to alter the Weave to give them more Power, and set them to explode together," she replied. "I'll bring them below when they're ready."

"Do so, and hurry," Titania ordered. Goldenmane touched her neck and disappeared.

"Captain, Send to Nightshade and brief her." Shatter nodded. "She must be ready before you leave." Shatter nodded again and turned, Sending as she walked to the Ring.

Titania turned to Conwenne. "Your idea?"

"Celia and I think it will work, but it's risky. It could overload the whole defensive Ward. Then we would be defenseless." She looked at Min and Elanor, still in their Circle. "And we'll need someone to be the focus."

"I'll do it," Celia offered. *"It's my idea. And I'm the strongest."*

"But you're injured," Titania objected. *"That would pull some of your energy."*

Conwenne spoke up. *"And you'll need all you have. Regent, I will be the focus. Foul magic like this killed my Twins. This is a chance to strike back."*

"Do not let your anger and grief cloud your judgment," Titania cautioned. *"But I think you're the best option for the job."* She waved away Celia's objection. *"When Min and Elanor are done with the alterations, speak with Min. She designed most of this. She'll know what needs to be done."*

"Yes, Regent," Celia said, and broke the connection.

"Yes, Regent," Conwenne echoed, and went to stand beside Min and Elanor. She put a hand on Min's shoulder and requested entrance to the Circle.

"And Goddess protect us all," Titania beseeched. She returned to the cliff's edge, took the spyglass back from the soldier there, and focused on the distant Blood Ring, as another bolt lit up the sky.

☾ ♒ ☼

Elanor and Min came out of their Circle to find Conwenne and Obsidian standing before them. Conwenne helped Min to her feet.

"Do you have the Weave?" she asked.

"Yes, we do, but someone has to go down and make the connection." Min rubbed at her arms. "I'll go."

"No," Elanor said. "It's my turn." She took three bundles of rope from Obsidian.

"I agree," Conwenne said. She gestured to the seventeen Paramounts still in their Circle. "I need you here. Make sure everything goes as planned. And if anything goes wrong, you can compensate."

Min frowned, but nodded in agreement. Two Paramounts — a man and a woman — came up from the Ring. Soldiers stood at their shoulders.

"These two will go with you, Elanor," Conwenne continued. She held out her hands. "I will relay the changes to the other groups."

Min took Conwenne's hands. "There's something else," she muttered as the information flowed.

"Yes," Conwenne agreed. She went to Send. *"I have a plan to use their energy to not only strengthen our Wards, but to strike back at the invaders."* She Sent the information.

Min paled. *"That's dangerous. It could burn out the guide stones, or the bands in the tower. Or a backlash could hit the focus."*

"I know the dangers. That's why I will be the focus."

Min began to argue, but Conwenne cut her off. *"There's no time to argue."* Another bolt hit the Ward. Sparks flew in all directions. The Circle of Paramounts flinched, and almost lost their connection. *"I am High Paramount. This is my responsibility."*

Conwenne broke the connection. She Sent the information to the two Paramounts standing behind her as Obsidian passed out more rope.

"Yes, there is no time," Min agreed, grabbing Elanor. "Be safe," she told her, before kissing her.

"I will be," Elanor replied afterward. She motioned for Tiger-Claw and Foxruff to follow her.

Min took one more look at Elanor's retreating back, then rejoined the Circle. "Well, Fairies," she said, forcing lightness. "Let's show those bastards what true Servants of the Moon and Sun can do."

"Moon and Sun," they echoed, as they followed Min into the Circle.

《 ∭ ☼

"We'll start at the inner ones," Elanor told the others. "And work our way down."

They nodded, and moved to the right and left, their escorts on their heels.

Foxruff spoke up. "I should go first. I don't fly, so much as plummet. I've been working on my gliding but. . . ." He left it at that. He tightened his weapons nervously.

"I'm sure you'll do fine," Elanor told him in a soothing voice. "I'll see you at the bottom."

He darted a look at the sky, making a silent call to the Goddess, and stepped off the cliff.

"Something new every day," Elanor quipped, watching him fall.

"What's that?" Tiger-Claw asked in confusion, walking to the edge with her.

"A Fairy afraid of heights," Elanor said, and jumped. Tiger-Claw followed, laughing the whole way down.

Chapter Seventeen
Flying Before the Storm

They were on the way to the last guide stone, with Tiger-Claw on point, his bow raised. Elanor followed, holding the Shadow over everyone. Foxruff came behind, playing out the rope, making sure it didn't get snagged.

The sky lit up again and again, casting fierce shadows on the rocks and small trees around the mountain. Elanor wished it would stop, as panic was clawing its gnarled hands into her belly. She concentrated on her steps and keeping the Shadow over them all. The area adjacent to the mountain had been evacuated when the first invading flyers had appeared, so there was no one about. The silence — when the lightning wasn't crackling — was ominous.

"Just a few more steps," Elanor Sent. Tiger-Claw Sent back understanding, while Foxruff merely grunted at her back.

They walked around a tree, and the guide stone appeared before them. There was no one else visible, but the Ward glowed faintly in their Sight. Elanor began to move forward, but Tiger-Claw stopped her.

"Something," he Sent, then arrows streaked from above a boulder behind the guide stone. Their blackblade tips hit the Ward and sparked, but did not penetrate.

Elanor dodged back behind the tree.

"I don't See them," she called. Then she heard the sound that haunted her dreams: the cocking of a crossbow. A large male Fairy in red and blue armor stepped from cover, aimed at her, and fired. The bolts hit the Ward, showering the ground in sparks. He emptied his weapon and began to reload.

Elanor could see a hole begin to form in the Ward. Then she remembered the twist Min had put into the Weave. She strung her bow, and Sent to her soldiers. Two more of the False Sisters' troops rose from cover, aiming their crossbows directly at her. She stepped from behind the tree, arrow notched. The first crossbowman was still reloading. He saw her, smiled, and gestured for his men to fire when she made a door in the Ward, then went back to loading, utterly unbothered by her presence.

Elanor took careful aim and fired. Her arrow passed through the Ward, striking the lead crossbowman in the chest. He dropped his weapon, looking at her in amazement. Another arrow was already in the air as she announced to him, "I can shoot through." The second arrow took him in the head, forcing his limp body back against the rocks. Tiger-Claw and Foxruff rose and shot the other two invaders. Foxruff's arrow threw his target completely from his feet.

"Hurry!" Tiger-Claw called. "There might be more!"

Elanor scrambled to the guidepost, tying the rope around the base and beginning to alter the Weave.

"More!" Tiger-Claw warned, his bow singing. Elanor glanced up, and saw more soldiers charging from the right. Two fell, but one — in black armor — appeared behind the others and cast a lightning bolt directly at Elanor. Sparks flew, and Elanor jerked back, feedback burning her hands. She saw the black-armored attacker's smile as he prepared to cast at her again.

Then a storm of arrows took him and all his other soldiers from behind. After a crash and some pained grunts, Nightshade and two others materialized out of a Shadow into the sudden silence. The spy looked to Elanor.

"I'm okay," she reported. "Just a few more moments."

"Good," Nightshade replied. She gestured to the others. "Sweep along the perimeter, and make sure the other teams have finished." They moved off, rippling as they disappeared.

Elanor returned to the Weave, twisting and manipulating the lines of Power within it. Then, suddenly, she was done.

"Good," Nightshade said again, looking around. "Shatter has a plan. I'm going to join her. Goddess keep you safe, Elanor." Then she was gone.

"Done," Elanor Sent to Min.

"Thank the Goddess. One more to go, and then we'll be ready." Her Send was garbled, as another lightning bolt hit.

"Min!" Elanor called.

"I'm all right. The last team is done. Get back here. I need you. If this whole thing falls apart, I don't want you in range of the backlash."

"On the way," Elanor Sent.

She looked at Foxruff and Tiger-Claw.

"I can fly with you," Tiger-Claw offered.

"I'll make my way to the cave entrance," Foxruff said. "My wings have had it for today. I'll make sure the others are out of range."

"We'll have to practice with you," Elanor chided him. "We'll make you a flyer yet. You can carry satchels of Silverfire stones."

"Yes, Ma'am," he agreed, moving off, following the curve of the Ward.

"Hurry!" Elanor shouted after him. Then she looked up. "Well, let's go."

She and Tiger-Claw spread their wings, and fought the currents up the mountain.

☾ ∿ ☼

Elanor joined Min's Circle. "Next time you have an idea that will take a total reworking of the Weave, remind me to support you instead of complaining."

"So it worked," Min said, squeezing her tightly.

"Like it wasn't there."

"Thank the Goddess," Min said. She looked around the Circle. "This will work, too," she assured them.

"Another lightning bolt is building," the Iridescent on her right advised.

"Paramounts," Min announced. "Goddess guide us." Min implemented the necessary changes to the Ward. She watched as another bolt hit it, a hammer of red light. Instead of breaking into sparks, though, it birthed a bloom of color, opening like a flower.

"Hold it!" Min called. Everyone in the Circle threw their strength into the Ward. The colors flowed, swirling over the Ward's dome.

"Push it up!" Min commanded. Together, they Pushed the energy to the apex of the dome. There it flowed like a whirlpool down into the watchtower. Min felt the Power crackle and sing on the stones. It tried to leap away, to smash through the bonds, but Elanor and the others pressed it into the stones of the tower. Min held her breath, waiting.

Nothing happened. The Power was contained.

A glad cry rose from all around.

Titania strode over to Min and the Circle. "We're all still here, so I guess it worked."

"It did," Min agreed.

"Another coming!" one of the Circle called out.

"Mab!" Min called to a Feather-wing outside the Circle. "Ready your Illusion."

The bolt hit, and to those on the outside, it seemed as though the usual rain of sparks filled the air. Inside, however, the Circle watched the color bloom and saw it flow to the tower.

Min shook her head. "This will sap our energy quickly. We'll need replacements for the Circle soon."

Titania nodded. "I'll call for more. How long to build up a counterstrike?"

Min shook her head. "You'll have to ask Conwenne. She's keeping herself closed off. She needs all her concentration, up there in the eye of the storm."

Titania brushed Min and Elanor's arms. "Well done, all of you," she called to the Circle, then moved toward the tower.

"No time to revel in our success," Min told them. "One wrong step, and we'll all be burned blacker than one of Shatter's soldier feasts."

A laugh flowed around the Circle as another bolt hammered into the Ward.

☽ ∿ ☼

"*Captain Hooklance!*" Captain Shatterstaff's Send, augmented by the Power of the soldiers arrayed around her, stabbed across the field. She stood at the edge of the lake, the

171

waterfall crashing beside her. All around her stood soldiers in green and purple armor. Though some of it had been hastily painted, all stood proud, weapons in their hands, wings spread to soak in the sun. They were few, facing the growing masses of troops of the False Sisters across the field. Lightning flashed over their heads, hitting the Wards behind them. A few flinched, but most had mastered their fear and stood still.

"Captain Hooklance!" Shatter Sent again. *"I know you're there. Come out. We didn't finish our duel. Come out. Prove to all your soldiers that you have at least a tiny shred of integrity left.*

"I challenge you to single combat for the honor of my Queen!" A pause. *"Come out. I beat you once before, with my hands bound. See if you can beat me now! Or are you without sufficient honor to face me in a fair fight?"*

Shatter's soldiers bashed their swords against their shields and yelled: "No honor! Coward! No honor!"

A rumbling grew among the troops facing them. Lightning flashed over Shatter and her forces, forked and red as blood. Their cries rose, becoming louder, through both Send and voice. "No honor! Face her! No honor!"

"I have no need to prove my strength!" Hooklance Sent back, more weakly, but still at sufficient volume to be heard by everyone on the field. *"I outnumber you! I have no reason to come out. Come to us! And we will show you our strength!"*

"I've come out from behind my Ward!" Shatter replied. *"Come out from behind yours! We are few, but we are mighty! Face me!"* Shatter paused; amusement filled her Send. *"Or do I need to send out a champion? There's a young Feather-wing girl up on that mountain who could beat you. Or wait a moon, and my child will be born. She'll be more than a match for you, even fresh from the womb!"*

Lightning crackled over her head. It was so close, if she had had any hair, it would have stood on end.

"We aren't afraid of your cursed lightning. We are Servants of the Moon and Sun! We fly before the storm! We defy your darkness!"

172

Shatter raised her hands up high. Cries of, "We fly before the storm!" and "Servants!" rose around her.

She let them build, rolling over the field to the now nervous and angry troops of the False Sisters. Shatter dropped her hands, and the cries ceased. She brought her gauntleted hands together. The clash echoed like thunder.

"No honor!" Shatter cried, bringing her hands together again. "No honor!"

Her troops took up the cry, smashing their own hands together, building a rhythm to the words. "No honor! No honor!"

Captain Hooklance heard his troops begin to mutter, "No honor," and saw their eyes begin to dart furtively toward him. He turned and yelled, "Bring me my helm and shield!"

"Don't be a fool!" an Iridescent in black armor said, grabbing his arm. "They're trying to goad you."

Hooklance pulled his arm free. "I can beat her. I've done it before."

"Something has changed," the black-armored Fairy reasoned. "Their Ward was close to breaking, but now it's stronger. They're planning something. Don't be a cursed fool, Captain."

Hooklance laid his hand on his sword. "Don't insult me! I am in command here. Queen Tra gave me a free hand. You may be the son of a powerful Lord, but you are not a soldier." He waved to the Fairies all around them. "Look at their eyes. I cannot let this insult stand." He took his helm from his lieutenant. "Stay here. Put up a Ward around the Ring if you're afraid."

"The scouts looking for the anchors of their Wards have not returned," the Fairy in black told him. "My husband hasn't returned either. There is something rising. You're a fool if you cannot see that."

Hooklance ignored the other Fairy and slipped on his shield. "When I've killed the bitch, sweep the field with your lightning. Then we can use their blood and bodies to finally break that cursed Ward." He patted the blackblade at his belt and chuckled. "Or, I may just disarm her, and let her watch all her friends die." With a final tug on

173

his belt, he strode away from the Blood Ring and toward the mountain.

The black-armored Fairy turned. "Cease your lightning," he told the other four in similar armor. "Bring up the Wards," he ordered, stepping fully into the Blood Ring. "Be ready to strike them when Hook fails."

"At that low an angle," one of the others argued, "we'll hit our troops, too."

Waving off the protest, the leader said, "Hook was right about one thing: we need more blood and bone to fuel this Ring. It doesn't matter whose blood and bone." He pulled a black crystal from his belt. *"Zahadune,"* he Sent. *"Beloved?"* After a pause, *"Father."*

Behind the black-armored Fairies, there was a shimmer at the edge of the flowing, ever-moving Blood Ring. A small plop disturbed the flowing current, unnoticed.

☾ ∾ ☼

Across the field, Shatter watched Hooklance emerge from the press of his troops. He walked proudly across the grass, a lieutenant at his heels.

With a motion, Shatter stilled her soldiers' chants. She turned to a lieutenant. "Lastlight, spread the word: the plan is in motion. I will buy us as much time as I can. Watch for my signal." He nodded, and entered a Send. Shatter turned to her soldiers. "Be prepared for anything. Hooklance and his troops were once honorable, but we don't know what they'll do now. Be ready. Protect your Brothers and Sisters. EagleClaw, come with me."

"Yes, Captain," he agreed, picking up Shatter's dragon helm.

"The Mother of Waves protects us!" Shatter called out, beginning her walk across the field.

The chant followed her. "The Mother of Waves!"

Shatter smiled. *"I love you,"* she Sent.

"We love you, too, Staff," Saber replied. *"Make that bastard pay."*

"And come back to us," Stiletto added. A ripple of the baby's potential flowed into Shatter. *"Your daughter needs her mother. Make us proud."*

Shatter had no words, so she simply Sent her love and dedication to them both.

"Goddess keep you safe, Captain," Titania Sent. *"We'll be ready when you are."*

"Yes, Regent," Shatter replied, then broke all connections. She needed to focus now.

EagleClaw handed her her helm. "He'll cheat," he warned her.

"I know," Shatter said, fastening the helm. "Just be ready.""

"That lieutenant looks familiar, but I cannot place him. Treachery rolls off them both like a foul stench."

"That's just Hook. He never bathes."

EagleClaw laughed, but quieted as they got closer to Hooklance and his lieutenant.

"Make the circle," Hooklance commanded. His lieutenant and EagleClaw began to draw a circle in the grass with their spears, each starting off to their right. They stopped halfway through the arch, turned, and faced each other. Then they bisected the circle, the lieutenant passing with a sneer, EagleClaw with a smile. Finally, each turned and returned to where they had started, completing the dueling circle.

EagleClaw stuck his spear into the ground. "We stand in a circle of single combat," he called. "Let none interfere." He looked to Shatter. She nodded. "Until one is dead."

"Unless you prefer another condition?" Shatter asked. "Arms, maybe? Hands?"

"You'd start at a disadvantage, then," Hooklance shot back. "No!" he called louder, so all could hear. "Only one will leave this circle." He turned, raising his arms to his troops. "And it will be me!" A muted cheer followed. Hook turned, red-faced. He closed his faceplate, drew his sword, and readied his shield.

"The honorable one will leave!" Shatter called in response. A larger cheer rose. Shatter drew her sword, and held it two-handed before her.

"Need my shield?" EagleClaw offered.

"No," Shatter returned. With a snap of her chin, she closed her faceplate. "Just my bastard sword, for killing bastards."

"Don't get too confident," EagleClaw warned. He eyed the lieutenant across the circle.

"I won't. Remember your part."

"Yes, Captain."

"Less talk!" Hooklance called, banging his sword on his shield.

Both combatants stalked to the center of the circle. A hush fell over the troops on each side. Lightning stabbed across the sky one more time, then fell silent.

"Throw away that foul weapon," Shatter commanded, her voice hollow from behind the helm. "It has no place in this circle of honor."

"I have no honor," Hooklance sneered. "Or so you say."

"Prove me wrong then," Shatter growled. She stepped back, and brought her sword up.

Hook reached awkwardly across himself, yanking the blackblade from his belt and holding it up for everyone to see. All the nearby sunlight streamed into the black metal, pulled by its darkness. Shatter flexed her right hand, memories of another such blade causing a terrible ache in her arm.

Hook tossed the blackblade behind his back. The lieutenant caught it, and tucked it into his belt.

"Satisfied?" Hooklance asked, settling into a fighting stance, his shield up and sword ready.

"Not yet," Shatter replied. "As the Goddess wishes, only one of us will leave this circle."

"As she wishes," Hook agreed, then lunged at Shatter. Their swords came together and clashed. He pushed her back, but she dodged, striking his shield. He struck at her hard in response, but she turned his blade.

The clangs of metal on metal filled the air. EagleClaw watched the duel resolutely. Shatter was fluid, flowing around and away from Hooklance's blade with apparent ease. He came at her hard, chopping and lunging, then putting up his shield as her blows rained down, denting and chipping the surface. Then she would step back, letting him come at her again.

EagleClaw kept one eye on the opposing lieutenant. He was following the combat closely, wincing when Shatter landed a flat-of-the-blade blow on the top of Hook's head, rocking him. He stumbled, almost losing his sword. Shatter didn't follow through, though, allowing him to shake it off and regain his footing.

"I still have my honor," Shatter declared, then struck with an overhand blow, denting Hooklance's shield further.

Hook pulled free, waving his blade wildly to keep her away as he did so.

The lieutenant began to frown. He turned slightly, and EagleClaw felt a Send. Uneasy movement rose among the troops behind Hooklance.

EagleClaw Sent back to his own soldiers. He received answers — from all around and above — confirming that they were ready. He clapped his hand to his thigh, and Shatter nodded slightly in recognition.

Then she lunged at Hooklance again, coming at him overhanded. He smiled beneath his helm, noting her mistake. His shield came up, and as the blow fell, he wrenched to the side, leaving Shatter's blade tangled in the dented metal. Hooklance slipped his arm out of the shield and kicked at Shatter, catching her in the stomach. She stumbled, losing her blade. Hook loomed over her and raised his blade.

"Die, bitch!" he snarled.

Shatter burst into high speed, deflecting the descending sword with her left arm, and punching him under the ribs with her right. Hooklance gasped as her armored fist continued through his chest, smashing his lung and heart. Through the slits on his helm, she could see his eyes widen.

177

"Don't call me that," she said, twisting her arm. He gasped again and went limp, his eyes going dark. Shatter rose, pushing the dead body off her arm to fall to the grass with a thunk of wet meat and metal.

The lieutenant was staring at her with wide eyes. Behind him, she heard angry cries and the dark clanging of weapons.

Shatterstaff raised her blood-stained right arm and closed her fist.

A line of Silverfire stabbed from the mountain, striking the Ward around the Blood Ring. For a moment, the red dome held, but then it collapsed under the intensity of the attack. With a rolling boom, the Blood Ring detonated in a spray of grass, blood, and fire. The False Sisters' troops were flung into the air.

The lieutenant turned back, just in time for EagleClaw to hit him in the face with his spear. The lieutenant fell in a clatter.

"Now I know you," EagleClaw spat. "You broke my arm when I tried to join Air." He turned to Shatter. "I couldn't fly for weeks."

"Lucky you," Shatter told him, picking up her sword. "Ware!" she cried. "They're coming!"

☾ ∭ ☼

Nightshade huddled in her Shadow. The corruption of the Blood Ring at her back was giving her a headache. She waited, breathing low and slow. The black-armored Fairies were nervous. They held their Ward tight, pulling Power from the Ring to feed an already strong Weave.

'Fools,' she thought. 'You make my job so much easier.'

The leader, in his fancy armor, was pacing the perimeter across from them. She could tell he was worried. He kept fingering a black crystal. Then Nightshade recognized the armor. It was ornate and expensive. The man she had cut down to save Elanor had been similarly attired. In her Sight, she could See a protective Weave infused within the armor. She would have to hit him with more Fire than the others.

A pit of worry opened in her gut. 'Vengeance,' she thought, 'is a powerful thing.'

178

"Ready?" Steel Sent through the crystal under her armor.

"Ready," she affirmed.

Two heartbeats. *"Now!"* Steel cried.

Nightshade burst into action. Her knives flew, taking two of the Blood Cultists in the back of the head. They fell, tangling with the others as they tried to turn. Nightshade kicked the third in the knee, and rammed a blade under the chin of the fourth.

Their leader was also turning, raising his hand, as the sky lit up silver.

Nightshade threw Silverfire stones, scattering them around the Ring and activating those she had placed there earlier when she had arrived. Then, she wrapped herself into a ball, her wings tight around her. She locked a Shield tightly around herself as well. As she closed her eyes, the world exploded in flame. She felt herself flying, then rolling, and then, landing with a thump, she knew only blackness.

$$\left(\!\!\!\!\quad\text{≈}\quad\text{☼}\right.$$

The False Sisters' troops, shocked by the pillar of Silverfire rising from their Blood Ring, held for a moment, then charged. They screamed, bearing down on the dueling ring and the Regent's soldiers across the field.

Silverfire exploded in their front ranks as flyers — swooping out of Shadows — dropped Silverfire stones on them from above. Bodies flew, and the charge faltered.

A powerful Send burst over the troops. *"Hold!"* A cloud of arrows smashed into their right flank. More fell, trampled by those following.

Belladonna and her archers appeared to Shatter's left. They drew back for another volley.

A weak, uncoordinated volley of arrows from the False Sisters' troops fell on the right flank of the Regent's soldiers. Most were deflected by Shields, but a few found their targets, piercing soldiers and spilling their blood. A determined rumble rose, as others stepped up to fill the new gaps in their ranks.

179

The False Sisters' flyers began to rise, but not before the Regent's dropped another barrage of stones on the invaders' trailing ranks, leading to more cries and flying bodies. Then, the flyers broke formation, fighting for air as their enemies followed.

Another Send from Titania hit the Regent's forces. *"Hold!"* Powered by Min's Circle of eighteen, it reached the whole battlefield. Belladonna fired again, the wave of arrows eating further into the invading troops.

The cries of the remaining officers began to rise. "Stop! Hold!" The charge slowed, and then stopped.

"Throw down your weapons!" Titania ordered.

The False Sisters' troops looked first at each other, then at the carnage surrounding them. Another group of archers materialized from their left. Shatter and her soldiers, shields up, were bracing to receive the charge. Spears glittered in the sun.

Titania's Send burst over them. *"I said, weapons down!"*

Steel, leading another group of soldiers, jogged up, ready to charge the right flank.

"No more Fairies have to die today," Titania declared. *"Surrender, or face our wrath."*

With a clatter, the False Sisters' troops dropped their weapons and held up their hands. Above, the invading flyers drifted slowly down, under the watchful eyes of those loyal to the Regent.

"Captain Shatter," Titania ordered. *"Separate the officers from the rest of the troops. You should have enough cuffs for them. Lay down your Ephemeral Ring, and Mab will come through with more temporary bindings for the rest."*

Shatter motioned, and her soldiers moved in. They gathered the lieutenants and the sergeants, binding their hands with Power-blocking cuffs.

"Shieldbreaker and the Healers are on their way," Titania informed everyone. *"Captain Steel, please see to the Blood Ring. I can't see it. There's too much smoke."*

Steel called to her soldiers, and began moving up the field to the smoking ruins of the Blood Ring. Belladonna gave command of her archers to her lieutenants, and ran past Steel. *"Nightshade!"* she

Sent desperately. Steel quickened her pace, running behind her, as she realized there had been no response.

Shatter forced an uncooperative sergeant to his feet and pushed him at EagleClaw. She looked slowly over the mounds of arrow-pierced and burned bodies on the field and felt sick. She had trained with many of these soldiers, and fought beside them. Now, she had to kill them.

"Shatter," Min Sent to her. *"Are you all right?"*

"Yes, Sister. I am."

"Is he dead?"

Shatter remembered the panic in the corridors beneath the palace on the day of the False Sisters' coup. *"Yes, he is,"* she said decisively.

"Bring me his sword," Min commanded. *"I want my daughter to have it."*

Stiletto broke in. *"Our daughter has a stronger claim to it."*

"She's right," Shatter conceded.

Min was silent for a moment. *"Then bring me his armor. We'll make it into something more useful."*

Shatter returned to the trampled Ring and kicked Hooklance's body. *"It's only fair quality,"* she Sent back.

"All the more reason to make something better with it. I want his helm for my chamber pot," Min Sent with a smile.

"But I want that," Steel cut in.

"Nightshade?" Elanor asked. *"How is she?"*

"Dizzy, bruised, burned, a few broken bones, and missing a piece of her wing," Steel reported. *"But otherwise whole."*

"So, a normal evening then," Belladonna commented dryly.

"I'm the pregnant one," Min argued. *"I'll have more use for the pot."*

"Yes, little mother," Steel acquiesced, cutting her connection to focus on Nightshade.

"Looks like we won," Min Sent after a few moments of silence.

"No," Shatter replied. *"We just held on. This war will continue."*

Chapter Eighteen
Finding a Way Through

"Lady Min," Titania called brightly as Min entered her chamber. "How are you?"

"I'm fine, Regent," Min said with a bow. She took the seat Luna motioned her to, then took the cup Luna pressed on her. She held it between her hands, inhaling the familiar scent and enjoying its warmth.

Titania stayed silent, sitting back in her chair. Min held her cup, waiting for the Regent to speak.

Luna finally nudged Min in the shoulder and cleared her throat.

With a long-suffering sigh, Min drank the tea, draining it in two swallows. She set the cup down, made a face, and coughed.

"Horrible stuff," Titania finally commented.

"Yes, Regent," Min agreed.

"But we must do what is right for our children," Titania said. She looked up at Luna. "Isn't that right?"

"Yes, Mistress, it is," Luna confirmed, pouring another cup — from a different pot this time — for Min.

"Thank you, Luna," Min said gratefully, taking the new cup and drinking heartily. "Flora always makes me drink two."

Luna tutted. "She's overprotective. But I'll be sure to tell her."

Min frowned, somehow caught in a trap she had not seen.

Titania laughed, an honest sound Min hadn't heard from her since before the Queen's Pyre. "You may go, Luna. I can serve myself."

"Yes, Mistress," Luna agreed with a bow, and left the room.

"How any of us survived without those two sisters," Titania marveled, taking some fruit, and offering the basket to Min, "I do not know."

"We would never have survived without Flora," Min said vehemently. She took a tiny melon with a nod of thanks and began to chew on the rind.

Titania realized her jest had held more truth than she had intended. She sat back down, sipping her tea.

"How is Conwenne?" she finally asked.

"She's better," Min reported, making the Sign of the Three. "Not mindlost, thank the Goddess. But she'll be unable to think clearly or do very much for a while. Celia and the Healers are debating whether she should be put into an enforced sleep so her mind can heal."

"I must speak with them," Titania said. "A decision like that must not be made quickly. She's a valuable part of my court, and I would not have her asleep when I need her."

Min started to reply, but dropped her head, looking into her cup.

"It was her decision," Titania reminded her. "She is High Paramount, and she was needed there. You and Elanor were needed in the Circle. Do not blame yourself."

"I just wonder if there was more I could have done. Maybe held the backlash, or channeled it in a better way." She sighed. "I also feel guilty that it isn't Elanor in that bed."

"Your guilt does you credit, but do not let it overburden you," Titania counseled. "Sometimes others have to take the risks. We must let them." She brushed the two bracelets on her arm. "You will learn that as your children grow."

"Yes, Regent," Min said, sitting up straighter. "The Wards are back to full power. All the damage that was done has been repaired. I think it's a good idea to maintain the outer Ward at all times. It'll provide an early warning for any approach. I had to alter the Weave again, so it would be two-way, instead of just a one-way Shield. But it can be restored swiftly if necessary."

"Celia agrees with you," Titania said, nodding approvingly. "How many will it take to maintain?"

"Only two or three. I've set up a schedule." She pulled a scroll from her side, but Titania waved it away.

"I'm sure it's fine, as long as you aren't taking too long a shift."

"Yes, Regent," Min agreed, putting the scroll away. "I'm not. Flora won't let me. Or Elanor," Min said, mostly as an aside.

Titania smiled again. "That's partly why I wanted to see you. With Conwenne unable to perform her duties, the position of High Paramount must be temporarily filled."

Despite herself, Min felt a surge of hope, pride, and — deep down — fear.

"No," Titania said, hiding a smile. "That would truly be reaching beyond your wingtips. One day, maybe."

"I'm sorry, Regent," Min apologized, lowering her head in embarrassment.

"No, don't be. Your ambition is good. But remember, you just attained the rank of Paramount. You have much to learn yet."

"Of course, Regent," Min said, raising her head again. "It has been difficult."

"I understand. And I need you to continue overseeing the mountain's Wards. That will be a great help to all of us." Titania paused. "I will be calling Lady Bethia to be my High Paramount."

Min took a moment to absorb this information. "I thought my mother was busy in the north."

"She is, and your father will remain there. She will split her time between here and there. But I need a strong hand. Conwenne was that. Lady Bethia will be, too."

"The children need a strong hand," Min joked, instantly regretting it.

"Yes, you do," Titania agreed, "but not because I do not trust you and all the other Paramounts here. All of you need the guidance that she can give. She's served longer than I have. She was one of my teachers in the Tower." Titania chuckled. "I was afraid of her for so long. Then I got to know her. Not as well as I knew Miranda, of course." A darkness passed over her face, but she shook it off. "But enough to understand her. She guided me down the path I now follow." She sat back, and took a sip of her tea. "I thought the two of you were getting along well."

"We are," Min admitted. "We seem to be the only ones who are," she said with a smile. "But there's always that worry. She's never really spoken to me about my pregnancy. I just feel a distance between us. Both her and my father. I'm just not sure."

"Not sure of what?" Titania asked, gently.

"What they'll look like," Min admitted. "There are so few Iridescent Elenites. And their father is half Leather. Will they have wings? Will that matter?" Min shook her head. "I wish I could See."

"There are more Iridescent Elenites than you know," Titania noted. "But I understand. I went through the same thing."

"But it's not the same: your children were sure to have wings," Min interrupted. "Forgive me, Regent," she said, immediately realizing her misstep.

Titania reached out and took Min's hand. "Let me be just a mother right now. An aunt to you, if you will." Min nodded. "I felt the same worries about my children. Yes, it's not the same, but I could still hear that voice in my head. My mother asking me, what will my grandchildren look like? Will they carry on the line? Will they bring honor and respect to our family?" She gripped Min's hands. "And do you know what I decided?"

"No," Min said faintly.

"That it does not matter. My children will be their own Fairies. They will follow their own paths. They will each be who the Goddess and their own conscience direct them to be. By doing that, they will bring honor to themselves and their family." She smiled. "I saw the eyes of some of the Fairies of the court, when one was a Feather-wing. But it doesn't matter. He will be a powerful Fairy. He makes his mother and father proud. Even if he does make a mess every time he toddles into a room."

Min smiled. "I understand," she said. "I just wish she would make her feelings toward me clear."

"Let me tell you a secret," Titania offered. "Mothers do not have all the answers. We do the best we can with what we have. She might not even know her own mind. What I'm sure of is that she loves you. And she will love her grandchildren. How they look — and whether or not they can fly — does not matter."

'I'm not so sure,' Min thought, but she smiled back at Titania. "Thank you, Regent . . . I'm sorry, Titania. I will think on all that you have said."

"Her first question was, 'Is she safe?'" Titania confided. "She's eager to join us."

"When will she arrive?"

"She has a few details to take care of first. The next moon, I think. Until then, and unless Lady Bethia decides otherwise, Celia will act in her stead."

"Elanor won't like that," Min blurted before she could think.

"Lady Elanor has no choice," Titania said firmly, returning to being the Regent. "The two of them will work together." She narrowed her eyes at Min. "Make sure she understands that."

"Yes, Regent," Min acknowledged with a bow of her head. "I'll make sure she understands."

Titania held her gaze for a moment, then smiled. "And I will make sure Celia understands it, too. We must work together to defend our Sisters and Brothers. To keep safe all those we care about."

"Yes, Regent," Min agreed. "We must."

☾ ⌇⌇⌇ ☼

"Lord Troilus, the younger," Titania greeted her prisoner, stepping into the well-guarded room. Belladonna — in grey armor — stood to her right, and Steel — in her green and purple armor, except for the helm — stood at her left. Shatter shut the door firmly and put her back to it.

Across the room, an Iridescent man rose. His hands were firmly bound in front of him with strongly glowing cuffs. Fairysilk ropes — also faintly glowing — bound his chest, and were wound around his legs for good measure.

"I demand to speak to my father," he said arrogantly. "And I demand to see my husband." He looked from face to face.

"Your husband is dead," Titania informed him, her tone matter-of-fact. "And you are in no position to make demands."

Troilus sat back down on the bed, slumping. He closed his eyes, and brought his bound hands to his face. Belladonna watched him closely, her hand on a knife. Steel watched him as well, her hand on the hilt of her sword, her face grim. Titania was still and calm, her staff of office providing the only movement in the room, as she held it, swaying a bit, in the crook of her arm.

Troilus looked up. "How did he die?"

"He was killed attempting to break the Ward around this mountain," Titania reported simply, but not without compassion.

"I demand to see the body," Troilus said, sitting up straight, and pushing away any emotion.

"That isn't possible," Titania explained. "It's being held with those of the others who died. We're preparing for a Pyre of Return." She looked at him. "If you wish to hold Vigil with him, I'm sure we can arrange. . . ."

"You will return his body," he interrupted, "when you send me back to my father."

"What makes you think you're going back?" Steel asked, truly curious. Titania glanced at her, and she fell silent.

"I am a lord of the highest birth and caliber," Troilus replied haughtily, ignoring the others, and focusing solely on Titania. "As is my father. You will of course ransom me back." He gestured around the room with his bound hands. "A little silver would do this place good."

"And that's what your life is worth, a little silver?" Titania asked.

"On the contrary! My life is worth more than all of yours," Troilus replied. "Far more. But I'm sure my father will provide you with adequate compensation."

Belladonna bristled, but Titania settled her with a look.

"You are a traitor to your Queen and a practitioner of the most foul Magic," Titania stated. "There will be no ransom. You will be held and tried here."

"I do not acknowledge your authority over me," he replied with heat. "The True Queens are back at Fae-Treval. If you had a Queen, she would be here." He waved his hands. "I see no Queen, just an old woman pretending to rule."

"She is the Regent of the one true Queen," Belladonna snapped. "You will show her respect."

He sneered. "I will show her nothing of the sort. You are all rebels and traitors. I was sent here by the True Queens to return you to their justice." He looked them over. "Or, failing that, to kill as many of you as I could."

"There were no terms offered," Titania argued. "No calls for surrender. Your flyers appeared, conjured that foul Ring, and then attacked us. Those are the actions of brutal killers. Not agents of a true Queen seeking justice."

He simply shrugged. "The messages must have been lost, or garbled by your Wards. You can ask Captain Hooklance: he sent them. He was in command here. I was merely an observer."

"You created that Ring," Steel snapped. "You murdered prisoners to do it. Your foul Magic is a stain on the honor of all Fairies." She took a step forward. "I should kill you now, for all the suffering you've caused."

"Leash your bitch," Lord Troilus said casually. "She barks too much."

"You will leash your mouth, boy," Titania said, losing patience with him. She motioned Steel back. Titania took a step forward, pointing her staff at Troilus. "You are accused of treachery to your Queen, and foul practices before the Goddess. How do you plead?"

"You have no authority to accuse me of anything. I serve the True Queens." He spread his hands, as much as he could within their bindings. "I have taken no blood. You are no Keeper, to accuse me of acts such as those. Where are they? Where is she? She hasn't been seen in many moons. Or have you usurped that authority, too?"

"I do not need a Keeper's cloak to see the corruption and rot in you," Titania replied. "What do you plead?"

"I will see my advocate," he said smugly. "That is, if you have any Law Masters here. They've been missing, too."

Steel growled. Troilus smiled at her, baring his own teeth. "It would be better just to send me back to my father. All this trouble, all this Magic." He gestured to his bonds. "All those guards."

"The Queen's Justice will find you an advocate," Titania said shortly.

Troilus smiled mockingly at her. "If you will not treat me as my status demands," he continued, "I will consider myself held by enemies, and shall do everything in my power to escape."

"Try it, boy," Belladonna said low. "See how far you get."

"Yes, I will," he told her, making a kissing face at her. "Might stop in your bed first. Show you the true meaning of pleasure."

Belladonna's sharp Send stopped Steel's angry retort. "You would not survive," she told him simply.

He lost his smile at her cold stare and returned his gaze to Titania. "I will allow you a day to decide. After that, I cannot be responsible for my actions, or those of my father." He sat back on the bed. "On my Oath, if you return me, I will not raise a hand to you or your rebels for a year. Standard ransom conditions," he told her. "You do remember your former position, don't you, Regent?" He curled his lip, making her title a mockery.

"I give you a day to answer these charges," Titania told him, ignoring his insult. "After that, I will treat you as the murderer you are."

Steel knocked on the door, and Shatter opened it. Without a backward glance, Titania swept out of the room. Belladonna pinned Troilus with her gaze, made a kissing motion at him, then followed the Regent. Steel trailed behind, laughing, and shut the door behind her.

"At least free my arms," he called out, too late.

Joel C. Flanagan-Grannemann

Chapter Nineteen
Aftermath

Elanor walked to the edge of the shaft in the heart of the mountain. She could have gone below by using one of the Ephemeral Rings, but sometimes she just needed to fly. On the sides of the shaft, Fairies were working on rebuilding the spiral staircase that had once curved up the wall. Upon hearing all the banging and yelling, Elanor pushed down her memories of the area, once happy, now colored with betrayal.

"I just have to get over it," she told herself out loud. A Feather-wing worker, lowering supplies, looked at her with puzzlement.

"Long way down," she told him.

He nodded. "Bothered me, too, at first, but now. . . ." He went to the edge, stood on his tiptoes, and looked down. His wings spread, balancing him. "I'm fine." He slipped, but Elanor have him a tug back with her Power.

"Thank you," he said breathlessly. "Apple?" he offered.

"No thanks," she said. "My Sister who loves them isn't here." Then, with a jaunty wave, she stepped off the edge. With the wind singing in her ears, Elanor wondered why some things were so easy, and others — like falling — brought so many bad memories. She extended her wings to land in a puff of dust.

'Maybe they used to be good memories,' she thought, waving to the guards, whose numbers had increased. She stepped into the vast cavern.

Before, it had felt big, but now, it was cramped. It had been converted into a combined holding area and infirmary. The False Sisters' troops sat or lay on the floor. They were being tended to by Healers and watched over by the Regent's soldiers. In the far corner, where the chora pen used to be, the captured troops who were unharmed sat on the cold rock floor, looking tired and dejected. Most kept their heads down, but a brave few looked up, meeting the eyes of former comrades or acquaintances among the Regent's soldiers.

They were always met with cold indifference, followed by pity when they looked away.

Elanor stopped, sighting someone she knew across the cavern. She hurried over.

"Scarlet!" she cried happily, grabbing the young Medic's arm. "I didn't know you were here."

He turned. Scarlet looked much younger than Elanor remembered. "Your feathers," she gushed. "They came back. And they're silver," she said with wonder.

He smiled and shook his wings at her. They shone, a silver wash glowing over his originally pure white feathers. "Yes, they are. Right after you left, they began to come back, and all of them had this silver shine. Goddess wonder." He turned to the other Healer beside him. "Give her more of that tea. It will clear her lungs."

"Yes, Healer," the other Fairy replied, helping the injured soldier sit up. Her face was burned, and her wings mangled.

"Thank you," she croaked.

"It is my duty," Scarlet replied. He took Elanor's arm and pulled her away.

"She was caught in one of the Silverfire blasts," he explained as he led Elanor toward the door. A fence had been set up there, but the guards waved them through. Scarlet went down to the edge of the lake. There, he reached into the water and splashed some on his face.

"Shield called me when they first attacked. There was nothing I could do at what was left of Holly's tower, and Silverflow's Healers had things well in hand there. So, I came here." He looked around. "This place is beautiful."

"Yes, it is," Elanor agreed, watching him.

"I'll be headed back to Silverfire in a few days. I'll take some of the worst ones with me. We'll have time to work with them there and get them back on their feet."

Elanor was confused. "But I thought the False Sisters were attacking there."

"They've let up. I guess, to attack here," he admitted. "Maybe they'll return. But the cold season is coming. Should give us a few moons of relief." He sat down on a rock. "I saw Flora briefly. I'm sorry. Such a tragic story."

Elanor just nodded, sitting down beside him. "But you seem to have risen. Those wings make you look more handsome. I wager you're being propositioned by many, looking for children with those wings."

He blushed slightly. "Most of the children born at Silverfire now have similar wings," he told her. "Must be something in the air."

"Don't be modest," Elanor chided. "Shield told me you're well liked. Two?" she asked.

"Children? Yes," he confirmed. "But not with partners, just. . . ." He lost the words. "I've been finding it hard to bond with anyone. And many just want comfort in some form."

"And, of course, you're glad to provide it?" she teased.

"Don't be so flippant," Scarlet said angrily. "I was there long before you and your Heir arrived. You don't know what we endured."

"I'm sorry," Elanor apologized swiftly, leaning back. "I was just trying to lighten the mood. I'm sorry if I offended you."

"Yes, of course," Scarlet said with an equally apologetic sigh. "I've just been seeing so many maimed and dead lately. I guess my edge is closer to the surface than I thought." He looked up at her. "You didn't come out here to ask me about my bed habits," he remarked, trying to smile.

"Maybe," she said, almost reaching out to touch him. But she pulled back. "Actually, I was looking for Shield."

Scarlet sighed. "She's further along this path. The officers are being kept apart from the regular troops. A few of them were badly hurt. She's been tending them."

"Thank you," Elanor said. "I'm sorry. I should have been more sensitive."

He stood, helping her up. "I shouldn't have snapped at you, either. All of us have been hurt."

She let her arm stay in his grip for a moment. "And there are many ways to ease that hurt."

He smiled. "It's a long path back," he told her, taking his arm back. "I must return. If I don't see you before I go, walk with the Goddess, Lady Elanor."

"You also, Healer Scarlet. But don't slip away without seeing Flora. She'll fly all the way to Silverfire to tweak your feathers if you do."

He laughed. "I won't." Then, with a wave and a twitch of his feathers, he returned to the cavern.

Elanor followed the curve of the mountain. Across a crude bridge, she saw a group of their soldiers standing guard at a depression in the rocks. On the other side of them, an angry male was yelling, "Get your hands off me!" from within a smaller knot of soldiers.

"If I don't treat that arm," a familiar voice replied, "it will fester. You don't have the Healing Power to fix it on your own. It's barely keeping up."

"You and your fellow traitors did this! We will Heal our own."

Recognizing Shield's voice, Elanor hurried her steps.

"Then lose the arm," Shield said, standing. "And I am not a traitor. I serve my Queen."

"As do I," the man replied to a chorus of similar cries from his fellows.

The voice of a Sergeant in green armor cut through. "Silence!" The dissident voices quieted. "Don't be a stubborn bastard. I can't remove the cuffs. Take her Healing."

Elanor came up behind Shield, brushing her wing. Shield Sent a thanks.

The Fairy on the ground glared up at them. His left arm was badly burned, the skin black and flaking. It was bound with the remains of his blue tabard. Behind him sat more invaders, all in the remains of blue and red uniforms. They all had their hands bound. Some were chained together, while others were bound at the feet and gagged.

"Then, when you're too weak to resist," Shield told him matter-of-factly, "I'll be forced to cut off your arm to save your miserable life. Then you can feel the pain our soldiers are going through."

More ugly voices rose among the prisoners.

"Healer," the Sergeant told her, "it's best you go." *"When it's time, I'll send for you. Or if he comes to his senses,"* he Sent with amusement.

Shield glared one more time at the man on the ground. Then she turned, pulling Elanor with her back toward the entrance to the cave. Shield stopped on the narrow bridge and sat down, hanging her feet above the water.

"What was that about?" Elanor asked, sitting down beside her.

"Those are the officers," Shield explained. "The ones who are unrepentant. They've either fallen for the lies of the False Sisters, or want to believe them. Others whose cruelty fits with theirs."

"Mostly men," Elanor noted. "And I saw many Air tabards."

"Shatterstaff did the Realm a great service when she killed that cursed bastard," Shield swore. "His men murdered and ravaged. Killed. . . ." Her voice broke.

Elanor put her hand on Shield's arm. "He will be judged before the Mother's Throne."

"I want to bury him," Shield said savagely. "Hold his spirit here, so he'll never be allowed to bring his corruption back."

Elanor gasped at the intensity of Shield's hate. She slipped one arm around the Healer's shoulders and gripped Shield's hand with the other. "That is what they want us to feel."

"I don't care," Shield said, pulling away from her. "I hate them!" She stood. "They don't deserve to Return. Any of them!"

"Then why try to help them?" Elanor threw back, also standing. On the other side of the bridge, a group of soldiers was waiting to pass. Shield noticed them and strode away from Elanor, walking fast. As she brushed brazenly through the group, they let her and Elanor pass, stepping politely out of their way. One soldier did not move, however. Instead, he planted himself directly in Shield's path. His green armor was battered, as if he had rolled down the mountain, and his right sleeve hung empty.

Shield stopped, looking up at him, annoyed.

Once he was certain he had her attention, he spoke. "Thank you, Healer Shieldbreaker," he said earnestly. Then he stepped aside to let her pass. A chorus of similar thanks rose from his companions. Flustered by the attention, Shield hurried on, Elanor hastening at her heels.

Shield didn't stop at the entrance as Elanor expected, but continued walking around the mountain instead. Elanor followed, sensing both her immense need to be alone, and her equally strong and contrary desire not to be. So, around the mountain they went. Finally, Shield turned, taking a small trail up the side of the ridge. Elanor followed, slipping on the loose stones. Shield never looked back. She climbed, grabbing outcroppings and trees along the slope to help her up the steep trail. Elanor climbed after her, following Shield's lead.

They climbed for what seemed like a long time, until the trail ended at a wall. Without stopping or looking back, Shield began to climb further, finding hand- and foot-holds in the rock that were invisible to Elanor, who watched her ascend in amazement. Finally, Shield scrambled up onto a ledge, without ever looking down. Elanor followed, using her Power to find the handholds Shield had used and to secure herself to the mountainside to avoid falling. After much exertion, an exhausted yet exhilarated Elanor finally pulled herself up over onto the ledge, where she found Shield sitting cross-legged at the far end. The remains of an old fire lay beside her.

Elanor walked over to her and sat down. "Why didn't we fly?" she asked after she caught her breath.

"Doing it the hard way is the point," Shield informed her.

"More Keeper wisdom?"

"No. My father," she said simply. She stared out over the land, sloping down before them.

"It's a good view."

"If I told you to go, would you?" Shield asked, looking at Elanor for the first time since the bridge.

"No. I like this ledge. I can see the whole lake, and the mountain behind us." She took a deep breath, then began to cough.

Shield pounded her on the back. "You need to get out more. You've been cooped up in the mountain for too long."

Elanor nodded. "I forget how hard soldiers are."

"I am no longer a soldier," Shield reminded her.

"Yes, you are," Elanor disagreed. "In the way you're a Leather-wing. It's part of you. What you do is different. You'll always be a soldier. Just as I will always love her."

"It always comes back to her," Shield said savagely. She picked up a stone and threw it. It bounced off a tree with a wooden ping.

Elanor didn't comment.

They sat in silence, watching the sun move across the sky. Shield picked up stones and built little cairns, then took them apart and started over. Elanor just sat, watching the birds fly by and listening to the chattering of the small animals scrambling about. One little brown creature — with a white stripe down its back and a short tail — watched her from a tree. It jumped at any move Elanor made, but always came back, watching her with little black eyes. Elanor was wondering if she had anything in her pouch to try and feed it, when the call of a Briarrose Hawk overhead sent it skittering for cover. Elanor went back to waiting.

Her feet had gone to sleep, and Elanor was wondering if Shield was going to be stubborn, when she finally spoke up.

"I started coming up here not long after the Queen's Pyre. I couldn't sleep. I kept hearing Nova's final goodbye. And the noises in the library and the mountain only made it worse. So, I came up here. I followed a black and brown creature I saw outside the cave entrance. He seemed to know where he was going, and I didn't, so I followed him. He led me to the base of the wall. Then he turned and chittered at me. Despite everything, I laughed. He was so offended. I told him, 'Sorry, little Brother; I just needed quiet.' He looked at me again, and I swear he understood me. He stood up on his hind legs and pointed up the wall. Then he scampered off into the woods. So, I climbed. I used to climb with my father, and it came back to me easily. Soon, I found this ledge. Might have been a watch point in the Exile Queen's time, or just a ripple in the stone. But I found peace here. I sat, and tried to feel the stone like she did. But I felt nothing." Shield shrugged. "It's just stone to me. Nothing like she used to describe. A living — though frozen — river. And then I began talking to her. Telling her everything that had happened. Like I used to when we were on the road. And I felt better. It helped to talk out loud. Then, Longstride arrived, and I found I could talk to him, too. I told him about this ledge. He wanted to see it; feel the peace I had found here. I told him about watching you and Min setting up the guide stone. How it kept sparking, and lit your dress on fire. How you took it off, and. . . ." She stopped.

"That happens to me a lot," Elanor said wryly.

"It happens because you make it happen," Shield said forlornly. "So, I brought him up here." She brushed her hand through her short hair. "Now I understand why he came," she said savagely. She pointed down the slope. There, glowing faintly, stood one of the guide stones. Elanor saw a soldier standing guard. After a moment, he disappeared, and another soldier appeared in his place.

"Understood why," Shield said again, as tears flowed down her cheeks. "So he could set a trap to try and kill Min. Betray my Sister, and my Regent." She struck her fist on the stone. "I was such a fool. I wanted comfort so bad. Wanted what you have. And I failed again."

"You didn't fail," Elanor countered. "Min is still with us. The Ward didn't fall. If it wasn't you, he would have found another way. He could have found any other stone easily."

"But it was me," she said. "When I was training, a kid fell asleep on guard duty as part of an exercise. An exercise," she stressed. "And he was thrown out."

"I do not blame you," Elanor stressed. "Neither does Min." She struggled, looking for the words that would make Shield understand. "A betrayal isn't about the one betrayed. It's about the betrayer. Longstride made his decision, however manipulated and coerced he was. He chose to use what you felt for him against you."

"You know so much about betrayal," Shield said cruelly. "Why did you let it happen to you?"

"I came up here to try and help you," Elanor said, standing.

"I never asked you to."

"If you need to fight, well." She looked around. She reached out, and wrenched a branch from a nearby tree. It flew to her hand, dry leaves dropping as it flew. She took the branch like an ill-shaped spear and shook it at Shield, more dry leaves rattling and falling on her. "Well, then, fight me, brave soldier. Beat me, when all you want to do is beat him."

"Get that away," Shield said, batting the branch away from her face. Elanor pulled it back out of her reach, then lunged again. Shield batted it away with frustration. "Leave me alone," she said, getting angry. She stood up. Elanor pulled the branch back, but Shield grabbed the end of it.

"I won't until you fight me," Elanor said, dancing back, shaking the branch. Leaves covered the ledge, crunching under her feet.

"I don't want to fight you," Shield said, letting go and backing up.

"Then what do you want to do?" Elanor asked, advancing again, pushing Shield back against the mountain. "You can't end it like I end all my fights with Min."

"Leave me alone, you foolish trollop," Shield swore. She finally grabbed the branch, ripped it out of Elanor's hands, and threw it over the edge.

"Ow," Elanor said, holding up her hand, blood flowing from a slash across the palm. "That hurt. I think I got a splinter."

"Serves you right," Shield said, folding her arms.

"If you don't want to fight, and you don't want to get naked with me," Elanor said, getting closer to Shield. She held up her bleeding hand. "What do you want to do?"

"I have to Heal that cut," Shield said, reaching for Elanor's hand.

Elanor snatched it back. "I can Heal it. We trollops need to know how to Heal. We break our own hearts all the time. I have much practice."

"I can't heal a broken heart," Shield said. Then she dropped her hand. "I can't heal a broken heart," she cried again, slumping to the ground, her arms covering her head. She tried to wrap her wings around herself, but Elanor was there, holding her.

Shield began to sob. "Why? Why? I don't understand."

Elanor held her, wrapping her wings and arms around Shield. Feeling her sobs reverberate through her body, Elanor held her tighter. She opened her mind to Shield, offering her a safe place to rest. Someone who understood.

Shield rushed in like a little child, taking the embrace, and letting her pain flow. Pain from the betrayal of Longstride. Pain from the loss of Nova. Pain from the loss of all their Sisters. It almost overwhelmed Elanor, but she held firm, holding Shield steady and letting her pain wash against Elanor's strong wall.

The two Fairies huddled together as the sun moved across the sky.

Chapter Twenty
Under the Dancer's Stars

"He's right."

"Yes, curse him," Titania agreed, setting her cup down. "We can't hold him, and we can't let him go back to his father either. I would hold no faith with any Oath he would give."

"But what repercussions will arise if we do what must be done?" Celia asked.

"His father's powerful," Shatter said. "His army came up from the south, joined with the False Sisters, and quickly drove the loyal groups out. Now he helps hold Oberon pinned in Elen."

Titania swore. "And now we also know he's a Blood Cultist. I always had my suspicions about Lord Troilus the elder, but they were always about pushing things over the line of consent, or abuse of his people. Not this. And we all know the rumors about what he did in the Human Realm."

"It could be said that our current problems arise from his actions during and immediately following the war," Celia commented.

"Their roots were in place long before that," Titania said, waving her hand dismissively. "But I take your meaning." She looked around the room. Celia — still bound to her board — was lying at an angle so she could see everyone. Shatter nursed a cup of wine and a plate of food, while Nightshade ate heartily, the only quarter given to her injuries that she lay reclined on a couch. Obsidian kept running back and forth to keep her plate full.

Nightshade spoke up. "You need to say it, Regent."

Titania's face became very still. "How will he react if I execute his son?"

Silence filled the room.

"The man has other children," Nightshade said.

"But he is a man of vengeance," Celia stated. "He might send more powerful attacks against us. Or kill others in retaliation."

"We've been lucky," Titania noted. "But if he goes mad with grief, who knows what he might do!"

"Will he really go mad — throw caution to the winds — to get vengeance on us?" Shatter asked incredulously.

"There's no way to know," Titania replied.

"We need more allies," Shatter stated. "Holly's tower has fallen, but Silverflow still stands. After much loss, that Ring was destroyed, and the False Sisters' troops have been captured or driven back. We need to secure that line of approach. Make them unwilling to fly over."

"How do we do that?" Celia asked. "Troops from the north? Or further west?"

"The cities in the west are few and small, and their governors are an independent lot," Titania told them. "They've been unwilling to move or choose a side in this war. They prefer to remain concerned solely with the safety of their own people."

"They wait to see who wins," Nightshade said shrewdly.

Titania nodded. "We'll get no help from them. And as to the north: Lady Bethia and Lord Johan are holding, but they have few troops to spare."

"What of Bell-Oak, and the Lord there?" Nightshade asked. "You know him, Shatterstaff."

"He is also unwilling to commit," Shatter reported wryly.

"But he can't be," Nightshade argued. "If the False Sisters march troops right by his castle, he'll be forced to take a side."

"I don't think so," she disagreed. "He seems happy to sell supplies to everyone and keep his garrison behind the walls."

"And with the Opal River bringing trade from the west, he has no reason to do otherwise," Titania commented. She shook her head. "Then there's the Mistress of Shadows." She raised an eyebrow at Nightshade.

"I don't know what she'll do," Nightshade admitted. "I haven't spoken with her since before the Human King died. She keeps herself closed off."

"She has attacked us," Celia argued. "Many times."

"Rogue Shadow Agents," Nightshade replied.

"You don't believe that mound of chora dung," Shatter said angrily.

Nightshade glared at her. "I am not prepared to believe that she is a traitor."

Shatter moved to speak again, but Titania held up her hand. "We have debated this. There's no sense in fighting about it further. There's no way to get to her. Goddess, but I hope she hasn't fallen completely under the sway of the False Sisters and this foul Blood Cult."

"And if she has?" Celia asked.

"Then we must deal with her. As we must deal with both Lord Troilus the elder and the younger. Thank you all. I will spend the night in contemplation and seek the wisdom of the Goddess." She rose, and headed to the door. "Good night. And let the Goddess guard us."

☾ ∾ ☼

"Elanor!" Min called.

Tiger-Claw, ahead of her on the trail, looked back. "She went this way."

Min struggled up the path, Foxruff supporting her from behind. She Reached out, searching for Elanor. She sensed her, ahead and above. Elanor felt different. Not hurt or in peril, just different. Her mind was full of bright colors and the chirping and singing of birds.

"I feel her," Min said, relieved. "She's up ahead, but she seems odd."

"Enemies?" Foxruff asked.

"No," Min said, confused. "Just off. Let's keep going."

They reached the end of the trail and hit the wall. Min looked up. Elanor was still there, almost floating above her.

"Elanor!" Min called again, beginning to worry. She looked up the sheer wall.

With a small shower of stones, Elanor's head popped over the edge above. She smiled and called down. "Hello there, small, pregnant, pale, beautiful Fairy woman." She folded her hands and set her chin on them.

Expecting more, Min waited, but Elanor only stared down at her, smiling.

"What are you doing up there?" Min finally called up.

"I went looking for Shield," Elanor yelled back.

Again, Min waited for more of an explanation. There was none forthcoming. "I know that. You left eons ago, and it's getting dark." Elanor pivoted her head, looking at the sky. She smiled and nodded. "Well, did you find her?" Min finally asked.

Behind her, Foxruff and Tiger-Claw shared a smile and a soft laugh.

"I think so," Elanor replied. "Let me make sure." Her head disappeared. "Shield!" Her yell echoed off the stones. "Did I find you?"

There was silence, then Elanor reappeared. She put her head back on her hands and stared down at them again. "She thinks so." Her eyes wandered for a bit, then focused on Min. "Hello there, Beautiful. What are you doing here?"

"What is going on?" Min wondered aloud to the two soldiers with exasperation. They shrugged. "I don't feel she's in trouble, or under any strange influence." She yelled up again. "Are you okay?"

"I'm more than okay," Elanor gushed back. "I'm perfect." Her head lolled to the side. "I'm perfect here, on this warm stone, under the setting sun. Come up," she called, waving to them. "There's room for all. Well." She frowned. "Maybe not the big one. He might have to sit in Shield's lap. Or she on his. Not sure how she'll feel about that." Her head disappeared again. "Shield!" she called. "How do you feel about lap sitting?"

There was another — longer — pause, then Elanor appeared again. She looked down. "Hello there," she flirted. "What's a good-looking little Fairy like you doing on a mountain like this? Come on up and see me sometime." She patted the stone beside her.

Tiger-Claw burst into laughter. Min whirled on him. "She's drunk," he managed to gasp out. "Or something." Foxruff covered his mouth.

Min glared at them until they could control themselves. "Keep a watch," she told them sternly. "There might be troops of the False Sisters still about." That got their attention, and they regained their composure. Hands on weapons, they scanned back down the trail and into the woods below.

"I'll go up," Min decided. "I'm coming up!" she yelled.

"About time," Elanor replied. "I've been waiting."

Min spread her wings and flew up, in a somewhat wobbly fashion. At the top, Elanor had moved back from the edge and was sitting, an inviting smile on her face. Min landed and went to her. Elanor grabbed her hand and kissed it.

"Thank you for coming," Elanor gushed, pulling at Min's hand as she laid back. "It's so pretty up here. I want to share it all with you."

Min resisted being pulled down and looked around the ledge. Shield was sitting cross-legged, her back to the mountain, her eyes closed. She moved her hands in slow circles in front of her. Bits of nut shells danced in the air there. Elanor flopped over on her side. "It's a bit hard," she said, "but the view is good." She winked at Min. Then she sat up. She spread her arms wide, and carefully laid on her back. "Look at that sky!" she exclaimed. "The stars will be out soon."

Min knelt at Elanor's side and grabbed her head. "What's wrong with you?" she asked, trying to find a way through the bright colored fog around Elanor's mind. Her consciousness was there, but pushed far into the background. Feelings of happiness and bright light filled the front of her mind. Min began to feel a similar euphoria. She Sent a sharp thought through the fog.

"Oh, hello," Elanor said in response. Her voice was closer to normal. "I found Shield." Elanor gestured. "We had a fight, then a cry. When we came out of the Circle, Shield's friend had brought us some nuts." She gestured to a pile of shells on the ground. "He was a handsome fellow. Brown, black, and grey. And friendly. He piled up the nuts and left. We were hungry, so we ate them. A bit bitter at first, but after that." She waved her arms, bumping into Min's leg. "It

204

was like a rainbow and sunset were wrestling in my mind. And I don't know who won."

She beamed at Min. "Hello there." She sat up. Rubbing Min's arm, she got closer. "The stone is warm," she said suggestively.

"What kind of nuts?" Min asked suspiciously. She slid back out of Elanor's amorous reach. "These?" she asked, picking up some of the shells lying about. "Brown, with little spikes, and a darker brown nut inside?"

"Yes," Elanor said in triumph. Then she frowned. "Were you here? I didn't see you." She turned her head. "Shield!" she yelled, making Min jump. "Was Min here?"

Shield did not open her eyes. She kept the shells before her dancing in the air.

"Elanor," Min said, with all the disapproval of a mother. "Flora uses those to make a paste to kill pain. You aren't supposed to eat them." She grabbed Elanor's arms. "Elanor," she said desperately. "Look at me!"

"He was wearing a mask, so maybe I shouldn't have trusted him," Elanor said vaguely, then drifted off. It took a moment for her to focus again. "Hello," she said. "Has the sun set yet? I'd hate to miss it." She tried to get up, but Min held her down. Grinning, she tried to kiss Min.

Min let her go, and Elanor fell happily back to the stone.

"Tiger-Claw. Go and bring us a tent and blankets for the night. These two are in no condition to climb or fly."

"Yes, Lady Min," the bodyguard replied. His amusement filled the Send.

"I'll Send to Flora and see if they need an antidote."

Tiger-Claw signaled his understanding and set off down the trail.

"I'll stay here," Foxruff announced. Elanor heard him and laughed.

"Come on up!" she called. "She's small. We can make room."

"No. Stay there," Min commanded. "Goddess's mercy," Min swore under her breath, as she pushed Elanor's roaming hands away.

"Flora," she Sent.

It took a long count for Flora to respond. *"Yes, Lady Min? Did you find her?"* Flora's tone was light at first, but feeling Min's concern, quickly turned serious. *"What's wrong?"*

"Elanor and Shield ate some of the nuts with the spiky shells. They're acting loopy."

"Are they throwing up? Trembling? Unconscious?"

"No, just acting strange. Elanor can't keep her hands off me," Min said, batting Elanor's hand off her thigh.

With relief, Flora Sent, *"That's not strange. But I understand. Shield?"*

"Sitting with her eyes closed, making the nut shells dance."

"They'll be fine," Flora reassured her. *"Might be just what they needed. Now, don't you eat any of them."* Flora shook a mental finger at her. *"Might harm the babies."*

"I won't. I sent Tiger-Claw back for shelter. These two will only hurt themselves if they try to come down in this condition."

"That's wise. I'll send something back with him. The morning might be rough. They should drift off to sleep soon. Just keep an eye on them. Usually bad reactions happen right away, but you never know."

"I will, Mum. Anything else?"

"Might have to tie her hands," Flora mused. *"I remember one time, I shared half a nut with someone. We. . . ."* A sudden grief hit Min, stronger than anything Flora had ever Projected before. Then, before Min could examine it, the feeling was gone. *"Well, we spent a long night."* Joy coated in sorrow replaced the grief. *"She won't remember much. So don't tell her anything important."*

"Mum," Min began. The intensity of Flora's emotions had confused her. Min wanted to ask about them, to understand.

But Flora's guard was up, and she soon became all business. *"They'll be fine after they sleep. Bring them to me when you return."* Then Flora cut the connection.

Min sat back, her image of Flora suddenly turned upside down. What kind of pain was she hiding? The grief was far more intense than anything they had shared, for sure. What long-held and deep-seated sorrow rested under her grey hair?

Min's thoughts were interrupted by Elanor grabbing her and kissing her, rapidly and repeatedly. Finally, Min had to push her away.

"Enough," she said, more harshly than she had intended. Elanor frowned. "I mean," Min recovered, "we must look at the sky. The stars will be coming out soon."

"Yes," Elanor agreed, leaning back on her hands. "We must see them. They sparkle so. Shield!" Elanor yelled. "Stars!"

☾ 〰 ☼

"I need to stretch," Elanor said suddenly, and stood, exiting the tent so fast that Min almost fell over. They had been resting in each other's arms, not talking, but staring at the reflections of the fire on the tent wall. Min followed her.

The night was cold, and the stars looked down from the darkness. Elanor raised her arms and spread her wings. She turned in a slow circle, on unsteady legs. Min pulled her away from the edge and back toward the fire Tiger-Claw had made against the mountain.

Shield had resisted — silently — standing or moving. She also did not want Tiger-Claw to touch her, holding up crossed hands whenever he tried. Finally, Min had wrapped her in a blanket against the cold and let her be. Shield didn't seem to mind Tiger-Claw sitting beside her. She hummed a quick melody off and on throughout the night, the only sound she made.

Foxruff had stayed at the base of the wall, despite Min's worry. "I'll be fine," he assured her. "After the cramped quarters in the storeroom barracks, this is a wonder."

"Do you think he's cute?" Elanor asked in a loud whisper. "I do."

Min darted a quick glance at the bodyguard, embarrassed for Tiger-Claw, but he simply smiled.

"If I could think about a man touching me without screaming, or throwing up, or throwing up screaming, I might ask him to join us," Elanor continued. She gave a full body shudder. She bent, whispering in Min's ear, "But you know." Then she looked at Tiger-Claw. "Sorry. Next life?" she asked casually, as if she were offering him a cup of soup.

"Of course," he replied. "I'll see you there."

"I can see the Dancer," Elanor said abruptly, pulling away from Min again. She went to the edge of the ledge. Min watched her. Elanor made no move to leap off or fall, so Min turned back to Tiger-Claw.

"I'm sorry," she said helplessly. "That was much too private. She. . . ." Min stopped, unable to go on.

"I understand," Tiger-Claw said. "Flora warned me." He made a brushing motion across his forehead. "See? Already forgotten."

"I haven't forgotten," Elanor interrupted. "And I will hold you to it. Next life. You will be one of my husbands. Or wives." Elanor sat down on the edge, her feet dangling.

Min joined her.

"I love seeing the Dancer," Elanor said, taking Min's hand. She raised it, tracing the stars. "There are the three stars of her belt, and that brush of stars is her sash. Father always pointed them out to me. He taught me all their names." Elanor stopped; her voice began to quaver. "I don't remember their names," she admitted, sobbing.

"It's all right," Min said, comforting her. She pulled Elanor's head into her lap, gently stroking her hair. "We can make up names for them."

"We can't do that," Elanor objected through her tears. "They already have names. I just can't remember them."

"Nonsense," Min said. "They still have their names. They won't forget. We can just call them something else. Something just for us. Like Fairies, who take on other names as they grow."

"I don't know," Elanor said doubtfully, her tears stopping. "Are we allowed?"

"We are strong, powerful Fairies," Min declared. "But they are the stars. They'll forgive us."

Above them, a shooting star streaked across the sky.

Chapter Twenty-One
Negotiations

Titania sat down. Behind her, the door to the room was Locked and Warded. An Ephemeral Ring lay in a Warded circle before her. Its Song was very weak, barely reaching her. Celia had warned her about this.

"That's exactly what I need," Titania had assured her.

She stared at the circle and the Ring within it for a long time. Then, with a frustrated sigh, she stood up and went to the door.

At her knock, Shatter opened it, looking concerned. Titania said, "I need another chair."

Shatter looked over the Regent's shoulder at the empty room.

"We should always offer courtesy," Titania explained. "Even when none will be afforded us in return."

"As you say, Regent," Shatter said, still unsure. She motioned to the other soldiers and Paramounts milling about the hallway. A soldier at the end of the line ran off, returning a moment later with a wooden chair. Titania nodded in approval, and took the chair from the soldier's hands and set it inside the door.

"Thank you," she said, as he bowed and returned to his place. Titania acknowledged Shatter's bow. "Captain. I hope all these Fairies will not be needed."

"It is better for them to be here regardless," Shatter said decisively. "The stones are ready?"

Titania smiled. "They are. Warded and Shadowed."

Shatter nodded. Titania smiled again and shut the door. She restored the Wards and returned to the center of the room carrying the new chair. With a wave, she collapsed the Ward around the Ephemeral Ring, then placed the chair behind it and restored the Ward, enlarging it a bit this time.

Finally satisfied with her preparations, Titania sat down, taking a Warded box from under her chair. Speaking the words that had been relayed to her by the messenger who had delivered it, she opened the box. Inside she found a pale crystal in a bed of red Fairy silk. She smiled grimly at how the fabric turned the crystal as red as blood. Titania Sent the Frequency of the Ephemeral Ring through the Geode Web and waited.

After a short delay, an answer came to her. Titania sat up straighter. The Ephemeral Ring surged, and then a tall, silver-haired Iridescent woman appeared within it.

"Greetings, Lady Perrault. I was expecting Lord Troilus."

She nodded in greeting, then ran her hands over the Wards, testing them, before pulling the chair across the Ring to sit closer to Titania.

"Is everything to your satisfaction?" Titania asked.

"Yes," Perrault replied. "The Wards and the Ephemeral Ring are all as was agreed." She looked around the room. "I do not remember agreeing to the Silverfire traps around the Wards, but I would have expected nothing less."

"I'm sure you have your own contingencies in place," Titania replied coolly.

"I do," Perrault agreed. "I would see my son now."

Titania gestured, and a door on the other side of the room slid open. Out stepped Steeltrap, leading the gagged Lord Troilus, the younger. His hands and feet were still bound with Power-nullifying cuffs, and glowing Fairy silk cords wrapped around most of his body. He looked like a child's doll, wrapped in yarn.

Perrault looked at Titania in surprise.

"He has a foul mouth," Titania informed her. "It was either that, or we take his tongue out."

Perrault sighed. She looked at her son with a hard eye. "I taught you better than that. Keep a civil tongue. We are guests here."

He glared at both her and Titania, but nodded. At Titania's gesture, Steel removed his gag.

"Are you being treated well?" Perrault asked him.

"Yes, Mother," he replied sullenly. "The food these bitches feed me is adequate."

He would have gone on, but Perrault snapped, "I told you to keep a civil tongue! Another insult, and I will leave you to their mercy."

Troilus snapped his mouth shut and gave a sharp nod.

"On second thought," Perrault said to Titania. "Gag him and take him away. I know that is my son." She waved dismissively at him.

Troilus tried to speak, but Steel gleefully stuffed the gag back in his mouth and dragged him away, sliding the door shut behind them with a snap.

"My husband was too angry to come," Perrault said, answering Titania's earlier question. "Too angry at you, the Queens, and his son to maintain the temperament these negotiations require."

"I thank you," Titania said with a nod.

"But do not take my temperance as weakness," Perrault warned sharply.

"I will not," Titania agreed, just as sharp.

Perrault sat back in her chair. "Set my son free, and I am prepared to take your surrender to the True Queens. They will be merciful. You and your family will go into exile. Certain others of your council will be able to go with you. Others will be bound for trial. Some executed — as is proper — and most will be held for an appropriate time. And all this unpleasantness will be forgotten."

Titania let the arrogance of the other woman wash over her. Saw the amusement and hardness in her eyes, and in how she held her feet.

"Instead," Titania countered, "I will execute your son as a traitor to our Queen. And as a heretic before the Goddess. His wings will be removed before his head. I do not know who will do the deed. I might have a lottery. So many wish to hold the blade. Then, his body will be burned — as is proper — and his ashes shall be returned to you."

"Then we will surround this little mountain," Perrault returned with a sneer, holding her composure via a tight mental leash. "With more force than you can imagine. We will grind you and your people into bloody dust. Then we will bury you so deep under the rubble that no one will ever find your bones."

"You can kill us," Titania said calmly. "You and your false Queens may use your foul weapons. Those evil Rings could surround us. All of us may die here. But the resistance will go on. The evil that is your Queens will be clear to all. Word of our resistance will spread. Nothing you do will stop that. The truth will win in the end."

"But you will be dead," Perrault said with a shrug.

"But my spirit will go on. Others will take up the standard of the true Queen."

"Where is this true Queen?" Perrault asked suddenly. "You speak as her Regent. Why isn't she here? What is she running from?"

"She is following the path the Goddess has set for her," Titania replied tartly. "She will return and be the Queen we all need. Until then, we hold the line."

"You hold very little," Perrault said insultingly. "What, this mountain and a few strongholds? Little towns and castles? We have all of Fae-Treval and beyond, to the border. Your husband sits in one of those dusty little towns. Have you seen him recently?"

"I asked you here to negotiate in good faith," Titania informed her. "If you're only going to insult me and my people, then there is no point in our speaking further. I will execute your son, and you can retaliate. More blood will be spilled. Lives lost. Mothers and fathers will lose their children. Children will lose their parents."

"Blood of your people," Perrault stressed. "Blood of Leathers and Feathers," she said dismissively.

"Then go," Titania said, rising. "I will send you the ashes."

Perrault did not move. "Then what do you offer in ransom for my son?"

"I will return him to you," Titania said, sitting down again. "In return, you will withdraw all support — all troops, all material, and all silver — from those you call your Queens. You and your husband will return to the south and stay there. You will have no contact with Dina and Tra."

"For how long?" Perrault asked suspiciously.

"Fifty years."

212

Perrault laughed. "That is a long time, even for Fairies." She rested her chin on her hand. "They are our Queens. We owe them tribute. Taxes and goods."

"You owe them nothing. They are false Queens."

"Then do we send our taxes to you?"

"If you wish, but that is for the Queen to decide."

"When she returns," Perrault said with interest. "That would be a tremendous change to how the Realm is presently governed. I do not know if it will survive."

"You know as well as I do that the south has governed itself for a long time. The cities to the west are doing so now, too. They're staying neutral in all of this. I want you to do the same."

"Where will we send our wares?" Perrault asked. "Our silk and other goods? Do you expect us to trade with you? You can barely afford to keep your own people fed."

"Sail them to the west," Titania suggested. "Or ship them upriver. The Opal comes down not far from Bell-Oak. I'm sure something can be arranged. Some tax or fee to bring your goods through our territory."

"The cost would be prohibitive," Perrault argued.

"Or trade with the Humans. They need goods, too. Their silver is as good as ours."

"I would kill my son first," Perrault swore.

"Then let me tell you how it will be done," Titania began. "As a criminal, he will be stripped of his wings first. Then he will kneel, and a random Fairy will take his head. I will find every crystal and Geode I can. I will Project this execution to everyone I can." Titania fixed the other woman with a cold, hard stare. "Then the bits will be burned, and the ashes scattered. Then, I will send messengers to every corner of this Realm. They will Share this execution with every Fairy who will listen. Even into Elen and the Human Realm. Your son's death will be witnessed by countless others. They will see the fate of criminals and traitors to our Queen."

"And you call us foul and cruel! What will that do? We will retaliate. More will die. For every cut my son endures, we can kill ten, twenty. Mothers will drown in their children's blood. And it will all be your fault!" She stabbed her first finger at Titania.

"With every death, more will see the evil of the False Sisters, and more will resist. A tower built on sand cannot withstand a siege. They will fall," Titania said with certainty. "Will you be atop the tower, or safely far away, when they do?"

Perrault took a moment to contemplate the offer. "You have no right to call him a criminal. You are no Keeper."

"I have spoken to my Law Masters," Titania said confidently. "The Queen may act as the representative of the Goddess in these matters when the Keeper is unavailable. And since I act for the Queen, the decision is mine."

"You have no proof of his participation in what you call foul acts."

"I have plenty of witnesses, among both my soldiers and your son's own troops, to his use of Blood Magic." Titania sat back, folding her hands.

"Fifty years is too long," Perrault bargained. "Ten years at the most."

"Every Fairy in this mountain has lost a loved one — whether a parent, a child, or a partner — to the foul weapon your son wore openly." Titania leaned forward. "I could take his wings and then give him to them. Let vengeance be enacted on his body for all his crimes. That would be neither pretty nor quick." She sat back. "Forty."

Perrault became angry. "You claim the high ground here, but you seek vengeance, too."

"I do," Titania admitted. "I would like nothing better than to hack off his arms and let him live as other blackblade survivors do. Or sever his legs, and let him crawl around on his belly. Make him live with the pain he has inflicted on so many others." She made the Sign of the Three. "Goddess forgive me, but some don't deserve mercy."

"Do such a thing, and you will deserve no mercy," Perrault threatened.

"If you or your agents come for me," Titania assured her, "then you'd better kill me, my husband, and my children. Leave any of us alive, and you and your family will know no further moments of peace in this life."

"We can threaten each other. . . ." Perrault began.

"This is pointless," Titania interrupted, standing. "Where should I send your son's ashes?"

"Thirty," Perrault said quickly. "Any more, and the Sisters might go to war with us."

"And then you will feel their cruelty." Titania sat down. "Agreed."

Perrault let out a breath of relief. "He will be returned to us. His wings will not be damaged. Not clipped, nor damaged in any way."

"They will not be damaged," Titania agreed.

"And his husband's body will be returned with him."

"If you wish," Titania said, with a bitter thought that they wouldn't dare bury an Iridescent. "What of the troops we captured?"

"Did the captains survive?"

"No. Hooklance died in single combat with Captain Shatterstaff," Titania told her with quiet pride. "The other captain died when the Blood Ring was destroyed." Titania's voice dripped with disgust.

"Pity. He was good at only a few things, but killing was one of them. And the rest of the Iridescents in my son's. . . ." She paused. "Group?"

"Unfortunately, they were all killed in the Blood Ring," Titania reported, with more disgust twisting her features. "Otherwise, they would be facing charges, too."

"They were of good families, too," Perrault replied conversationally. "The blood price for them could be high. For some concessions, I might be able to negotiate on your behalf."

"What do you have in mind?" Titania asked carefully.

"Passage for southern goods through your territory," she answered quickly.

"After a suitable tax," Titania countered, just as quick.

Perrault smiled, genuinely impressed. "I will speak to my lords, but I believe an agreement can be reached." She paused to consider. "There was a soldier. He was Hooklance's Second, I believe. He was a useful man. If I could have him?"

"I'm sorry," Titania returned. "There have been charges of many crimes leveled against that one. He was always protected by Hooklance and his status in Air before this. But no longer."

"Never mind," Perrault said, waving her hand. "And the rest, you may do with as you wish. They're mostly the Sisters' troops. And any of mine who let themselves be captured, I do not want back."

"As you wish," Titania agreed calmly, as inside she recoiled at the callousness with which Lady Perrault treated her own people. No wonder she was an ally of the False Sisters.

"I would take my son with me," Perrault announced, standing.

"There are details still to be worked out," Titania countered, also standing. "He will be returned to you soon."

"I will send the scrolls and other papers to this Ring for your signature," Perrault replied. "Two days. Any more, and the lightning my son sent against you will feel like a gentle spring rain." She looked hard at Titania. "Or if my son is killed trying to escape."

"He will be returned to you in the best shape that can be managed. He's a real bastard, though, and I cannot be held accountable for the repercussions of his foul words and actions."

Perrault narrowed her eyes. "Then see that he is protected. His wings undamaged. His mind whole. Any less and. . . ."

"I understand," Titania interrupted. "It will be as you ask."

"Then I will return and set this in motion." She pushed the chair deliberately into the Ward, watching the sparks fly from the point of contact. She stepped back onto the Ring. "It has been a pleasure dealing with you, Lady Titania. My husband will be glad to have our son returned." Then, with a short bow, she disappeared.

Titania took a moment to regain her composure. She took several deep breaths to return her heartbeat to normal, purging her body of its built-up adrenaline. When she was calm again, and the shaking in her legs had stilled, Titania focused on the Ward surrounding the Ephemeral Ring. She reached out her hands and brought her palms together in a swift clap. The Ward contracted, crushing the chair, and anything else that Perrault might have left behind. There was a tiny burst of light, and a small pop. Titania kept her palms together, rubbing them against one another. When she was satisfied that the area was safe, she released her hands and returned the Ward to its original shape.

Behind her, the door opened, and Shatter strode in.

"So, it's done?" she asked.

"Yes," Titania said with a sigh. "And I know what you're going to say, Captain. I hate making deals like this. I hated it when I was Queen's Justice, and I still hate it now."

"But that is what a leader does," Shatter said with resignation. "Makes compromises for the greater good."

"Yes," Titania agreed. "But this one sticks in my throat like none before it have." She stood up. "But we got what we need. Time. And the removal of an enemy." She faced Shatter. "I was having nightmares about more of those Rings appearing on our front doors."

"This will give us some breathing room, and a chance to strike back," Shatter reasoned.

Titania smiled grimly. "There is more justice to dispense, but I have lost the taste for it today. I will return with the sun."

"Yes, Regent." Shatter bowed. "We're still culling out the really bad ones from among those we captured anyway. We'll be ready in two days."

"Good. I will speak with Celia and the others about our contingencies." She looked concerned. "I know Lady Min is up to it, but I do not know about Lady Elanor. After her experience."

"She admits to some trepidation," Shatter said. "But she understands why it's necessary." Now it was Shatter's turn to look concerned. "It may not be my place, Regent, but this is a very grey area."

"Yes, Captain, it is, but I see no other way. I can only trust them so far to uphold their end of the bargain."

"The wrong thing for the right reason," Shatter suggested.

Titania nodded. "Goddess forgive us. But I will do all I can to fight this evil."

Chapter Twenty-Two
All for Nothing

There was no window in the room he had been put in, and the guard had neglected to light the Fairy Lamp that hung from the ceiling. It didn't matter. Longstride didn't need light. It was better to sit in the dark, his food lying cold by the door. Hunger didn't matter either. He would be dead soon. He wished he were dead now. But how could he stand before the Mother of Waves and face her judgment? His only hope was that his daughter's death had been quick, and they would meet again. But what if those cursed bastards had buried her? Her spirit would be trapped, and all this would have been for nothing.

He leaned his head back against the wall. The pain, fear, and despair were almost too much. His fingers found the stone Min had rammed into his forehead, and he applied pressure, drawing tears of pain. The chain connecting his cuffs rattled, and the stump of his right arm ached, but he couldn't do anything about it.

"Forgive me," he muttered. "Forgive me, Swiftdive. I was only trying to save you." He let go, his hand falling limp at his side. Eventually, Longstride closed his eyes, falling into something like sleep.

Noises outside the door woke him. It was still dark, but it was always dark. He didn't recognize any of the voices. It didn't matter: there were always voices. He stopped listening, and returned to his self-torment.

Then an imperious female spoke clearly and close. "I will see him."

"Are you sure?" a second woman asked.

"No," the first voice answered. "But I will see him all the same."

The door opened, letting in light. Longstride blinked, then lowered his head.

"I'll stay," Steel offered.

"Remain outside," Shield told her.

"He's not worthy of your pain," Steel said. "He. . . ."

"I know what he did. Now, Captain," she said with barely-contained emotion, "I would like to speak to the prisoner alone. If I need you, I will call. He is bound and Warded. He is no longer a threat to me."

"If I had known," Steel began.

"Captain," Shield said more sternly. "Leave me."

Steel frowned, but gave a sharp nod and closed the door.

Shield lit the Fairy Lantern, bringing the light up slowly. She stood, her back against the door, watching him. He still wore his uniform, but his rank badge had been ripped from his breast. The chain connecting his left hand to the stump of his right jiggled as he listlessly moved his arms to block the sudden light. All Shield could hear was his breathing.

"Why?" Shield finally asked.

Longstride did not look up.

Shield raised her voice. "Why did you betray me? Betray all of us?"

"I wanted to save her," Longstride said. His voice was flat. "They told me if I did what they asked, she would be freed."

"You must have known they were lying to you," Shield said.

"I couldn't take that chance. She might be alive. I had to do what they demanded."

Shield wanted to press, but the despair in his voice made her reconsider.

"Then what we shared was part of it, too?" she finally asked. "You lied to me, and manipulated me, for your foul masters."

"I didn't mean to," he said defensively. "It just happened." He finally raised his head. "What I felt — feel for you — is real. What I told you, that morning, I meant."

"I don't believe you. You used me. You used my pain to find out where the guide stones were. Used me to gain access to the Paramounts. Used me," she repeated. "Used my pain against me. Used my foolishness to betray the Regent and my Sisters. You tried to kill Min. My Sister!" she cried. "Someone I am sworn to defend. You knew about my earlier failure, and you used it against me."

"I did not use you," he protested weakly.

"Then what was the time we spent together?" she asked. "I was falling in love with you, you bastard. Do you know how hard that was? To trust again? To allow you into my heart, and then my bed? You knew about the sleepless nights, and the nightmares that haunted me on those rare nights when I could sleep. I thought you would help me heal." She stepped closer. "Look at me! I trusted you, and you betrayed me."

"What do you want me to say?" he asked, looking up. Shield stepped back. The naked pain and despair in his eyes cut her. "I loved you. I didn't mean to, but once I started, I couldn't stop seeking you out. I wanted to be close to you. To help you. I truly wanted to."

"And you thought betraying me and my Regent would help me heal?" she cried back. "You thought, what? After the False Sisters broke the Wards, that we would just fly away? That they would let you leave?" She knelt so she could look into his eyes. "That your daughter would be waiting, and we would be this perfect family?"

"I don't know," he said, shaking his chains in frustration. "I just knew I had to save her. I had to do anything necessary. And that included hurting you." He drew a shaky breath. "I almost told you. That morning. I almost did."

"When did you almost tell me?" Shield asked. "When you were waking me up with your kisses, or taking your pleasure on my body? Or when you laid in my arms after? When I cried, remembering again, Nova's last words to me?" She grabbed his chin, forcing his eyes up. "You should have died."

"I deserve to," he agreed. "I wish Min had killed me. I can't bear this pain."

"You will live with it," Shield swore. "You will live with it, like I live with my pain. I couldn't save them." She let go of his face. "I couldn't save them. And you can't save me."

Longstride looked down. His hand went to his forehead, pressing the stone. He began to bleed.

"That won't help," Shield assured him, standing and going to the door. She banged on it until Steel opened it. Shield pushed past her, and walked swiftly up the hall. Steel stood in the doorway, watching Longstride for a moment. He didn't move.

"I should kill you," Steel pronounced without emotion.

"Yes, you should," he agreed.

Steel looked at him for another moment, then closed the door, locking it with a heavy snap.

☾ ⌁ ☼

"Get up, soldier!"

Shatterstaff's voice pulled him out of a dream. He looked up at her angry face, groggy and confused.

"I said, stand up!" She grabbed his shoulder, hauling him up and pushing him back against the wall.

"Is it time?" Longstride asked, shading his eyes from the bright Fairy Lantern.

"Tell me your story," Shatter demanded.

"What?" he asked in confusion, still half asleep. "My story?"

"How did they catch you? What did they promise you? How did they contact you?" She shook him, as his attention wandered.

"What does it matter?" he asked, despair filling his voice.

"I should kill you," she said. "For what you did to my Sister. For your betrayal of our Regent and your fellow soldiers."

"Then do it," he said, tired. "I want to die."

"You don't deserve that honor," she said, slamming him against the wall. "You deserve to live with this pain."

He just stared at her.

"So, tell me your story," she said slowly. She released him. He stood, swaying. Shatter led him to a chair that had suddenly appeared in the room and pushed him down into it. She stood in front of him, her arms crossed. "If you want a chance at redemption, then tell me everything."

"I don't deserve redemption."

"No, you don't," Shatter agreed. "But the Regent demands that we give you a chance anyway." Shatter bent close, her nose almost touching his. "I will use you as you used her."

There was little Longstride could do, so he told her.

"It wasn't long after the Night of Black Wings. Halfwing sent me for some supplies, and I took the chance to find my daughter. She was serving as guard for a Law Master at one of the nearby plantations. But when I got there, the False Sisters had already taken it. I was captured, and someone recognized me as one of the Queen's Guard. And some cursed bastard knew my daughter was stationed there." He looked up at Shatter. "It was either betray you and the Regent, or watch her die slowly." He dropped his eyes. "I made the only decision a father could."

Shatter growled. Longstride flinched, expecting a blow, but none came. He looked up. She stared at him, her mouth a thin, cold line, but there was something in her eyes.

"How did you contact them?" she asked without feeling.

"I only spoke to them through another. She relayed the information to the False Sisters."

"Sunserri," Shatter stated.

"Yes. I told her everything. She was supposed to take me to my daughter when this was all over." He put his head in his hand. "Now, because I failed, they'll kill her." Through his fingers he muttered, "So I deserve to die."

"What if she isn't dead?" Shatter asked.

Longstride looked up at her. "How could she be alive?" he asked. "Why? You're right: they would have killed her after I agreed to betray you."

"What if I gave you a chance to avenge her, then?" Shatter asked. She grabbed his chin, forcing him to look at her. "You're a soldier. You were a good one once. Stand up, and either help to rescue her, or avenge her. Or." She let go of his chin. "Just sit there and let her killers go unpunished."

Longstride looked at the stump of his right hand. He remembered Swiftdive's hand in his as they flew on the currents above the Diamond River. Heard her cries of joy. Slowly, on shaking legs, he stood. He tried to straighten his filthy uniform.

"What do you want me to do?"

Joel C. Flanagan-Grannemann

Chapter Twenty-Three
The Regent's Justice

The library had been cleared of all its tables. Titania sat in a chair under the crystal dome, with most of the high-ranking Fairies of the mountain in a semi-circle around her. To her right sat Min and Elanor. Beyond them were the Paramounts who had defended the mountain, both in the Circle and in the short battle. Behind Elanor, Captains Shatterstaff and Steeltrap stood at attention. At their shoulders stood various lieutenants and sergeants, all on guard and alert. To the left of Titania, Celia was standing upright, still strapped to her board. To her left were Law Master Willis and her staff from Silverfire. Titania had requested their presence to deal with the captured troops of the False Sisters. Willis was chatting with Nightshade while Belladonna and a group of her archers kept a close eye on the two hooded prisoners kneeling at the opening of the semi-circle.

Behind Titania stood Merry-Weather, fierce hawk of this Fairy court in exile. Flora and Luna — with the help of Obsidian — had made sure everyone was prepared and knew their place in the drama about to unfold.

"I'm glad you're safe," Willis whispered to Obsidian as the girl brought her a cup of water. "I was afraid for you, but I trusted Merry-Weather would keep you well."

Obsidian returned the woman's good wishes with a smile and hurried on to deal with Nightshade's impatient wave for more bread.

All present were dressed in their finest, though some of it was worn and threadbare. The soldiers' armor gleamed in the mid-morning light filtering in from the dome. The wings of the Iridescents radiated an inner fire, casting a warm glow over everyone.

Titania struck her staff on the floor, and the murmur of quiet conversation stilled.

"We are here to pass judgment on traitors," Titania stated. Even though everyone in the room had been warned, a gasp still ran through the crowd. "These two have betrayed their Queen. Betrayed their Sister and Brother Fairies, whom they were sworn to defend. Their actions led to the deaths of many brave Fairies, the destruction of vital and irreplaceable material, and the compromise of places of safety for those of us who fight the evil of the False Sisters."

One of the prisoners began to struggle with her bonds and shake her head under her hood. The guard behind her muttered for her to be still, but she kept trying to stand and speak.

"Let her up," Titania called to the guard. "It is time for her to have her say before this council."

The guard roughly pulled the prisoner up and removed her hood. Sunserri blinked in the sudden light and spat as the guard removed her gag.

"I am not a traitor," she called out. "I serve the True Queens. They are the legitimate rulers of this Realm." She gestured around the room. "All of you are the traitors."

"We are not here to debate. Nor will I argue my legitimacy as Regent," Titania decreed, stilling the rising dark mutterings around her. "You have been found guilty of numerous counts of betrayal and murder, both direct and indirect. You revealed my location to the False Sisters several times. Your treachery led to the deaths of many brave soldiers. You perverted one of my own guards for evil. You tried to disable the Wards protecting this mountain. You released foul Magic in this safe place."

"All my actions have been proper. You defy the true Queens," Sunserri said with arrogance. "It was my duty to fight you, and my job to prevent you from rebelling against your proper liege. It was my pleasure to try and kill you." She gestured at Titania with her bound hands. "You and your people. All of you are traitors!" she yelled.

"You will find no agreement here," Titania said calmly. "Even if the False Sisters were the legitimate Queens, they use foul and evil Magic. They bury dead Fairies and use the spirits of our Fallen for their own twisted plans. Even if I was not the duly appointed Regent of the Queen, it would be my Goddess-granted honor to fight such cruel rulers."

225

"You condemn yourself with your own words," Sunserri taunted.

"Proudly," Titania declared. She stood. "We are Servants of the Moon and Sun. It is our duty to fight the darkness."

"Servants of the Moon and Sun," all the loyal Fairies in the room replied. Sunserri flinched, and tried to sneer, but her face only twitched.

Titania returned to her seat, her pride in her people clear on her face. "Is there anything else you wish to say before we pronounce judgment on you?"

"I demand," Sunserri began, but her voice broke. Recovering, she said, "I demand trial by combat!"

A murmur arose among the surrounding Fairies. Emboldened by the sound, Sunserri spoke louder. "I have that right! The Goddess gives me the right to prove my truth on the body of my accuser." She pointed her hands at Titania. "You, false Regent of a false Queen. I challenge you!"

The muttering boiled over with rising anger. Sunserri stood at the center of it all, beginning to smile.

Titania raised her hand, and the room fell silent. "I doubt the Goddess wants anything to do with a foul Blood Cultist like you, but I am an honorable Fairy."

Cries of "No, Regent!" and "I will be your champion!" rose from all sides.

Feeling suddenly trapped, Sunserri looked around. Titania smiled and waved her hands till the cries stopped.

"Yes," she said smoothly, addressing Sunserri. "You will have your duel. And as I am of higher status than you, I will choose a champion."

"Afraid to face me?" Sunserri jeered.

"No," Titania said, sitting down. "But I do not have my sword. It defends my children, far away." Titania smiled and laughed as Fairies called out for her to use their blades. Sunserri looked around, her hope for sympathy dashed by the hostility being thrown her way.

"No," Titania decided, standing. "I have had my exercise for the day. I call upon Saber. Come forward, and be your Regent's champion!"

Saber stepped forward from his place beside Shatter. He gave a wave to the Fairies who were yelling and stomping their feet. With a grand gesture, he slipped off his cloak and tossed it smoothly to Stiletto. She caught it, and wrapped it around her arm. He walked to Titania and bowed to her.

"My blade is yours, My Regent," he said, offering her the hilt of his curved sword.

She took it, and pointed the blade at Sunserri. Looking down its sharp length, she asked, "Is this champion acceptable?"

"I have little choice," Sunserri replied.

"You always have a choice," Titania told her. She returned the blade to Saber.

Sunserri held up her bound hands. "I cannot fight with these. Will you dishonor yourself by binding me?"

"You long ago dishonored yourself, but." Titania gestured. Belladonna stepped forward, removing Sunserri's shackles and replacing them with single cuffs for each of her hands.

"These still take away my Power," she complained, rubbing her wrists.

"Then I shall wear the same," Saber announced. Belladonna moved to him and placed similar cuffs on his wrists.

"It's still unfair," Sunserri complained, as a soldier handed her a blade matching Saber's.

"It is tradition when different wings fight," Saber reminded her, taking practice swings with his blade. "The cuffs take away our Power and leave us with just our skills."

"I am not the warrior you are."

"Then withdraw your challenge," Titania said, losing patience. "And accept my judgment. The False Sisters say we must return to the old ways. This is one of them."

Sunserri clenched both her teeth and her fists, but eventually she nodded. Two soldiers quickly drew the dueling circle.

"I can use my off hand," Saber offered, tossing his blade to his left hand. "Or hop on one foot, perhaps?" Laughter flowed around the room.

Sunserri glared. "You mock me, Leather," she hissed. "I will show you my skill."

Saber only nodded, and returned his blade to his right hand.

"Enough," Titania commanded. She rose. "Both of you, stand in the sacred circle. Let this combat decide who is the true Servant."

"When I win," Sunserri said, "you will release me."

"I am an honorable Fairy," Titania agreed with a nod. "Conditions for the duel?"

"Till she yields, or can no longer fight," Saber said with confidence.

"Till he is dead," Sunserri said. A hiss from Saber's wives and the other survivors made her turn pale, but she leveled her blade and faced Saber across the circle.

"As the Goddess wills," Saber said with a shrug.

"As the Goddess wills," Titania echoed. "Let Her guide your hands."

With a sharp cry, Sunserri lunged forward, striking with surprising speed. Saber easily parried, and parried again as she struck lower the next time.

The clash of silksteel on silksteel filled the room. Shatter watched as her husband neatly parried and evaded each of Sunserri's attacks, with either a subtle twist or a graceful step.

"I forgot how good he is," she whispered to Stiletto.

"He's been training," Stiletto whispered back. "Not much to do with all the hands you hired."

"I wanted to make sure the farm was well run."

"We can take care of ourselves," Stiletto whispered back fiercely. "I was fine before I met you, and all the times you've been away."

"Kila," Shatter began, reaching out to her, hoping the use of her pet name for her wife would melt some of the ice between them. Stiletto brushed her hand away.

"Keep your focus!" Stiletto snapped. "This was your plan."

Shatter returned her eyes to the duel. "He's playing with her, tiring her out."

Stiletto's sniff was her only response.

"She's getting more desperate," Steel noted. "Look: her blows are becoming more and more wide. Won't be long now."

Shatter wasn't so sure. Saber wasn't striking back, just parrying and evading. Sunserri was breathing hard. She pulled back from another failed strike and took a few steps back as Saber stood his ground.

"Yield?" he asked.

Sunserri only shook her head. Then she gathered herself and lunged. Saber parried easily, but her attack was a feint, and her blade struck his left arm. He twisted desperately to avoid having a hole ripped in his wing. He transferred his blade to his left hand and clamped the right over the wound as a small trickle of blood flowed down his arm.

In the sudden silence, Sunserri taunted, "First blood."

Saber spared a glance at the wound. It was shallow, and was already closing. "And last," he said firmly. With a skillful burst of speed, he struck her in the face with the hilt of his blade, grabbed her sword hand with his right, and brought his blade down. Her sword hit the ground and skittered away across the floor, her hand still clutching the hilt.

Sunserri's eyes registered shock as he held her, his hand over the stump of hers. Saber looked to Titania.

"Take the other one," she commanded.

Sunserri tried to scream, but it became a gurgle as her other hand hit the floor. Saber grabbed the other arm and forced her to her knees. His fingers skillfully found the pressure points on her stumps and slowed the flow of blood.

"Yield?" he asked again in a calm voice, looking into her wide eyes and at her rapidly paling face with a neutral expression.

She tried to shake her head in denial, but then the pain hit her, and she screamed.

Taking that as agreement, Saber released her and backed away, letting a Healer step in to stop the bleeding and close the wounds. Saber gave the hand on the ground a contemptuous kick, sending it sliding across the floor to stop in front of Nightshade. She gave it a nudge with her boot and gave him an approving smile.

"Why bother?" Sunserri asked, as the Healer eased her to the ground. "You're just going to kill me."

"Not yet," Titania informed her, as she walked across the floor, avoiding the small pools of Sunserri's blood. She stopped in front of the prisoner. "I think we will take your wings instead, and then send you back to your chosen Queens."

Her words penetrated Sunserri's shock. "You can't!" she begged. "They'll kill me, and then bury me." She reached her arms out to Titania, pleading. "Please, kill me here. I beg you."

Titania knelt. "Why should I give you that mercy? You would certainly deny me if our positions were reversed. You have betrayed everything we believe in. Why should I grant you mercy?" Titania stared into Sunserri's eyes. "Why?"

"Because you are honorable," Sunserri replied lamely. "I can tell you anything you want. All the secrets I know." Sunserri begged. "Please. I know more names. Names of other Shadow Agents and their Tethers. Boltholes. Rings." She reached out again, but saw the stumps at the ends of her arms and dropped them. "Goddess, please have mercy, Regent."

Titania appeared to consider. Then she stood. "No. You had your chance for mercy." Sunserri tried to cry out, but Saber stuffed a gag into her mouth and hauled her to her feet by the upper arms.

Titania looked over her court. "Shieldbreaker," she called. Shield started. She had been hiding behind Elanor, not looking at the duel or the other hooded Fairy still kneeling under guard. "Sunserri has betrayed us all, but her treachery was more personal for you. Would you care to take one of her wings?"

Shield looked coldly at Sunserri as she struggled and pleaded through the gag. Saber finally had to drive a thumb into her shoulder, the pain from the pressure point quickly silencing her. Sunserri's eyes teared as she stared at Shield's impassive face.

"No, Regent," Shield finally said. "Thank you for the offer, but I have taken an Oath not to draw blood in anger. And I am very angry at her." She stepped back, taking Elanor's extended hand.

"As you wish," Titania said. She turned to Steel. "Captain."

Steel stepped forward and drew her sword. "Her betrayal killed many of my soldiers at Holly's tower and Silverflow. I will gladly take her wings." She slowly approached Sunserri.

Sunserri was shaking her head, her whole body trembling. A soldier came up behind her and grabbed her left wing, stretching it out. Saber's hands were unmovable on her arm and head.

Steel smiled, locking eyes with Sunserri. "Tell the False Sisters I will see them soon."

Sunserri's muffled scream was mixed with yells from behind. A suddenly free Longstride was running across the floor. He tackled Sunserri, yanking her out of the steady grip of Saber and the soldier. Then they disappeared.

It took two shocked breaths until Steel could yell, "That was a Torc! He can't be far!" She looked around. "Find them!" That broke the crowd's paralysis, and the soldiers and Paramounts all ran or disappeared on the search.

Shield tried to follow, but Elanor held her back. "Wait," she whispered at Shield's confused look. Soon, the library was clear, except for Titania and her council.

Steel sheathed her sword with a snap. "Oh, no," she said, sardonically unconcerned, "he got away."

Shield looked at Elanor and Min with a mixture of betrayal and confusion. Before she could speak, Celia did.

"Regent," she called imperiously, "what is going on, and why am I the only one not to know about it?" She looked around the circle. Nightshade, Belladonna, and Steel smiled openly. Shatter had the good grace to lower her head while helping Stiletto see to Saber's wound. Elanor smiled, and was about to say something when Min gave her hand a tug.

"I am the Queen's Justice," Celia told Titania. "If a deal was to be made, I should have been consulted."

"You are Queen's Justice," Titania confirmed, "but I am the Regent. Captain Shatterstaff and I made a deal with Longstride. In exchange for his life, he will lead us to the Shadow School. Sunserri was obviously deep in the False Sisters' plans. Longstride has assured us he will not let her escape."

"Of course, Regent," Celia said with a bow, "but. . . ."

"You and your Fairies have been busy with the False Sisters' troops and their officers," Titania stressed, ending the conversation. "The opportunity was presented to us, and we took it."

"Then he is forgiven," Shield said darkly, pulling her hand from Elanor's.

"No, Healer," Titania stressed. "His crimes will take much to forgive. But he is on the path to our forgiveness. Yours. Only you can say."

"As you wish, Regent," Shield said with a bow. "You are wise."

"You want to say I'm a fool," Titania responded with a smile.

"No, Regent," Shield denied, aghast at the implication.

"I'm sorry we didn't warn you, but we needed your honest reaction."

"And if I had wanted to take her wing?" Shield asked honestly.

Shatter spoke up. "I doubted you would. But we were prepared for that. Steel would have taken the other one."

Shield would have responded, but Belladonna spoke up first. "Come, Healer," she said, gesturing. "You will have more duties soon." She looked to Titania. "The officers are next, correct, Regent?"

"Yes," Titania confirmed. "They should be gathered at the entrance below by now." She waved to everyone. "Precede me. I will be there in a moment." They began to file out, headed to the stairs and the Ring. "Paramount Min, would you stay a moment?"

Min nodded to Elanor, who sighed mightily and went to help move Celia to the Ring.

When everyone else had gone, Titania turned to Min.

"I wanted to tell you; your mother will be arriving in the morning. Circumstances delayed her journey."

"Nothing bad, I hope?" Min asked, concealing her anxiety.

"No, just minor things that grew bigger." Titania smiled. "You know Lady Bethia."

"I do," Min replied. She managed to smile. "I must clean my room."

"We will make sure you have sufficient time," Titania said with exaggerated grace. She took Min's arm. "Now, Paramount, let us go and dispense more justice."

Chapter Twenty-Four
Fools and Traitors

"Where are we?"

"A cave."

"I can see that," Sunserri sneered. "Where is this cave?"

"Just north of Bell-Oak. I found this place on a scouting mission," Longstride explained as he piled wood for a fire.

Sunserri tried to stand, but her lack of hands and weakness from blood loss made it impossible, and she just fell back to the sandy floor.

"How did we get here?"

"Someone slipped me a Torc and removed my bonds," he said, raising his bare arms. "I took us through a couple of Rings before arriving here. The Ephemeral Ring I had stashed here was used up in the journey."

"Where is it?" she demanded. "Maybe I can grant it more Power."

"I burned it."

"You fool!" she snapped. "Without it, we're trapped here."

"There's an exit above you." He pointed. "After we rest and you recover, we can leave."

"But without a Ring. . . ," she started.

"You can't use one anyway," Longstride pointed out. "Your cuffs."

Sunserri snarled, and banged her arms against the stone. The pain almost made her pass out.

"I could just cut them off," Longstride offered. He pulled a knife from a hidden pack. "A few more inches won't matter."

"That's what she told you," Sunserri mocked. Longstride's hand whitened on the knife hilt. "Fool. These cuffs are anchored to my blood and bone. They neuter my Power regardless." She moved to tap her head, but thought better of it. "A precise Weave must be used to remove them. I know it, but I can't use it."

"Then I guess we'll have to walk."

"Where?" Sunserri asked. "You saved me, but why? I thought you'd roll over and die for that slut Healer."

"Do you want me to kill you?" Longstride asked. "Keep talking like that, and I will."

Sunserri gingerly folded her arms and glared at him.

"You're going to take me to my daughter, and then to the Shadow School."

Sunserri's eyes widened, then she laughed. The sound was cold and cruel. "You're a bigger fool than I thought. Is that all you think about, your daughter and that Healer? You think I'll take you there?"

"If not, I'll find a patrol of the False Sisters' troops and offer you to them," Longstride said matter-of-factly, sitting back down. "You were terrified of being returned to them before." He tested the blade on his thumb. "Or maybe I'll just open your arm and let you die here slowly." He gestured. "Something lives here during the winter. I doubt it will object to eating your dead body."

"You wouldn't dare," she said. "You don't have the guts. Without your Captain and traitor Regent, you're nothing. It was so easy to manipulate you. I wish I could have seen Shield's face when. . . ."

Longstride hit her, driving her head into the stone. She lapsed into unconsciousness.

When she opened her eyes again, Longstride told her, "You will take me to my daughter. Then you will take me to the Shadow School. I'm an outcast. The Mistress takes in all of those she can." He raised the knife. "Or, I will kill you."

"Then you'll never see your daughter again," Sunserri slurred. "She might already be dead."

"The Goddess wills," Longstride said, rising. "If she's dead, then you will follow her." He placed the point of the knife on her neck. "I'm tired. Yes or no. Death or life."

Sunserri looked into his eyes. In the dim light of the fire, she could see nothing but his deadly resignation. "Don't you want to use me first?" she teased, sliding her legs apart. "See if it's true what they say about Iridescents? I can tell you, it is. There is no pleasure like what's between my. . . ."

He hit her again.

She woke with an intense ache in her leg. She tried to move it, but the pain flared.

"The blade is keeping the wound closed," Longstride informed her from one side. "Move too much and you'll re-open it. You'll be dead before I can close it."

"You're a fool," she snarled, her head spinning from the acute agony.

"I know. I trusted you." He placed his hand on the blade and pressed. Pain shot up her leg, and hot blood began to flow down her thigh. "Now, decide."

"I'll help you," she agreed quickly. "Just Heal the wound."

Longstride looked into her eyes. Then, with a contemptuous motion, he pulled the blade out and clamped his hand over the gash as Sunserri's vision began to go black.

"I don't trust you," he hissed, as his Power began to flow into her. "So I weakened the muscles of your heart. Betray me, and you will die before you take two steps." At her raised eyebrows, he added, "My death will also trigger yours."

"I guess you aren't such a fool after all," Sunserri whispered. "Maybe this will work."

Longstride growled, and sent her back into unconsciousness with a thought.

☾ ⌇ ☼

"What now?" Longstride asked as he fed her stew.

"When I'm stronger," she replied, after swallowing with a grimace, "we'll go west and cross the Opal River. On the other side, I have a bolthole. If we had an Ephemeral Ring," she stressed, stopping as Longstride almost shoved the spoon down her throat.

Coughing, she continued. "There I have a device that will hopefully remove these cuffs. Then we can use my Ring to get close to the Shadow School."

"My daughter comes first," he reminded her.

236

"She's there," Sunserri said, turning her head from the offered food.

"Why?" Longstride asked in confusion, returning to the pot and filling his bowl. "She doesn't have a strong Shadow ability."

"The Mistress had other uses for those such as her," Sunserri said, and flinched as Longstride almost threw the bowl at her.

"What do you mean?"

Sunserri smiled. "You remember that strange attacker at the Regent's original stronghold, the one Dark Glider let in through the Ring? Your daughter hasn't been there long enough for that to have been her, though. I think that was a young man, anyway." She shrugged.

Longstride stared at her, disgusted. After a moment, he stammered out, "How could you do such a foul thing?"

She shrugged again. "Easy. It's just conditioning. Take any child — or any adult, for that matter — and with the right lever, you can make them do anything. Look what I did to you."

Longstride barely resisted hitting her again. Bravely, Sunserri laughed.

"Why can't we just go directly to the School from your Ring?" Longstride asked after a few bites of his stew, once he had regained his composure.

"The School isn't in this Realm," she explained, as if speaking to a child. "It's so wrapped in Shadows and other Wards that it is a place all to itself. The only way in is through one of three gates. I know one." She cocked her head. "It will be a long walk. Are you sure you don't want to get to know me better? Might make the nights warmer." She smiled lustily. "It will be difficult without my hands, but we can make do. The one handed and the handless. Sounds like one of the Keeper's boring parables."

"I wouldn't defile myself with you," Longstride said forcefully, his face filled with disgust.

"Your choice," she replied offhandedly. "It'll take about a moon for us to walk there, and then time for my hands to grow back. It will be boring just staring at each other."

"That's a waste of time and Power."

"I need my hand to activate the gate," she told him arrogantly, holding up the stump at the end of her right arm. "And we'll just have to hope that the Weave recognizes my new one."

Longstride barely restrained his nearly overwhelming desire to scream in frustration. He sat down and began to eat mechanically, not noticing as the stew burnt his mouth.

"I'm still hungry," Sunserri complained. Longstride ignored her, eating without emotion.

Sunserri questioned him. "Who passed you the Torc? And how did you hide your unbound hands?"

"I have secrets of my own," Longstride told her. "We escaped, didn't we?"

"It couldn't have been your little hussy," she said. "Not with that look of naked betrayal in her eyes. Who? I wasn't told of any more Agents."

"Where was your partner?" Longstride asked, turning her questions with one of his own. "Shadow Agents always work in pairs."

"He died," Sunserri said with anger. "Your Captain killed him. Delivering your mountain hiding place was the price for me to be let back in." She glared at him. "I hope what I've learned will be enough. Otherwise, we might meet a bloody reception at the Shadow School."

Longstride managed to smile. "I will mourn you."

"They'll kill you too, fool," she snapped. "And you'll never see your daughter again. In this life, or any other."

"Then we must make sure we have enough to be let in," Longstride said smugly.

"What do you know, Leather?" she said contemptuously. "What could you possibly know that would be of worth to the Mistress?"

"I keep my own counsel," he replied, going back to his food.

"If you tell me. . . ," she began.

"Be silent," he growled back at her. "Or you will have to regrow your tongue, too."

Sunserri snapped her mouth shut and glared at him. Longstride only smiled and returned to his meal.

Chapter Twenty-Five
Dark Looks

Titania climbed the stairs of a hastily built platform. In front of her, the loyal soldiers of the Queen were spread out, filling the space from the mountain to the lake. Among them were three carefully guarded groups of the False Sisters' troops. The largest was mostly the regular troops, with a few flyers sprinkled in. The second group was mostly the sergeants. They stood, hands bound, but otherwise free. The third group was the rest of the False Sisters' officers and the surviving members of Air. All were tightly bound, and many were kneeling. More than a few of the men were gagged. They were surrounded by heavily armed soldiers of the mountain. Most of the prisoners glared at the Regent, standing on the platform above them. Their dark looks filled the space between.

Titania's eyes swept over them as she addressed them. "Troops of the False Sisters, I am the Regent of Queen Talia Zellandine Corwyn Fae-Sidus-Lumen. Many of you know me from my former role as Queen's Justice under Queen Zellandine, may she return swiftly." She paused to make the Sign of the Three, echoed by both her soldiers and many of the False Sisters' troops. "I have always been fair in my judgments, reaching out with empathy and compassion when needed." She paused again, sweeping her eyes over the prisoners. "And righteous justice and punishment when a closed fist was the only option left."

Murmurs of both assent and denial rippled through the crowd. They stilled when Titania raised her arms.

"The Goddess calls upon us to be merciful. To answer injury with compassion and understanding. As She led us out of the waves to this Realm, we should lead those who trespass on their fellow Fairies back to a path of light, away from the darkness." She gazed out at the crowd. "We are Servants of the Moon and Sun."

"Servants of the Moon and Sun," the crowd repeated. Many of the troops of the False Sisters bowed their heads, though others did not, and stared at Titania with hard eyes instead.

"I have spoken with many of you," Titania continued. "Both personally and in groups. I understand most of you were misled. You were following the orders of corrupted leaders." There Titania stopped. "I would remind each of you," she said, her voice turning hard, "that despite any Oath you take, your duty and honor as Fairies is to defend the lives and spirits of your Sisters and Brothers. You have an obligation to speak out against orders that do not lead you to the light."

"We would have been killed!" one voice objected.

"They threatened our families!" another cried.

"You are all traitors!" a harsh voice yelled from the bound officers' group. "You deserve death!"

Angry shouts arose from Titania's soldiers, and the crisp clap of a slap echoed across the field.

"Leave him be!" Titania commanded before another blow could fall. She found the dissenter, who had been pulled away from the others and was surrounded by soldiers in green armor. She met his eyes. He held her gaze angrily, trying to shift his bound hands out of the grip of the soldiers holding him. Titania held his furious stare and returned only compassion with her own eyes. He finally settled, but continued to glare at her.

"Yes," Titania acknowledged. "We are traitors, to the eyes of the False Sisters. But they are the ones who have betrayed us. They killed our Queen. Used foul weapons against their own sister and liege. Their captains killed loyal soldiers. They have looted and defiled the Shrine of the Goddess. Denied those who died their proper Return to the Cycle. They use the bodies of the Fallen in foul rites that betray everything we are as Fairies."

"Lies!" the dissenter called. "We serve our Queens." Murmurs of assent rose from the prisoners. "Zellandine betrayed us to the Humans. Tried to fill our court with half breeds!"

"Silence, traitor," Steel said firmly, striding forward. "Do not speak our beloved Queen's name! She died in front of me, a blackblade in her heart."

"Lies," the enemy officer replied. "You are all turncoats!" He began to struggle as a soldier tried to gag him. "You try to silence me?"

"Let him speak," Titania called out. "Captain Steeltrap," she said, looking down. "Please step back. Truth will win out." Steel mastered herself, and stepped back to the base of the platform.

"Whatever beliefs you have," Titania continued, addressing the man. "What is your name?"

"Lieutenant Swift-Talon, of Air," he said proudly.

Titania questioned him. "Swift-Talon, do you deny that dead Fairies were buried? Those who fell on the Night of Black Wings and after?"

"I haven't witnessed any burials," he replied quickly.

"That is not what I asked you," Titania shot back. "Do you have any knowledge of Fairy bodies being buried, and not Returned, as is proper?" He hesitated. "On your honor as a soldier of Air," Titania pressed.

"Lies and deception by traitors," he finally replied.

"Then how many Pyres have you witnessed?" Titania asked. "Hundreds died that horrible night. The fires should have gone on for days." She looked to the other bound troops. "How many did all of you see? Who lost Sisters and Brothers, then stood Last Vigil with them?" Silence filled the field.

One brave voice finally spoke up. "They told us it was a waste of valuable time. That we were needed to fight the traitors. There was no time to mourn."

"They took the bodies away," another voice added.

"We were told they would have private Pyres," another voice called out, breaking with the sudden realization of the truth.

Titania stepped to the edge of the platform. "Captain Shatterstaff," she called. Shatter stepped up and raised her sword to the Regent. "You fought at Brine Hill?"

"Yes, Regent," Shatter confirmed, loud enough for all to hear.

"How many died there?"

"Too many to count," Shatter replied. "The chaos of the battle prevented us from compiling an accurate tally."

"All those dead, were they brought back to the Realm?"

"No, Regent," Shatter called out. "It took days, but all the dead were Returned. Then, we burned the entire field, seeking to release any who had been missed or buried under the mud and detritus of the battle."

"Days!" Titania called. "I remember seeing the rising smoke. I remember the smell. The stench of that smoke followed us back to the Realm and filled our noses for moons." She looked out over the prisoners. "Did such fires rise over Fae-Treval in the days after the Night of Black Wings? Did clouds of smoke hide the sun, as they did at Brine Hill?"

"No," came the tortured cries of hundreds of Fairies just now realizing the truth of the matter.

"No," Titania echoed. "I watched for them. I hoped." She looked down. "And when I did not see them, I mourned our lost Sisters and Brothers."

"Lost!" came the heartbroken and then angry cries. Some of the False Sisters' troops still retained enough honor to lower their heads, but others just looked defiant. Titania swept her eyes over those men, memorizing their faces.

"Former Lieutenant Swift-Talon," she called, returning her eyes to the dissenter. "What do you have to say now?"

"I do not acknowledge your authority over me," he cried. "You are all traitors to the True Queens and have no right to judge any of us!" A small number of prisoners — mostly his fellow officers — called out in support.

"I have every right to judge you. You have committed crimes against your fellow Fairies," Titania shot back. "Who your Queen is, does not matter. As soldiers, you are expected to act with honor on the battlefield. To refrain from striking a helpless opponent. To accept the honorable surrender of an enemy. Not to strike them down," she called angrily. "Not to slit their throats, and use their bodies to fuel those foul Blood Rings of yours." She fixed Swift-Talon with her hard gaze. "Do you deny participating in these crimes? Did you step in to stop any of them?"

Swift-Talon just stared back at her.

243

"Crimes have been committed," Titania called out. "By all of you." Her gaze swept the three groups. "Some can be forgiven, with proper Oaths and other measures. Others require severe punishments. Some of you are guilty of assaults and rapes. Others are guilty of murder, and the use of Fairy bodies in foul blood rites. Crimes so horrible there can be no forgiveness in this Realm. I must send you to Her and hope She will grant you mercy before Her throne, because I have none to give you."

"It's not a crime to kill traitors!" Swift-Talon yelled, struggling with his guards. Other officers also stood. Some struggled against their bonds, while others simply yelled insults. The soldiers of the Regent looked to Shatter and Titania for orders. But before either could act, one of the other bound officers strode up to Swift-Talon, who had managed to get his arms out of the grasp of his guards and was opening his mouth to yell more insults.

"Silence," the officer said, hitting Swift-Talon across the face with his cuffed hands. "You're only making it worse."

Looking betrayed, Swift-Talon turned his attention on the officer. "How dare you!" he cried. "Turncoat!"

The officer only shrugged and hit Swift-Talon again, pushing him back into the arms of the guards. They took Swift-Talon, struggling, to the ground. The attacking officer then raised his hands in surrender and knelt. Around him, the action swirled as soldiers of the Regent tried to control the False Sisters' troops.

"*Kneel!*" Captain Shatterstaff's yell and Send crashed over them. *"Or you will be knelt!"*

A few did, but others still struggled, yelling insults and threats. The group of sergeants began to look at each other, wondering if they should join in. A few moved toward the melee, pushing their guards.

"Paramounts!" Titania called out calmly.

With a gesture, Min, Elanor, and the other Paramounts activated a Weave in the struggling troops' bonds. As one, they stopped fighting, stiffened, and fell over. Loud snores began to rise from their fallen forms.

Nervous laughter flowed through the remaining troops as order was restored.

"Captains," Titania ordered, "please take them away."

Under the hard eyes of Captain Steeltrap and her lieutenants, the sleeping troops were removed from the field in good order. A tense silence settled as Titania stood calmly looking down at the remaining prisoners. Most of the kneeling officers kept their heads down. A few looked up with defiance, watching their comrades being hauled away. At Shatter's command, more soldiers emerged from the mountain, and others drifted down from above. Three squads of flyers hovered overhead, their bows ready.

Satisfied her captains had restored order, Titania stepped closer to the edge of the platform.

"To be blunt," she Projected to all present, "it is my right to execute all of you. You raised your hands against your rightful Queen. By law, I should remove your wings and then execute you, in any manner I see fit. Throwing you off this mountain has been suggested."

There was a collective gasp, torn from even the most stoic of throats. Titania held the moment, as all eyes turned to her.

"Do not take my mercy for weakness," Titania finally said, once she was sure they were all listening and watching. "Some of you, I must execute. Your crimes — against the Throne and your fellow Fairies — are unforgivable. Your wings will be removed, and then you will receive a quick death by skilled swordswoman." Utter silence, deeper than before, covered the prisoners. "Others, I will allow to take your own lives. Hopefully, this will balance the scales when you stand before the Throne of the Mother of Waves." Her gaze seemed to reach each of the kneeling officers individually. Some dropped their eyes, shameful tears falling. Others stared back at her stoically.

Then Titania turned her eyes to the regular troops. "For others, I offer the mercy of a second chance. Enough blood has been spilled. I will not kill you out of hand, as the False Sisters do." Hopeful inhalations rose, prompting Titania to speak further. "You will submit to a full reading of your mind and memories. All will be bound with strong Oaths, and you will be watched." She gestured to Captain Shatterstaff. "All of you know the Captain, either directly or by her reputation." She paused, gathering steel into her voice, and Projecting it out. "Any betrayal will be met with swift justice." Shatter folded her hands on her sword hilt to punctuate the declaration. "I will speak with each of you. Have your answer ready." She looked out over all the Fairies before her.

"We are Servants of the Moon and Sun," she cried, in a voice that sent ripples over the lake. "We bring light to the darkness. We bring hope."

"Moon and Sun!" came the response from the crowd, rising to break on the mountain behind her.

"We stand before the storm!" Titania continued. "We are guided to a better day!"

Cheers followed her hopeful proclamation.

Chapter Twenty-Six
You Take After Your Mother

"How do you feel?" Min asked Elanor as she helped Min into one of the new, larger, dresses Flora and Luna had found for her.

Min sighed. The color was wrong for her complexion, but it was the best they had been able to find.

"After two nights' sleep and too much tea from Flora?" Elanor continued. "And we can't forget those dark looks from Merry-Weather! I feel better." She leaned in, brushing her lips on Min's hair. "That'll teach me to eat nuts brought by strange animals."

"Seems like that's something they teach at the Tower of Learning," Min bantered, twisting her hips, and easing the fabric over her belly.

"I must have been off flying that day," Elanor replied, tightening the ties. "Is that too tight?"

"No. Thank you." She turned around and took Elanor's arms, gripping her elbows. "I was afraid for you, when I couldn't find you. Then your mind was so odd." She seemed on the edge of tears.

"You shouldn't have worried," Elanor tried to say, but Min interrupted her.

"Not worry?" she said sharply. "You run off and eat some nuts and wind up loopy as the moon. What if you had fallen off that ledge? Shield was too out of it to help you. You could have been hurt or killed, or found by some of the False Sisters' troops!" She let go of Elanor's arms and glared at her. "I love you, you foolish Fairy, but if you keep putting yourself in harm's way." She stopped, pulling her emotions together. "I don't know what I would do if you got hurt."

"And who went down the mountain with that traitor?" Elanor shot back. "Who could have been hurt then?" She pointed to Min's belly. "You're responsible for more than just yourself now, remember." She grabbed at Min's arms. "I love you, too, you foolish Fairy. I don't know if I could go on without you."

Min tried to stay stern, but a smile crept onto her face, and she let Elanor pull her into a hug. "Then we must both be careful."

Elanor answered her with a kiss, slow at first, but with increasing passion. Min's arms tightened around Elanor's waist, pulling her as close as was possible in her condition. They lost track of everything but each other, existing only in the moment, in each other's arms.

A firm knock at the door and a shout from a strong voice broke their kiss. "Minuet. Flora said you were still in here." Another knock, louder this time. "Minuet!"

Min pulled away, her nerves jangling. "Yes, Mother. Just a moment." She smoothed her skirts and her hair. Elanor playfully batted at her braid. "Stop that," Min whispered. "Your own hair is a mess."

"Whose fault is that?" Elanor asked, but she tried to smooth down her own loose strands and straighten her own dress.

Min took a deep breath. "Come in," she called, gesturing the door open.

A small female Fairy entered. She was slightly shorter than Min, with the same white hair and pale skin. Her Iridescent wings radiated a silver light that dimmed as she walked over the threshold. She looked around the room, taking in the scattered books and scrolls. Her eyebrows rose at the stack of cups and plates under a chair. She projected strength, filling the room far more than her small stature warranted.

"Now I know where you get it," Elanor whispered, standing up straighter at the woman's sharp look.

"You're early, Mother," Min said, stepping up and trying to hug her. Lady Bethia stopped the hug by grabbing Min's arms and squeezing them.

"I always try to be early," Bethia said. "You know that." Her gaze turned to Elanor. "Paramount Elanor," she greeted, politely, but not warmly.

"Paramount," Elanor replied with a bow. "I hope your journey was smooth."

"It was, thank you," Bethia said, then turned her attention back to Min. "And how are you, Minuet?"

Min frowned at the use of her full name, but then smiled politely. "I'm fine."

Bethia turned her eyes back to Elanor. "How is she, really?"

"She doesn't sleep enough, and she works too hard," Elanor replied with a smile.

Bethia released her daughter. "I thought so. You take after your father."

"And you, Mother," Min replied, more harshly than she meant. "There is so much to do. The protection of the Regent and this mountain are of the utmost importance."

"And you have done a superb job," Bethia told her. "I'm here to guide you and support you."

"We've been doing pretty well on our own," Min replied.

Bethia's eyes narrowed. She turned to Elanor. "Paramount, would you speak to the other Paramounts and gather up all the information on your Wards and other protective measures for me to review?" She glanced at Min. "I would like to speak to as many as is possible, as soon as possible. Maybe at the mid-day meal?"

"I could bring them all to the top of the mountain," Elanor suggested. "So the Circle maintaining the Wards won't be left out."

"Excellent," Bethia praised. "I'm sure Merry-Weather and her staff can be of help. Especially that young Feather-wing girl. What's her name?"

"Obsidian," Min supplied.

"Yes, that's her," Lady Bethia said. "I would like to speak to as many of our Sisters and Brothers of Power as I can. I'm sure you can arrange that?" she said with confidence.

Elanor understood the order and said, "Yes, Paramount," with a bow before heading to the door.

Bethia's voice stopped her. "Aren't you forgetting something?"

Elanor looked back, puzzled. Bethia nodded slightly at the mildly fuming Min. Smiling, Elanor returned and kissed Min on the cheek. "I'll see you later," she whispered at Min, who was too caught up in the swirling emotions brought on by seeing her mother to do anything more than politely nod back at her. Elanor understood, and

Projected love and support at her. Then, with another bow to Bethia, she left.

"Mother, I. . .," Min began after the door shut.

"Minuet. Mara. Marigold. Fae-Luna-Major," Bethia said over her in the strongest matriarchal voice she possessed. "I am not the mother that Celia is. You will not treat me as if I were." She fixed her daughter with a hard eye. "And if I ever treat you as badly as Elanor has been treated, you will have the right to turn those fiery eyes on me. But not now." She folded her arms.

"I apologize," Min said low, looking at the floor. "You've been away, and I haven't seen you since I returned."

Bethia motioned her to sit, and pulled the other chair closer. She sat, and took Min's hands. "I'm sorry," she said. "But it couldn't be helped."

"I know," Min said, still not meeting her mother's eyes. "It's just. . . ." She lost the words. "You haven't said anything about my children. In all our conversations over a Geode, you haven't spoken of them. Haven't even asked how they're growing." She looked up. "And Father! He hasn't spoken to me at all."

Bethia sighed. She gripped Min's hands harder. "I'm sorry. I. . . ." It was her turn to be at a loss for words. "I'm trying, my dearest. Your father is, too. Is this the father I wanted for your children, for my grandchildren? No." Min opened her mouth, offended, but Bethia raised her hand. "But you loved him, and by all I have been told, he was a good, honorable man."

"He is a good and honorable man," Min corrected. "He's still alive."

"We can only hope, and ask the Goddess for her mercy," Bethia said, wanting to spare her daughter the pain of the probable reality. She smiled brightly. "Captain Shatterstaff and Steeltrap both speak very highly of him."

Min blinked and cocked her head. "I know Shatter cares for him, but I didn't expect Steel to say such things. She always drove him hard in training."

Bethia lost her smile. "They say only good things. Though mostly in the way a soldier speaks of a fallen Brother."

"He's not dead," Min declared sharply. "He can't be. No matter what anyone says. He survived." She began to cry. "He made it back to his Forest, and his family there. Maybe Spear is with him. Or maybe he's alone." She raised her eyes, looking at her mother with desperation. "No matter. He will see his children one day."

Bethia knelt, taking her daughter's hands. "I hope you're right."

"The Goddess is cruel, if she takes him from me again," Min said bitterly.

"Do not say such things," Bethia admonished her. "We must have confidence in Her mercy and Her path for us." She touched Min's belly. "She has given you the gift of his children." She spoke more sternly. "If he is gone, then you will have this part of him. Do not let bitterness poison the love of these innocent children."

"I'll try," Min said. "It's just hard. Everyone looks at me with such pity. Even Elanor sometimes. I'm the widow mother. But. . . ."

"He is not dead," Bethia finished for her. "You are a strong and powerful Fairy. You are my daughter. Your line reaches back to the First Fairies. If anyone can will it to be so, you can."

"Our line," Min said bitterly, sitting back, and letting go of her mother's hands. "It always comes back to that. Is that why Father hasn't spoken to me?"

"I cannot speak for your father's inner thoughts, but we are trying." She returned to her chair. "These are unknown times. Everything we thought we knew has been turned upside down. And you come back from the wilderness bearing the children of an Elenite."

Min's eyes darkened. "Celia has said many unkind things. She calls me an Elenite's whore. Is that what you think of me?"

Bethia sat back, stunned and speechless. She struggled with the shock that Min had spoken so plainly and that, deep down, she understood Celia's sentiment.

"That woman," she finally said, low and fierce. "We will have words. I do not understand how our beloved Queen allowed Celia to act so. . . ." Her words stopped, overcome by her anger. "I'm sorry. I had no idea."

"Yes, you did, Mother," Min said levelly. "All the Iridescents do. Most of them have the decency not to say it. But they think it." She gestured to her belly. "They look at me, and just see some half-breeds growing inside. They tut and give me sympathy, but it's all from the other side of their face."

"No," Bethia disagreed. "I can't believe you're treated so." She stood. "I will speak to the Regent. No daughter of mine will be looked at in that manner." She headed to the door.

"No, Mother," Min said, also standing. "This is my fight. All I need from you is your support and love."

Bethia stopped. She turned, looking at her daughter with new eyes. All her memories of the flighty young Fairy who had danced, and flirted, and slept with flyers — and all the other handsome and beautiful Fairies who had caught her eye — were replaced by the strong woman now standing before her. There was steel in Min's wings and determination in her eyes like Bethia had never seen before. Time away had wrought multitudinous changes in her daughter. Many of them were horrible, but others had allowed her to access the raw strength and Power that had lain dormant within herself. Bethia felt overwhelming pride.

"I see more of your father in you now."

"I see more of you in me," Min countered. "And don't worry about Lady Celia. Flora gave her a full meal of humility, and demanded that she change her ways or else."

"Really?" Bethia said with wonder. She sat back down. "Do tell."

Chapter Twenty-Seven
The Regent's Mercy

A Fairy Lantern and a pile of glowing stones in the center of the tent held the darkness and the cold of the night at bay. Titania only had a few more Fairies to speak to, but the weight of moons fighting to preserve the honor of the Fairy Throne was too heavy. She sent Celia and her Law Masters away, telling them she needed time to clear her mind. She settled into her chair, trying to meditate. Finding her center had been hard lately. Every time she closed her eyes, she saw Miranda's face and heard her last words. Pushing aside her grief, as Miranda had taught her, Titania reached for peace.

A Send from Shatter interrupted her.

"What is it, Captain?" she replied sourly.

"I'm sorry, Regent, but I have someone who needs to speak with you."

Titania took a moment to swallow her anger. *"I trust this is important, Captain."*

"It is, Regent."

"Then come in."

Captain Shatter entered, leading one of the False Sisters' officers. Titania recognized him as the one who had struck Swift-Talon. She nodded a curt greeting.

He stood before her, his hands folded in front of him, his wings still. His whole manner exuded quiet resignation. In Titania's Sight, his aura was grey, shot through with dark red. He looked slightly familiar.

"Well, Captain," she asked, "who have you brought me?"

"My name is Gauntlet, Ma'am," the officer said. "I was a member of the Queen's Guard. To my dishonor, I left to join the False Sisters in their bloody coup."

"I recognize you," Titania said. She narrowed her eyes at him. "Why did you make that choice?"

The guilt in his aura increased. He lowered his head, unable to meet her eyes.

"You spoke out against Swift-Talon and further violence. If you have come to me for mercy," Titania told him, weary from all the other judgments she had given today, "you must speak."

"Helm was my niece," Gauntlet stated. Titania glanced at Shatter, looking for her reaction. The Captain's only visible response was a tightening of the eyes. "She was the last of my family," Gauntlet went on. "Everyone else died before, or at, Brine Hill. When news of her death reached Fae-Treval, the False Sisters used my anger and grief against me. They lied to me. Led me down a path to betray my Oath. I was angry that the Heir and the Queen had allowed my niece — the only family I had left — to die for nothing." He bowed his head, his voice dropping with shame. "Captain Shatterstaff has Shown me that she served and died with honor."

Titania began searching through her papers, looking for this officer's name. She remembered it coming up in a few statements.

He heard the papers rustling and raised his head. "If you're looking for proof of my guilt, I give it freely. I was brutal. I killed my Brothers and Sisters. I stood by as others committed horrible acts." He took a breath. "I prevented Shrinekeepers from taking the dead away during the Night of Black Wings."

Titania suppressed a shudder at his words. Others had told similar stories. Some with pride, and others, like this soldier, with shame.

"Then why do you come here?" Titania asked. She held up a page. "I have statements about your actions. They are. . . ." She set the page down, unable to read it. "What you now call lies, you once firmly believed. You acted on them. You raised your hand against your Queen based on them. You took the path, and now you stand at the edge of a cliff. Something within you wanted to believe those lies. Now you stand before me, seeking what? To save your life? Save your wings?"

"No, Regent," he said, shaking his head. "I deserve the punishment you will level on me. I have betrayed my family. I deserve death."

Titania looked at Shatter, wondering why she had brought this man to her. He was like many of the others, full of shame. She had decided they would be allowed to take their own lives. She was tired of retribution.

"Gauntlet," Shatter prompted, "tell the Regent what you told me."

He gathered himself. "Since I was a lieutenant in the Queen's Guard, the False Sisters looked to me for all the information I could give them. I was in many of their councils. I know many of their plans."

Titania waved her hand. "As do many others. Tell the Captain. Then you will be allowed to take your own life."

He persisted. "Regent, I was in several councils when the Mistress of Shadows was present."

This got Titania's attention. She waved for him to go on.

"She supports the False Sisters. Anything else she's told you is a lie and a deception."

Titania looked at Shatter. She nodded, smiling.

"This is welcome news," Titania said. "I will call for Paramount Celia to read your memories."

"I have more," he offered. "I was once sent to take the Mistress a message. I know the location of one of the gates to the Shadow School."

Titania leaned back; her enthusiasm was blunted by active suspension. "And you will trade this information for your freedom?"

"No, Regent. I will give this information freely." He dropped to one knee. "My path ends here. I can only hope the Goddess will grant me mercy and give me a chance to be better when I Return."

Titania contemplated him for a long time. He bowed his head, calmly kneeling. The red in his aura faded away. The grey lightened, becoming the silver of summer rain clouds. Titania Sent to Law Master Willis.

"Soldier Gauntlet," Titania said, as she stood and raised him to his feet. "An old friend once told me that, even if it is dark and we cannot see the path, it is still there." She held his hands, absorbing his emotions. "Times are very dark, but we remain Servants of the Moon and Sun."

"You Sent, Regent?" Willis asked, poking her head into the tent.

"Yes, Law Master. This brave soldier has information we desperately need. Please relay him to a room so he can tell us everything he knows." She shook Gauntlet's hands. "Thank you."

Surprised, Gauntlet could only gape at her.

She smiled at his confusion. "I think the Goddess has more work for you in this life. I understand your pain, but sometimes we must rise above it. Our Sisters and Brothers need us. Your next life can wait, soldier."

"Is that an order, Ma'am?" he asked with wonder. His aura brightened. "I came here expecting to end my life, and now you're offering me another chance? After all I've done?"

"Yes, I am, soldier. If we threw away every broken sword, there would be none left. Broken blades can be reforged. Lives rebuilt."

He dropped to his knees again, pressing her hands to his forehead. "I pledge myself to you, Regent."

"And I accept your pledge," she replied formally, "in the name of the Queen."

Gauntlet stumbled to his feet — with Shatter's help — and left with the Law Master. Shatter stayed, watching as Titania returned to her chair.

"Is that wise, Regent? By his own admission, he's a criminal. He should die."

"I would expect those words from Captain Steeltrap," Titania said in surprise.

"She is blunt," Shatter admitted. "But he's still a danger."

"And he will be watched." Titania shook her head. "We must mark all those we give a second chance. Something like what Paramount Min did to Longstride. Do you have any suggestions, Captain?"

Shatter considered. "Removing hands would be too much. We want them to be loyal to us. That might drive others away."

"It must be something clear. Obvious to all," Titania said, tipping her head back in contemplation. "A clear statement of who they were, and why they're still alive."

Shatter's hand drifted to her arm. She contemplated her rank tattoo, and how it showed her journey. She pressed a finger to Talia's name, written in Old Fairy, underneath it.

Shatter had an idea. "The deathmark. It can be added to their rank tattoo."

Titania blinked, considering, then smiled. "Brilliant, Captain. We'll combine it with the symbol of sunrise. A new day, but also a warning."

"Not sunrise," Shatter objected. The sharp and painful memory of Talia sitting on the edge of the cliff alone, the bundle of bones in her lap, intruded on her mind. The recent revelation that Sunrise wasn't dead, but only stolen, did not mute the pain of that scene. "First crescent moon," she suggested. "The emergence of light from the darkness."

Titania smiled widely, truly impressed. "Are you sure you're not a Keeper, disguised as a soldier?" she teased. "That's an inspired thought. Make it so. Maybe it will become a symbol of pride."

Shatter smiled, moved by Titania's praise. Then she became serious. "Regent, you are wise. . . ."

"You soldiers keep saying that," Titania said, slightly annoyed, but also amused, "when you want to call me a fool."

Shatter smiled, remembering happier times. "I used to call the Heir one of my foolish ladies." She lost her smile. "Before."

Titania nodded. "I understand, Captain," she stressed, needing her to understand as well. "Maybe I'm tired of death, but something made me give that poor Fairy another chance."

"I hope we won't regret it," Shatter remarked with a bow.

"Goddess willing," Titania beseeched. Then, she drew a deep breath and straightened her back and wings. "Send in the next one."

☾ ⁓ ☼

Lady Perrault gasped as her son stumbled out of the Ring. "What did they do to you?" He carefully set the wrapped body of his husband on the floor, then sat down. He wore a look of utter exhaustion and despair.

"Take the body away!" Lord Troilus, the elder yelled from his chair. Two Elenite servants rushed to do his bidding. As the first one reached for the head of the body, the young lord moved to strike him. The Elenite leapt back in fear. Then Troilus mastered himself.

"Just be careful," he said. After a moment's hesitation, the servants lifted the body carefully and took it out of the room. Troilus watched it go.

"And bring my son back wine!" the older Troilus yelled. He was shaking so much with contained rage that even his lame wing seemed ready to lift him off the ground.

"They will pay for this," he swore. "Send to the Queens. We will gather more Eclipse knights. We will cover that mountain in blood," he spat, "and drown them." He continued cursing and yelling, making less and less sense as he went on.

Lady Perrault stood. She walked on shaking legs to her seated son. Her hand reached for his wing, then pulled back, forming a fist. "They betrayed me," she hissed. "She broke her word. That Regent will pay for this outrage."

"Where is that cursed half-breed!" Troilus yelled. "And where are the Queens?"

"They will pay," Perrault said again. She turned, but her son grabbed her arm.

"No, Mother. Titania did not break her word."

Aghast, she pulled away from him. "How can you say that? Your wings are. . . ." Words failed her.

"They are undamaged, as was agreed," Troilus said simply. He extended his wings. "I can still fly. They are unclipped." He smiled bitterly. "They read the wording to me several times. They wanted to be sure I understood." He shook his wings. Once brightly Iridescent, they were now white, the color of unspoiled snow. "'This in no way violates our agreement with your mother,' Regent Titania told me."

"That bitch!" Troilus the elder snarled. Spittle was forming on his lips. "That daughter of a buzzard. I will kill her myself." He tried to stand, but his legs shook so much, he fell back into his seat.

"Calm yourself, Father," Troilus cautioned. "Or your heart will burst."

His mother glared at him. "How can you be so calm? Your beautiful wings have been polluted. I can barely stand to look at them."

"It gets worse, Mother. That little slut Paramount said this color will deflect the light of the sun and lessen my Power." His hands clenched. "I can feel it. They practically castrated me."

"Then we shall answer this insult." Perrault turned toward the door. "Guards!" she yelled. "Call the Captains. Prepare to fly."

"No, Mother!" the younger Troilus said, rising. He turned as white as his wings and dropped to his knees. He grabbed his chest, laboring for breath.

Perrault rushed to his side, grabbing his head, and extending her Power into his body. She was jolted back by a spark of pure white energy.

The elder Troilus watched, his anger cooling as he opened his Sight and examined his son's aura. "What has been done to you?" he asked, shock and fear filling his voice.

"They put controls in my mind," the young Fairy said. He sat down heavily on the floor. His breath was returning to normal. "If you violate your agreement with Titania, either directly or in spirit, I will fall ill. I'll gasp for air, eventually dying like a fish on land." His face twisted. "One of those bitch captains was so proud of that."

"And they cannot be removed?" Perrault asked, reaching toward her son again. He shrank back away from her.

"No. And don't touch me." He moved back, further out of her reach. "No one can touch me with Power." He slammed his fist on the floor. "Not without causing great pain for both of us."

Perrault sat back, shock and livid anger twisting her features. "This is a betrayal of all the laws of Fairies and Power. To implant controls without someone's consent." She shook her head. "It goes beyond anything."

Troilus shook his head. "I agreed. I had to." He looked at his mother, tears in his eyes. "They were going to bury Zahadune. I couldn't lose him forever."

Lady Perrault slapped him.

Troilus the elder laughed, cruel and mocking. He waved his arms. "This is what a son of mine has been reduced to." His anger bled away, replaced by ridicule. "Well, your wife won't be happy about all this. I guess there's nothing to do but go home."

"What do we tell the Queens?" Perrault asked, rising.

"Nothing," Troilus the elder replied. "We will simply leave them to the fight. We have time. One side or the other will win, eventually." He shrugged. "It doesn't matter. We have access to their source of Power. Their cruelty will keep it well stocked." He gripped his left arm, suddenly in pain.

"Go get his Healer," Perrault commanded, running to her husband. "Moonserri is down the hall."

Troilus the younger hesitated for a defiant moment, then went in search of his father's new — and very pretty — Healer.

Chapter Twenty-Eight
When You Are Ready

Min stood outside the door to Celia's rooms. Tiger-Claw was chatting with the guard further back down the corridor. Min had knocked as hard as she could on the locked door. She couldn't sense anything beyond it due to its Wards, and was about to knock again, when she felt an exit form in the Wards as the door opened.

A tall, willowy male Iridescent stood in the doorway. "How may I help you, Paramount?" he asked in a sweet, melodious voice. He folded his long-fingered hands in front of his chest gracefully and smiled brightly down at her.

His beauty took Min's voice away for a moment. She had seen him a few times from afar, but had never been this close to him. She thought, 'He's the kind of Fairy the Humans worry about.' He stood gracefully on the line between male and female, liable to seduce either with skill and fluency. His aura was bright flowing colors, swirling with both hard and soft tones. One of his sleeves rode up, and she could see the white lines of dueling scars on his forearm.

He noted where her eyes were directed and twitched his sleeve down, covering the scars while he continued to look at her.

Min finally realized she hadn't spoken. "I'm sorry," she mumbled. "Is Paramount Elanor here? I was supposed to meet her for dinner."

"I'm sorry," he replied, unconcerned with her staring. "She and the Queen's Justice went to their private work room a while ago." He gestured down the hall with a graceful hand. "Elanor didn't tell me you would be coming by. They're probably still there."

"As I thought," Min said with a sigh.

"It is a confusing walk," he said. "Let me Show you," he said, reaching out and taking her hand before Min could protest.

As his fingers tightened on her wrist, his eyes widened. He let go immediately, and shoved his hand under his other arm. "Oh my," he said, with a hint of both wonder and pain.

"I'm sorry," Min said again, stepping back. "They don't like anyone at first." She placed a hand on her belly. "It just takes time."

He blinked at her, holding her gaze. A swarm of emotions flowed over his face and through his aura, too fast for her to follow. He wrung his hands together.

"I have never felt such a reaction from such a young child," he finally said, wonder coloring his words. "You're only a few moons along?" he asked, with obvious understanding of how children grow.

Min simply nodded. Her twins murmured in her mind, irritated, but not angry.

"And I have never felt such a reaction from Elenite children." He shook his head. "Even among Fairies, very few react this strongly this young." He made the Sign of the Three. "You will have powerful children, Paramount. Full of potential. It is almost blinding." He passed a hand before his eyes.

"Yes," Min said with a wistful smile. "I've felt it, too."

"I have spent a good deal of time in a midwife house in an Elen town. I have helped many mothers with their Elenite children. Helped them find the peace to make the choice whether to bear the child or not. Then, to find their path, whether that meant keeping the child or letting it go to another. Mostly Humans, but a few Fairies as well." He smiled. "I was the only man there. But for some reason. . . ." He raised his arms, his robes flowing around him, and said, in mock confusion, "I was never seen as a threat, and helped many of them through their trauma." He looked at Min with understanding. "I seem to have a gift for it."

"Those mothers had endured much," Min said, sidestepping his unspoken offer.

"Yes, they had," he agreed. "I'm proud to have helped them find a way around the violence that fathered so many of their children." His aura became red for just a moment, then settled back to its normal peaceful colors. "I used my status and birthright to open doors that would otherwise have been closed to the Elenite midwives. Some of them even called me a midhusband." He smiled. "The woman who ran the house named me an honorary woman."

His smile became bittersweet. "I was in love with her, but she did not see me that way." He shrugged his shoulders. "Another life."

"You've honored yourself and the Goddess with your good deeds," Min told him.

He nodded his head modestly. "It was the only thing I could do. I was forced to leave when the Queen closed the borders. I ask Her every night to keep those women safe. I hope I can return soon. There is so much work still to do. I want to see how my children are. I helped new mothers find new lives with their babies. Or, helped them find better lives elsewhere."

Something in his voice caught Min's attention, but before she could speak, he held out his hand once more.

"Shall we try again?" he offered. His aura dimmed, and he Projected a sense of safety and greetings.

"Behave, children," Min said under her breath, and took his hand.

It was like grabbing a warm coal, for him, but after a moment, he smiled and bent down. He moved his other hand toward Min's belly, asking for her permission to touch her. Min nodded, and he gently put his hand on the curve of her growing belly.

"Greetings, children," he said out loud and in a gentle Send. "I am a friend. I look forward to meeting you both under the moon and sun."

Min felt a surge, and her children's colors reached out and wrapped his hand in an embrace.

"Treat your mother well, and don't kick her too much," he instructed them. Then, with a gentle goodbye, he took his hand away and stood.

"You do have a gentle touch," Min remarked. "I'll have to remember that."

"I am always at your service," he replied with a bow. "Whenever you need me."

"Thank you." Min stumbled, realizing she didn't know his name.

"Perrault Willow," he said quietly. "Though those names might not sit well with you." He looked up, considering. "You may call me Malachite. My grandmother called me that."

"Willow," Min muttered. Grief and shame crowded in on her, pushing aside the good feelings this man had brought. Unconsciously, he held out his hand, and she took it. Warm support flowed into her. She still felt her grief; it had not been pushed away, but merely wrapped in his compassion and blunted, just enough to be bearable. For the first time, Min found she could think of Willow with a smile and not tears.

"I knew her aunt," he said slowly. "She made beautiful blankets and sleeping wraps. I always sent my new mothers away with one of them. It was a horrible thing what was done to them."

"Horrible does not seem a strong enough word," Min replied. She pulled her hand away. "Thank you, Malachite."

"There is much hurt in you," he noted. At her frown, he added, "When you are ready."

Min could only nod. Then something else entered her mind. "Perrault?"

"She had me when she was very young, and before she married Troilus." The naked hatred that suddenly lit up his aura forced Min to take a step back.

"I'm sorry," he said, tamping his anger down quickly, as though he had much practice. Then he smiled. "So, I guess you know why I'm working with the Queen's Justice."

Despite the instant spike of distrust at learning who his mother was, Min couldn't help but smile and laugh. "She's keeping an eye on you."

"Yes," Malachite admitted. "But how I could support anyone who treats their Sisters and Brothers in such despicable ways? The betrayal of my mother. . . ." His lip twisted. "Would be nothing compared to the betrayal of everything I believe in if I were to bow to the False Sisters."

Min nodded. "I know what it's like to be torn like that."

"I was never close to her," he confessed, shrugging. "She didn't understand my desire to help others. Troilus wanted to disown me, but she just wanted to be sure I didn't father any Elenite children." He looked at Min with compassion. "I haven't decided if I will honor her wishes."

Min sighed. "And I thought Elanor and Celia had a strained relationship."

Malachite laughed. "Yes, there is always a deeper hole." He brushed off his knees. "But I have kept you too long. I was trying to Show you where their workroom is." He took her hand again and Gave her the directions.

"Thank you," Min said. Then she leaned close. "You said you found new places for these Elenite children. . . ."

He broke the connection and stepped back. Strong Wards sprang up around his mind. "I've said too much. I am bound by strong Oaths to say no more."

"But," Min cajoled, "you must have sent them. . . ."

Malachite made a sharp motion. "I will say no more," he declared, all his flightiness falling away. He stood taller, towering over Min like the tree he was named for. Tiger-Claw felt the change and turned, his hand on his hilt. Malachite noticed, and folded his hands before him, bowing in silent apology.

Min frowned, but she could see that she would get no further information from him now.

"Unless," he said, "you wish to send your children away and never see them again." He paused. "Many do."

Shocked and horrified, Min could only stutter, "I would never."

"Yes, Paramount," he acknowledged with a bow. "I can tell you, though," he said with a conspiratorial whisper, "that unlike Conwenne, I am not worried."

Min wanted to press him further, but saw he would not be moved. "I understand," Min said. She bowed to him. "It has been good to meet you, Perrault Willow Malachite. Your gifts are something I will remember." She made the Sign of the Three. "One day. . . ."

"When you are ready," he agreed with a nod. "I'm here when you or your Sisters," he stressed with understanding, "need me. I live to serve all who are in need."

"Do you have any brothers? There are many in need," Min asked, joking, but as the words left her mouth, she realized her error.

"Unfortunately, I do," he said.

Min tried to take her joke back. "I'm sorry. I was being too flippant."

"I take your meaning," Malachite said with sympathy. "There are many in need."

"We should go, Paramount," Tiger-Claw said, stepping in. "Flora just Sent. Dinner will be ready soon."

"Go with the Goddess," Malachite said, flowing back to the doorway. "And tell Flora I will see her soon." With another bow, he closed the door.

Min stared at it till Tiger-Claw pulled at her arm. She yanked herself out of her contemplation with conscious effort and took the bodyguard's arm to lead him up the corridor.

"He is unlike anyone I have ever met," Tiger-Claw commented as they walked. He radiated confusion, but admiration as well. "And I have met many Fairies."

"I think I was meant to meet him," Min said, her voice slightly puzzled, "but it is too soon."

"I'm only a soldier, Paramount," Tiger-Claw told her. "He's deeper than I'm prepared to go."

"Right now," Min admitted, "neither am I."

Chapter Twenty-Nine
Many Paths

As they wound their way through the corridors under the mountain, Min felt the rock above pressing down on her. "I've never been this deep," she muttered, feeling the sudden desire to spread her wings. Tiger-Claw seemed to feel the same way; he kept clenching and unclenching his fists.

"We must have missed a turn," he finally said. The corridor before them was dark, lit only by their Fairy Lights.

"It's only a little further," Min said, going over the directions. She took a deep breath and started forward again. Tiger-Claw lagged. Min turned another corner, and came upon a silksteel door. She had to shade her eyes, the Wards around and over the door were so bright.

"What are they doing in there?" Min wondered as Tiger-Claw caught up with her.

"It's making my eyes hurt," he complained.

"Mine, too," Min said, as pain began to bloom in the back of her skull. She was ready to turn back, when the light of the Wards dropped, leaving only the shining door. As Min took a cautious step forward, the door opened, and Elanor stormed out. Her face was pale and streaked with tears. She came up short when she saw Min in the corridor.

Celia's voice came from beyond the door. "You must be more careful. The Weave is fragile, and so is the globe." Her voice turned hard. "We'll have to start over."

"Not now," Elanor said. "I'm hungry." She grabbed Min's arm, and without another word, pulled her back down the corridor, away from the door.

"But what about your mother?" Min asked, helpless to understand the waves of emotions coming off Elanor.

"I'll help her," Tiger-Claw offered, as he watched his charges flee down the corridor. Celia answered in a barely polite fashion.

"Stop pulling me," Min complained, after they had moved a bit further away.

"I just want to get back," Elanor said, not letting up.

"What were you doing?" Min asked.

Elanor didn't answer.

"We missed a turn," Min informed her imperiously. "It's back that way."

Elanor clenched her hands in frustration and turned, almost hitting Min with her wing. She stomped back to the junction, then stopped and looked back at Min.

"Are you coming?" Elanor asked.

"No," Min said, folding her arms.

"Fine," Elanor huffed, and turned and walked away.

☾ ∼ ☼

"I hear you met Lady — excuse me, Paramount — Min," Flora said with immense pride.

"Yes, I did. She's a remarkable Fairy. And the potential radiating from her children." Malachite paused. "I wonder if they're the ones."

"You were always obsessed with those stories," Flora said, waving her hand dismissively. "I never understood a word of them."

"You always understand more than you let on, Lady Flora."

"Don't call me that," Flora snapped. "I am no Lady."

"Then Dame Flora," he replied with a smile.

"That's my mother's affectation. I am simply Flora."

"Never that," he replied, still smiling.

"Foolish old man," she said with affection. "You haven't changed a bit. How do you do it?"

"The only gift my mother gave me," he admitted with a sad smile.

"Those stories," Flora pressed. "Is that why you spent so much time in the Elen towns? Why you took so much interest in the Elenites?"

"That, and my own sense of honor. I couldn't stand by and let our children be treated so."

"Very few feel that way, unfortunately," Flora said in a low voice. Then, her tone rising, "There was also her."

Malachite could only fold his hands.

Flora let the silence stretch, then asked, "Do you really think it's possible?"

"'She will be born on the shore of the sea,'" he quoted. "And now you tell me, she isn't dead, but merely lost. Stolen by the False Sisters. 'She will stand in the place between, a hand out to both.' Seems clear enough."

"But there's more," Flora pressed.

"Yes. 'They will be her hands and wings. Swirled colors of past and future. He will betray and be betrayed. She will close the circle and begin again. Thorns and green fire. Red fire and purple sparks. Mothers must gather. The ancient betrayal shall be freed from bondage.'"

Flora shook her head. "I'm glad you find something in those words. It was always just bad poetry to me."

Malachite nodded. "It is that. I wish I could see the original text, but the Tower of Learning is lost to us, at least for now."

"You should look through the Exile Queen's histories Ta. . . she found. There might be something there."

"I will. Do you know where they are?" he asked eagerly.

"The Regent took them. I'm not sure if they're here, or in one of her strongholds."

"I am to meet with her in the morning. I will ask her."

Malachite bowed and moved to leave, but Flora grabbed his arm. *"You didn't tell her, did you?"*

"I gave my Oath. I will not break it." He paused, looking at her from under his long lashes. *"Unless you want me to."*

"Don't look at me with those big empathetic eyes. I made my decision, and I stand by it. Despite the pain."

"I never doubted your choice."

"But you think I should have made another?"

"My path is to counsel, and then guide when a path is chosen. I do not judge."

"But you do," Flora said out loud, as she dropped his arm.

"I don't mean to. I was younger then," he apologized, then asked, "How is your wound?"

Flora's hand moved automatically toward her left thigh, but she stopped herself before she reached the scar. "It's the same as always. You, of all Fairies, should know that."

"I offered to Heal it completely."

"Go bother someone else," Flora said suddenly. "My neck is hurting from looking up at you."

"Yes, Mum," Malachite said with a bright smile.

"Don't call me that either," Flora fussed, then turned and glanced about the room, looking for someone else to speak to. She spied Shatter, and walked off in her direction.

Malachite smiled again, then drifted away.

☾ ⌇ ☼

"Stop," Min said, pushing Elanor away and sitting up.

"Don't you. . . ," Elanor began, leaning forward, but Min pushed her away again.

"No, I don't. You ignore me and are rude all through dinner, but now you want to make love. As if you haven't been cruel to me all day."

"I haven't been. . . ."

"Yes, you have. All through dinner. You rolled your eyes at me when I asked the simplest things." She sat up straighter, adjusting her shirt.

Elanor leaned back. She stared at the blanket, picking at the seam.

"And now you pout," Min accused.

"I'm not pouting," Elanor responded, still not looking up.

"I kept trying to tell you what happened to me today, but you wouldn't listen."

"I'm just tired."

"Then go to sleep."

Elanor looked up. "But you couldn't keep your eyes off that Fairy. What was his name?"

"Malachite," Min told her with frustration. "He was who I wanted to tell you about."

Elanor's eyes narrowed. "He's too old for you."

"What do you mean?" Min asked, her frustration with Elanor rising to anger.

"He's at least as old as Flora. Maybe older! I heard them talking. They seem to have known each other for a long time." Elanor looked at her. "He's just your type, though. Long and lean. I bet he flies all the time." She clenched her fists. "Is that what you wanted to tell me? That you want to have a go with him?"

Min almost slapped her. Containing her anger, she hissed, "Get out of my bed. Get out of my room. Find someplace else to sleep tonight."

"I can't," Elanor whined. "Shield's using my room."

"Then sleep with Shield," Min said, pulling the blanket off Elanor and hoarding it on her side of the bed. Elanor was looking at her with a mix of shock and hurt.

"Go," Min said again. "I don't want you around right now."

Elanor got out of bed and pulled on her dress. "When will you want me?" she said hurtfully.

"When you start acting like the woman I love," Min shot back. "I thought healing the rift with your mother would make you happy!"

"Well, you were wrong," Elanor replied angrily. "You don't understand."

"No, I don't," Min agreed, bowing her head, her hair swinging forward to cover her face.

"Min, Beautiful," Elanor started, suddenly realizing how far this argument had gone. She took a step closer. "I'm sorry."

"Go," Min said with anger. "You're disturbing the children."

"It's always them," Elanor shot back, her own anger overcoming her desire to apologize. "You use them as an excuse."

"I said, go," Min said low. "Or I will call Foxruff, and he'll throw you out."

"You want that," Elanor challenged. "Have a big strong man in here with you."

"Go!" Min shouted, Pushing at her. Elanor stumbled out the open door to the other room. She raised her hands, as if to strike back, but then turned and stalked out. The slam of the door seemed to shake the whole mountain.

Min took a deep breath so she wouldn't break down and scare her twins, who were huddled in the back of her mind, uneasy.

"It's all right," Min muttered. It took all her concentration to push back her tears. "She's just upset."

Min was in the middle of a breathing exercise that was calming both her and her babies when she heard a voice from the outer door.

"Dearest?" Lady Bethia called.

"Back here, Mother," Min replied.

Her mother appeared in the bedroom door, looking slightly disheveled. Min realized it was later than she'd thought.

"Are you all right?" Bethia asked, sitting on the bed. "I heard you yell, and then saw Elanor storm out of here as if she were being pursued by a troll."

"Yes," Min admitted. "We were just having an argument." She shifted, trying to rise. "I should go after her."

"No," Bethia said, catching her arm. "Both of you need to cool down first. In the morning, things will be much clearer."

Min wasn't so sure about that, but let her mother ease her back into bed.

"Now," Bethia said. "Now that we're all awake, I would hear more of the father of my grandchildren."

Though her residual anger almost made Min refuse, the look of gentle, but stern, urging on her mother's face — and her bright, inquisitive aura — made her quash that impulse. "That chest over there," Min said, pointing.

Puzzled, Bethia crossed to the simple silksteel-bound wooden chest. "It's Locked with a Weave," she said, as she tried to open it.

"Elanor," Min said, exasperated. "She thinks keeping him away from me protects me."

Bethia only shrugged. "There's a tune Woven into the binding." She began to hum.

Min closed her eyes, listening, and searching her memories. Bethia began the simple, sad tune again. An image of the Twins singing in front of the fire somewhere on the road came to Min's mind. She pushed back tears, but also smiled at Elanor's wit.

"'From my finger never part,'" Min quoted, looking at her mother.

Bethia repeated the words. The binding fell away, and the lid opened. She looked inside, a puzzled tilt to her head.

"Bring it here," Min said, trying to steel herself. Bethia complied and returned to the bed, setting the worn satchel beside Min.

Now Min did cry. She ran her fingers over the leather and cloth. The tarnished buckles resisted her, too blinded by tears. Bethia finally reached over and undid them for her.

"It's all he left me," Min said, reaching inside. "A shirt, a few spools of thread." Bethia watched her remove each item, letting her daughter take her time to explain. "A scroll." Min pressed the rolled paper to her chest. "All he left me." She mourned. "Why didn't he leave more? A note." She looked at her mother, searching for answers. "We didn't know what would become of us. He must have known he might not make it. The Curse." Min stopped.

"Who can truly know another's mind?" Bethia finally said. She took Min's hand. "All the men I have known always thought they had more time. Even when they did not."

"But," Min argued, "he wrote so much." She shook the scroll. "Every day we were apart, he wrote me something. I don't understand."

Bethia gathered Min into her arms. "I don't know. If he didn't leave you anything, then he must have been sure he would return to you. Hold tight to that, dearest."

Min tried, but she could only cry.

Light snoring woke Min. She kept her eyes closed, hoping. But her hopes were quickly dashed. The snores weren't a roaring waterfall, only the babble of a small stream. She opened her eyes.

273

The dim Fairy Light in the other room — which she had forgotten to dispel — dimly illuminated the form in bed with her. It was her mother, who had her arms and wings wrapped around herself in a cocoon.

'And she will emerge into a beautiful Fairy,' Min thought. She was very hungry. Elanor's Projected emotions had made it hard to eat the night before. The twins were still sleeping, filling her mind with formless dreams, so she wasn't in a hurry to get up. Soon, they would wake, and fill her mind with their strangeness. She reveled in these rare moments of peace.

A spike of pain behind her left eye made her wince and clench her entire body.

"Beware," her mother cried, sitting up. She pulled herself clear of her own limbs, almost falling out of bed in her haste. But she quickly caught herself and turned her attention to Min.

"What was that?" she asked, pushing her hair out of her eyes.

"Nothing," Min replied hastily. "Just a twinge."

"No, it was not," Bethia disagreed. "You were in pain. A mother knows."

Min tried to divert her. "It was just you, crowding me in bed. You didn't have to stay."

"Yes, I did," Bethia replied, getting to her feet. "Though my back will regret it later." She poked at the bed. "Why is this so hard? And you and Elanor sleep together on this? Fool around on this?" she asked, making Min blush. "You should have a better bed. At least for the children."

"No, Mother," Min said, sitting up. "This is the best we have. Others have far less." She pushed back the blanket. "It wouldn't be seemly."

"Since when have you started worrying about being seemly?" Bethia joked. "And only one blanket? And you couldn't share with your old mother?"

"I'm the pregnant one," Min bantered back. "And," Min announced, standing, "Elanor and I create enough heat that we don't need more."

It was Bethia's turn to blush. She opened her mouth.

"Paramount Min," the Regent's Send interrupted. *"Are you with Healer Shieldbreaker? She was supposed to see me this morning, but she hasn't come. And she isn't responding to my Sends."*

"No, Regent," Min replied. *"She isn't here."*

"Captain Steeltrap is eager to return to Silverfire. Shieldbreaker was supposed to go with her."

"I'll find her," Min said out loud, for her mother's benefit. "She was sleeping in Elanor's old room."

"Please find her, Paramount. The Captain is getting impatient." A burst of emotion filled the Send, then Titania broke the connection.

"I saw Elanor headed that way," Bethia told her, as she combed through her hair with her fingers. Min marveled as her sleep-rumpled mother transformed before her eyes. Wrinkles in her dress faded away, and her body straightened. She shook her arms and wings.

"The Regent calls," Bethia said, her eyes losing focus. She gestured, and a dress floated across the bed to Min.

Min took off her nightshift and dressed, with her mother's help. She wished for the days when she could roll out of bed, leaving whoever was in it, and be presentable before she crossed the threshold.

"Life is change," her mother advised.

"Too much sometimes," Min said. "What did the Regent say?"

"That I should come to her. She wants a group of Paramounts to go with her. She wants Elanor. I didn't tell her she wasn't with you last night."

A spike of fear hit Min, coupled with a dark flash of jealousy. 'Elanor wouldn't,' she thought. 'Shield wouldn't.' But her anxiety rose just the same.

"Go find them," Bethia urged from the door. "I will speak with the Regent." Then, with a quick kiss, her mother was gone.

Foxruff wasn't at the door. Perhaps he was off looking for Shield, or Bethia had sent him away. Down the corridor, Tiger-Claw was standing at Elanor's door, shifting from foot to foot. He looked relieved when Min hurried up to him.

"The door is locked and Warded," he answered her unasked question. "Paramount Elanor ordered me out of the way last night. Then, she went in, and Warded and locked the door. Healer Shield was in there already."

Min put her hand on the door, feeling the Wards.

"They haven't come out," Tiger-Claw continued. "Nor have they left by Torc, but."

"With these Wards, you might never have sensed her using one," Min finished for him. She took a deep breath. "I'm not blaming you. She's strong. Curse her." She returned to the Wards. They unraveled under her hands. A surge of mixed relief and fear filled her stomach. She carefully pushed open the door.

The small room was empty. Shield's gear and bedroll were gone, as were Elanor's. On the chair lay a rolled piece of paper. Min picked it up with trembling hands.

"Min. I'm sorry. I do not have the words to explain all that I am feeling. I thought I could contain it, but I cannot. I must find a way to close this circle. Find a way to be the woman you need me to be. Please don't try to follow me. Shield is with me. I will return when I have found a way through this pain. Take care of your children and our Sisters. I love you, Beautiful."

Min could hear Elanor's voice as she read the lines. Pain, sorrow, and anger built in her breast. Her vision blurred, the pain level rising even higher. She sat down in the chair, crumpling the paper in her hand.

Tiger-Claw, still at the door, looked at her with shock. "Paramount? What's wrong?"

"Alert the mountain," Min said, pushing through the despair. "All the Rings. She left, and took Shield with her." She looked at Tiger-Claw, who hadn't moved. "Go," she urged, sharply. "The Regent and the others must know." He darted away, Sending to the captains.

"You ran away again," Min said darkly. "Left me alone. Curse you."

"Paramount," Celia Sent. *"I cannot find Elanor. Where is she?"* There was irritation and panic in Celia's thoughts.

Min wanted to project all her fear, pain, and anger at her in reply. 'This is your fault,' she wanted to scream. 'You pushed too far too fast.' Instead, she simply Sent, *"She's run away again. As she always does."*

"What did you do?" Celia Sent sharply. *"This is your fault. If harm comes to her. . . ."*

Instead of arguing, Min broke the connection. She pressed her fist, still holding the crumpled note, to her forehead.

"I will not cry," she muttered.

"Dearest," Lady Bethia called from the door. "The mountain is a kicked bees' nest. Elanor and Shield are gone?"

Min simply passed her the note. "I will not cry," Min repeated. "This is her choice."

Bethia read the note quickly, then turned to Min. "We'll find her. They must have used one of the Rings. We'll find them."

"No," Min declared, standing. "They'll cover their tracks too well. We were well trained. No." She sighed. "She will be back." Her voice broke. "When she comes back." She shook off Bethia's sympathetic grasp. "I must see to the Wards. If she's captured or compromised, we must be ready." Min smiled grimly at her mother, then touched her Torc.

☾ ≋ ☼

"I don't like it here," Shield complained.

"I don't either," Elanor replied. "But I need time to decide where we go next."

Shield wanted to say more, but the dark look on Elanor's face made her decide against it. She checked the door into the Ring chamber again, then sat down on the threshold. She ran her fingers absently over the sword Elanor had made her bring.

Despite her words, Elanor didn't feel any unease here, in the broken tower Ring, where Talia had violated both her body and her mind. She could still see the claw-like marks she had made in the dirt and sand. Still hear the echo of Talia's vow to never return. Still feel the blankness overtake her own mind as Talia violently pushed her consciousness aside to take control of her.

Elanor didn't understand it, but despite that painful betrayal, this still felt like a place of refuge to her. She didn't have time to examine her feelings just now. She needed to find a Ring they could use.

"Should we be doing this?" Shield asked again.

"You agreed that we need to find where they make the blackblades," Elanor argued. "So we can stop them from producing more of those foul things."

"Yes," Shield said, "but alone?"

"We can go places others can't. You're tired of having your patients die, or needing to cut off their arms and legs to save them," Elanor explained brutally. "If we find the source of the blackblades, we can stop them from hurting anyone else with them."

Shield nodded in understanding.

"I just have to find another Ring." She frowned down at the one at her feet. "All the ones I know are Locked, or in places held by the False Sisters," she griped.

Shield wrung her hands. Elanor had burst into her room, waking her, and babbling about finding the source of the blackblades. Before Shield had been able to think clearly, Elanor had convinced her to agree to accompany her, and now she was sitting before the broken tower Ring. Her mind recoiled at the dark emotions that filled this room. She was almost ready to demand that Elanor take them somewhere else. Anywhere else.

"I found it," Elanor said triumphantly. She stood, and held out her hand. "Let's go."

"Where?" Shield asked, climbing to her feet, and joining Elanor in the Ring.

"To where it all started. Elen-Gold."

As Elanor reached into the Ring and prepared to take them through it, she felt a presence behind her. Panicked, she turned, raising her hands, ready to defend herself.

Three Fairies were standing in the door to the Ring chamber. Two of them were Leather-wings, dressed in simple robes, and carrying well-used staffs. The third was already over the threshold. She was a short Feather-wing with silver and purple hair in a tight braid starting at the crown of her head. She spun a flail in her hands, filling the room with a whine as the silksteel weapon passed through the air.

Elanor met the woman's eyes. Recognition dawned in both of their minds.

"What are you doing here?" they both asked in surprise.

End of Book Three

If you've enjoyed the adventures of the Fairies in this book, please remember to sign up for my news and updates list at https://www.ServantsoftheMoonandSun.com and review this book on Amazon.com or your preferred platform to help others find my work. Thanks!

Also, if you haven't already, please read Book One, **Talia: Heir to the Fairy Realm**, and Book Two, **Talia: On the Shore of the Sea**, available at Amazon and wherever books are sold, in hardcover, paperback, e-book, and audiobook formats!

And be on the lookout for Book Four: coming Fall 2024!

Author Bio

Joel C. Flanagan-Grannemann has been writing since childhood, and has a B.A. in writing from the University of Pittsburgh at Bradford in Bradford, PA. He has lived in Columbia, SC for more than twenty years with his wife and editor, Jay-Jay Flanagan-Grannemann, and a coterie of cats. Joel has a day job in back room operations at a major national retail chain where he has worked in various capacities since 1995. For more information, please visit www.ServantsoftheMoonandSun.com.

www.ingramcontent.com/pod-product-compliance
Lightning Source LLC
Chambersburg PA
CBHW051247260626
47162CB00002B/644